RED'S PERIL

Part 2

Satan's Devils MC - Las Vegas Chapter #2

COPYRIGHT

Published 2021 by Trish Haill Associates

ISBN: 978-1-915106-04-9

www.mandamellett.com

Disclaimer

This is a work of fiction. Names, characters, businesses, places, events and incidents are either the products of the author's imagination or used in a fictitious manner. Any resemblance to actual persons, living or dead, or actual events is purely coincidental.

Warning

This book is dark in places and contains content of a sexual, abusive and violent nature. It may not be suitable for persons under the age of 18.

PRODUCTION ACKNOWLEDGMENTS

Cover Design by Wicked Smart Designs

Edited and formatted by Maggie Kern @ Ms.K Edits

Proof reading by Darlene Tallman

Photographer: Golden Czermak of Furious Fotog

Model: Andrew Flanagan

SATAN'S DEVILS MC

CHAPTER ONE

RED

I stand in the doorway to Cheryl's apartment, for once in my life at a loss for words. I've just, and that only briefly, met my son for the first time in his life, and now his mother, the woman I'd once loved and lost, is refusing to let me in to talk to him. More than that, she's accusing me of having the ability to hurt him. *What the actual fuck?*

The only reason she's able to give me is that I'm the prez of the Satan's Devils MC.

Sure, Cheryl and I hadn't had much time together in the past, but surely she'd learned some of my character in that time, or enough at least not to judge me without giving me a hearing. But all she sees is the patch on my cut.

"What the fuck? What the hell type of man do you think I am? Me, hurt my son? Woman, what's gotten into you? I'd fuckin' *die* before I saw a hair of his head harmed. He's my *son*. A kid I've been wanting forever…" I pause, trying to consolidate my thoughts about the family I never knew I'd had. "Sure, I never expected to miss the first fifteen years of his life, but I can deal with the here and now. And nothing, *nothing*, is going to stop me from getting to know him." Realising I must have some parental rights, I decide to overrule her. Raising my voice, I call out, "Zeke, get out here now."

Cheryl might not think I have any sway over him, but surely, as his father, I can order him around? Or at least, request his presence.

But our first interaction as parents is set for us to go head-to-head.

"Stay in your room, Zeke. I've got this handled." Cheryl's instruction is equally loud.

No footsteps sound. However curious Zeke might be about his old man, it's his mother he's listening to for now. *Goddamn it.*

My rage rises. "Do I have to get a fuckin' court order? Get a blood test to prove he's mine? Hell, woman, if you're going to make this difficult, how about I get the law to say I can take over now. You've had him for fifteen years, now it's my time."

Yeah, I might be shouting, but all I want to do is talk to him, have a chance to know him. Is that too much to ask?

"Mom?" a plaintive voice sounds.

"I've got this, Zeke," she calls back, and turns to me with fire in her eyes. "You want the truth? You want to know why you're no fucking good for your kid?"

"You've made it obvious," I spit back. "It's because of the cut that I'm wearing. It's because of my club."

"It's because of what that makes you," she rasps in a similarly heated response. She shakes her head and turns her back on me—a sign that while I might bluster, she's not physically afraid of me. Then she seems to gather herself and turns back. "If you were a normal man, with a nine-to-five job, I might try and explain to you." She shrugs. "I always thought I would if I ever bumped into you again. But now?" She eyes my cut, and again her head moves in a negative gesture. "I just can't. You'd never understand." Reminiscent of the past, she tosses her still long blond hair back.

"Understand what?" If she was talking in riddles, I might be better able to comprehend. All I'm hearing is she's judging me and my club without giving herself a chance to get to know the man I've become.

I'm faced with a momma bear who wants the best for her child. It angers and frustrates me that's she's not affording me a fair trial. "You know fuck all about me."

"I know enough!" She's the one angry now. "I know I want you and your kind nowhere near Zeke."

I approach her, crowding her, boxing her in with my arms. My eyes blaze. "Give me a fucking chance. That's my kid in there. I already know I'd die to protect him."

It's not because I've caged her against the wall—I'm certain she's got more fire than that—but tears form in her eyes and she slumps as the fight goes out of her.

"Please, Red. It's best you don't know. Just walk away, and never look back. Please, Red. I'm begging you. Forget any idea about having a child."

Nope, she never knew me at all. I grit my teeth. "There's no way in hell I'm going to do that." Turn my back on the family I thought I'd never have? No fucking chance.

"Don't hurt Zeke." Her voice is pleading. Hell, her eyes shimmer. "Will you promise me that once you know the truth, you'll walk away and not try to interfere?"

What the hell can be so bad I'd want to turn my back on my own flesh and blood? Has he committed murder or something? If so, I'd help him cover it up, bury the body if need be.

"Nothing you can tell me will make me walk out that door." I stare at her with sufficient intensity that she can be left in no doubt. Hell, if she doesn't start to explain what she's talking about in the next few seconds, I'll push her out of the way and go and see my son for myself.

When I make a move to do just that, she puts both hands on my biceps. "If I tell you, will you go? Will you leave us alone?"

What the fuck could she tell me that would make me want to do that? Sure, Cheryl's proving herself not to be the woman I'd built up in my head. I've already determined a relationship between her and me would never come to pass, but one between me and my son? Nothing is going to prevent that.

It doesn't help that the walls are thin, and in the sudden silence, I can hear gut-wrenching sobbing from the next room. *She's making my son cry.*

"Fuckin' explain to me now." I've never laid hands in anger on a woman before, but I'll be fucked if I'm not coming close to it.

"Alright!" she cries. Her mouth opens, shuts, and for a moment no words come out. Then a tear rolls down her cheek. In a quiet voice she starts, "Zeke is not your son—"

"A blind man would see that he is. Try again," I snarl. "I don't need the bloodwork to prove it—"

It's her turn to interrupt me, now hissing, "Zeke is not your son. They're your child. And don't refer to them as he. They prefer the pronoun they."

What? I don't get what she's saying. My lack of comprehension shows on my face as she gives a huff, as if my reaction was exactly what she'd expected.

"You're a biker, the epitome of a masculine man. You'd never be able to understand what Zeke is."

I'd had enough of going around in circles. "So fuckin' tell me."

She sighs heavily. "The term for it is nonbinary." She pushes away from me, wraps her arms around herself and continues speaking. "I don't blame you, it's hard to grasp. Why do you think I've had to move so many times? It's to protect Zeke from people like you, people who want to change them. Bullies who reject who and what Zeke is."

What? A myriad of emotions goes through my mind. Is she saying what I think she is? I'm worried, confused, and not the least, angry. Non-fucking-binary? What's she talking about? He's only fifteen, for fuck's sake. Of course, he needs to be set on the right path. I eye her differently, assessing her ability as a mom. What the fuck has she been doing to him? Screwed up his head so he doesn't know whether he's male or female? Well, I'm here as the cure for all that. I'm going to set him right. I just need to talk to him.

Suddenly, the air seems to have been sucked out of the room as I find myself wanting to kill her for what she's done to my son. It has to be her. Kids don't just decide on a different way of life, to follow the latest fad. Christ, at his age, he's far too young to make such far-reaching choices in life. I do the math in my head. Yeah, he's fifteen years old, but only just.

As his mom, she should have guided him, corrected him, shown him what's right. She's fucked up and fucked up bad.

My fists clench, my hands one moment away from reaching out and throttling her. My cheeks blaze and it's hard to keep hold of my temper. Though I have such a fragile hold on myself, some instinct screams at me. I'm so angry there's no way in hell I can talk calmly to my son right now. If I stay one second longer, I might even hurt the mother of my child.

I spin on my heel, go to the door, and walk out, slamming it shut behind me.

CHAPTER TWO

CHER

"Mom!"

"Oh, Zeke." I turn, opening my arms as they run toward me seconds after the slamming of the door. "I'm so sorry."

They sob, their hands clutching at me. "I knew how it would turn out. I knew he wouldn't want me." Zeke might have thought they were prepared, but their reaction shows differently.

"He doesn't know what he's missing," I tell Zeke, meaning every word. "You're everything a parent could want, honey." I mean that with every fibre of me. If I had a choice, I'd never change them.

"He didn't even give me a chance."

Of course, Zeke had high hopes. Even though I'd carried an image of Red in my head, I'd thought that time had maybe distorted it. My memory of Red often morphed into Zeke's face, but I hadn't been wrong. They look so alike, there's no way I could have hidden that Red was Zeke's father.

Have I played this wrong? I could have let Red talk to Zeke, I suppose. I could have at least let him get to know his child. But I'm used to reactions such as his, used to having the blame heaped on me for the way my child has turned out. Zeke's heard enough crap about being abnormal.

I rest my forehead against Zeke's—they're just as tall as me now—and allow myself to drift back to where it had all started.

I was sitting in the diner, waiting for Red to change his clothes, shivering so hard my teeth knocked together. I could never remember feeling so cold.

Red's wetter and must be far colder, I thought guiltily. At least I'd been wearing his waterproofs.

But is this what it's going to be like? Somehow, my romantic dream of riding off into the sunset doesn't seem so attractive anymore. What am I doing? I don't even know him.

My hands are stiff, my ass sore from riding. I'm miserable and my shivering just won't stop.

For the first time, I question the wisdom of just taking off. Somehow, in thinking I'd landed the man of my dreams, I'd expected the sun to shine forever. Is this worsening of the weather a metaphor for what my life will be like?

Red's still not back, so I take out my phone, wanting another perspective.

"You alright, Cheryl?"

"I don't know," I tell her.

"You crying?" Her voice sharpens.

"Shivering. I'm cold."

My mom humphs. "Doesn't much sound to me like that man's looking after you."

He is, I go to refute. But I stay silent.

"You don't sound happy, Cheryl. If it's that bad, you better come home."

But I was happy earlier, says my traitorous self.

"Is he with you?"

"No, but—"

"Cheryl, he's left you shivering and alone. You clearly can't trust him to take care of you."

She's wrong, I think. But what do I know?

"I'll let you know what I'm doing." Ending the call, I realise I've resolved nothing at all.

Glancing out of the window, I see the rain's still falling, harder, if that's even possible. I shudder. Not one part of me wants to get back on the road.

I miss my mom. I miss my home. I miss being warm and comfortable.

I was a stupid young girl, I think to myself as I hug Zeke to me. I'd let my momentary discomfort shape the rest of my life. Had I spoken to Red, explained to him, he might have agreed to delay our journey until the weather had turned in our favour.

Even then, my reasoning, *I want to be warm,* had seemed lame. I hadn't even been able to explain to Red why I wanted to go home. It hadn't been until I was at the bus station that I realised I didn't have his number, and I hadn't given him mine. I had no way of contacting him, no way of catching up with him on his journey.

Waiting for the Greyhound, I'd sat, crying for the man I'd known such a short time, but in those few days, had sensed he'd become someone important. I'd wept at the thought I'd lost him, already ashamed of my weakness, and already knowing I'd made the wrong choice. Even more so as the sun reappeared while I was waiting.

I'd been twenty years old, the first time away from my home. I've no other explanation for turning my back on him. It didn't dawn on me until later, I had no way to ever find him again. How could I have found a redheaded man who goes by the name of Red in the whole of the US? Okay, it was the southern half where he was headed, but even he had no idea which state. Why hadn't I asked his real name? Why had it not seemed important?

My mom meets the Greyhound. As I step into her cheap Ford Focus, I examine her carefully. Her lips are pursed.

"Aren't you happy to see me?" I've left Red, and I've returned, but *something seems to be different.*

"Of course, I am." She glances quickly at me. "But there are things you need to know."

"What things?"

"You were set on your own life, just as you should have been." Glancing at her, I see her shrug. "So, I moved on with mine."

I narrow my eyes at her. "What do you mean?"

Mom blushes, and I can't remember her looking so awkward before. "Joe and I have been seeing each other. When you left, well, we moved it on to the next level."

The home I returned home to wasn't the home I'd left only a couple of days earlier. It soon became obvious this affair with Joe hadn't suddenly blown up. It had been going on for ages. For some reason, Mom had preferred me to think of her as a strong grieving widow rather than a woman with natural urges and a desire for another man. Joe, I was certain, had enjoyed the benefits of a warm, willing body to keep him company, without the responsibility of a family. When I'd left, Joe had immediately taken advantage.

He'd moved in.

Was that when she'd changed? Or was she never the free spirit she'd pretended to be?

My relationship with the man who was to become my stepfather was uneasy. Partly because I think he'd have preferred if I'd stayed away.

The lack of warm welcome had made me understand how foolish, young and naïve I'd been. *I should have spoken to Red and stayed.*

The sense that I'd lost something special didn't leave me. Day after day, week after week, I missed Red and all I could have been with him. When two months had passed and I had my confirmation that he'd left something with me, it became clear exactly what a huge mistake I had made.

I knew about contraception, of course, I did. It was why I'd been taking the pill every day. Every single day, until the night I'd gone home with Red and had forgotten to take them with me.

I'd thought at the time, the protection would last until I could get my script filled again.

I'd been wrong. I was having the baby of a man who was, by now, in another state, and I had no way to trace him.

I cried, full of regret, not for the baby I carried, my memory of Red, but for the fact its father would never know its existence. At first, all my concern was about what he was missing. My gut told me he would have stood by me if he'd known he'd left me in this state. At least I had my mom beside me. She was a free-spirited woman, thumbing her nose at conventions. I didn't think she'd care less that she had a pregnant, unmarried daughter.

But I'd overlooked that I lived in a small town, where everyone knew everybody and all their business. I'd also ignored her budding relationship with Joe and his strict morals.

Their solution? To marry me off to the first man who'd take me.

While I was in fits of laughter, turning down Bob's proposal —a widowed man nearing his sixties—I'd noticed he was keeping his face straight. It took me a moment to realise he was serious.

"Of course," he ignored my fit of giggling, "you can keep the child, bastard though it is, and I'll give him or her my name. But I expect you to keep the kid away from me. Shouldn't be hard. All you'll need to do is cook and clean, and sleep in my bed." He leered at the end of his sentence.

All my mirth had fled, especially when Mom and Joe had become angry that I'd thrown their perfect solution back in their faces.

Packing my bags, this time with more than would fit in Red's panniers, I left the very next day.

Just three months pregnant, I knew life wasn't going to be easy, but if I couldn't have the man I wanted with me, I'd live for my kid. Perhaps one day I'd find another man to take Red's place. The one thing I'd never do was lie to my child. Whatever they needed from me, I'd give to them.

Zeke sniffs loudly, wiping their nose on their sleeve, which brings me back to the present. My few moments lost in my head seem to have helped Zeke put theirs together, as they now say firmly, "We'll be okay, Mom."

I swallow a sob of my own. "Of course, we will." Trying to inject confidence in my voice, I continue, "You and me, kid. Against the world." It's the way it's always been. It's been fucking hard at times. So, so many times, I'd wished I'd someone beside me.

Zeke's different, and it shows. They dress as a boy, more out of habit than anything else, but their features and the way they move are feminine. Their voice, although broken, is still high pitched. From an early age, they were bullied for being gay.

That's why I hadn't wanted Red to meet Zeke, especially when I found out who, or rather what, Red was. He'd never be able to understand, just as walking out just now has proven.

It's impossible to hide that Zeke is different. Hell, I should know, they've changed schools more times than I can count, and we've moved locations. Too often when I've started to find my place in a community, Zeke hasn't fit in. Too many people have wanted to change them, to cure them for being simply what they are. A mix of male and female with no real definition. A boy too feminine to be male, a girl too masculine to be a woman.

There is nothing wrong with my child, and I'll fight anyone who tells me different, even if that comes from the man I've dreamed about for the past fifteen years. I always thought should fate ever put him in my path again that I'd immediately lay all my burdens on him.

Red, being a member of an MC, had thrown me for six. Learning he was the prez had amplified my mistrust. As soon as I'd found out about the very male-dominated environment he was immersed in, I knew he would never accept Zeke as they were, and would blame me for them being that way.

I'd gotten exactly the reaction I'd expected.

I can't deny part of me is disappointed. That the other part is relieved, I'll own that. He'd want to fix them when there was nothing about Zeke that needed changing.

There's a loud knock on my door. Tensing, knowing it has to be Red returning, I tell Zeke, "Ignore it. He'll go away."

"Cheryl, open up, or I'll break the fuckin' door down!"

Oh shit. The mild-mannered man I met fifteen years back wouldn't have, but the prez of the Satan's Devils? Well, I expect he just might. A tremble of fear runs through me. *He won't want Zeke, will he? Not when he knows who they are? He won't try and take Zeke from me?*

The door shudders under the assault from his fists.

"Let him in, Mom. And this time, I'm staying. We face him together," Zeke says determinedly from beside me. But I can feel them shaking even though they're trying to be brave. Zeke's words make sense, but they've already been subject to so much ridicule and bullying, I don't want them to hear more of the same from their dad.

"Zeke…" Red yells.

Zeke visibly stiffens beside me. "Let him have his say, then we'll get along as we always have. We're a team, Mom. We don't need anyone."

God, how I've prayed for a good man beside me, one to help me, to help Zeke make their way through life. I know Zeke's wanted a father, and somehow knowing there was one out there Zeke could build up in their dreams was better than being faced with the reality that seems set to bring so much disappointment.

Crashes, like a foot or shoulder hitting the door sound. I look at my child and see the jut of their chin. I think Zeke's as prepared for rejection as they'll ever be.

"I won't let him hurt you," I promise.

"Open the door, Mom," Zeke says tiredly. "Let's get this over."

Taking in a breath and letting it out on a sigh, reluctantly, I go to the door and pull it open.

Red all but falls in. He pushes past me and goes straight to Zeke. He stops in front of them. Again, I take air down into my lungs and this time, I hold it. I'm ready to run and go protect my child, just like I've always done. Moving forward, I go to Zeke's side, effectively standing between the two of them.

Red's eyes glisten as they gaze at my child. He reaches his hand out as though to touch them, but then lets it fall back to his side as if he has no right.

He clears his throat, then starts speaking, his voice sounding choked. "Zeke." He pauses after saying the name, shaking his head as if he's overcome with emotion. "If I'd known about you, I'd have always been there." He gives a sideways glance toward me, then looks back at Zeke. "It's not your mom's fault I never knew about you. Nor was it mine."

Zeke shrugs and replies cautiously, "I know. You guys got together then parted without exchanging details or numbers. It happens." If Red is bothered by their slightly feminine voice, he doesn't show it.

Red's eyes harden. "If you're thinking you're the result of some casual hookup, let me tell you, you're not." Again, his eyes come to me, and this time, he leaves his focus there. "I've never been able to forget your mother. I'm single, and always have been. You know why?" He pauses theatrically for a moment, a silence that neither Zeke nor I fill. "I could never find anyone her equal. That I didn't search for her, well, that's on me. I probably knew where to find her, but the way we parted, well, I'll admit that stung my pride. Then I got tied up in making a new life for myself. As the years passed and I still couldn't fuckin' get her out of my head, I thought she'd be settled in her own new life. I'm so fuckin' sorry I never came looking. If I'd known about you, I'd have been there from the start."

They give another shrug. "I've done okay without a father."

Again, I hold my breath. This is when Red is going to tell

them that they have not. That they'd have turned out different with a father's guidance. It's something I'd often heard before, as if a single mother can't bring up a well-rounded child.

But Red surprises me. His attention fully on Zeke, he grins widely. "Fuck yeah, you have. Might not know much about you, but I'm sure I'm going to like what I find out. Your mom's done a stellar job with you. I'm fuckin' proud of you both."

"I'm not your son." Zeke broadens their shoulders and adds forcefully, "I'm your child." Zeke's eyes go wide as if they'd surprised themself with their own outburst. I all but burst with pride at how they've ripped the Band-Aid off.

Red half-smiles, then turns to me once again. "Can we sit? I'd like to have a conversation."

I suppose the way we're standing is confrontational. I gesture behind him to the table and four chairs. He takes the invitation. When Zeke starts to follow him, I take their hand and squeeze it.

Red sits, and Zeke puts himself opposite. Once again, I put myself between them. Red drops his head into his hands for a moment, then gathers what he wants to say and takes the lead again.

He catches my eye. "I'm sorry I walked off. Your explanation, well, I was going to react badly. Needed a moment to myself to put it into perspective."

"And now you have?" I'm still preparing myself.

Red shrugs. "I'm the prez of an MC, voted into the top spot because, heaven help them, all the members trust me." He gives a self-deprecating smile, which is reminiscent of the man I used to know. "An MC attracts all types of members." He grins slightly. "Society might call them rejects, but I prefer all sorts looking for a home."

I could ask questions, but I sense there's more coming, so I keep quiet, pressing my nails into the palm of my hand.

"It's part of my role to look out for the members. Years back, we patched a man in." At Zeke's look of confusion, Red shakes his head. "Okay, let's step back a bit. If a man wants to join, he works with us for a year as a prospect to prove he's going to fit in. Well, this man did. He was loyal and trustworthy, but there was always something different about him. I couldn't put a name to it. There was a sadness about him that I couldn't put my finger on. Out of everyone, I think he was trying his damndest to fit in."

"Where are you going with this, Red?" I give a wary glance toward my child.

Red raises his chin. "I'll give you the short version. Joker, yeah, that was his name, hiding his sadness by being a comedian, well, he relocated to Tucson. I didn't find out until a year or so later what was behind the move."

"What was?" I snap, wondering why the man was chased off.

"He'd been brought up in a strict family, one who had their own ideas of what a son should be. Told him anything different to the norm was a fuckin' aberration. Joker knew early on he was gay and thought he had to hide it from everybody." Red pauses and his mouth quirks. "He was successful in most cases, all except for one man. A man who pursued him to Tucson, a man who loved him. Both of them had their doubts about the club accepting them, so they kept it to themselves."

"What happened when the club found out?" They did find out, that was obvious, as Red wouldn't be telling their story.

"Fuckin' anti-climactic," Red states, chuckling. "They thought they'd be chucked out on their asses, but nothing happened. Brothers said, okay, and moved on. Didn't give a fuck about gay members."

"Your club's inclusive?" Zeke's eyes have widened, and they give me a hopeful look.

"As I said, we accept oddballs and rejects. We don't judge anyone by the person they love."

"I'm not gay," Zeke tells him.

Red smooths a hand over his beard. "Can't say I understand the situation, but I hope you'll give me the time to learn. One thing I do know, no one should try to change you. You, Zeke, are who you were meant to be. Isn't a case of your upbringing, it's your nature to be you."

A whoosh of air leaves me, and I feel like crying, but Red hasn't finished yet.

"If it hadn't been for Joker, maybe I'd need more education." His face tightens before he continues, "But Joker, well, his parents didn't accept him for what he was. Tried their fucking best to change him." His mouth twists. "Conversion therapy, the works. When that didn't work, they disowned him, always hating him for the supposed choice he made, while not understanding it wasn't any desire of his to be different. Lady? Well, he's Joker's husband. He was brought up by his mom, just like you. He was far more accepting of his sexuality because he never had to pretend to be anything other than himself."

"But he did with you." That contradicts what Red had said earlier, that the club didn't know they were gay until they were found out.

Again, Red shrugs. "Lady's bisexual. It wasn't so hard for him, but he'd taken his cues from Joker, so kept the gay side of himself hidden." Now he stares Zeke in the face. "I accept whatever you are, Zeke. Whatever you want to be. I'll support you in any way. You will need to help me to understand it, but one thing I won't do is try to change you." He coughs, and once again, sounds choked up. "I might only have met you less than an hour ago, but I already know that I love you."

My eyes go wide. Zeke's lip trembles as if they're going to cry.

"I'm me," Zeke starts, clearly commencing Red's education.

I think it's up to me to continue. "Zeke started to have a hard time at school when they were just out of kindergarten. They had more in common with the girls, and the boys seemed to sense there was something different about them. They started to be bullied, and of course, as a mom, I stepped in and complained to the principal." Red sits back, crossing his arms, and nodding at me to continue. "The first suggestion was that *he* should toughen up. Their *help* was to make sure Zeke was picked for sports teams, trying to force them to meld in with the boys. That only made the insults worse, and then it turned physical. When Zeke started coming home with bruises and black eyes, I needed to move them."

I see Red's nostrils flare as Zeke looks down at their hands.

"The next school was a little better, though they commented Zeke was quiet and reserved. They even mentioned depression. So, I took Zeke to a therapist they recommended. He said there was nothing wrong, that Zeke was playing up to get attention. The bullying started again. Boys had gotten bigger, and the damage was worse." Zeke seems to flinch as they remember.

"You changed schools again?"

Nodding, I agree. "And the town, and therapist. This one was more interested in Zeke. Saw them as an experiment. Looked at them and immediately decided they should transition."

"Transition? Become female?" Red turns to Zeke. "Did you consider that?"

Zeke huffs. "Not for a moment. It didn't appeal to me. I'm not uncomfortable with the body I've been given. Luck of the draw that I got a dick instead of breasts, but I have no inclination to change it."

I take over again. "When the therapist wanted to prescribe hormones to change Zeke's development, I got out of there immediately." Pausing, I then add, "If Zeke had wanted to transition, I'd have supported them."

"But I didn't." Now Zeke sits forward and speaks for himself. "The next therapist was brilliant. She introduced me to the concept that gender and sex are entirely different. She recommended some reading material that made me understand while my biological gender might be male, I don't need to identify as such. And not doing so doesn't mean I want to be female."

"She didn't influence Zeke," I say quickly, in case Red thinks Zeke was brainwashed. "She gave them the tools and let them work it out for themself."

Red shifts in his seat as if he's itching to ask questions but is wary of voicing them. I'm so grateful he's affording Zeke a level of acceptance that I hadn't expected, and now I'm annoyed at prejudging him as I had.

What I do think is that we need a break from this deep conversation. Pushing my chair back from the table, I stand. "Anyone want a drink or something?"

CHAPTER THREE

RED

I t must be hard, difficult, impossible for any parent to hear that their child is different, that they don't fit into the norm of society. It must take time to come to terms with the notion that in this prejudiced world, their life will never be easy.

Cheryl's had years to accept what's just been sprung on me. I've only had moments to realise for the first time, I have some sympathy for parents who try to put their child back into a box where they think they belong better. Not that I give a damn what people think about me, but who the fuck would want their kid to go through hell just for being born different?

I would have called myself a tolerant person. When Joker had come out, I'd been hurt by the lack of trust he'd had in me. The fact he was gay hadn't bothered me at all. Yet my initial reaction to Cheryl's revelations about Zeke was that it had to have been her fault, something she'd done wrong, or somehow had used her influence.

My brain had whirred with what she'd just dropped on me, my emotions spiralling out of control. Fuck knows how I'd kept my criticism of her locked inside, but somehow, I did. Before I'd said something I'd never be able to take back, I'd gone outside to process everything she'd thrown at me.

I may not be highly educated but I'm a man of the world, and I know people come in all shapes, colours, sizes and pre-dispositions. It's not Cher's fault that Zeke's different, unless you blame the combination of mine and her genes. It's in Zeke's DNA, and nothing I can do or say would ever change that.

I'd stood by my bike, wishing I had a cigarette to smoke, wondering what I was most upset about—Cheryl's reaction, her preconception that I wouldn't cope, that I'd let prejudices guide me, that because of the cut that I wear, she'd prejudged me? Or was it because I've found the son I'd often dreamed about, only to find they were something different entirely. Or could it be that I'm scared, not on mine, but on Zeke's behalf, knowing their life won't be easy.

Could I consider walking away because I couldn't box up my life in a nice, neat package?

Fuck no. I'm an MC prez. If I wanted easy or a long straight road with no bumps or bends, then I wouldn't be a fucking biker.

I'm not upset that Zeke isn't the son I dreamed of having. It's just going to take me a minute to make some mental adjustments. It's hard for me to get my head around.

Zeke's my child. Fruit of my loins. I determine there and then that I'm never going to be ashamed of them, nor apologise for them, nor be anything but proud as fuck of them. Zeke's different. It makes them no better nor worse than anyone else.

I'm also not blind that others won't so easily accept the situation. My brothers? Well, I've got hope there. Joker and Lady are gay. From time to time, I've had my doubts about Rope and Cuff, and in Utah, there's a big question mark hanging over Honor and Duty. But as far as I know, the majority of the members couldn't give a fuck what their sexual preferences are. They've proved themselves as men you can count on to have at your back.

We've even now got a member without a dick, Swift, the enforcer in Utah. While some brothers were upset that that set a precedent, it is unlikely we'd patch in any other woman. But hell, if a female with her capabilities turned up in Vegas, I'd probably give her my vote.

It's the person that should be accepted, not judged by the genitals they're born with, or how they choose to use them.

At the end of the day though, as Zeke's dad, I'm bound to come in for some criticism. How Cheryl's coped makes her grow in my estimation.

Like being an MC prez, I can't go into being Zeke's dad if I'm not anything but committed, but that won't be difficult. I might not have been able to categorise why, but from the moment I met Zeke, I'd sensed they were different. But that didn't matter one damn. Something in Zeke immediately called to me. This kid carries my blood and has my DNA, nothing could make me walk away.

However, I'm going to have to change my thinking. *They, their, them.* Staring down at my hands, I impress those pronouns on my mind. To use others would hurt my child. It would imply I was trying to fit them into a mould that was formed only in my own limited brain.

There's a wealth of things I don't know. I use electricity with only the rough idea of how it's made, how its power is harnessed, and how a light comes on when I flick the switch. I've been brought up with the idea if you have a dick you're a man. It just so happens Zeke is wired differently.

Now, as Cheryl leaves the room to get us a drink, I'm alone with Zeke for the first time. I feel like I'm walking across a minefield and have to watch every word out of my mouth. The thing that's bothered me most is how they've been treated.

"I hate hearing how you've been bullied."

Zeke shrugs, then focuses their green eyes, so much like my own, on me. "Kids get bullied all the time. It's not just me." A chuckle comes but it's without mirth. "I've had kids try to beat the gay out of me. I'm not even gay, you know?"

"You don't like men?"

Zeke frowns, taking my question seriously, then a faint red tinge spreads over the face opposite me. *Kid's like me.* I inwardly grin. *Same complexion, same giveaway traits.* "I like both girls and boys."

Like Lady? "So, you're bisexual?"

Zeke's face goes a darker shade, and while I know I've only been a parent, or that I've known, for a couple of hours, I suppose it's not something a kid discusses with their dad.

"I'm only just fifteen." They shrug. "I've got time to find out. It's more that gender doesn't matter to me." Now they grin and I think they're getting back at their newfound old man by adding, "I can admire a nice ass whether it's male or female, or gender fluid like me."

I frown. "But you're not transgender. You don't want to be a woman?"

"Nope." Zeke pops the p. "Having a pair of tits doesn't interest me." Their brow furrows, giving them a demeanour older than their years. "See, you're making the normal mistake, mixing up sex with gender. It's not about who I may have a relationship with, it's about how I feel, and how I identify." The look they send me now is one of sympathy. "It's confusing to straight folks, I know."

I'm the one who's confused? I slap that thought down. Zeke's got their own normality, and I can't change them to mine. If I want a relationship with them, then I have to bend.

Conversion therapy, rejection, nothing Joker's parents had done had changed him. No, they'd only succeeded in making him an unhappy and guilty man. Zeke needs my support and understanding, and so—I glance behind me where I can see Cheryl busying herself in the kitchen—does their mom.

I suddenly realise getting to know my kid isn't going to happen if I focus on their sexuality or worry about what gender they class themself as. So, I sit back, stretch my legs, and interlace my fingers in my lap.

"What do you like to do, Zeke?"

It feels like the atmosphere has been lightened. Zeke leans forward, elbows on the table, and rests their chin on their hands. A wide grin appears on their face. "I like to dance."

Dance? Well, that was unexpected, and something I know nothing about. Football, hockey, cars, bikes… any of those I could talk on for hours. Their reply has me flummoxed.

Cheryl chooses that moment to reappear. She places a coffee in front of me and sets a cup down for herself. Zeke gets a soda.

She speaks as she sits down. "Zeke won't tell you this, Red, but they're good. They've got an audition for one of the shows on the strip."

"Really?" I let my face glow with pride, and I eye them again. Dancing isn't for wimps. They're lithe but they have to be pretty muscular under their clothes.

"Zeke's always danced, ever since they were little." Her eyes go vacant, and a look of distaste twists her mouth. "You'd think it was a crime for a kid with a dick to want to dance with the girls. I'd be a millionaire if I had a dollar for every time I've been told I shouldn't encourage them. This was even before Zeke had any idea why they were different. People with dicks should be into sports."

I frown. I hate that anyone tried to interfere in my kid's life. It's time I step up to be a dad. Zeke needs someone by their side, someone who'll give the shit-talking people something to think about.

"When's the audition? I'd like to be there."

Zeke's eyes light up. "You would?"

Cheryl's looking at me, but I can't read her expression.

"Of course, I fuckin' would." I mean it. *But perhaps they don't want me there?* "Unless you don't want me to go, or parents aren't allowed."

"I'd really like that… Dad."

Cheryl's eyes widen and her jaw drops. Me? Well, I feel a hundred feet tall and start beaming.

"Haven't you got homework to do?" Cheryl asks Zeke while sending me a look which I can't interpret.

"Mom, I've done it."

Her obvious plot to speak to me alone having failed, she tries again, "Well, I'm sure there's something you should be doing."

Zeke grins. "If you want to talk to Dad privately, why didn't you just say?" They stand, start to move, then hesitate. "Will you be hanging around, Dad?"

I swallow hard, hearing Zeke give me that title. It's not something I've ever been called in my life, unless it was by one of the brothers messing around. For a second, I'm so choked up I can barely speak.

I place my palms flat on the table and cough to clear my throat. "Your mom and I need to have a conversation. To say I didn't expect things to turn out how they have when I came here today is the understatement of the century. But whatever, you'll be seeing me around. Now I know I'm your dad, I'm not going to stay away." *Whatever Cheryl has to say about it.* I've lost fifteen years with my kid; I'm not going to lose anymore.

I'm a fucking dad. I might be able to say the words, but my brain still hasn't processed it.

When Zeke disappears into their room, I pick up my coffee. It's gone cold, but I drink it anyway. I notice Cheryl's biting her lip and know she's got something to say. I'm not to be disappointed.

"I didn't purposefully keep Zeke from you."

Placing my cup back down, I breathe out a sigh. "Wasn't your fault you couldn't get in touch, that's on me. I'll beat myself up until my dying day that I never came back for you." I turn to look at her. "Bringing Zeke up on your own can't have been easy." Her expression confirms it without needing words. "But I am fuckin' annoyed you tried to keep them from me once we reconnected again."

She has the grace to look down. "A long time ago I met a man called Red, went with him for a few days. Sure, I liked him.

Possibly more than that. Then I made the worst decision of my life and left. I've regretted that every fucking day." She looks up. "I didn't realise I had no way of contacting you until you'd ridden away."

And that's on me too. I'd been annoyed and disappointed and hadn't hung around for lengthy goodbyes.

"I was stupid." Her voice is low and strained. "My only excuse is that I was young, and never before had been away from home." She grimaces. "I missed my mom, missed my creature comforts. It wasn't until I watched you ride away, that I knew I missed you more."

CHAPTER FOUR

RED

Sitting back, I put my thumbs in the belt loops of my jeans and look at her carefully.

The strain of the years that have passed are written on her face, as they probably are on my own. But if I squint, it's like those years disappear, and she's still the woman who'd caught my attention and held it. She retains the same assets that attracted me back then, though her breasts are slightly larger, possibly because they've nurtured my child. There's no doubt in my mind that my body still wants her.

But what makes us us, our souls and our brains, are they still the same? We've both been through shit that the other wouldn't understand. Has that shaped us into different people?

She says she regretted her leaving, but I still don't understand why. Or is it that she's missed having a father for Zeke that makes her feel that way? If our child wasn't in the picture, would she have forgotten me?

Could we pick up where we left off? Or maybe, start all over again? She's honestly the first and only person to ever hold my interest. Or am I fooling myself? I always wanted a wife and family. Am I just tempted to step into one ready-made?

Whatever, I've a child in my life now. Whether Cheryl and I

could have anything between us is a totally different matter, and there's one big thing coming between us. I broach the elephant in the room before it gets too much bigger.

"You're worried about me being in the club." She hasn't had to say the words for me to know she finds that distasteful.

She glances at me gratefully as if she's pleased I've been the one to raise it. "On two levels, I am. Firstly, I'm wary of motorcycle clubs. I've never heard anything good about them. And secondly, you say they're your family. Would you tell them about Zeke? How could you explain?"

I snort. "I think they'd understand that I was too damn thoughtless and didn't use a condom. I assure you darlin', they know how babies are made." And more than that, how to prevent them.

Her eyes roll. "I don't mean that. I mean, Zeke's perfect to me, but there's no denying they're different to the norm other people expect. You say now that you can accept them, but other people might not feel the same way." She shrugs. "They might influence you to look at Zeke as if there was something wrong with them."

"If my club has a fuckin' problem with Zeke, they'll have me to answer to," I growl. "Once I decide on something, I can't easily be swayed. I don't pretend to be an expert on who Zeke is, but they're mine, and that means I'll be behind them all the way." I soften my eyes. "I can't imagine the life you've had, Cheryl, but I've picked up enough just from the fact of you having to move around. One thing shouts out at me—both you and Zeke need people in your corner. Being mine means Zeke will have all my brothers on their side."

"You make it sound too easy."

In my eyes, it will be. Why wear the prez's patch if I'm not prepared to lay down the law?

"And how will this work?" she continues. "You want to make this formal, have visitation rights?"

It sounds so cold, putting it so starkly that it pulls me up. I haven't had enough time to think this through. In truth, I don't know how I see it playing out. Do I want to join them and play happy families? I think, in my head, that's exactly what I naturally thought we'd do. The idea of only seeing my kid on specified days of the week doesn't sit right with me. The vision of knocking on the door and her passing Zeke into my care, then shutting the door in my face is not what I want. While it would give me a chance to get to know the child of my blood, I wouldn't spend time with their mother. They come as a pair, and as Zeke's father, my gut feel is that I've got responsibility for them both, and a lot of time to make up for.

I brush my hands back through my hair. "What about you?" I ask suddenly, leaning forward a little. "When would I get to see *you*?"

She looks at me blankly. "When you collect Zeke and when you bring them back."

"No." I give a deliberate shake of my head. "That won't do. First and foremost, I'm Zeke's dad, but I also want a chance for us to reconnect. To explore what might have happened if we'd never parted, or had been able to keep in touch."

A wave of sadness crosses her face. "That boat has sailed, Red. I'm not the same person you knew. And you," she waves at my cut, "you're someone totally different."

I stiffen as she again reminds me of how little she thinks of all that I've achieved but giving her some allowance for her ignorance of my club, I try not to let my annoyance show in my voice. "I know we can't pick up where we left off, but, Cheryl, there's something about you that I can still feel today. It calls to me just the same as it did years back. I know we can't resurrect the past, but what if we could create something new?"

"I can't," she all but whispers.

"Why not?" I challenge, raising my eyebrows. "Is there somebody else?" There's a chilled feeling inside me at the idea she's got another man. While this apartment bears no evidence of anyone else living here, that's not to say there isn't someone around. Someone who could challenge me for the right to be Zeke's dad. What if someone else could step up and prove to be better for them? How much influence would blood really have?

For a moment, I don't think she's going to answer. There's a silence long enough that I have time to wonder how I'd cope if that was the situation. Not that I come up with anything other than an assurance I'd hate it.

Finally, and with reluctance, she puts me out of my misery. "No, it's always been you." She looks like she's sucking on lemons as she forces those words out. "Oh, I've tried, don't think I haven't. Being a single mom is a lonely life, particularly with all that Zeke and I have gone through." She raises her shoulders level with her ears then drops them again. "It was hard dating with Zeke around. First, they were a baby and I found it hard to leave them. When I did start looking around, I found most men who appealed to me didn't want to step into a ready-made family. And those that did, well…" Again, there's that sour twist to her mouth, "They didn't match up to what I'd built you up to be in my memory." She shrugs. "Though I do think my memory might have been exaggerating. I'm not sure I ever knew you at all."

I don't take it as an insult. It's the same way I feel about my feelings for her. We'd met and parted in such a short time, some of the things I believed I knew could turn out to be pure fantasy.

"It's the same for me, darlin'." I feel brave enough to use an endearment. "I've been with women, of course I have, but none were ever you." Shaking my head, I add, "If you want the truth, I'd given up looking. Thought the club was the only family I'd ever have."

Her head tilts as though she's questioning whether I'm serious but must believe the sincerity in my eyes as she says, simply, "Then you saw me."

"Then I saw you," I reply huskily.

Our eyes meet and hold. For a few seconds, neither of us can look away. She's the one to break it first and does so with a dismissive gesture.

Her voice is full of want and need. "It's too complicated. Zeke could do with a father in their life, but are you the right man?"

"I'm their blood," I state firmly. "There's no way you're going to get rid of me now." She's got to know how the land lies. I'm not going to take any easy way out she might think to offer me.

She nods slowly. "If you're serious about playing that part, then you need to know it can't be half-hearted. For their sake, you've got to be all in. If you can't commit to that, then it's best you don't start."

"I'm committed," I spit out. I knew that the moment I first saw Zeke at the door, looking so much like a younger, softer version of myself.

Her shoulders slump as if she realises she's no option, and for a second her eyes close. "Then you'll be around as Zeke's father, but as nothing else." I open my mouth to protest that she should give *us* a chance, but she gets her views in before me. "If," she points to herself then to me, "if you and I don't work out, it could destroy your relationship with Zeke, or at the least, make it awkward. I can't risk it. It wouldn't be fair on Zeke."

"And what's fair on you?" I raise a querying brow. "What about your life, Cheryl? I get the impression you've put yourself on hold and lived for your kid for the last fifteen years. Am I right? Fighting people to get everyone to use the right pronouns, getting between them and bullies, fighting for their right to their own way of life." Again, her expression says it all and that her life's been just as I've summed up. "You also need someone to be on your side, to have your back and help ease your path. Why not let me be that for you?"

A look of longing comes into her eyes as if she's been yearning to have someone take the weight off her shoulders, or at the very least, share it. While she's biting her lip, clearly fighting within herself, trying to decide whether she can chance taking something for herself when for the past fifteen years she's lived unselfishly, I examine her with fresh eyes.

Rather than seeing her as the girl of my dreams, I look at her for who she is now. I fucking admire all she's had to do. Bringing up any child is hard, but when the one you birthed disregards all society's rules, it must be horrendous. She has to be strong with a backbone forged of steel, and I doubt she'd take shit from anyone. She's exactly who I need as an old lady. *Nah*, I tell myself, mentally trying to take a step back, *that's too much, too fast*. There's a wealth of issues to deal with before I let myself go there. As well as Zeke, I've other responsibilities, and I've got to consider what's right for my club. But it's not stretching the bounds of possibility too far to say what's right for me could also be right for them, and that it could be her.

She's tempted, I can see that. So, I consider how to make it easier for her, and give me a chance to get my head straight as well. "Look, we don't have to jump into a relationship from the start. Let's take time and get to know each other again. We'll date, talk, share our dreams and desires, but out of bed, not in it like we did before. Let me take both you and Zeke out. Let me discover all there is to know about the two of you. We'll take this one step at a time. If it goes nowhere, no harm no foul, but there's always the chance we could make a relationship work."

She stays quiet, her forehead creasing, smoothing, then her brow furrows again. The lines around her eyes deepen and relax. Busy thoughts must be crossing her mind.

It's a few minutes before she speaks, but I allow her to have them. I've said my piece, now it's up to her to decide.

Finally, she looks up and meets my eyes. "It's too much like a fairy tale, Red. The handsome prince returns and wakes sleeping beauty after fifteen years."

I can't completely suppress the grin at the implication she

still finds me attractive and acknowledge that the word beauty accurately describes her. "Fairy tales must be based on some kind of reality."

"Or unfulfilled dreams," she returns.

"We won't know until we try, Cheryl."

She pouts as though I've said something distasteful. At my raised eyebrow, she asks, "Could you do one thing for me?"

She doesn't know it yet, but there's probably no limit to what I'd do to ensure her happiness. I give her a chin lift.

"Call me Cher? I'm not the Cheryl you used to know."

That's an easy one. "Cher." I try it out, rolling the name over my tongue. "You know, I like that for you."

"Good." She gives me a smile, one that carries genuine warmth and shows at last I've done something to please her. "I like it too."

That expression makes her look carefree, just like the girl I met all those years before. It doesn't help that it makes me admit my feelings are still exactly the same. *Christ, I still want her.* Being friends and keeping my hands off is going to be fucking hard, but if dating her is what it's going to take, I'll go slow and endeavour not to let the attraction that's never died show. My hands twitch in an urge to reach out and touch her. In my head, she's already mine.

Forcing myself to be sensible, I restrain myself. The clock can't be turned back. What we've got to deal with are the changes that have been wrought in the minutes, hours, days and years that have passed. It's best if I treat her as I would someone I've just met.

She's biting her lip and looking nervous. As I brace myself, waiting for more limitations to be put on our fledgling relationship, she surprises me and hesitantly asks, "You want to stay for dinner?"

The out-of-the-blue question forces a grin to appear on my face. It sounds like a great place to start. A chance to sit down and begin to get to know them both. "That sounds fuckin' good to me… Cher."

"I could do meatloaf." Her wink says it all.

Hell, that was the meal I'd first eaten at the diner. I reply with a laugh, "Meatloaf will do fine."

CHAPTER FIVE

RED

Sharing that first dinner with Zeke and Cher has to be up there with some of the greatest moments in my life.

I could have wasted energy internally ranting about what I've missed, how I lost out on knowing Zeke as a baby and all of their formative years, but with determination, I put that to one side. If anyone had blame, it was me for not going back for her. Life has dealt us these cards, and what's important is how we play them now.

Zeke might be different to me in many respects, and of those, there are a number I don't fully understand, but despite that this is the first time we've met in our lives, it's far from like talking to a stranger. They've got some of my quirks, not the least being quick to flush red in the face, something I regret passing on. Their eyes crease the same way mine do in the mirror, and as for freckles, it's hard to say which one of us has the most.

The evening hadn't felt odd. The conversation wasn't stilted and flowed, though for much of the time, I was content to sit and listen to the interaction between mom and child. It felt completely natural as if this was my place—me sitting, eating with the fruit of my loins and, however much I may be pre-empting the future, with my woman.

My family.

The one I've always longed for in my head.

A few times, I get a pang for the years I've missed, regret that I didn't see her body grow round with my kid, or that I hadn't been there to witness the miracle of birth. I'd missed the first smile, the first steps, the first day at school. I wasn't around to step in when the other kids became cruel. But what point do regrets serve? I've been given this chance to make recompense, and that's what I'll grab with both hands.

As I eat, I'm full of pride for what my genes have produced. In character, Zeke's different from me. Their relationship with their mom is easy and relaxed, whereas I used to give my mom and dad shit in my teenage years. But I guess that comes from it being them against the world for a while, which must have formed a strong bond.

Their easy interaction also makes me frown as I realise getting fully accepted into their loop isn't going to be simple at all. I'll need to make myself a place.

As Cher's cooked, Zeke and I wash the dishes, having a friendly chat as we do. I note they like hockey and mentally note whether I can get tickets to a Golden Knights game. Football isn't one of my particular passions, but when they informed me they follow the Las Vegas Raiders, I decide I'm going to too. I picture father and kid's day out at a game or watching away matches on the television. While Zeke has no aptitude for play-ing, spectating is something they enjoy.

When conversation falters, I ask what else they like to do. They start reeling off Xbox games, some of which I've heard of. I tell them Trist and Tom, Rosa's kids, like to play too. When I hear Zeke doesn't easily make friends, I again think of the twins. *Would they accept Zeke?* They're brats, but good kids too. I've a feeling they might, as long as the club does. For the moment, I put to one side any anxiety on that account.

After dinner, Cher puts on a film, a comedy which has me laughing despite my initial dubiousness at the subject matter.

Even though my place is to one side on a chair by the couch while she and Zeke snuggle together, I feel part of their team, and can't remember an evening when I've felt so relaxed.

When Zeke finally takes themself off to bed, I know it's time I should make a move. Though I'd love to, I can't stay longer and push things too soon. When I tell her I'm going to leave, I read regret warring with relief on her face.

I take out my phone, unlock it and hand it to her. "Put your digits in there."

Her eyes come to mine for a second, then she snorts a laugh. "Not going to make the same mistake again?"

Not fucking likely. I'm not going to wait another fifteen years for fate to put her in my path again.

She does as I requested and her phone pings. "Now I've got you too."

"I'll call you. Arrange a date." Already, I can't wait to see her and Zeke again.

"I'm working the next few days." Cher tells me something I already knew, but I don't admit I have access to her schedule. I'm just grateful she hadn't asked how I knew her address.

"We'll sort something out," I tell her as I pick up my helmet and extract my gloves. Passing by me, she opens the door.

I hesitate, knowing what I want to do. *Damn it if she thinks I'm moving too fast.* I cup my hand around her cheek, wait a pause for an objection, then receiving none, give her a kiss on the lips. Just our mouths touching, no tongues involved, but she can't quite suppress a little gasp, or hide that her pupils have dilated.

Hell, just that brief touch has affected me too. *I want more.* I want to stay, push her back onto that couch, kiss her the way I always have in my dreams. Instead, I've got to prove I'm a man of my word.

I pull back, politely wish her a good night, and then I leave.

I'd promised her slow.

I'm not going to give her a reason to doubt me or give her any excuse to run. I've lost her once; I'm not going to risk doing that twice. Even if that brief kiss has me adjusting myself in my pants as I stride toward my bike.

As I ride back to the clubhouse, a grin appears on my face and sticks like glue. Not only have I found the woman I thought I'd forever lost, but I've found something else too. Something I thought I'd never have. I'm a fuckin' dad. While not in the most ideal of circumstance, I have a family of my own. Now, I've just got to work on keeping it.

The streets fly past, and soon I'm turning into the clubhouse gates, backing into my spot and kicking the stand down on my bike. Before I dismount, I'm blasted again by that thought in my head.

I'm a fucking dad.

I'd never expected to see Cheryl again, let alone the bonus that came with her. Still unable to believe this isn't all a dream, I swing my leg over the saddle, and head to the clubhouse, wanting little more than some time to myself to process what's happened today.

But when I push open the door and step inside, Crash waves at me from the bar. Sighing, I know that I can't cut and run on my VP. I walk over to join him.

Crash takes one look at my face and elbows Twister. "Hey, Prez got laid." He eyes me again. "I don't know what else would have put that fucking smile on his face."

What I have with Cher and Zeke is too new to be shared. I feel selfish, wanting to keep my news to myself. So, neglecting to tell him I barely reached first base, I just smirk and leave them to reach their own conclusions about where I've been and what I've been doing.

"Hey, I'm considering new pipes. What d'you think of these?" As Twister slides a magazine across, I try to pay attention to it.

I shoot the shit for a while, listening to Crash's beef about the oil leak on Cobra's bike which needs fixing. When there's a lull in conversation and I feel I've done my part, I make my excuses and take myself upstairs, proud that I'd been able to function like a normal human being, when most of my mind was back with Cher and Zeke.

I step into my room and look around for a moment, my lips once again curving. My accommodations are now lavish compared to what I previously had.

Once Clare and Delly had moved on, Rosa had stated in no uncertain terms that she no longer needed to keep a room for herself and the boys at the clubhouse. So, I'd moved into Brick's old room—well, it's more of a suite really—two bedrooms and a private bathroom. *Fucking ideal for Zeke and Cher to stay in.* Assuming, that is, that Cher will be sharing my bed.

I stand for a moment, unable to stop myself imagining her there. Will I notice any changes? *Does she bear evidence of carrying my kid? Stretch marks?* I'd already noticed her larger breasts. *Would she be as soft as I remembered? Would her pussy still feel the same?*

Remembering how it felt to slide into her depths, my cock thickens. I reach down to reposition it, then find myself lowering the zipper. Freeing my cock, I begin to stroke it, my mind becoming full of memories of Cher and I in that motel room, her lying on the bed all wanton and waiting for me.

What a fucking novice I'd been. My pace slows and my face reddens with embarrassment as I remember. How had it gone? Oh yeah, I'd gotten her off, fucked her, and that about sums our encounters up. Now my mind imagines all the things I could do to her were I to have her at my mercy again, and how I could have her screaming instead of merely moaning my name.

As I imagine going down on her, pre-cum leaks. I use it to lubricate my hand, then again speed up my rhythm. Closing my eyes, it's not hard to picture her head thrown back in abandon nor hear her startled gasp as she comes undone. The picture in my head has my spine tingling. With my free hand, I fumble for a t-shirt I'd earlier discarded and hold it to catch my cum.

Jesus. Even using her as a muse to jerk myself off, my release was more intense than when I'm watching porn. *What would it be like when I have the real thing in front of me?* Fuck knows if I can imagine it, but I'm determined on one thing—the day will come when I have her naked and I find out for myself. Maybe it will have to be delayed gratification as I wait for her to trust me again, but it will happen. I've just got to come up with a plan and put it into action.

The first step is not allowing her time to reconsider the decisions we made this evening. I can't afford to waste time contacting her. The very next day, I call the number she'd programmed into my phone. When she answers immediately, regret again slams into me, *why hadn't we exchanged numbers back then?*

Life would have been different for sure. Better? Who the fuck knows? I damn well know I wouldn't be where I feel I'm meant to be, the prez of the Vegas Chapter of the Satan's Devils MC. Maybe fate plays out for a reason, and maybe back then our stars weren't aligned.

"Hi."

"I'm working today," she tells me hurriedly, and before exchanging pleasantries.

"Six to two, yeah?" I've seen her schedule but let her think it's an educated guess. "What happens to Zeke when you're not there?"

"They stay by themself. I've got good neighbours. They watch out for them, and Zeke's got their numbers to call." I can tell by her strident tone she expects me to accuse her of neglecting them, when how the fuck can I criticise when I left her to bring them up alone?

Having known she wouldn't be around this evening, I already know what I'm going to suggest. "Want to catch something to eat before you leave for work? You and Zeke? I presume they'll be back from school?"

When my remonstration about childcare arrangements doesn't come, her voice lightens. "School ends at three, but they've got dancing practice. I'll be taking them there, then bringing them home when they're done. Today's not a good day, Red." The undisguised disappointment in her voice shows me she's not putting me off, but just stating practicalities.

I want to offer to take Zeke myself, wanting to immerse myself in their world, but it's too soon, so I tamp down my impatience. "Tomorrow?"

"Tomorrow would be great." The slight breathlessness shows me her relief that I've understood and that she hasn't chased me off. She might not know it yet, but that will never happen. Where she's concerned, I'm fully committed.

What's one day? Twenty-four hours to wait, time which seems to go far too slowly. I find it hard to concentrate, anxious to see them both again. I curb my impatience, hoping no one sees anything different about me, trying not to snap at the slightest thing going wrong.

At last, Tuesday afternoon comes around and I meet up with them both once Zeke's home from school. Seeing as my only knowledge about what teenagers like to eat comes from being around Rosa's twins, I take them to an all-you-can-eat buffet, which proves a good choice. Zeke's appetite appears to be legendary.

It blows me away to be out as a family. As I watch Zeke pinching fries off Cher's plate and generally fooling around, I can't stop myself from grinning. And when they have the audacity to try to steal a piece of fried chicken from mine, I whip my plate away with a growl. Zeke cracks up, and their laughter makes me think I've never heard a better sound. The thought that this could really be mine sends delightful shivers through me. *We could do this all the time.*

I know I'm getting ahead of myself, but I'm determined that I'll win Cher around. While her arguments are valid, one day soon, I'm certain I'll call her mine.

I honestly can't remember when I've felt so relaxed and carefree. I normally avoid these types of restaurants. Bikers have no place where little kids are running around, and to be honest, they used to annoy the hell out of me. But this feels right, and with how Zeke's stuffing their face, I'd made a good choice.

Keeping the atmosphere light, I don't probe, don't ask questions, just let the conversation flow. It dawns on me, I don't just love my child as they're part of me, I'm starting to love them not just because they're mine, but for the person they are.

I already know I'll do anything to protect them. When Zeke gets a sideways glance from a man who frowns, I focus my best prez stare on him, which quickly makes him back down.

I arrive back at the clubhouse, trying to replace my face-splitting grin with a frown, and glare at Crash when he tries to question me.

Not pushing my luck, Wednesday I leave them alone. Thursday, though, well, that's one of the days Cher doesn't work. Like the previous occasion, I take them both out to eat first, then, drive them home.

This time, though, on Zeke's assurance that they're fine on their own, and indeed some encouragement directed toward their mom, I again leave the apartment, this time with Cher beside me.

It's then I curse that I haven't brought the bike with me. When she comes out of her room, wearing jeans that fit her like a second skin, and a pretty top that frames her perfect boobs, I wish I was going to have her riding behind me. I satisfy myself with the thought that I'll have that soon.

She's quiet in the car as we transition from being a family unit and talking as parents, and hell yeah, I'm getting one hell of a kick by counting myself one of that number, to being two people out on a date. I'm not sure that's quite how she'd name it, but that's what I believe this is.

We've eaten already, so I take her to a bar I know to be fairly quiet, one where the background music isn't too loud and where we'll be able to talk without shouting or straining to listen to any reply.

I do everything that I think a woman like her would expect. I tell her to wait once I've parked the car and walk around to open her door. Then I place my hand on the small of her back and direct her to the entrance, where, of course, I reach forward, open and hold the door for her. Then, when we get to a booth, I wait for her to seat herself first. See, I might be a biker, but I can be a gentleman when I want. I enjoy these little gestures, showing I can take care of her.

We sit and start to talk. She tells me about Zeke as a baby, and I'm sure glosses over the less pleasant parts of her life. In turn, I tell her about meeting Wraith, and how I originally joined the club. I share some amusing stories about the characters I've met and some of the pranks that were played on me while I was prospecting. Time seems to move fast, and before I know it, she wants to get back home. I understand. Zeke's left alone most nights when she works at the casino, and she feels she's abandoning them on her night off.

As I pass her her purse and wait for her to get it situated comfortably on her shoulder, I ask, "Are you happy always leaving Zeke alone while you work? Would it help if I came around or something?"

The way she bristles shows me she's taken it as a criticism. "They don't need a babysitter, Red. I think they'd be upset if they thought their dad didn't trust them."

Backtracking, I change my suggestion. "Well, make sure they have my number and know to use it if anything comes up. If they need something while you're at work, I, or one of my brothers if I'm not available, will be there."

"Your brothers?" She raises her eyebrow in question.

Viewing her seriously, I explain, "I told you, Cher, the club is a family. And family backs each other up."

The expression on her face shows her it's something she's not experienced. Right then, I know I want to introduce her and Zeke to the club, and let her see what I mean for herself.

"Sunday you're off, aren't you?" She nods. "We're having a

barbeque Sunday afternoon. It will be a family friendly affair. Why don't you and Zeke come along?"

No such barbeque is planned, well, not as yet but it will be after church tomorrow evening. I doubt many of the brothers will have other plans or turn down a chance to party. All PG of course, until my kid goes home.

She doesn't immediately jump at it. "Can I talk to Zeke first?" Her brow creasing shows her concern that my brothers might not be as accepting of Zeke as I am.

"Sure you can." But my offhand response belies the unease inside of me. I'm not going to pretend Zeke's anything other than what they are. If Zeke can put up with the shit they get thrown at them, then I'll have to step up and do the same. But I won't allow any disrespect to be shown to their face. I'll just have to make the brothers understand they'll answer to me if they don't toe the line. Belatedly, I realise I'm forcing the issue before I'm ready to make my relationship with Cher public. But would there ever be a good time?

Shaking off my concerns, I decide for now, I'll enjoy the rest of the evening. As we approach the car, I reverse what I'd done before, opening her door, waiting until she's settled and help with the seatbelt. Then I go to the driver's side and start the drive to her home, while wishing I was driving her back to my bed. Nothing about today has turned me off her. Nothing she's said or done has lessened my physical feelings, nor the respect I hold for her. I've been entertained all night and have found no parts boring. As I drive, I go over the evening in my head, hoping to fuck she could say the same thing of me.

Never in all my interactions with a woman before have I been so worried about how I'd come across. I was Red, prez of an MC, and cocky even before that. A woman either wanted me or she didn't, and if it was the latter, it didn't bother me. But Cher? She's under my skin and how I come across to her is important.

I'm not going to pretend to be something I'm not. I'll let her see the good parts and bad. But at the end of the day, I hope that it's the man I am that she wants.

Halting the car outside her apartment building, I walk around to open her door, giving her my hand to help her out.

She turns and looks at me, and tells me softly, "I had a good time tonight, Red."

Feeling a wave of relief, I tell her the truth. "So did I."

She does that adorable biting of her lip for a moment, then the creases fade from her brow as she comes to a decision. "If it's okay with Zeke, I'd like to meet your club on Sunday."

It becomes even easier to breathe. "And I'd like to see you there." Taking a risk, I place a hand at the back of her head and pull her toward me. Lowering my mouth, I pause hopefully. I'm not disappointed as hers comes up to meet mine.

It starts off as a gentle kiss, just like the last time, but now I can't hold back. I want more. Applying pressure, I groan when she opens and lets me in. My tongue invades, and I lose sense of where I am as I plunder that soft cavern. Her hands clutch at my biceps, her fingers digging into my skin as her tongue battles with mine.

Wrapping my hand around her hair, I tug her close, angling her just how I want. Of their own accord, my hips move in close, my hard-as-nails cock pressing against her. If she was in any doubt as to whether I want her as much now as I had fifteen years ago, she has to be aware of the proof.

Little mewls are coming out of her mouth. The taste of her, the sounds she's making, makes my cock want to burrow out of the confines of my jeans and straight into her.

She's been taunting me all night with that form-enhancing top. Swept away by the passion suddenly erupting between us, I squeeze my hand into the small gap between our bodies and palm her breasts.

I might have lost all sense of where we are, but she hasn't. Wrenching her mouth away, she cries, "Not here."

It's not a no, I process, it's an objection to the very public parking lot we're in. It brings me back to reality. "Let's take this inside."

"I can't…" She sounds as disappointed as I feel, but her explanation is sound when she adds, "Zeke."

Fuck. They're a little cockblocker. My thought isn't fair, and I know where she's coming from. Hell, I've never been embarrassed about doing it in front of anyone, but something pulls me right up at the thought of my kid hearing me getting it on with their mom.

"Fuck." I lean my forehead against hers, noticing both of us panting as though we've run a marathon. "Fuck," I repeat, but less desperately, willing my cock to get the message that he might as well stand down as he won't be needed this evening.

"I just can't, not with…"

"I understand." I do, but in my head, I'm running through options. Instead of taking her to the bar, I should have taken her to a motel room.

But she's worth more. And she's worth waiting for.

Still with the top of our heads touching, I smile down at her. "Soon, Cher. Soon."

She glances up slyly. "I thought we were taking this slow."

"Slow? When you all but ravished me?" I cock an eyebrow.

Her fist hits my chest. "I thought that was what you were doing to me."

"Fuck slow, Cher. I want you." My desperation must show in my voice.

When she looks away and doesn't answer, I feel a kernel of fear. "Don't you want me?"

"I've got Zeke to think about. Nothing's changed. If this is just getting fifteen years of waiting out of your system, then I can't go there. Not with them to think about."

This isn't what this is. But how can I, here and now, promise her a forever? I can't. She's not met my club, and she's still suspicious of my life. While I have hope, I can't hand on heart say it's certain my new family is going to fit in.

Worried I've jumped the gun, I ask cautiously, "The barbeque, Sunday. Will you still be there?"

"I want this to work, Red, but I need to put Zeke first."

I know what she's saying. I overstepped the boundary when I kissed her. And it's as true for me as it is of her. We should be friends, not lovers. I don't want to risk pissing her off and losing access to my kid. Not when I've only just found them.

"Cher, I would never do anything to upset Zeke, and if that means keeping my hands off you, then that's how it will have to be."

"You're a good man, Red."

A good man? Good men don't plan to go home and jerk off to the image of the woman they've just kissed. Good men don't study her ass as she walks off, wondering whether she's ever been taken there.

And good men don't howl with frustration and rage when they drive out of sight.

I want Cher.

CHAPTER SIX

RED

I've sat back and listened as the normal updates have been given at church, laughed in the right places, and scowled and frowned when a brother started being an ass, which happens more frequently than I like, particularly tonight. Despite my impulse, I've not rushed anyone. But as Crash sits back, having finally finished speaking, I'm determined to get my piece of other business in first.

I bang the gavel. "Listen up." When I'm sure I've got their attention, I continue, "We're having a barbeque on Sunday."

"Yeah?" Twister folds his arms and stares at me. "Not that I'm objecting, but that's two days away, Prez. What's brought this on so fuckin' suddenly?"

Indian chuckles and raises an eyebrow toward me. "Better come clean, Prez. You don't normally call a party for no fuckin' reason."

Titch narrows his eyes. "Prez is up to something. It's not for our fuckin' benefit, it's for his."

"True that." Crash looks thoughtful. "And since when has Prez ever arranged anything? Shit like that is always down to Rosa."

"What would Prez get out of it?" Sarge wonders aloud.

Crash's eyes gleam as he leans forward. "Could be he wants to introduce someone to the club." One look at the betraying flush of my cheeks and he slaps his hand on the table. "By fuck, that's it," he declares triumphantly.

"Yeah, he's been AWOL most of this week. Bet he's found a bitch." Roller's disrespectful tone makes me frown.

Before I can remark on it, Cuff shakes his head. "The prez? Nah, he wouldn't step out on us. We're all his bitches."

"Speak for yourself!" Hammer calls out.

"I'd be his bitch." Rope looks thoughtful, and for a horrible moment, I wonder whether he's being serious.

"Come on, Prez. Fess up. Why do you want to get us together?" Cobra's staring at me intently.

Hmm. I should have thought this through a bit more. There'd have been better ways to handle it. I could have gotten Rosa on board first, got her to say it was her idea. Cautiously, I eye my brothers.

"Can't I just want you to let down your hair and enjoy yourselves?"

"We do that every day." Hammer snorts.

Crash is tapping his fingers against his teeth. "There's more to it. He's bringing someone to meet us, and whoever it is, he wants us on our best behaviour."

Cobra slams his hand on the table and says, "Fuck me. Prez has found himself an ol' lady."

All eyes snap to me.

"I haven't," I deny fast, then hate myself for belittling what I hope will be between me and Cher, but I don't want her to be put on the spot on Sunday.

"Jeez, that will put Rosa's nose out of joint." Ignoring my denial, Petty shakes his head.

"Whoa." I hold up my hands to stop the speculation right there. I glare at them until they stop speaking, then rub my temples. "For some fuckin' reason, I thought it would be good to introduce a woman and her kid to you fuckers, and that the best way to do that was at a barbeque."

Cobra holds out his hand, palm up. "I called it, bitches. We're going to have a new first old lady." He waits expectantly for money to be passed to him, but there are no takers.

I've a specially reserved scowl for comments which annoy me, and I use it now. "It's not like that."

"Well, what the fuck is it?" Twister leans back in his seat and rests one foot against the table. "Talk to us, Prez."

"We've got your back, Prez." Crash glares at the rest of the brothers and once he's received chin lifts or nods, turns back to me. "You need us? We'll be there. But give us something to go on." He shrugs. "You have to agree, you've not introduced anyone to us before, so this person has to be special."

"He said a kid as well," Rope points out.

Sighing, I realise I'm nervous about their reaction. I need to prepare them for who they're going to meet on Sunday, and I have to do it carefully.

"Okay." My brow creases as I gather my thoughts. "I've met a woman. I like her. Want to see if she's a fit with the club."

Keys snorts. "It's the bitch from the casino."

Crash's eyes widen. "Her? Your old friend?"

Fuckers. "Alright." I hold up my hands in surrender. "Let me explain." When they all sit forward like fucking kindergartners at story time, I take a breath. "You all know my background, about how I left Vermont, rode south, and ended up prospecting for the Satan's Devils."

"You going to give us your whole fuckin' life story?" Titch challenges. "'Cos I need a fuckin' smoke and this is going to take too long."

A growl comes from my throat, but Twister has already reached over and cuffed his arm. "Shut it, old-timer." Then to me, he waves his other hand. "Carry on."

Crash snorts as the enforcer gives me permission. I just shake my head and continue.

"I hooked up with a girl in my travels, not long after I'd left home." I frown, wondering how to phrase it. "She rode with me a few days, and we clicked. It was soon, it was fast, but hell, I knew I wanted to claim her."

Multiple pairs of eyes are now staring at me.

"You didn't though. So, what went wrong?" my VP asks, sitting back and folding his arms. "Didn't she want you?"

"Life happened," I tell them. "Fucked-up shit meant she left my ass, and I rode on alone." I grimace. "I was pissed, which meant I left without leaving her my number, and not getting hers."

"And she's the bitch you met at the casino?"

I glance at Crash's wide eyes head-on, there's no point in denying it. "She is."

"Aw fuck, Prez." Sarge places his hand over his heart. "That could be in a romance novel. You meeting up and falling in love after all this time." He, for one, looks pleased for me.

"You fuckin' forgive her?" Petty doesn't look so impressed. "If a woman walked out on me, that's the last chance she'd have." Growls from a few of the brothers indicate they'd feel the same way.

"She had good reasons for leaving?" Roller asks sceptically.

I glare at Petty while I answer Roller, rubbing my hand over my face. "The weather turned. She was young, wet and cold. Being on the road was too much for her. She was too young to tell me how she was feeling, and I was too hotheaded to ask for her reason."

Shadow scoffs. "Life of a biker, Prez. She couldn't hack it. Maybe you were better off without her."

Titch, though, seems to see it from her side. "Sounds like she was giving up everything to be with you, Prez. Must have been one hell of a decision to make, and with the weather batting against her, no wonder she let doubts change her mind."

I raise my chin toward him gratefully. "She regretted it immediately, just as much as I had known I'd done wrong when I rode off and left her."

"That's fuckin' sweet." Rope grins widely. "You reconnecting after all this time and now wanting her to be your ol' lady."

I open my mouth to say it's too early to say where this is going, when Petty snorts.

"Sweet? It's fuckin' obvious now she's found out Red's the prez of an MC, like most women, she can't wait to drop her fuckin' panties. I'd stick well clear if I were you, Prez."

I slam my hand on the table. "It's not fuckin' like that," I snarl. "If anything, it's because I'm prez she's not jumping into my bed. She's wary of the club, which is why I want her to come meet you assholes." Though listening to them now, I have to ask myself why. If Petty suggests to her she's a patch chaser, she'd run a mile.

Indian sits forward and does his sergeant-at-arms stare. "If Prez has found his woman, you better not fuck it up for him, Brothers." He says it in general, though his eyes land on Petty.

"How does that shit work?" Sarge asks, genuinely. "I mean, only Rosa and Tiff are old ladies. No one else has gotten close."

"We'd have to vote on her. Can't take in just anyone, which means we'll have to get to know her," Crash reminds everyone calmly. "Which is why Red's setting it up to bring her here and wants us all in attendance."

I rub my temples. "Look, yeah, I suspect she could make a good ol' lady, but I'm not pushing for that. Not right now. I've only just reconnected with her. Who knows where the fuck this is going? But unless she meets the club, and yeah, Crash is right, you meet her too, we can't consider going anywhere."

Hammer frowns. "So why do you want a special get-together so we can meet her? Shouldn't you be sure before you bring her around?"

"Didn't you mention a kid earlier?" Cobra shows he's been paying attention. "She's not exactly remained faithful to you, Red. You stepping in on another man's property?"

Breathing in deeply, I bite the bullet and tell them the rest. "When I left her, I left something with her. Something I didn't know about at the time." I pause to take another breath. "Something that's just fifteen years old."

The table goes as silent as I've ever experienced it. You could hear the fucking proverbial pin drop.

"She kept your kid from you?" Cobra's the first to break the silence with widened eyes.

"That shit's not right, Prez," Crash says with a frown. "How could you ever forgive her?"

"You had a right to know. She should have fuckin' told you." Twister's face has gone as black as thunder.

As various other remonstrations come from all around, I have to resort to banging the gavel. "She didn't have a fuckin' chance," I say, loudly, then in a scoffing tone, add, "How the fuck was she to find a man called Red, somewhere in any of the southern states of America? We hadn't exchanged surnames or as I said earlier, numbers."

"Jeez." Crash regards me, his jaw dropping. "She's never been able to find you. So what, you've got a kid and you've only just found out?"

"Son or daughter?" Indian asks, also looking shocked on my behalf.

"Zeke. My kid's named Zeke."

"Well hell, Prez, congrats." Titch seems to be coping with this better than some of the others. "And you escaped the baby phase. Got a ready-made junior Devil right there."

Could I picture Zeke wearing a patch? Hell no.

"Of course, we want to meet him," Fox, quiet up to now, says. "And I suspect I'm right in thinking whether or not you and this woman make a go of it, you want your son in your life."

I nod, grateful someone understands. "That's where I want them," I confirm. "And hence the request for a family friendly barbeque."

"You sure he's yours?" Shadow asks. "Done any paternity testing?"

I take no offence, it's a natural question to pose. My lips curve. "It's like looking in a fuckin' mirror, Brother. No testing required."

"Shit." Keys pretends to look horrified. "Can we cope with a mini-Red?"

"Lock up your daughters," Rope states with a grin, then looks around. "Oh, we haven't got any."

"Or none that we know about," Cuff finishes for him, getting a laugh.

"What's he like?" Titch seems to be the one most interested. "You click with him, just like you did his mother?"

I think of the time I've spent with Zeke this week. Hell yes, we've clicked. There might be shit that I don't quite understand, but as a parent, I'm fucking honoured to be able to say they're mine. I let that show on my face when I speak.

"I'm fuckin' proud to have them as my child."

"Then I want to meet him." Twister grins. "See if he's a chip off the old block. I say fuck yeah to the barbeque."

"A mini-me Red? This I've got to see," Indian states, grinning widely. He glances at Titch. "Me, I think I'd prefer a baby rather than be thrown in the midst of the teenage years if Tom and Trist are any example. Aren't they about the same age? Hell no to that."

Titch shrugs as if he's conceded the point.

"Hey, now I'm looking forward to this barbeque." Shadow's comment is echoed around.

Rapping my knuckles on the table, I get their attention. "Zeke's my kid," I tell them, my face growing stern. "I want a chance to get to know them. I don't want anyone fuckin' this up. If I bring them here, I've got to be able to trust you around them."

"What do you think we're going to do? Scare him off?" Cobra snorts.

"I just don't want you fuckers to crowd them."

Crash's brow creases, then he chuckles. "Think your English has left you there, Prez, unless you're saying you've got twins."

"Nah, he's talking about the pair. The kid and his mom." Indian rolls his eyes.

I was wondering whether to keep this to myself, but out of respect for Zeke, I want to prepare them. I take a deep breath. "No. I'm talking about my kid, and you lot being respectful to them." I take a deep breath. "Zeke's nonbinary, and they prefer gender-neutral terms."

It takes a moment for the penny to drop. Even so, it doesn't for everyone, judging by the looks on their faces. Petty though, well, he's quick to the mark.

"What the fuck? You're bringing a fuckin' freak here, Prez? You want us to accept him?" He thumps the table. "Kid should be in a fuckin' nut house not anywhere near this club."

"You show some fuckin' respect!" I snarl at him.

But he won't stand down. "We got rid of the last two perverts to Tucson. And now you're bringing one more around? Well fuck that, Prez."

I don't even know what the others are thinking or whether anyone else would support him. I just see red and roar, "I'll fuckin' have your patch!"

"Have my patch?" Petty's on his feet now. "I doubt anyone here wants your deviant kid anywhere near the club."

"Now hang on." Crash's hand shoots out to my arm and forces me back down. "You don't speak for all of us, *Brother*. I never understood why you hated Joker so much when he came out. What the fuck did he ever do to you?"

"It's not fuckin' normal," Petty shouts. "Joker was fuckin' gay. At least he had the sense to hide it when he was around. Anyone want to meet this kid who doesn't know if he's a boy or a girl? Little fucker's twisted. And you?" He points to me. "You should step up as his dad and sort this shit out, not fuckin' expect us to pander to him."

"You're dead," I announce in a chilling tone, brushing Crash's hold off and starting to stand. "Fuckin' dead, you got me? Your patch isn't enough. I want your life."

"Calm the fuck down!" Indian's now on his feet, gesturing to Twister and Crash. When Petty snarls and tries to come at me, Roller and Shadow hold him back. "If anyone's going to kill anyone, it will be in the fuckin' ring, you hear me?"

Flexing my muscles, I get out of the hold of the VP and enforcer. "Suits me down to the fuckin' ground. You're going down, fucker. You think I want you anywhere near my child?" I roll angry eyes and look around the table. "You think my child's weak for coming out? You think they've fuckin' chosen to be like they are? If you do, you can't understand how fuckin' strong someone has to be to be true to themself. Or how tough it is living in a world alongside people like *Petty*." The man's name comes out as a snarl.

They all talk at once, but Titch manages to raise his voice and speak above them. "What the fuck do you think we are?" he shouts, drawing attention. "We're seen as society's misfits. All of us. Petty mentioned Joker and Lady. Well I for one, am fuckin' ashamed they were too damn scared to admit what they were." He thumps his chest. "I don't care what's inside a man once he's proved his loyalty. It's what's in here," he bangs his heart, "that matters, not what he does or doesn't do with his sexual organs."

Petty rounds on Titch. "Well, I fuckin' care." He looks around the table for support. I study the brothers carefully, but don't think he's getting any.

Shadow, still holding him, snarls, "Joker and Lady were grown fuckin' men. We're talking about a kid here, Petty—"

"A kid who should have the truth knocked into him—"

"Take him downstairs," I say, menacingly. "He's the one who needs to be taught a lesson."

Shadow gives a sharp nod and yanks at Petty's arm. As he walks him out of the door, Roller, I notice, goes with them.

I wait to see who else is going to leave, but the rest of the brothers stay sitting.

"You sure about this, Prez?" Crash asks, his eyes moving from the closed door back to mine. "He's not bad on his feet."

"I can take him," I growl. Petty might have his younger age going for him, but I've got right on my side.

"It's a lot for me to get my head around," Indian states, calmly. "Kid seems mighty young to make a decision of that sort. But if it is what it is, or he is who he is, Titch is right. Devils don't give a damn about society, and it's not like we're being asked to patch… *them* in. Nah, this is just Prez asking us to be friendly to his kid. Where's the fuckin' harm?"

"Petty's worried it's going to brush off on him," Rope states. I look at him quickly, but I don't think he's joking.

Instead, Cuff nods. "I've often thought Petty protests too much."

Hammer snorts. "Rather you than me tell him."

"I think Prez is gonna teach him a lesson," Crash says, shaking his head. "We've just got to make sure it ends up the right way around. Red, Brother, you haven't been in the ring recently."

It's the truth. Prez's tend to step back. It doesn't matter them taking a brother down, but vice versa, it shows weakness. I grimace, acknowledging the point. I work out, I'm fit, but Petty's not slow on his feet.

"He's got a weak left side," Cobra says, tapping his chin as he considers. "His left knee is likely to give out."

"Yeah, he's easy to unbalance if you focus on that side," Hammer offers.

Twister shakes his head. "Technique's not going to win this, Brothers. It's going to hinge on whose rage is worst. Why don't you just take his patch, Red?"

It might come to that if I can't teach him better manners. A man only loses the patch if he disrespects the club. For a personal insult against the prez? That's debatable, but I fear not sufficient. Wanting to know what I'm up against, I ask, "Anyone else going to have a problem with my kid?"

"Fuck no," Titch seems to answer for everyone. "But you might have to cut us some slack. Fuck knows if I'll remember what to call him… it."

"Now I'm picturing a fuckin' clown," Cobra states, making the others laugh.

Most seem to be like Titch, wondering what all the fuss is about, but one or two are quiet.

"I'll judge him when I see him," Sarge says. "Ain't going to be treating him any different to Tom or Trist. He earns my respect? He's got it."

"They," Crash corrects.

Sarge just shrugs. "I'll try, but it ain't like I'm gonna remember." He taps his head, and while it could be an excuse, his brain injuries give him an out.

Hell, it had taken me a moment to accept Zeke, and that was only by acknowledging you couldn't change someone, however much they didn't fit into the ideal of what you wanted them to be. Would it be easier if Zeke fit the norm? Fuck yeah, but I can handle it. I'll have to.

"Barbeque Sunday then," I tell them. "Attendance not obligatory. But if you're there, I want you to show respect. Zeke's only fifteen for fuck's sake." They've already had enough ridicule and bullying. They don't need more.

I hope they'll all be there, but if not, I'll be taking note of who doesn't turn up. I'm incensed anyone could dislike my kid before they even met them simply for the way they were born. Zeke's Zeke as far as I'm concerned, and having gotten to know them, I wouldn't want to change them for the world. Or if I do, only for the fact it would make their life easier.

Unable to forget I've a lesson to teach Petty, I stand and dismiss them. "Now I got a place to be."

I might swagger confidently in the direction of the gym, but mentally, I'm already preparing myself for a world of hurt. This fight is going to be serious, not a simple test to show who's got more prowess. After the threat I made to him, Petty's going to do his best to kill me. I've got to be prepared to incapacitate him first.

I'm no stranger to fighting, though it must be said, my skills in the ring are probably rusty. I could do with some practice if I'm honest. But this is a fight about honour, the right to respect my child for whatever they are.

It seems no one is going to miss out on seeing their prez kick some ass or having his own handed to him as men flood down to the large basement and surround the ring. Indian takes me to a corner and prepares to wrap my hands. Crash comes up alongside and whispers into my ear, reminding me of some of the ploys Petty tends to use.

I nod, knowing I'm here for business not entertainment, and I'm not going to hang around. If I get the opportunity to take the asshole down with one punch, then I'll take that chance. Taking off my cut and t-shirt, I get ready.

Roller's the only person with Petty, and I wonder whether I should read anything into that. Just because no one came out and backed him up, doesn't mean they're not of the same mind.

Twister pulls himself up through the ropes and gets into the middle of the ring. "No knives, no guns, but no holds barred," he tells everyone. "Winner is the last man standing."

Petty catches my eye and mimes cutting my throat. I keep my face impassive. When Twister moves out of the way, Petty wastes no time, throwing himself across the ring and coming out swinging.

He's sloppy. I can work with that. I neatly evade him and land a fist on his right kidney as he flies past. He bounces off the ropes and comes back for me.

I take a stance, he feints, I raise my arm to block him and get in a punch under his guard. Spitting blood from his mouth, he snarls at me.

We're fighting dirty. There won't be any time-outs. Only a

madman would try to get in between us as we prowl around, each appraising the other and seeking an opportunity.

I dart in, he blocks, I slide out from under his arm and spin quickly. He raises his leg, pivots and lands a kick in the small of my back. It's me hitting the ropes now, using the momentum to spin myself around.

Petty's fuelled by adrenaline and hatred, and if I can't tamp down my rage, I'm going to lose this fight out of my desire to hurt him as much as I can. I can't afford to be sloppy. I take a moment as we circle around to draw breath down into my lungs, hold it, then breathe it out again, trying to calm myself down. To focus all my attention on taking down the enemy rather than hitting out in pure anger.

My movements become more targeted, my approach more methodical as my vision tunnels and I've only one task in mind.

We trade punches, some hard, some fleeting. I try and analyse his moves, and notice soon, the brothers were right, he has got a weak side. I wait for an opening then go for his left knee. It slips out from under him, and he comes crashing down. Wasting no time, I launch myself on top of him. He gets in a lucky punch, and I reel back but let the pain soak into me as I draw back my right hand.

I hit him, hard.

There's no retaliation. He's out.

Wearily, I leave him and stand. "Get him out of here."

"Then what do you want us to do with him?" Shadow, already in the ring, asks, while simultaneously gesturing to Roller and Cobra that he could do with some help.

"Keep him out of my fuckin' sight," I rasp out, looking at the hand I've just wiped over my face. It's covered in blood. Seems I've got a cut over my eye that's copiously bleeding.

Crash gestures me toward him. When I get there, he hands me my shirt and cut, then puts his forefinger and thumb to my jaw, moving my head so he can see my injury.

"Don't think you need stitches, but you could do with some butterfly strips."

"I'll sort it."

"Prez, you're the man." Sarge fist bumps me as I walk past him.

"Good one, Prez," Hammer calls out.

With not a little concern, I examine all the faces. No one seems to have been upset about the outcome, though I suspect that after having seen me take Petty down, any adverse comments they'll have the sense to keep to themselves.

I lower my head and walk out to get myself sorted. I'd taken a risk here today. This was personal between me and Petty. If the brothers hadn't sided with me, I might have split the club. Might still have if the objectors are staying silent.

"It had to be done." Titch is waiting by the door for me. "Who the fuck are we to judge anyone?"

I meet the old-timer's eyes. "Which would mean I've got to accept Petty, and all the fuckin' judgemental shit that comes out of his mouth."

"Think you already do, Prez. But you weren't in that ring fighting his views. You were fighting for respect to be given to your kid, and for that, you have every right." He sighs and looks weary. "Sarge's PTSD is known, and we make allowances for it. Petty's got some deep-seated shit he's carrying around. Who knows what reason lies beneath." He pauses and shrugs. "Either that, or he's just a total ass."

"An ass who just got his handed to him." I allow myself my first grin since leaving the ring. "And now I'm going to get this sorted before I get too much blood on my cut." I gesture to my forehead, and he steps out of my way.

CHAPTER SEVEN

CHER

"Mom." Zeke steps closer, their eyes narrowed as they examine me carefully. "It's going to be fine."

"I don't know what I'm doing," I admit to my child who often seems much older than their years.

Zeke's eyes roll. "You're going to see the man you've loved forever."

Therein lies the problem, I have, but my love's for the man I knew so fleetingly, not the stranger I've recently met.

I've often wondered whether my failure to move on was part guilt I bore his child and he knew nothing about it. If no reminder had remained of our liaison, would I have forgotten about him, found someone else and had a different family? Had I built Red up in my mind because of the constant reminder I'd had of him?

This past week has been great, that I can't deny. Red's all that I remembered and more, but I can't shake this thought he's only wanting to get to know me so he can have a relationship with his child that had, through no fault, but definitely mistakes of our own, \been kept from him.

Red's come into his own. I might be wary of his position in an outlaw MC, but if that's his chosen career, he's reached the pinnacle of it. I, on the other hand, have gone from one unskilled job to another. The only success I can count in my favour is bringing up Zeke.

If I hadn't had a baby, maybe I'd have been more ambitious, but in no world would I be blaming my child for that. That Red's been the man I've measured all others up to, well, yeah, I own my mistake there.

Now my dreams have become a reality. Red's reappeared in my life, and far from hating that he has a child he never knew about, he wants to embrace them with open arms.

Zeke, I can understand. They have a presence that belies their years, a confidence born of needing to meet the world head-on, though underneath lies such vulnerability. Zeke has a charm that draws people in, and I'm not surprised that Red's been brought under their spell.

But as a mom, I understand how it's all too easy to hurt them. Zeke needs acceptance and unconditional love, and that to my surprise, I've become sure Red can give them.

What about me? What can I offer a man such as Red other than memories? I'm thirty-five, no longer young. I'm not naïve. I know Red's in a position of power which is an aphrodisiac for many people. There's a new confidence but also a hardness in him that allows him to take on the life he's chosen, and while he's shown glimpses of him to me, I worry about how much remains of the younger man I fell for.

I'd be worried about going to the barbeque today even if I was going alone. Red's matured and it hasn't done anything but enhance his attractiveness. He's not hidden that he's been active sexually, but never found anyone he'd wanted to commit to. If he's got a big field to choose from, why should he settle for a frumpy mom with stretch marks?

With each time I've seen him, my barriers have come down, until I've finally admitted to myself, I still want him. I hate my younger self who ran, but have to question, where would we be if I'd stayed?

Happily married? Or divorced by now? Who can tell? Would I have stayed beside him, encouraged him on? Or would he be less of a man than he is now because I'd have dissuaded him? *He wouldn't have joined the Satan's Devils if I'd been around.*

Or it's them he might have chosen, and me he'd left behind.

Zeke's right. I still love him. The emotion rekindled over the last few days, a dying ember flickering back into a roaring flame. But am I just setting myself up to lose him all over again?

Today we're seeing him in his element. Half of my heart leaps that he's letting me into the life he's chosen, the other half scared that he'll soon see I won't fit there.

I've preconceived notions and I'll admit to them. Bikers roaring around on their oversized metal horses scare the fuck out of me with their masculinity enhanced by the muscle machines between their thighs, their reputation for violence and the way they raise their middle fingers to polite society.

How could I fit in? One look at me and his friends might keel over laughing. It's plain to see Red could crook his little finger and have any number of women running to him, so why should he settle for me?

I put the last touches to my makeup, just a little eyeliner and mascara, and foundation to cover my broken veins.

"You look great, Mom. Red's going to love you."

I smooth down my t-shirt, hoping it's doing its job to hide the fold of my belly that defiantly pokes over the waistband of my jeans. I've dressed down deliberately. It's only a barbeque I'm going to. Discreetly, I turn and look over my shoulder into the mirror. My ass is not as perky as it was once before. I sigh at Zeke's comment, knowing my kid is biased. In the same way I think that they're good looking, they've got the same rosy-eyed view when it comes to their mom.

Turning back to the front, I grimace, and draw in a breath for the conversation I need to have.

"If at any time you feel uncomfortable, Zeke, we're leaving."

"Dad will be there," they reply, as if that will make every-thing fine.

Experience, however, tells me otherwise.

I've sat in PTA meetings, listening to people debate that as my child has a penis, they should be using a male bathroom, without a thought to the bullying to which they're then exposed. Perfectly polite people unable to understand how someone like Zeke doesn't fit into their world, nor that their thoughtless actions have implications.

I've met parents who act as if they understand, but then deny Zeke the sleepover with their female friends or male for that matter, as if they're going to corrupt their precious daughters and sons.

I've even spoken to medical professionals who are deter-mined they can fix what they see is wrong.

I've spent the last ten years defending Zeke.

Now I'm voluntarily taking them into a situation where I'm certain they won't belong. Red's friends will never understand my child.

Bullying is Zeke's way of life. I know it and hate it. I can't control what happens at school, but I can control what happens out of it. I've taken desperate measures and moved when it's become too much to fight against. That's how I ended up in Vegas. It goes against the grain to take them somewhere they won't be appreciated.

We can just stay five minutes, I console myself.

"We're going to be late," Zeke reminds me.

As I slip my wallet and phone into my pockets, and pick up my keys, I eye my child, wondering yet again whether I should tell them to go and change. Zeke's wearing harem pants, and a tie-dyed shirt over them, and on their feet are Doc Martens. Sexless clothes in which they feel comfortable. *They're not going to fit in.* But they're them. I keep my mouth shut.

"Let's do this then. But remember—"

"I know, Mom." They roll their eyes. "If anyone makes me

feel uncomfortable, then we're gone. Same goes for you, Mother."

I start for the door, then pause. "Have you—?"

"Yeah, Mom." Once again, Zeke's eyes find the ceiling then look back down.

I needn't have asked whether Zeke's used the bathroom. When they're out, Zeke limits their liquid intake, and would rather risk bladder infections than need to use facilities where people question them on their choices. They've been chased out of the female bathrooms before and faced molestation in the male one.

Shaking my head, I follow them out to the car. I'm convinced I'm going to make an impression, but it's going to be the wrong one. They'll look at me and wonder just what Red's invited.

I pause before starting the engine. "Red's friends don't have to like us," I remind Zeke. "You and your dad will continue to get along, whatever happens today."

"Same goes for you," Zeke replies chirpily.

But they're wrong. Red might have reason for continuing a relationship with Zeke, but if his friends don't like me, then it will make things too difficult for him, and I'll be gone.

He's the prez, for fuck's sake. He can't bring back just anyone.

I follow the directions Red had given to me, and all too soon am approaching a forbidding-looking old warehouse with a large parking lot out front. The gates are closed. I draw up, wondering how I'm going to open them when a man approaches.

"Ma'am," he greets me politely, looking into the car. He raises his chin toward Zeke.

"I'm Cher. I'm here to see Red."

A grin spreads across his face. "Kind of guessed you were. Prez warned me to watch out for you. I'm Meat, by the way. You need anything, you just holler." He turns, shades his eyes from the sun and then points. "Park the car over there."

Over there is a rough unpaved area where there's a truck and an SUV. The asphalt appears to be reserved for the bikes which are in pride of place outside the clubhouse. When the oddly named Meat slides the gates open, I drive through and park where he's said.

"Well, he seems alright." Zeke peers backward to look at the man now closing the barrier between me and the outside world. "It says Prospect on his cut."

"Red told us about that, remember? It means he's not a full member until he's proved himself."

"Oh, yeah. Cool," my kid replies, then gets out, quickly losing interest in the man who let us in through the gate. "You know where to go?"

I don't. But there's the sound of male laughter and some shouts coming from around the back of the vast intimidating building. I guess that's where the barbeque's happening, and I'm just wondering whether I should just head that way when my saviour walks into sight, sliding his phone back into his cut.

"Meat told me you'd arrived." The welcoming smile on Red's face is tinged with relief, and I realise he'd half thought I'd back out. "Zeke, good to see you." They bump fists. "Come on, we're out back."

I hold back. "What the hell has happened to you?" Red's got a black eye and a bruise on his cheek.

"You should see the other guy." He winks. "It's nothing for you to worry about." But maybe it is. Violence in his world is something that concerns me. My alarm must show on my face as he adds, "Sparring between brothers. It keeps us fit."

It's an explanation, but can I accept it? I cast a glance toward Zeke.

Red notices. "Nothing is going to happen to them," he says, firmly.

Struggling for something to say, I ask, "Did you win?"

A flash of pain crosses his face so quickly I'm not sure if I imagined it. "I won, babe. I always win."

He takes my hand as though it's the most natural thing in the world, and I hold on to it as though it's a lifeline. I'm a confident woman, but today I feel totally out of my depth. The sheer number of bikes parked up makes me nervous about who I'll be meeting. I'm actually glad Red wears the prez badge on his vest, surely that's the uttermost protection I could have in this place.

As we move around the building, the sounds become louder. I hear some kind of roar, and a loud shouted, *Fuck that.* I feel as much as see Red grimace, and I wonder, not for the first time, whether I really want my child around these type of men.

Two youths round the corner so fast Red has to block their way with his arm to stop them from crashing into us.

"Tom," he growls at one, then at the other, "Trist. What have I told you about tearing around?"

"I'm Trist, he's Tom," the first one says with a cheeky grin.

It's obvious they are identical twins. Red's face scrunches as he considers for a moment, then cuffs the first boy lightly around the head. "Nah, I got it right in the first place."

I reckon this pair could easily give people the run around, they do look very much alike. The only way I can immediately tell them apart is by the colour of their shirts, and that Tom's hair is fractionally lighter.

Zeke moves slightly behind me, and I wince realising why. Tom and Trist are very masculine boys, young men, really. They're already tall, taller than Zeke, and brawny with it. If I had to guess at a hobby, I'd said they were on a football team. The very epitome of the type that like to bully Zeke.

"Hey, how you doing?" Trist pushes past his brother and, ignoring me, moves to greet Zeke.

"You're Zeke, aren't you? Mom told us you were coming." Tom steps forward as well. His eyes narrow slightly, and in them, there's a flare of recognition. "I've seen you around. You go to our school."

"I'm in the year below you." Zeke's voice comes out as a squeak. They cough to clear it.

Trist frowns, turns to his brother and they seem to have a twin thing going on—a form of silent communication. "You stick with us from here out, Zeke. We'll look out for you."

The other nods, then asks, "Want to see our bikes?"

"You've got bikes?" I ask, speaking for the first time. They seem a bit young.

"They turned sixteen a few weeks back and nothing was going to stop them," Red explains with a roll of his eyes. "Rosa's got a few more grey hairs though."

"Less than two years before we get our prospect cuts." Tom, I think it is, grins at Red.

Red snorts, but it's hard to tell whether he's in agreement or not. While I wonder what their mom would think about their desire to join the club, I also worry about Zeke going off with the pair. What if they get them alone just to torture them?

I notice Red glancing toward Zeke who's looking unsure, and then, more consideringly, toward the twins. He gives Tom and Trist a chin lift, then turns to my child. "Up to you, Zeke. You can come with us, and I'll introduce you to everyone, or go with the twins."

Tom rolls his eyes. "We won't be long. We'll be back when the food's ready. Come on, Zeke, what d'you say?"

When I see Zeke straighten their shoulders and reply, "Yeah, I'd like to see your bikes," I can read them like a book. If Tom and Trist are going to tease them, they feel they might as well get it over with.

"I'll be here if you need me." I communicate more with my eyes. *I've got your back, Zeke.*

Zeke, looking a little reluctant, follows the boys while Red squeezes my hand. "They'll be okay with the twins, Cher. They're a fuckin' handful, but good guys. It's not often we have someone their own age on the compound."

"I didn't realise they went to the same school," I tell him, conversationally, as I allow him to steer me along. But then, I didn't know about them at all, so couldn't be expected to.

"It's a small fuckin' world," he replies.

It is. I just wish it was a lot smaller, and I'd run into him again much sooner—back before he became a Devil. Then I wouldn't be about to walk into this lion's den with the feeling I'm going to be eaten alive.

"Are there any more kids here?"

"No," he replies, not breaking a step. "Rosa, their mom, was married to the old prez. She's kind of a mother hen to us all. There's only one other old lady—that's Tiffany. She's married to Fox who'll you'll meet later."

CHAPTER EIGHT

RED

She's here. In my world. Having more than half expected she'd chicken out, I've been a bag of nerves waiting for her to arrive. Now she's here, I'm hanging on to her hand, not letting her go in case she decides to run.

Zeke, well, my relationship with them is sound. I'm their dad, and for them, I'll always be around whatever way I can. If they don't like my life, I'll make time for them in theirs.

It's Cher who I'm most concerned about. If she's going to be a part of my life, she's got to fit in with it, and whether we can make it work depends on her taking the first step that she has, showing she's open to exploring it.

I didn't organise Tom and Trist to abduct Zeke as soon as they had appeared, but I had briefed Rosa. Those boys have a good heart and take after their dad. Brick was always protective of the underdog. It hadn't surprised me they wanted to find Zeke first and initiate them into their circle. I've no worries about how they'll treat them, and when Zeke meets my brothers, it will be with their new support around them.

Cher glances over her shoulder in the direction the boys have disappeared.

"They'll be fine," I tell her again. "No need to worry." I encourage her to get moving.

Her hand grips mine as if she's scared of losing me, and I see this afternoon through her eyes. She's expecting to be greeted by a band of ruffians, and I couldn't correct her on that. Petty, I notice, has kept himself out of the way since I beat his ass, and if he has any sense, will not be making an appearance today. My other brothers? Well, they might be rough at the edges, but if they respect me, they'll be on their best behaviour.

My concern? Well, she's wearing jeans that hug to a perfect ass, and her tee, while long, hugs those tits which I itch to get my hands on. She's wearing barely there makeup that only serves to enhance what nature gave her. She's so fucking beautiful I'm not only proud to be walking in with her, but I'm already devising ways of dealing with anyone who tries to take her off me.

And they will. How could anyone resist her?

As a mark of possession, I pull her closer, dropping her hand and instead curling my arm around her waist. If anyone wants to make a move, they'll have to get through me first—if, that is, anyone's foolish enough to challenge their prez.

As we round the corner, the first thing I see is Hammer twisting Cobra's arm around his back, and Cobra screaming for mercy.

"Give it back." Hammer's demanding.

"Fuckin' won't." Cobra's eyes are watering, but he's not going to give in.

"You tell him." Keys is egging them on.

For fuck's sake. I wanted to make a good impression. "Hammer," I snap. "Let Cobra go. Cobra, if you've got something of his, return it. Keys, stop fuckin' encouraging them."

Like guilty school kids, they jump apart, Cobra rubbing his arm ruefully. I stand with my eyebrow raised, waiting.

Cobra snorts, then reaches into his pocket, pulls something out and throws it at Hammer. Unfortunately, it lands on his head, and now my brother's standing with a pair of clearly worn panties slowly sliding down his nose.

Undeterred, Hammer takes hold of the flimsy material, holds it to his nose and breathes it in, his eyes closed as he relishes the perfume.

"Oh, hi. Cher, isn't it?" Cobra, letting go of his elbow reaches out his hand.

Hammer comes to and realises what he's doing and hastily shoves the panties into the pocket of his cut. He, too, holds out his hand.

I bat it away. "She doesn't want to shake it now, fucker. Or yours, Cobra. What the fuck are you doing?"

"It's only a souvenir from last night," Hammer explains, as if it's perfectly natural with which, if Cher wasn't standing beside me, I'd be in agreement.

Christ, she's going to think we're a bunch of perverts. I quickly glance around, trying to spy someone normal, but my eyes land on Rope putting a pair of handcuffs on Cuff, and hastily turn Cher to face the opposite direction. *Thank fuck, there's Crash.* Hastily, I lead her toward my VP.

In time to overhear his conversation.

"...and I'm just saying it was all wrong. If he wanted to take him out, the knife should have gone in like this..." He breaks off to demonstrate thrusting a blade up into Twister's chest. "Then he should have twisted it like this—"

"VP," I snap. "I'd like you to meet Cher."

Cher steps back into me as though seeking sanctuary.

"Oh, hi, Cher. Good to see you again and meet you properly."

Twister salutes her, then turns back to Crash. "Should have used a fuckin' stiletto. I tell you, that film studio ought to have us as advisers on set."

Ah, thank fuck. There's Fox and Tiffany. "Come, we'll go meet Fox."

"Red!" A high-pitched voice calls to me.

Swinging around, I wish the ground would open up and swallow me. Tottering across the uneven ground in impossibly high heels, wearing only sheer panties on her bottom and a top that barely contains anything, is Jinx. *Just kill me now.*

"Reeeed," she draws my name out pleadingly as she draws closer. Ignoring the woman glued to my side, she bats her eyelashes at me. "The girls and I want to party. Crash said we weren't allowed. We are, aren't we?" Behind her I can see Angel and Pixie, dressed to impress any cock in the vicinity. And fuck me, they're giving finger waves and tilting their heads pleadingly.

Crash and I will be having words later, I decide, knowing it's just one more thing to embarrass me. Now do I tell them to get lost? Or would their obvious disappointment go the worse for me?

I glance down at the woman I'm holding on to, seeing her head bowed and her shoulders shaking. I can feel her rage vibrating against me.

I gesture with my free hand toward Jinx, letting her interpret that anyway she wants, then hurriedly lead Cher away. I take her back around the side of the building, then once alone, push her back against the wall.

"I'm so fuckin' sorry." I raise her chin so I can see her face, ready either to wipe tears away or to receive a well-deserved smack around my head.

But to my astonishment, it's not sadness or ire that I see. Cher's laughing her fucking ass off. Surprised, I step back. Freed, she bends double, straightens, glances at me, then more laughter bursts from her again.

"Your… your face, Red." She giggles uncontrollably.

A nerve twitches in my cheek. "I wanted them to make a good impression."

"Oh, they made an impression alright," she jokes with me.

"They're not always like that." I try to defend them.

"Don't lie to me." But she smiles as she speaks. "There you

were, wanting them to be on their best behaviour, but they didn't take any account of me." I open my mouth, but she puts her hand against it. "Don't you see it's better this way? I thought I'd be an exhibit in a zoo."

"Instead of which, you're visiting one." I'm fighting hard, but her mirth is infectious.

Suddenly I give up, pulling her to me. I can't help myself. My mouth crashes down onto hers. My relief that even the sight of the club girls hadn't sent her running make me lose my inhibitions and any sense I was hanging on to. I push her back against the wall, plundering her gorgeous lips as though my very existence depended on it.

She tangles her hands in my cut, pulling me closer, giving as good as I'm giving her. It's not a delicate dance, it's dirty, it's rough. My tongue's pushing in, demanding, taking, my mouth ravishing hers.

I growl, she moans. The sound goes straight to my cock, and I press into her soft belly, letting her know what she's doing to me.

Her leg rises and goes around mine. It's an invitation, and I take it.

Her scent, her taste, the sounds she's making all drive me wild. Forgetting myself, I pull down her shirt, revealing her gorgeous breasts to me. Lowering my head, I start to feast on them.

Does she push me away? Does she hell. Her leg rises, her jean-clad pussy rubs against me and I'm seriously considering how quickly I can get us both naked when multiple pairs of footsteps and the sound of young voices approach.

Rapidly, I raise my head, pull up her tee, and step away from her. *Fuck.* She looks as though she's been thoroughly ravished. Her pupils are dilated, her chest heaving, her cheeks are a pink that have nothing to do with the warmth of the day. Hurriedly, I put her behind me.

"Hey, Red. Food ready?"

With my body in front of hers, I turn to the three pairs of

curious eyes watching me. "Yeah. Go check it out." *Get out of here kids*, I translate.

"Er, Mom?"

"Yes, Zeke?" Cher's breathless voice sounds cautiously from behind my shoulder.

"I told you, you had nothing to worry about." I turn to my kid to see they're fuckin' beaming. They winks at me. "Don't mind me, Dad."

There's a loud giggle, then the three tear off again.

I turn back to Cher. "Busted." I grin at her, smoothing my palm down her flushed cheek.

"I…"

I don't want apologies. I don't want regrets. "What was Zeke talking about? Why were you worried?"

She grimaces and looks away. "We're older, Red. You're in your prime, I'm a woman—"

"You're fuckin' beautiful. Sexy as hell, Cher." I need to shut that shit down now. Reaching for her hand, I put it on my engorged cock. "See what you do to me? I want you every bit now as I did back then."

She jerks her head in the direction we'd so recently come from. "Those girls, back there. I can't compete."

"I wouldn't fuckin' want you to. They're club girls, darlin'." I thought I'd have time to ease her into this, but there's no good way of letting her know. "They live-in and in return, ride biker cock."

"They ride yours?"

I have to admit it. "In the past, yeah. But not since we reconnected, Cher. There's only one woman I want, one woman I've thought of all these years. Sure, I used the girls when my hand wasn't enough, but that's only because you weren't there."

She's gone quiet, and I wait it out. Wait for her to say how disgusted she is. But what have I got to apologise for? Until I'd walked into the Lucky Fortunes, I'd never thought I'd see her again. Hell, I'd thought there was no chance since the moment she left. How could I have stayed faithful to something I thought I'd lost?

But Cher is full of surprises. Instead, she reaches for my hand, clasping it in both of hers. "Am I going to have to fight them off?"

Fuck yeah. I'm a man and for a second, I have precisely that image in my head. Then I shake it out. I won't have Cher rolling around, scratching and hair pulling with the likes of them.

"No fighting," I tell her. "You're mine, they know it. And they know that I'm yours."

"Are you?" She looks up, hesitantly. "What we just… When I came here…"

"Cher, it's pure fuckin' attraction we're battling against. That hasn't faded all these years. I lost control and I'm not going to apologise for it. I want you, Cher."

"Perhaps we ought to just fuck and get it out of our systems."

I'm all up for that, with one proviso. "I haven't gotten you out of my system for fifteen years," I remind her. "I doubt one fuck will do it."

CHAPTER NINE

CHER

I shouldn't have laughed, but it was obvious Red had wanted his club to make a good impression on me, but the first men I saw were fighting over a pair of obviously used panties. Then, there was another man trying on handcuffs, maybe practicing how to get out of them? I couldn't be sure, but that would be a handy skill for criminals. Then there were the pair who obviously knew a lot about knives.

And those girls.

Well, I'd lost it. There I'd been, worrying myself sick I was going to be paraded in front of a line of bikers, all assessing me and finding me lacking, and instead, I'd walked into a crowd who couldn't care less, a family making their own entertainment.

Red had been so mortified like a parent discovering their kids misbehaving. I couldn't help myself. The scene and his obvious discomfiture had struck me as hilarious. My relief, then his when he saw I wasn't upset, had us both losing our senses.

When he'd kissed me, I'd had to respond, there was no option about it. It was like a tide sweeping me away. I've never felt anything like it, never been closer to losing my inhibitions and begging a man to fuck me right there and right then. What came over me? What would have happened if those kids hadn't arrived?

I might have ignored my libido while Zeke's been growing up, but Red's reminded me I'm a hot-blooded woman today. Despite our interruption, heat runs through me and I feel wet at my core. I'm torn between relief we were stopped, and a visceral desperation to have this itch inside me eased.

When he successfully dismisses the kids and turns back to me, Red's chest is heaving, his hands fisted by his sides, his brow scrunched in concentration, but if he's willing his erection to subside, that tent in his pants just isn't going down.

I'm thirty-five, not a kid anymore, but there's nothing adult about me when I want to throw common sense to the wind. I watch Zeke walking off. They're relaxed, laughing at something Tom's said, while Trist is obviously intent on getting to the food. Zeke catches my eye and raises their chin, confirming they're having fun.

Looks like there's nothing for me to be worried about. Except, of course, for the state of the man standing beside me, and my own need, suppressed for far too long. The words come out of my mouth without my brain being involved.

"I need you."

Red's eyes flick open and come to mine. Silently, he telegraphs he's exactly of the same mind. He grabs my hand, holding it prisoner, then marches me back to where his friends are all gathered, ignoring everyone but zoning in on one woman, a matronly soul who looks to be in her fifties.

"Rosa?" he calls, as he approaches. "Can you keep your eye on Zeke for us?" I don't know this woman from Adam, but there's something about her—a tilt of her head, showing she's in charge and will take no nonsense from anyone. My initial reaction to her confirmed when Red leans down and explains, "She's Tom and Trist's mom."

I raise my chin toward her. Raising that pair has to be fun.

A knowing grin spreads across Rosa's face. "Won't be a bother looking out for one more. You two go and have fun."

Red wastes no more time. He pulls me back through the crowd, again paying no attention to anyone who speaks to him, just moving me toward the back entrance to the clubhouse. I blush as I feel the knowing eyes on us.

Kicking open the door, Red gets impatient. As if I'm moving too slowly, he sweeps me up into his arms, and even then, manages to take stairs two at a time. A short while later, he kicks open a door.

I don't care what room he's brought me to, whether it's his or if it belongs to someone else, there's a bed and that's enough. Need such as I've never felt before is coursing through me.

Fifteen years back, Red had been a polite lover, considerate enough to make sure I got off. I wasn't a virgin when I'd met Red and I had been with other men who'd had more of a repertoire, but what they didn't have was the intimate connection between us that had made simple sex so much more. Red and I had made love in Illinois, and against that, no other man has since measured up.

It was those feelings, my emotion for him that I'd buried but had never really forgotten that was going to make the next few minutes special. This is going to be more than the failed experiments I have behind me.

I expect Red to undress me politely, take me to the bed and worship me there. What I don't anticipate when he lets my feet slide to the floor is that he slams me back against the door, his mouth finding mine again and devouring me.

I feel his hands at the button of my jeans, then feel bereft as he takes his lips from mine, folds himself to the floor and drags down my jeans, taking my panties with them. Urgently he lifts one of my feet, pulls off my sandal and throws it away, then does the same to the other.

My lower half naked, he waits no more. On his knees, he

pulls my pelvis to him, and he does what he never had fifteen years back, puts his mouth on me.

With an expertise I didn't expect, his tongue finds my clit as a finger spears up inside me.

"Red," I gasp with the suddenness of the action I wasn't expecting.

Automatically, my hands go to his hair, holding him tight to me in case he gets the idea of moving away and stopping paying this glorious attention to me.

Christ. Has he become a sex god or something? He seems to know exactly how to play me. His first finger is joined by a second, and while his mouth licks, sucks and toys with my clit, he curls them around, finding a special spot inside me that I thought was only a myth.

My desire increases at such a rapid rate of acceleration, I'm breathless before my muscles start clenching. In a world record for certain, I lose all control.

"Red!" I scream, as he sends me over the top.

My legs are shaking, my muscles still rippling from the after-shocks when he gets to his feet, not letting go of me for a second. His eyes meet mine, then he grins, obviously satisfied with what he's seeing. With one hand bracing me, he undoes his fly and lets his cock come free.

Like a magician, he produces a condom, and smooths it on one-handed, and before I've regained my breath, lifts me and braces me against the door. My legs come around him for stability, putting the heart of me exactly where he wants it.

With one long push, he's inside me.

I sigh in satisfaction. He groans and pauses for a moment, his forehead resting against mine. Then, oh God, he starts moving.

Where has this Red come from? He never had such moves before. He hammers into me, his hips rotating, unerringly finding with his dick that secret place his fingers had found moments earlier.

I'm lost. I'm no longer a sentient human being. I'm just a

mass of feeling. Sensations go through me as my muscles tighten once more.

I've never come with a man inside me.

But this day seems to hold more revelations. When Red's mouth finds a tender spot on my neck and starts sucking, I discover there's a direct connection between that and the centre part of me that is soon clenching.

"Fuck, Cher. You feel fuckin' fantastic." His lips leave my skin for a second. "Babe, your pussy's strangling my fuckin' dick."

Never before had he spoken dirty for me. I discover I like it as my arousal ramps up some more.

"Come for me. Come all over my dick."

Impossibly, my body seems to obey him. My response astounds me. Whether it's him finding places I didn't know existed before, whether it's the position we're in or simply that it's the man himself, but I'm unable to resist him.

My skin feels on fire as the orgasm slams into me and I swear I see stars.

Red pauses to enjoy the sensations of my muscles clamping down, but barely leaves me seconds for recovery before he's pumping once again. Expertly moving his cock in and out of me, he unbelievably extracts another, albeit weaker, reaction from me.

Only then do I feel his strokes become erratic as he chases his own release, coming with a roar.

Like the aftermath of a tornado, all movement except for our chests heaving ceases. The only sounds are our mutual heavy breathing.

It takes me a moment to return to my senses. My body's needs sated for now, guilt slams into me.

Taking this slow? That's what I wanted wasn't it? Instead, I've let this man fuck me senseless.

Zeke? For heaven's sake, I've left them on their own with complete strangers.

I push at Red. With one hand holding the condom, he lets his cock slide from me, then lets my unsteady legs down to the floor. When he's certain I've got my balance, he steps back from me. I watch as he ties the condom and throws it into a bin. His cock, not completely flaccid, juts from his open jeans.

He didn't even get undressed to fuck me. The realisation makes me feel like a whore.

Reaching for my pants, I start struggling into them.

"Hey, babe. What are you doing?"

"I need to get back to Zeke." Hell, I can't even look at him.

But Red's not having that. He puts his hands to my waist and easily lifts me. "Not so fast, Cher. I haven't finished." His lips descend to mine, and this time, they caress me gently.

I may be fooling myself, hoping for something that's not there, but the kiss seems full of emotion. I allow myself to lose myself in it for a moment, then force my mouth away.

"We shouldn't have done this." My voice is emphatic.

"Don't run from me again, Cher." His intense eyes stare into mine. "And why the fuck shouldn't we have done what comes so fuckin' naturally? It was only a matter of time."

"I've left Zeke alone," I tell him, crying out my explanation, my eyes shocked and wide.

"Zeke will be fine," he tells me confidently.

Again, I push at him. "Let me go. I need to check for myself."

He tightens his hold on me. "I'm not going to let you go while you're berating yourself. We fucked? Yeah, it was inevitable. You going to deny the flame that was between us has been put out? Nah, we just flared it back into life."

"Zeke—" I start again.

"Cher, you've done an amazing job raising our child, but you're more than just a mom. You're my fuckin' woman." Is it so wrong that his caveman declaration sends fresh arousal shooting through me? "I want to take my time with you, get you naked next time." He gestures at our clothes and looks bashful.

The experience he's gained gave me pleasure, but I'm not

stupid and I know why. "I'm just one in a long line, aren't I?" Those girls outside, they've all probably shown him a good time.

He grips my hair, using it to pull back my head so I'm forced to look into his eyes. "Each pussy I sank my cock into was never mine. Most, I didn't want to go back for seconds, and none that I thought about all the time. You, Cher, you were different. Now I've got you back in my life, you're mine. I won't be looking for anything else. Why should I?"

"We barely know each other, Red."

"Have you seen anything you don't like?" He grimaces. "Apart from the behaviour of my brothers that is."

"I like you, Red, but I still think it's a mistake. If we fuck this up, we could damage the relationship you have with Zeke."

"And if this works?" he snaps back. "Zeke could have both a dad and a mom who are always there for them. For Zeke's sake, don't they deserve that we give this a chance?"

Glancing down I see Red's cock, now limp, still hanging out, and that my lower half is naked. Pulling away from his grasp, I again bend down and start pulling on my jeans. Red, realising his half-dressed state, tucks himself back in.

"Give us a chance, Cher. That's all I ask." His voice sounds pleading.

"This where you live?" I glance around. We're in a living room. Off to the side, I can see a bedroom and there are two more doors. One, I presume, leads to a bathroom. It's small, but comfortable. I've lived in apartments with less.

"It's where I live now," he confirms. "But if you want, we could buy a house. Choose one, all three of us."

He's offering that we become a real family. Something warns me it's still too soon. Even in the past, I barely knew him. Sure, we'd made an impression on each other, one we'd both been carrying around for fifteen years. Now we've got a chance, could dreams of a future become reality?

"Come on, let's go back down," I suggest, lightening my tone. "Introduce me to your friends properly. I'm willing to give us a chance, but that's all I can say for now. And I am worried about Zeke. Sometimes they're not good with new people."

Red snorts. "The twins have taken them under their wing. I wouldn't have left Zeke otherwise. Believe me, the brothers won't dare cross Tom and Trist. Let's just say, they can make life interesting."

Even on my short acquaintance, I suspect that he's right. "Come on," I encourage him again. "I'd like to meet the men you call brothers."

He grimaces. His head turned down, he looks up through his eyelashes at me. "Do I have to introduce you?" he almost whines.

Grinning widely, I respond. "Yeah, I'm intrigued as to the handcuffs."

"Oh God." He slaps the palm of his hand against his forehead. "That was just Rope and Cuff fooling around." Then he adds under his breath, "Sure way to make you fuckin' hate me."

"Come on," I say again, tugging at his arm while giving myself a visual inspection that everything's properly pulled up or pulled down. My flushed expression I can do nothing about, but I hope will be put down to the heat of the sun. Though with the way Red hurried me away from the barbeque, I'm pretty sure they'll all be well aware of what's gone down. "Let's get the worst over with."

Reluctantly, he takes me downstairs. I take the moment and more leisurely pace to glance around at what I'd not had time to take in before. It's a large clubroom, a bar to one side, mismatched tables, chairs and sofas, a pool table in one corner, and a couple of game machines.

But my scrutiny doesn't take long. Filled with growing guilt I abandoned Zeke and not understanding the reasons that made me do so, I hurry outside.

Zeke's been my whole focus for fifteen years, and I can't believe how I let myself be swept away by Red. It was as if time had ceased to exist, and we were back fifteen years ago without responsibilities. I lost myself just now, exactly the same as I had then—lost in sensation and forgetting everything which comes with being a mom.

Which isn't sharing personal time with a lover while leaving my child alone in a place where they know no one.

Suddenly, guilt crashes in on me. I turn horrified eyes to Red. *How could I have done that?*

CHAPTER TEN

RED

've fucked up.

What just happened between us had so not been on my agenda for today. I hadn't even been hopeful. What I had planned was on her arrival, I'd take her around and introduce her to my brothers who'd all be on their best behaviour, showing her what was my life, and trying to persuade her how she could fit in.

Instead, she'd had a baptism by fire as brothers were being brothers which, foolishly, I hadn't anticipated.

I'd been devastated, knowing for certain Cher was going to run, and who could blame her? I was hardly inducting her into civilised society. When she'd seen the funny side, when her last inclination had been to flee, I'd lost control of myself.

That kiss? Had she not responded, I could have stopped myself and pulled back. But as it became obvious her appetite for me matched mine for her, it turned into a repeat of what had happened when we'd first met. We'd been unable to keep our hands off each other.

Our first time together this go around should have been in a bed under soft lights, an occasion full of romance, of making love not just getting off. Instead, I took her against the wall, not even removing my pants. I'd just been so desperate to get inside her, I lost all rational thought and behaved like an animal, letting my baser instincts have full rein.

Have I scared her off? Or have I tempted her with how things could be between us?

Fuck, I hope it's the latter.

What I do know is what I've been searching for all my life has ended up within reach and I might already have blown it. Seeing her again only confirmed that no other woman has come close to the one I'd loved so briefly and lost.

I could have a real family—me, Cher and Zeke. But after today, is that still achievable?

We both neglected Zeke.

I'd been confident that with the twins Zeke was in good hands, but I couldn't be sure of it. Never having had responsibility for a child, I wasn't used to doing so and put my needs first.

As we leave my room, I sense a change coming over her, a transition from wanton woman to mom. I made her forget herself, forget her child—a crime in her eyes, mine too. Will she ever forgive me, or forgive herself?

I'd noticed she'd paused to glance over the clubroom, and I spared a moment to see it through her eyes—a masculine domain, one which wouldn't feel welcoming. It wasn't a surprise that she'd hurried her steps to leave it. Palpable anxiety is coming off her in waves, and I hope it's caused by concern for Zeke, and not what has just transpired between us.

Food's ready and being eaten by the time we arrive out back. Steaks, ribs, chicken, brats and burgers, Rosa's certainly gone to town procuring everything. Meat is behind the grills, cooking each carnivorous offering to perfection, his talent for butchery is how he got his name, and he's just as adept at the preparation.

Brothers are walking around with laden plates in their hands or seated at the picnic tables.

Cher's anxiously looking about. My taller height enables me

to see over everybody, so I tap her on the shoulder, turn her, and point her in the right direction. As soon as she spies Zeke sitting with the twins, she rushes over to join them. Seeing them smiling and clearly happy and talking animatedly, I hold back, taking a moment to fill a couple of plates, then follow her over.

Zeke's so intent on something Tom is showing them on his tablet, they barely acknowledge my approach. Cher's expression is now relaxed as she leans forward with her chin on her hands, fondly listening in on the conversation. Folding my body over the bench, I place a plate in front of her, then take a seat to her side. I can't help myself, wrapping one arm around her.

I half expect her to pull away, but instead she leans into me, clearly having relaxed again. *This feels so right. My woman and child with my club around us.*

The kids are discussing games. I quickly pick up, *Call of Duty.* As Zeke seems very familiar with it, I wonder for a moment whether Cher knows that one has an adult rating. Several brothers are into it, and it was hard to deny Tom and Trist taking part, but hell, they've been brought up around an MC, which unfortunately means there's not much about sex and violence they don't know. But Zeke? I tense a little, thinking this probably isn't what Cher wants them involved in.

Then, to my surprise when I catch some of what they're saying, Zeke's not only no stranger to the game they're discussing, they've gotten even further into it than the twins.

Now it's me who's frowning, wondering whether it's suitable for my kid, and whether I ought to have a word with their mother later when Cher leans into me. "Zeke spends too much time playing, I know, but he's not made any friends since he's been here."

"That game's 18-rated," I tell her.

"Oh, believe me I know." Her eyes hold pain when they meet mine. "Zeke already knows this is a cruel and violent world. How's an online game going to hurt them? They're far from the only one their age to be playing it, as you can tell." She inclines her head toward the twins.

Unwilling to become the heavy-handed dad who denies them anything, or at least so soon, I let it go.

"This is good." Cher moans around the rib she's tucking into.

My cock twitches as she licks, nibbles and sucks it. I start wondering whether I can get more time alone before she has to go home, then slap that thought down. I've pushed my luck too far already.

Owl approaches. "Can I get you and your lady drinks, Prez?"

I order a beer, and Cher copies me.

As the prospect walks off, she grins. "You get special treatment?"

I shrug. "The man wants his patch."

"So, he keeps you happy?"

Something like that. I reach for the beer Owl's just brought over and take a long sip to avoid answering. Does it make me a dick that my station gives me liberties?

Cher glances at Zeke, sees they're still deep in conversation, and then gives me her attention. "So, who is everyone?"

Glancing up, I raise my hand and point with my middle finger. "There, that's Crash, he's my VP. Next to him, the big man is Twister." I pause before naming his role, but then decide to hold nothing back. "He's the enforcer." When her eyebrows rise, I explain, "He enforces the rules of the club. And that's Indian—he's the sergeant-at-arms, and he looks out for everyone."

"Who's that?"

Following her gaze, I tell her, "Fox, he's our treasurer, and with him is his old lady, Tiffany." My eyes move on. "The old guy next to them is called Titch—"

"Titch?" Her eyes widen.

I snort. "Yeah, a misnomer for certain." Titch is tall and broad. "That's Shadow." Again, I point him out. "He's our road captain. He keeps us safe when we're riding out and makes sure we maintain our bikes."

"And the handcuff pair?" Her eyes sparkle with wickedness.

"Rope and Cuff." I grin. "They're into BDSM."

"Together?" Her eyebrows rise.

"Don't know, don't care. But they do like the ladies." I wink. I move on to a safer member. "Keys is the one who looks serious. He's our go-to technical expert. You want any information, just go to him."

"Who's that talking to him?"

"That's Cobra, and Hammer beside him."

"What do they do?"

"A bit of everything." I notice Sarge sitting on the sidelines. I'm grateful for him coming today, he usually avoids big gatherings. "That's Sarge," I tell her.

She regards him quizzically. "He upset about something?"

Grimacing, I explain, "He suffers from PTSD." It's no secret. It's easier if people know about it. A car back firing can set him off.

"Oh." Her face fills with genuine sympathy. "A vet?"

When I nod, she chuckles. "I don't know how I'm going to remember anyone's names."

Snorting, I tap the patch on my chest. "Pretty good clue right here."

Batting her hand against my arm, she asks, "Is this everyone?"

Frowning, I shake my head. Petty, I didn't expect to dare show his face, but Roller? Yeah, I'm disappointed in him.

She stares at me for a moment, gently raising her hand to touch the bruise on my cheek. "None of your brothers are sporting injuries, Red. Who did you really fight?"

I grimace. "He's not showing his face today, Cher."

"Why not?" Her intelligent eyes narrow.

I don't want to tell her the truth, don't want to make her feel uncomfortable that someone has a problem with our child. But I don't want to lie either, so I settle for picking up my beer and not saying anything.

"You hurt him that badly?" She looks shocked, jumping to her own conclusions.

"He's walking wounded, Cher. He's okay."

Her teeth worry her lip. "Will he retaliate?"

"I'm the prez," I impress on her, my tone and expression conveying he wouldn't dare.

"Hey, boys. Scat." Titch's loud voice booms.

"Need a seat, old man?" Tom gives him cheek.

Titch pretends to cuff his ear as Tom rears back. "Less of the fuckin' old, kid."

Tristan stands, theatrically waves Titch to his seat, then once he's seated, Tristan puts his arms around the old man and gives him a quick hug. "Take care, Grandpa."

"I'll grandpa your fuckin' ass," Titch growls, twisting out of his grasp. "Now get out of here."

"Come on, Zeke." Tom, laughing, beckons with a wave of his hand.

When Zeke queries me with his eyes, I nod my head. "Rosa's probably got some desserts hidden away. Why don't you kids go find them?"

"Fuckin' kids," Titch growls.

At Cher's obvious consternation, I snort. "This, Cher, is the man who all but helped Rosa bring those boys up after their father died. They do indeed look on him as their grandad."

One side of Titch's mouth twitches as he tries not to smile. "Didn't have much choice. Kids turned up everywhere I was. And I absolve myself of any responsibility for the way they've turned out."

"He always offered to babysit," I interpret for Cher, out of the side of my mouth.

"That he did." I startle slightly as Rosa comes up and joins us, I hadn't heard her approach. She pats Titch's arm. "Couldn't have done it without you." Her eyes rest on him fondly for a moment, then she turns to Cher. "You've got a good kid there."

"Looks like his old man." Titch snorts. "I see what you were talking about Red."

"No doubt to Zeke's heritage, is there?" I grin at him.

"What do you make of the club?" Rosa asks Cher.

"It's a bit overwhelming," she replies. "I doubt I'll ever remember anyone's names."

"Just call them asshole, that'll fit," Titch murmurs.

Rosa snorts. "Hey, Red. I'm going to kidnap your woman for a bit. Tiff wants to meet her."

Narrowing my eyes, I ask, only half-joking, "You going to run her off?"

I'm not completely comforted by the strange grin on Rosa's face, nor her words.

"Well, we might be letting her know what she'd be getting into."

Fleetingly, I debate within myself. Rosa's continued to be the first old lady even after her old man died. Could it be that she sees Cher as a rival? Could I take that chance? Or can I assume she's looking out for me just as much as any other one of her boys?

Cher's eyeing me quizzically, as though wondering whether I'm going to insist on her staying by my side.

When Rosa raises an eyebrow in challenge, I give in with a shrug. "If it's okay with Cher."

Cher grins. "It's fine with me if Rosa's going to spill the dirt."

And that is exactly what I'm afraid off. "Get gone," I growl, but before letting her go, I curl my hand around the back of her neck and plant my lips on her mouth.

"I think a discussion between us is well past due," Rosa remarks with a grin. She stands. "Come on, Cher. Let's go somewhere with a little less testosterone."

Cher chuckles as she stands.

"I'll be right here," I promise her.

"I'll be fine."

"Good-lookin' woman," Titch remarks. As I see his eyes on her ass, I reflect it's only his age that stops me following through on my urge to plant my fist in his mouth. When he, thankfully, turns away, he puts his attention on me. "From your disappearing act earlier, I take it she's not here just because she's your son's mom."

Hmm. I doubt I'd be able to hide what we did earlier. Our disappearance was hardly discreet, and the flush on her face when we returned, too recognisable for my less-than-saintly brothers.

I decide to be honest with him. "I like her, Titch. Always did. I just thank fuck I found her again. And my *child*." I emphasis the non-gender specific term I'd prefer him to use.

"Pfft. Child, son. Hell, Prez, I'm too old to remember shit like that. It doesn't naturally fall off the tongue."

"I'd appreciate you trying."

He raises his chin. "I can do that. But them…?" He tilts his head toward the rest of my brothers. "You think they're going to accept the kid as he… they are?" His forehead creases. "Petty and Roller ain't even bothered to turn up."

"That's not on Zeke," I retort. "Any issues the brothers have, they'll just have to deal. If, and it's still up in the air, if Cher will have me, then she'll have to accept the club, and the club her."

"If she'll have you?" His age-experienced eyes narrow.

I sigh. "She's not been around MCs before."

"Bit of a stretch bringing a civilian in as a prez's ol' lady."

"I know," I reply pensively. "I'm club, Titch. I can't give up the patch." I stare over to where Rosa, Cher and Tiffany appear to be animatedly talking and laughing. "But now I've found her, I'm loathe to give her up. As for Zeke? They're mine, whether or not Cher and I are an item."

"You'd choose the club?" Titch's eyes widen slightly.

"I'm surprised you'd question it." My jaw is tense as I reply. It's not only my personal inclination, it's all the brothers depending on me. I take the patch seriously. From the day I earned it, I was nothing other than all in. As prez, I can't see me leaving the club except in a coffin.

"This is a woman you've been yearning for, for fifteen years, Red." Titch regards me seriously, ancient wisdom in his weather-lined eyes. "Could say your loyalty to her goes back longer than that to the Devils."

"And where's she been?" I round on him. "Devils have been there for me all this time. Sure, I want her, more than I have any woman, but the club comes first. Always."

"She know that?"

I purse my lips. Not yet. I hope we'll never have to have that conversation. "If it's necessary, Titch, I'll make sure she does."

Boys' voices reach us. I swing around to see Tom, Trist and Zeke tossing a ball about. Zeke seems to be holding their own, I notice.

"Your kid's got a fuckton of problems."

I swing back at Titch's remarks and snarl, "There's nothing the fuck wrong with them."

"Whoa." Titch holds up his hands. "He… they're a good kid. That's not what I mean. The kids at his…," he catches my eyes, "their school, well that's understandable. Little fuckers will always come down on those who are different. But in Zeke's case, it will be with adults too. Just take Petty's reaction as an example."

"Where are you going with this, old man?"

He cocks his head to one side. "Whether or not you and Cher are an item, seems to me that Zeke needs the club. With new uncles around them, folks won't be so quick to come down on them." He's made a good point.

But I have to admit, I'm surprised. "You'd go to bat for them?"

"Fuckin' right I would." He shakes his head. "Never sat right with me all that shit with Joker."

My brow furrows. "There was no shit."

"And that's the problem," he muses, still eyeing the twins and Zeke having fun. "He didn't fuckin' trust us. When I heard about what his fuckin' parents did to him, well, that's when I understood."

"You can't change what's natural." I raise my chin toward him.

"That you can't," he agrees, then grins at me. "We'll just have to step in and educate people who think otherwise." His face hardens. "And never, ever, let Zeke believe there's anything wrong with them."

I think Zeke's got that handled already, courtesy of their mom. But it warms my heart to hear Titch say we'll have their back.

Sitting back, I fold my arms, and consider the oldest member of our club. He's always been there for Rosa's kids, took to Clare's baby when she stayed in the club. Now he's immediately on Zeke's side.

I'm curious. "You never wanted a woman, Titch?"

"Not so much lately," he snorts. "But in previous years? Every damn day." He palms the crotch of his jeans and winks.

Chuckling, I clarify, "I mean, a woman of your own."

"Had one," he replies, a darkness coming into his eyes. "Married her. A couple of years later, watched her give birth."

He's got a kid? My widened eyes show my surprise. "What happened?"

Titch's face tightens. "Kid wasn't mine." His eyes go back to Zeke. "Let's just say, he wasn't a chip off the old block, and when things came to light, well, I found the Devils and never looked back." His gaze returns to my face. "I've never trusted a bitch since."

I recall him being concerned Zeke wasn't mine. But hell, it's clear as day that they are.

Titch nods as though I've spoken. "At least you know Zeke's yours."

CHAPTER ELEVEN

CHER

I don't really want to leave Red and go talk to an unknown woman, but I don't make a protest for two reasons. One being purely to be polite, and the second is that I suspect Rosa wants to fill me in about the club. Though watching her, I've seen she seems to be some kind of Queen bee, and might try to run me off. Didn't Red say she was the old prez's old lady?

Nevertheless, it's an opportunity to hear about the Satan's Devils from a woman's point of view.

Rosa leads me through the brothers who, with hands still full with food, seem to be behaving themselves, and if they acknowledge me at all, it's just to give me polite nods. She heads straight for the man Red had pointed out as Fox. As we approach, I estimate him to be a similar age to Red, late thirties or early forties, and the woman by his side only a little less if that.

Unlike the club girls, she's at least fully dressed, though her skintight leather pants hug her ass and legs. Her leopard print top clings like a second skin, the neck low, revealing an admirable cleavage, and her bare arms are covered in tattoos. Hooped gold earrings hang from her ears, and her hair is held back by a bandanna covered in skulls. She's the epitome of a badass biker bitch.

Rosa, on the other hand, is a more motherly type, her figure rounded by being, I suspect, post menopause. She wears jeans, but boot cut and not figure-hugging tight. A loose floral blouse completes her ensemble.

Tiff's staring at me with an unreadable expression on her face and her hands on her hips. When we draw close, Rosa steps beside her and folds her arms across her chest.

"Er," I say, but with a smile on my face. "Is this an intervention?"

One corner of Tiff's mouth turns up. "That depends on whether you need one."

Rosa chuckles. "We want to know what your intentions are toward our prez."

They're being forthright. I, in turn, am completely honest. "I can't tell you that as I don't even know myself."

"No?" Tiff's eyes widen. "It didn't take you long to jump into his bed."

I blush, knowing there's no point in denying it, but hesitate to tell them the horizontal position wasn't involved. "It was always like that between us." Knowing these women can help make my mind up about the club, I add, half to myself, "Perhaps that was our problem. Too much sex and too little talking."

"And lack of protection." Tiff jerks her head toward Zeke, showing she knows our history.

Grimacing, I tell them, "I was on the pill. Young and stupid, I thought it didn't matter if I missed a couple of days."

Rosa's face softens in sympathy. "And you really had no idea how to find Red and tell him?"

"How do you find a man whose only name you know is his handle, and that he's heading toward one of the southern states?"

Rosa gives a ladylike snort as she realises the problem. "If you could have done, would you have wanted to find him?"

Still one hundred percent truthful, I admit, "With all my soul. I'd have never kept Zeke from him. I hated Zeke not knowing their dad. I always told them about him, and that it wasn't Red's fault he wasn't there."

"Pretty lucky happenstance he turned out to be the prez," Tiff casually remarks.

"You think?" I direct my gaze on her. "I know nothing about this life. All I know about MCs is from watching TV programs and documentaries, and what I saw I didn't like. I admit once I saw that patch on his back, I didn't want Zeke to meet Red." I wave my hand around. "Apart from the dangers and crime that I'm sure is involved, I never thought a club like this would accept them."

Rosa chuckles at that. "You never know what we'd accept, honey. Now your Zeke is no hardship at all to bring into our fold." She glances behind her, and her features assume a mother's pride as she watches her twins and my kid playing. "The twins have taken to him."

"Them," I automatically correct, then wait for the rebuttal.

"That's going to take some getting used to," Tiffany admits. "Though we'll try, for their sake." Her statement makes me shoot a look of gratitude toward her.

"Back to you." Rosa starts steering the conversation back to where she wants it. "Are you good enough for our prez?"

A laugh breaks from me. "What do you think?"

"Oh, honey. I think it's time to start your education." Rosa winks at Tiffany, then nods toward the clubhouse. "Follow us."

Bemused, I match my footsteps to theirs and let them lead me inside. We pass through a kitchen that I'd briefly noticed before, and gaze in awe at the industrial-sized appliances. Then, a couple of steps down the hallway, Tiffany places her thumb against a device on the wall, and a door opens. Stepping inside, I find myself in a totally different space.

It's a big airy room with a large screen television on the wall, and two cream leather couches covered in pillows that look so inviting you just want to sink into them. There's a games system, and a small desk with a computer on it, and against one wall, a bar. The main thing is, it's not masculine at all.

I tilt my head to one side and with my expression ask Rosa for an explanation.

Seeing my obvious approval, she smiles. "It's a women's area. Mine and Tiff's."

"Not the club girls," Tiff puts in fast.

Rosa takes over again. "It's where we come when we want to get some girl time. And," she nods to the computer and the games system, "where the boys can come, play and do their homework."

"It's a big room for just the two of you," I observe.

Grimacing, Rosa enlightens me. "I always hoped more of the boys would settle down, but for years, it's just been us two old ladies."

"That thumb thing on the door? Is it that only the two of you can enter?"

"All the men can, brothers and prospects," Tiff assures me. "But no strangers. Here, we're totally protected."

I glance around doubtfully, not seeing too much security until I spy two monitors on the back wall.

Rosa chuckles. "Here." She goes to the coffee table and slides the top to reveal a selection of buttons. Pressing one, a rattling starts, and metal screens begin to roll down to cover the windows. Honestly, it looks like something out of a Star Trek movie. *Shields up, captain,* I joke to myself.

"The walls and the door are reinforced steel," Tiff says, proudly.

My heart stops at the implications. "Do you have to use it often?" What the hell are the Devils into if they need this much security?

"Never used it at all," Rosa announces. "It was my idea originally to have a space for ladies only. I picked up the idea from another club. I spoke to Red about it after Brick passed as God love him, he'd never gotten around to it. Red made some adaptations, and this is what we got."

I look around. "It seems a lot of work for something that's unnecessary."

"It's insurance," Tiff states, pushing back a strand of her hair. "Having it makes the men happier."

"Yes," Rosa takes over. "If any trouble came to the club, they'd know we were safe and could focus."

"Wouldn't you want to be fighting with them?" I don't like the thought of women being seen as weak. Not that I know how to shoot or anything, but if it was my home, I'd like to defend it.

"Oh, honey," Rosa grins, "you've got a lot to learn. Satan's Devils protect their women and kids. They'd never have them fight by their side."

"Except for Swift," Tiff butts in.

As Rosa wrinkles her nose, I have to ask, "Swift?"

Muttering, *"I don't know what the world's coming to,"* under her breath, Rosa turns to me with a critical look in her eyes. "Swift's a member of the Utah chapter. She's a woman."

"Ex-forces," Tiffany adds, then shudders. "Scary woman."

"She's got an ol' man in the chapter, but I doubt she'd label herself an old lady."

"She's one of a kind," Tiff agrees.

That kind of revises my opinion of the Devils. "They let women join?"

"From what Fox told me, there's nothing against it. But they'd have to be special." Tiff shrugs.

"And Swift is?"

"She's definitely something." Tiffany grins. "Let's just say, when she visited, we didn't bring her in here."

Rosa snorts in a way that makes me think this Swift wouldn't have fit in.

Something still concerns me. "Did anything happen that made you think it was necessary to have a safe room?"

"No." Rosa walks over to the bar. "Drink?"

"A soda if you've got it. I have to drive."

She gets wine for her and Tiffany, then resumes her conversation. "Back in the day, before Brick was prez, the Satan's Devils mother chapter in Tucson was invaded by the feds. Not that they didn't deserve it. They were in some shit at the time."

"So was Vegas." Tiff takes her drink and sits down.

Picking up my soda, I do likewise.

"Feds killed a lot of members that day, including Bastard, the prez, and his ol' lady who'd stepped in front of him, trying to save him. Drummer, that's Bastard's son, took the helm and started to steer the club in the right direction. Their clubhouse was destroyed so they had to get a new one. Drummer was determined to get the Devils out of the shit they'd gotten into and for the main part, earn their money straight." Rosa pauses to swallow some wine. "As he ruled over the mother chapter, all the other chapters had to follow his lead. The raid had shaken the club badly, so no one baulked at the change. Since then, because we mostly play with others nicely, Vegas hasn't really had any trouble on its own account."

"But some of the other chapters have," Tiff puts in. "So, when Rosa mentioned a woman's room, Red, who'd prospected in Tucson, decided to make it a safe room to protect their property, just in case."

"Property?"

My narrowed-eyed question starts a conversation that goes on for the next half hour, involving concepts quite alien to a woman who's brought up a teenage kid on her own. I'm not necessarily brought around to their way of thinking, and when Tiffany brings down her *'Property of Fox'* cut to show me, which she wears when they're out riding or have other clubs visiting, I still have doubts. Though I have to admit, some visceral part deep inside me responds to the thought of the world knowing I belong to Red. Then, I shake that feeling off me. We're a long way from that.

Especially when Rosa opens a different subject. "I was the prez's ol' lady, Cher."

"You still are," Tiff remarks. "In all ways but one."

Rosa shrugs. "I act like it to fill the vacuum. The boys need someone to keep them under control and keep them fed."

"And kiss their boo boos." Tiff laughs.

Rosa chuckles then her eyes harden. "A woman taking on any of the brothers needs to be sure this life is for her. The prez's old lady? Well, she needs a backbone of steel. She has to be one hundred percent behind her man, whatever he does. And behind the club."

"And accepting she'll never know the reason for it," Tiff strangely adds.

"Ah yes, plausible deniability." At my look of confusion, she clarifies, "If you don't know what's going on, you can't be questioned about it. Or if you are, you can't give anything away let alone testify."

"The dreaded 'club business.'" Tiff rolls her eyes. "You'll have to get used to knowing to close down your questions when that phrase is used."

I don't understand. "But if what they do is legal, why should there be business that needs to be kept secret from us?"

There's no denying there's still an attraction between me and Red which has survived a gap of a decade and a half. The amazing sex earlier proved that. I'm a woman who, for once in her life, had her needs more than adequately met by a man, and if I'm honest, I want more.

But there's more than me now. There's Zeke to think about. If I was on my own, I might take a chance and jump into Red's life. But could I do that to my child? Should they complete their teenage years living in the shadow of what the law would define as criminals? I'm so torn. At the end of the day though, Zeke's needs will always trump mine.

Rosa gets up, grabs the wine bottle, tops off both Tiff's glass and hers before she replies, "Bikers live outside citizen laws.

They might earn their money legally, but they don't rely on the law to protect them or theirs. It's a dog-eat-dog world out there, Cher, and if someone hurts them, they hit back hard."

The thought of what she might not be saying sends a shiver down my spine. I try to laugh it off. "Next you'll be telling me they have a place where they bury the dead bodies."

"Ah, that," Tiff taps her nose, "would definitely come under the heading of club business."

My trouble is, I don't know whether she's joking or not.

Before I can think whether it's a good idea to even ask, the door bursts open, and in come the twins followed by Zeke. I notice Zeke's face is reddened, and sigh that they've been too long in the sun. They certainly inherited their father's complexion.

"You had fun?" I ruffle their hair as they flop down beside me.

"I have," Zeke confirms.

Trist raids the fridge by the bar and takes out three sodas. He throws one to his brother, then brings one over to Zeke.

"You're fast," he comments, handing the soda over.

"Fast?" I query, as they pull their head away from my hand.

"Zeke beat both of us in a sprint," Tom comments, then winks. "Can't catch a ball for fuck though."

"Language!" Rosa calls out, but neither of the twins look perturbed.

Zeke looks relaxed, happy, and though it makes me a bad mom to admit it, slightly sunburned. I should have topped up their sunblock earlier. They also look tired, and I realise how late it's gotten.

"Come on, kid. Let's get you home." Zeke goes to protest, but at my frown and pointed glance at the clock on the wall, they sigh. "Let's go find Red and say our goodbyes." And then I can leave to ponder on this afternoon that's turned out nothing like I'd expected, and despite myself, I've stayed not a few minutes, but darn near seven hours.

I've a lot to think about.

"Hey, Zeke?" Trist comes over to us as we stand. "Tomorrow, huh? Remember what we said. Anyone picks on you, just send them to us."

"Sit with us at lunch, yeah? Send them a message." Tom backs his brother up.

Zeke gives one of their reserved-for-special-occasion smiles. It makes their whole face light up.

"Sure thing." They stand and fist bump first Trist's, then Tom's bunched hand.

CHAPTER TWELVE

RED

Apart from feeling the first burst of parental pride when I watch my kid beating the twins in a running race around the compound, though I did note they can't catch a ball for shit. I'd kept a wary eye on Zeke for a while, but Tom and Trist seem to have taken them under their wings.

When Cher disappeared with Tiffany and Rosa, I made sure to stay in view, so Zeke knew where to find me.

I thought she'd soon reappear, but she was gone for ages, those hours I'd spent nervously wondering what the hell the other women were talking to her about. Were they warning her off me?

I need for her to get in Rosa's good books. Although obviously Brick's old lady is not a member of the MC, she's been a fixture in the clubhouse since before my day, and her opinion carries weight. I'm not blind to the fact that even though her man is dead, she's still considered to be the first old lady by all the men. As for Tiff, I think she'd be swayed by whatever Rosa decided.

"You doing okay, Zeke?" I grab for them as again they rush past me.

They stop and give me a huge grin. "Yeah, Dad. Tom and

Trist are amazing. I love their bikes. Can I have one?"

Whoa! My face goes blank at the unexpected request, my mind immediately going to what Cher would think. Then I realise that I, too, as their dad, am entitled to have an opinion.

"You wanna know how I got my first bike, kid?"

They nod enthusiastically, showing their appetite to find out all about me, as I want to do about them.

I indicate a bench and lead Zeke over to it. Once we're sitting, and their eager eyes meet mine, I tell them the story. "My dad, your grandad…" I pause, a lump coming into my throat as I wish my father had lived to meet Zeke. "When I was only a couple of years older than you, he was involved in an accident. He was never the same after that. It fell to me to look after him."

Their eyes widen at the thought of a grandfather they'd never met. "Is he still alive? Do I have a grandma?"

I soften my features and ruffle their hair. "Nah. My dad died before you were born. As for your gramma, well, she left and I've no idea whether she's dead or living." My expression warns them now's not the time to ask more. "Anyway, I looked after your grandpa for seven years, and I needed something to occupy myself but still be able to stay close to him. I couldn't afford much, so I bought myself a wreck of a bike, and started building her back up from scratch." I jerk my head toward the front of the building. "That's the bike I still ride today."

"Heap of junk." Crash winks at Zeke, having overheard as he's passing.

Without thinking, I shoot him my middle finger before I think better of it, but Zeke bursts out laughing.

"Kid," I tell them, trying out a dad's tone. "Do as I say, not as I do, okay?"

They snort and roll their eyes. "You think I don't know what flipping someone off means? I'm at school."

I have to grin. "Yeah, but don't do it in front of your mom, eh? Or me," I add, belatedly, realising I too should get in on this game.

"So, your bike?" Zeke tries to get me back on topic.

Hmm. My bike. Can I come up with a solution that Cher would be comfortable with? "How about I look around for something suitable for you to do up?"

"Like you did?"

I raise and dip my chin. "Exactly."

Their face falls, then they grin. "And you'll help me?" Zeke seems delighted to have landed on something that will involve some father and child time.

Me? Well, I too foresee it could lead to some bonding. "Of course, I will," I tell them. Then I consider the promise I'm making. "If your mom's agreeable, of course."

Deciding to overlook the condition I've just set, Zeke leaps to their feet and puts their arms around me. "Thanks, Dad." Glancing around, Zeke spies the twins. Running over they start yelling, "Dad's going to buy me a bike."

"You've created a monster." Indian plonks his ass beside me. "You know what you're letting yourself in for, Prez?"

Keys also joins us. "Heard the kid yelling about a bike from way over there. You grooming a new Satan's Devil?"

I lower my face into my hands. If he's leaped to that conclusion, would everyone else? Fuck my life, Cher's going to kill me.

"Probably a fad," Fox, also joining us, says wisely, to some extent putting me out of my misery. "Zeke's seen Tom and Trist with theirs and thinks it's a great idea."

"Yeah," I say, staring after them, wondering whether Zeke will really want to get their hands dirty.

"I reckon a Sportster would suit them," Indian states, his brow frowning. "Something fairly light to handle."

Relatively, foreign models are lighter. But then, what kid of mine would ride anything other than a Harley?

Fox props a foot up against the bench and leans over it. "Petty and Roller aren't here. You think anything of that, Prez?"

My good mood disappears immediately. "Petty's right to stay

clear," I growl. "If he showed my kid disrespect, I'd fuckin' end him. But Roller's a surprise."

"They're tight," Keys reminds me.

"If I have my way, Zeke will become a fixture on the compound." As, I hope, will their mom. "Those two will just have to suck it up."

Indian stares over to where Tom, Trist and Zeke have their heads together, then I watch too as they head toward the club-house. "Zeke seems a good kid. A bit strange, perhaps. I'd have said he was gay if you hadn't said different."

I notice the slip but don't remark on it. It's going to take us all a minute to get used to how to address Zeke.

"There's a difference?" Fox asks.

"Kid can't be gay if they're nonbinary," Keys responds knowingly. "Gays are men attracted to men."

Indian's eyes widen. "So, Zeke could end up with a woman?"

"Zeke's too fuckin' young to end up with anyone," I growl.

Keys snorts. "And how old were you when you first started playing with your dick?"

Luckily, Fox saves me from answering. "Don't give a damn about where a man, or nonbinary's dick ends up, as long as it's nowhere near me." He turns to stare at me. "It's not all in Zeke's head, is it, Prez? I had a quick word with them earlier. It's their manner, their actions. It's hard to put a finger on how to define them."

"Nonbinary does it," I reply, knowing that Zeke can't hide that they're different. "I just don't want anyone to judge them." I raise my eyes to encompass the others sitting around the table. "You think anyone else feels the same way as Petty?"

"They'll have me to fuckin' answer to if they do," Crash snarls. "But no. Maybe I had doubts about Zeke before I met them, but now I have, they can be whoever they want to be. Ain't no skin off my nose if they don't conform to my version of normality."

"They'll need us," Indian foresees. "But hey," he stands and slaps my back, "we'll be ready to kick some asses for them. With you as their dad, Zeke won't have to worry."

My heart feels like it's going to burst, and I choke up. My brothers have my back. In everything. Much as I, and they, seem to accept Zeke, their life won't be easy. Not in this world that only recognises two genders and nothing in between. Not for the first time in my life, I'm grateful to have the Devils around me.

Fox and Crash start a discussion that doesn't involve me. As I tune out, I look around, but Cher and the other women haven't yet reappeared. I start to get anxious.

Had I come on too hard and too fast? Of course, I fucking did. But Cher was far too much temptation for me, and once she was on my home turf, I hadn't been able to control myself.

Now Rosa and Tiff will be spilling all the dirt about me and the MC. I grow more and more worried about what her reaction will be. I hope she's getting more of a positive slant.

What would it be like having her as my old lady? For a moment, I allow myself the luxury of imagining her here, living with me. Splaying my legs, I turn my face up toward the sun, and let myself dream.

Am I really this close to gaining what I thought would never come to me? A wife, and a family?

Would she want more kids? Would I? Would Zeke be happy living here with me?

Should I buy a house off compound?

Others might think it's too soon, but this is a woman I've been carrying a torch for what seems like forever. Now she's gotten this close to me, I won't let her go.

Unless she doesn't think the same way about me.

At fucking last.

Rosa and Tiffany appear, closely followed by Cher, the twins and Zeke. As I rise, I can hear Cher preparing to leave. I'm pleased as fuck when I hear Tom and Trist promise Zeke they'll be their champions at school. At least that will make that part of their life easier for them.

But Cher? From here, I can't read what she's thinking.

Approaching her, I pull her to one side. "All good?"

She gives me a quick smile which doesn't quite reach her eyes. "Yeah, we're good. I've got to get Zeke home. They've got school in the morning."

I test the waters. "I'll come around tomorrow, yeah? Take you and Zeke out to dinner or something?"

"Not tomorrow. Zeke's got more rehearsals as it's coming up on their audition."

"When's their audition?"

"Friday. Right after school." She grimaces as she makes her apologies. "This week's going to be pretty full, Red. Is it okay if I give you a call?"

I'd be an ass if I didn't agree. "Sure. And if Zeke wants company when you're at work, they know where I am, okay?"

Her expression doesn't convince me anyone will be picking up the phone. Taking her to one side, I ask quietly. "Are we okay?"

To her credit, she doesn't lead me on. "I've got some things to think on, Red."

I shoot narrowed eyes toward Rosa and Tiffany. "What the hell have they been saying to you?"

Placing her hand on my arm, she shakes her head. "It's not just them, Red. It's you and me. I think earlier proved I can't keep my head around you."

And there's a problem with that?

"I need some space to think about this," she continues. "About what being with you would mean to me and Zeke, and whether it's a step I should take."

"Like what?" I demand. Personally, I can see no downside at all.

"You're an MC prez, Red. Rosa explained what you'd need in an old lady."

"You'd be perfect."

She shrugs. "And then there's the question of why you have a safe room."

I suck in air. "A precaution, Cher. And one we've never had to use."

"But it's there," she tells me, worry lines etching her face. "If the club isn't dangerous, why have one at all?"

"You leaving me, Cher?" I bite back the word *again*, but some part of me thinks she's running just like she did before. But this time it's different. "I will have a relationship with Zeke, whatever you and I do."

Her head bows. "I know. I haven't decided anything, Red. I don't know what to do. But yeah, I won't take your kid from you." She gives a tired shrug. "But it worries me. What will happen if they get too close to you?"

Like them and me fixing up a bike. I decide to keep that tidbit to myself for a while.

"Don't cut me out," I warn her. "Don't close doors which should remain open for now. Give me a chance to prove myself to you."

"I like you, Red. Too much. I've spent years of my life loving you. But you're the prez. It's more than a role, it's you. I've got to wonder what's best for me, and for Zeke too." She catches the tightening of my face. "This isn't goodbye. Just give me some space, yeah? Let me figure out what's best to do."

Does any man like a woman asking him to give her time? Not this one, that's for certain.

"Zeke's mine," I tell her through gritted teeth. "I'll be there for them, whatever you decide to do."

"I'll call you," she promises, and adds seeing the doubt in my eyes, "Red, I will. I'll call you."

I raise my chin. For now, there's nothing more I can do. I watch as she gathers Zeke to her side, and politely accompany them to her car. When she sees Zeke in and goes to the driver's side, I'm there too.

Without giving her a chance of evasion, I snake my hand

around her neck and pull her to me, planting my lips on hers—a chaste kiss for once.

"I know what I want," I hiss at her, sotto voce. "And sweetheart, that's you."

She nods, grimaces, and gets into her car. I wave to Owl who opens the gate and lets her through.

When the taillights fade, I storm around the back once more.

"Rosa!" I yell. "I want to talk to you."

She finishes her conversation with Twister, then comes across. "What can I do for you, Red?"

"Tell me why the fuck you called it the fuckin' safe room for a start," I hiss. "You've scared the shit out of her, Rosa. Or was that what you were trying to do? What the hell were you talking about?"

She draws back her shoulders and straightens her back. "If my opinion's worth anything to you, Red, I'm not sure she's the woman you need."

I rear back. "What the fuck?"

"She's a citizen through and through."

"So? You were once. Before you met Brick."

"I knew of the harsher side of life," she throws back, pointing a finger at my chest.

"You think Cher doesn't? She brought my kid up on her own, Rosa. Thrown out by her mom. That's not easy to do."

"But she's got to know what she's getting into if she gets together with you." Rosa shakes herself and seems to calm down. "I didn't bad mouth you, Red. I just told her about the club."

"And that we've got a fuckin' safe room."

Rosa looks unrepentant. "So? She'll know you take our safety seriously."

While that's true, Cher's clearly now worried about what we have to protect ourselves from.

I regard Rosa with a worried frown. Could she be worried about some other woman coming in and taking her role?

CHAPTER THIRTEEN

CHER

"So, you and Dad got on okay?" Giving them a sideways glance, I see Zeke's got a cheeky grin on their face. "Or so I presume," they adds. "Seeing as you were missing for quite some time."

"Not long," I correct, giving them a quick glance then turning my eyes back to the road while thinking just how fast and wild our illicit activity had been. "Your dad just wanted to have a private talk with me."

"Yeah, Mom," they mumble, knowingly. "I guess you and he are going to try to make a go of things?"

When Red and I were together, I never wanted something more. But after my conversation with Rosa, I'm really not sure. The sensible me says we need to slam on the brakes. Sure, I've met his club and while I still have concerns, I hadn't been made to feel awkward or that I was an outsider, though I remain far from convinced it's a place I want to have influencing my child. But I can't separate the club from Red, and that's where my problem lies. I want Red, there's no doubt about it, the man I've loved for almost half my life.

But a woman associated with Red would be drawn into his

world. Even if we all lived away from the club, as his woman, I'd be expected to play my part. I don't think I could keep me and Zeke separate from Red's role as prez. It's likely I'd be expected to be like Rosa, giving my all to the club.

Under other circumstances, I might enjoy being involved in my man's life, but whether or not I could be a good fit with an outlaw MC is something that weighs heavily on my mind. I've lived my life being honest, obeying all laws. I haven't even picked up a speeding ticket. Despite how personable the men Red calls brothers had seemed, I know they thumb their noses at authority. I don't want to live constantly worrying my man would end up behind bars, or worse, him being killed.

If it was just me, maybe I could bend a little more, but I've got Zeke to think of. The club's got a freaking safe room. Why would they go to such trouble to build it if it was unlikely it would ever be used?

"How did you get on with Tristan and Tom?" I ask, turning the tables.

"They're a laugh." Turning my head briefly, I see Zeke wearing a genuine smile. "They take no shit from anyone. Mom, you know, I've seen them around school? I didn't know at the time why they'd earned it, but they've got a reputation. It's like they're untouchable, and no one wants to get on their wrong side." Zeke pauses and gives a satisfied sigh. "Now they're going to be looking out for me."

"And that's good?" I'm slightly on the fence as Zeke's going to become known for associating with the kids of bikers.

"It's great, Mom. Hopefully no one will bully me now when Tom and Trist put the word around about who my dad is. And they'll ensure no one messes with me when they're around."

Grimacing, as I wait for a light to change, I know I'll have to factor that into what I do now. It will make Zeke's life easier to have kids such as the twins on their side, but I doubt whether Tom and Trist would have given them the time of day were it not for them being Red's child.

Still, I muse as I ease my foot off the brake, even if Red and I don't work out, Zeke will still have to have a relationship with him. There's no way I could, or would, stop that.

Arriving back at the apartment. Zeke's fast getting out of the car and walks ahead of me, while I sit a while longer, my thoughts still whirring.

How could I refuse to have a relationship with Red because I don't approve of his life, but then be comfortable letting Zeke be a part of it? Eventually following Zeke's path, I enter my home and put down my bag, wondering what I do now and regretting I gave into temptation with Red. We should have kept our distance, taken things slow just like I'd planned. Now I know exactly what I'll be turning down. A vibrator will be a poor substitute.

While Zeke disappears and shortly after I hear sounds coming from their room that tells me they're back playing one of their games again, I mentally go back over this afternoon. I think I made a big mistake not pushing Red away. While there are still so many other things we've got to sort out between us, jumping into his bed, or to put it more accurately, into his arms and wrapping my legs around his waist, happened far too soon.

My teeth worry my lip as I wonder if the concern is not all from my side, and whether Red, too, will have second thoughts. Red's obviously got more experience in all the years we've been apart, while I've remained the same naïve girl I once was. Sexually, could I ever be his equal, and is that what he wants? I'd tried to dismiss the club girls who'd he'd been totally honest about, but if that was the kind of performance he's expecting, I wouldn't know where to start.

My insides start to tingle at my memory of being in his room and being honest with myself, I'd love to experience more of what he's learned. If he was a normal man, I'd have no hesitation or doubts, but as he's not, I'm full of them.

Having checked that Zeke's getting themself ready for bed, I take a shower. Standing naked under the spray, I run my hands over my body, throwing back my head, remembering Red's touch and how much knowledge he now has about a woman's body. My fingers touch my clit. Just the thought of him turns me on. *Am I really going to give that up?* As my fingers strum, my actions and the memory of earlier today causing my muscles to tense and soon shoot me to the pinnacle and over the top, I realise if our sexual compatibility was the only thing I had to worry about, I'd run straight into his arms and do all I could to keep him.

But sadly, it's not. I've got Zeke.

While I think Zeke is the best child I could ever have, and utterly love and adore them, I'm not blind to the effect being nonbinary will have on their life. It's hard enough for other people to accept them. Would an association with an MC make that harder or worse?

When I get into bed, I've not reached any conclusion. My dreams are haunted by men in black leather, handcuffs and chains. Somehow, I even conjure up Red wearing nothing but his leather vest and jeans. When I wake, my body is drenched with sweat, and I feel needy all over again.

What is this power that Red has over me? Would it have been better if I'd never met him? But then, I wouldn't have Zeke.

My day starts completely normally. I wake with no inkling that anything's about to change. I get Zeke up. The only difference is that they're eager to get to school—one thing to thank Red for, well, more so Rosa's twins. I wave them off to the bus then do my chores. Again, nothing out of the normal.

When I pick Zeke up to take them to their practice, they start talking even before they've fully closed the car door.

"You should have seen people today, Mom." Zeke's bouncing in their seat with excitement.

I shoot a fond look their way. On a normal day, Zeke's mostly quiet when I pick them up from school. "Yeah?"

"Trist and Tom were waiting for me." Zeke's face is

animated. "They greeted me like a long-lost friend with back slaps and hugs. It drew quite a bit of attention. Then they walked beside me and escorted me in, right up to my first class." Zeke sniggers. "They glared around the room, then left."

"Uh-huh." I start the engine and start driving away.

"Then, at lunch, they were waiting for me. We sat at the same table. There was a kid behind us who spoke loudly, wondering why the twins were sitting with the freak."

I shoot my eyes toward Zeke. *Is this what they put up with every day?* They've never used that word around me. Well, not here. In the past, once I knew the bullying had proved too much to bear, we'd moved on.

Zeke's bouncing up and down excitedly. "Tom got up and punched him in the face." Again, I risk taking my eyes off the road. I don't condone violence, and I know the expression on my face shows it, but Zeke either doesn't notice or ignores it. "He told the kid if he wanted to see a freak, he should try looking in the mirror some time."

Despite myself, I have to hold back a snort of laughter. "Did Tom get into trouble?"

"Nah. He was clever, no teachers saw."

Clever? Is this the behaviour I should be encouraging? Though if I'd heard that comment, I'd probably want to slap the originator myself.

"Trist told them I was a Satan's Devils kid." Zeke sits back and folds their arms triumphantly. "I reckon they'll leave me alone from now on. Oh, and, Mom, when I got to my next class, a girl came up to me and asked if I could introduce her to the twins."

I can see there are benefits of being a Satan's Devils kid, which Zeke is, but I'm not sure I want them to garner that sort of reputation.

"You got everything with you?" I query, as we arrive at the studio. "Dance belt?"

"Yeah, Mom." They roll their eyes. "I'm set. You going to hang around?"

I know they don't like me watching, so I shake my head. "I've got some shopping to do. I'll pick you up in an hour."

Car laden with groceries, I return for Zeke at the allotted time, race home and pull together a meal for them and me. Then, ruffling their hair and planting a kiss on their cheek, I run through the rules I always repeat when I'm about to leave. Stuff like, don't open the door to strangers, call the neighbour if anything's wrong, and don't stay up too late. The words go straight over Zeke's head as they're used to the same litany.

After a moment's hesitation, I take out my phone and shoot a text to them.

"What?" Their eyes widen as they pull it out.

"That's Red's number, Zeke. I can't think why you'd have to use it, but if there's an emergency, you can call him."

"I think I'd feel awkward, Mom. I don't think we're at the stage of being able to chat over the phone."

Again, my hands run through their hair. "You don't have to do anything, Zeke, but you know his number is there. You can use it or not. It's up to you."

Just giving them their dad's number hits me that I'm letting their other parent into their life. While that's just how it should be, I feel like I'm losing part of my child. I try to balance that with the thought it will be good to have someone there to support me, to share the joys and the tribulations of a teenager's life. But they've been only mine for so long, part of me feels jealous, and a small bit resentful. All those years, all those times when I worked with Zeke as they tried to find themself and come to terms with what they are, well, where was Red then when I needed someone beside me?

He'd have been there if he could, I remind myself, as I straighten, pull away, and head to my job to earn us some money.

Working evenings was better when Zeke was a baby. I had all

their waking hours, and while they were sleeping, was happy enough to leave them with a trusted babysitter. That arrangement had continued until we came to Vegas, when they'd begged me to trust them to be left on their own, and in the end, I relented. It was money saved for me, and they're sensible. Even knowing that, it's hard to pull myself away, but money doesn't make itself, and we both need to eat.

Arriving at the casino, it's still the same as any other day. I strip off my coat in the locker room, revealing my smart, tailored black-and-white uniform. I put my purse away, then proceed to the blackjack table to take over from the daytime shift.

On autopilot, I don't immediately notice the two security guards waiting for me.

"Ms Samson? Could you come with me please? Mr Carson would like to speak to you."

Carson? He's one of the owners of the casino. What on earth would he want with me? I notice another croupier has taken over from the girl I'd been supposed to relieve. Seeing arrangements have already been made, nervously, I comply. Flanked by a guard on either side, I take the stairs which I've only used once before, the day of my interview.

What's this all about? I've nothing to be worried about, but still, I'm nervous. Quickly, I run through everything in my mind. I'm good at my job. I turn up on time. I've never been late or left early. I'm polite to the customers.

Maybe he wants to give me a raise or a promotion? But if so, why has he sent such dour security guards? A simple summons would have ensured my swift attendance.

I'm led into a boardroom. That's intimidating enough, but instead of just Carson, the man who'd originally employed me, sitting alongside him are the other three owners. While I've not been introduced formally, I recognise all of them immediately. Everyone on the floor knows who the big bosses are.

I give a nod and offer a pleasant smile of greeting. It's

Crossman who waves me to a chair. Having no option, I go over and take it.

"Ms Samson." He says my name, then pauses, and a flicker of emotion crosses his face. It's hard to interpret, a mixture of anger and sadness rolled up in one. "To say I'm disappointed is an understatement."

Rodgers takes over with a grimace Crossman's way. "We trust all our employees, and it hurts when they betray our trust."

They must be speaking about someone else, not me. I'm completely trustworthy. *They want information on somebody else.* Rapidly, I think whether there's been any wrongdoings I've witnessed, but can't think of any.

I sit forward, placing my hands on the table. "How can I help you?"

Carson snorts. "I expect bluffing on the casino floor, not in here." As my eyes widen, he continues, "Your game has been discovered, Ms Samson. You might as well admit what you've done."

I start to feel sick. My body tenses, but I try to keep my composure. "I'm not sure what you're talking about."

"No?" Crossman snaps angrily. "You're a good actor, I'll give you that. Wouldn't want to sit at a poker table with you. But we've been watching you for a while, and you're not quite as clever as you think. We know all about the arrangement you have with Parker Devonshire."

Now I'm completely lost. "Parker who?"

Greaves sighs as though he's disappointed and slides a photo toward me. When I pick it up, I see a customer who plays at my table quite a lot and wins more than not. I've thought he'd had the luck of the Devil with him. In the photo, I'm smiling as I deal the cards, and he's grinning back at me.

I always smile. It's not unusual for me to get home with face muscles which ache from trying to be pleasant all night. I pass the photo back.

"I'm sorry, I don't know what I can do to help you. I recognise him but didn't know his name. He's played at my table a few times."

Crossman's eyes narrow. "He only ever plays at *your* table, and he's cost this casino a few million dollars."

"He's lucky—"

"No." Now Crossman slams his hand down on the table, making me jump. "You're in cahoots with him. You're both playing a scam."

They think what? My voice doesn't sound strong when I try to protest. "I'm not—"

"Oh yes, you are. Tell us how you do it, and we'll keep the cops out of this."

"How can I tell you what I don't know?" I cry out. "I haven't done anything wrong. I do my job diligently. As for cheating the system, I wouldn't know how."

Carson shakes his head almost sadly. "Bring 'em in," he says in a tired voice.

Crossman stands, opens the door, and two police officers enter. My face goes slack. I'd already had suspicions I was about to unfairly lose my job, the last thing I expected was to be arrested.

"I haven't done anything wrong." There's a tremor in my voice, but I can do nothing about it.

"Ms Samson, I need you to accompany us to the station," one of the police officers tells me, his face impassive.

"But I'm innocent." My protest falls on deaf ears. The casino owners won't look at me, and the cops roll their eyes as if they're bored with always hearing the same thing.

When one whips a pair of handcuffs out, I feel like screaming.

This isn't fair. It's not happening to me. I freeze when I'm approached and asked to hold my hands out. Shakily I comply, knowing I've no other option.

"Can you at least tell me what I'm to be charged with?" I plead with my eyes, hoping the cop will take mercy on me, but he's not even gentle when the metal bands are snapped closed around my wrists.

"Theft from the casino," Crossman says coldly. He glances my way once, his eyes alighting on the cuffs, gives a satisfied nod, then ignores me as I'm led away.

CHAPTER FOURTEEN

RED

"Seeing your baby momma tonight, Red?" Crash comes over and slaps me on the back.

I pick up the beer Owl's just put in front of me and pick at the label. "Nah, she's working tonight."

He pulls out a stool and places it beside mine. "You and her all good after Sunday?"

I shrug. "I'll be fucked if I know." I grimace. I've heard all the comments going on around me and know brothers had put two and two together when we'd hidden ourselves in my room for a while. Well, that and the just-fucked look Cher was sporting when we'd turned back up, so I've no hesitation in telling him, "I think I might have moved too fast and fucked it all up."

Crash sniggers. "You were like two kids unable to keep their hands off each other. You're not usually so forward, Prez."

"Remember we've got history," I remind him, rubbing my hand over my short beard. "It's not like I just met her."

Crash nods as though he's guessing the words I left unsaid— that the attraction between us hadn't faded over the intervening years.

"Her problem," my eyes glaze as I try to explain, "is that she's not convinced this thing could work between us because of who I am. And I," I pause to take a sip of my beer, "I've got to be careful who I bring in as my ol' lady. I've got to think of the club. Then there's Zeke. If things don't work out, what would that mean to them? They come first. We both agree on that."

"I liked her," Crash states, and I feel some of the weight I've been carrying around lessen. "Zeke seemed okay too. Sure, he's a different type of flavour, but there was nothing about him, *them,* to dislike. The twins have taken to Zeke."

They have, and for that I'm grateful. Not so much when they'd cornered me earlier and told me some of the shit Zeke has to put up with in school. They'd never paid them any attention before, but today were confronted by the bullies themselves. Of course, the twins come as a twosome, and coupled with that they're Satan's Devils kids with the backup of the club, no one wants to take them on.

Now their classmates know Zeke's got the same protection, maybe their life will be easier with them on their side.

"Want me to beat your ass at pool?"

I grin at the VP's offer, drain my beer and place the bottle down. "I'd like to see you fuckin' try."

Winning the toss, I break first. By my third shot, I'm becoming confident I'll be able to clear the table. While Crash fidgets, Keys and Twister wander over. I play up to my audience, attempting a trick shot, which, of course, goes wrong.

Ruefully, I step back and allow Crash to take my place. I'm preparing to watch him clean up when my phone rings. It's a call from an unknown number.

"You got Red."

"Dad? It's Zeke." The choked sob tells me immediately they're upset.

"What is it, kid? Calm down and tell me." The seriousness in my tone makes Crash put down his cue and stand waiting expectantly while I finger the pocket in my cut, making sure I've got my bike key.

"It's Mom," Zeke cries out, making me go cold.

"She okay? She been in an accident?"

Twister's face turns my way, and his focus is all on me.

"Zeke?" I prompt when all I hear are sobs. My blood feels like ice running through my veins. *No, she can't be gone.* "Take a deep breath and tell me, kid."

"Sh-sh-she r-r-rang me 'cause I'm the only n-n-number she knows. She asked me to c- c-all you. She says she needs a lawyer, Dad. M-m-mom's been arrested."

What? Of all the things I expected Zeke to say, that wasn't even close to the top of the list, not even on it.

"What the fuck for?" My voice is too abrupt, and I try to calm down. I take a breath then ask more quietly, "What happened, Zeke?"

There's another sob on the line. "It has to be a mistake, Dad. She's been accused of theft by the casino."

The news takes a moment to sink in. I have no doubts that she's innocent of everything. I might not have been around her over the last fifteen years, but I'd stake my life on it. But my faith in her doesn't mean anything, she needs to prove it.

We have lawyers on speed dial, both locally and Alex in San Diego who we can call on for advice. "I'll get someone, Zeke. Leave it with me."

"What do I do, Dad?" Zeke sounds completely lost and I don't blame them.

"You hang tight, kid. I'll get news to you as soon as I can."

"Bring Mom home, Dad. Please."

Assuring Zeke I'll do what I can, I end the call and speak to Crash, Twister and Keys. "They've arrested Cher on a bogus charge of theft from the casino. Fuck knows why."

"I'll get on it." Keys is already moving toward his office. As security, he's got access to all the casino systems and can hopefully find everything we need.

Twister's got his phone out with his finger hovering over the list of contacts. "I'll call Jeeves."

"I'll come with you to the precinct," Crash states adamantly, knowing where I'll be headed. I raise my chin toward him. I appreciate his support. "Which one was she taken to?"

Shit. I didn't ask. I ring Zeke back immediately and get the information I need. As I repeat the destination, Twister, on his own phone, relays that information to the standby lawyer we use.

"Jeeves will meet you there," Twister confirms. "She got money to pay him?"

"I'll see to everything she needs," I confirm without hesitation. I want to see her properly lawyered up and not left to the mercy of a public defender. "Ready?" My question is directed toward the VP.

At his raised chin, I rush outside, heading straight for my bike and start her up. With Crash beside me, we're out of the gates almost before you can blink.

My mind races. She's been set up. She has to be. Sure, Cher probably makes little more than minimum wage, but her apartment doesn't scream money. From what I've seen, it's a pleasant enough home, but without many luxuries. Zeke's well fed, but their clothes are nothing special. If she's been stealing, I'll eat my fucking hat.

I grow angrier by the second. Driving on autopilot, I head the right way, unfortunately familiar with the direct routes to all the precincts in Vegas. I am the prez of an MC after all, but I never expected to go to one to retrieve my woman.

Hopefully they'll realise they've fucked up and made a mistake, and Cher will be set free with an apology. There's no doubt in my mind that's what this is.

When we arrive, I back my bike into the kerb with Crash beside me. Then we stride in.

The cop behind the desk views us suspiciously and I swear I see his hand twitch toward his gun.

"You got Cheryl Samson in custody?" I bark, hoping that she's already been released or maybe is in the process of being so.

"None of your business," the cop replies.

"No," a deep voice states from behind me, "but it is mine. Christian Jeeves." Pushing past me, the lawyer hands his card over the desk. "I'm here to represent Cheryl Samson who's my client."

"She's being interrogated—"

"Not without me," the authoritative lawyer responds, making me hope she had the sense to keep her mouth shut until her legal support arrived. But then she'd have to trust Zeke to have contacted me, and me to have responded fast.

As the cop gets up to let Jeeves through, he sets a hand on my shoulder and leans in to tell me quietly, "I'll see what's going on and come back out."

Yeah, he will. If he wants to be paid that is. I raise my chin as he walks off.

I go outside with Crash as he wants a smoke. As he lights up, I look on enviously. At times like these, I sorely feel the lack of nicotine. I stand downwind and inhale the second-hand smoke, not that it helps any.

While he puffs away, I take out my phone and update Zeke. They can't hide their relief at hearing from me.

"I'm at the precinct now. I can't see your mom, but I've got a lawyer for her. He's in with her now. I'll let you know as soon as I hear anything."

They've pulled themself together since I last spoke, but the voice which thanks me still quavers.

"I wouldn't have known what to do, Dad. I'm glad I could call you."

"Anytime, kiddo. Anytime." Simple words but I really mean them.

Fuck, but I'm grateful we'd reconnected. A nightmare scenario runs through my head of Zeke and Cher being alone. She's not the type of woman to have a lawyer on speed dial.

Crash finishes his smoke, and we move back inside. The cop glares at us as we take up two visitors' chairs.

I hate these places, been in them far too much. Normally, it's just to retrieve a brother who was arrested on a drunk and disorderly, but other times I've been out back myself on a trumped-up charge. All police stations seem to smell the same, an air of hopelessness hanging around them tinged with the scent of disinfectant.

My leg bounces uncontrollably. I'm tense.

"She'll be okay," Crash tries to reassure me. "They've got it wrong, and Keys will discover the truth of it. I doubt there's anything to hold her on, and she'll be back home with her kid tonight."

I fucking hope that he's right.

I'm jittery and find it hard sitting still. There's a fucking clock ticking on the wall behind the desk, but for all the noise it's making, the hands don't seem to move. A woman wanders in, giving us a wide berth, then, with glances behind as if expecting us to attack her, she explains how her purse was stolen to the bored cop behind the desk. He takes the details, then sends her back on her way.

Two cops come in dragging a guy who's singing tunelessly at the top of his voice. When he throws a punch at one of his captors, he's marched on out back obviously to spend the night in a drunk tank. The police officers shortly re-emerge presumably to go out on patrol and see who else they can pick up to enjoy their hospitality for the night.

At fucking last, Jeeves reappears. He looks harassed as he gestures toward the door, and strides outside. Crash and I waste no time following him.

"They've had the evidence for a couple of days," he starts. "Decided to wait until she turned up to her shift to pull her in. There's a search warrant for her place that's been issued."

"Zeke's there alone—her fifteen-year-old kid," I tell him. "They'll be worried sick if the cops come calling."

"She told me that," Jeeves says, his eyebrows raised in question.

"I'll go get Zeke," I respond immediately, understanding Cher will want me to be with them. Then I process he's said they've got evidence. While I know whatever they've got won't show fuck all when they examine it carefully, that they even think they've got something on her may mean she won't immediately be going home. "Will they release her while they investigate?"

"With the amount of money involved, it's unlikely until bail's been set. Even then they could argue she's a flight risk."

"She's actually been charged?"

"They think they have evidence," Jeeves replies. "And that it's an open-and-shut case."

Fuck, fuck, fuck. And there I was, hoping this was just a mistake that could quickly be cleared up. But now I've got to try to get to Zeke before the cops come calling and scare them half to death.

"Just get her out of there," I instruct him, extracting the key to my bike.

"I'll stay," Crash states. "In case there's a chance she's coming out."

I raise my chin to thank him, though from what the lawyer's said, it could be a fruitless night.

Going to my bike, I take out my phone and call Zeke. "The cops have a search warrant," I warn them.

"They're already here." Zeke's voice sounds squeakier than ever, and frightened.

"I'll be right there." I end the call, wanting to be on my way to reassure them in person.

Pushing the speed limit while keeping an eye out for blue flashing lights, I reach the apartment, pulling up just past a couple of cop cars. When I knock on the door, Zeke opens it and falls into my arms.

"You're too late if you're here to destroy evidence," a cop cockily tells me when he spies my cut.

I ignore him. "You entered when there was just an unaccompanied minor here?" My eyes accuse him.

The officer shrugs. "He let us in."

"I asked to see the warrant, Dad," Zeke defends themself. "They showed me the badges, and the warrant looked legit to me. They can search *anything*."

"You won't find shit," I tell the cop. "Cheryl Samson is innocent." Purposefully, I avoid saying Cher is mine.

"Then maybe we need a warrant for your club." The cop smirks. "Maybe she was working for you."

I try to keep a tight rein on my temper, but it's hard. Speaking through gritted teeth, I defend Cher. "You won't find anything because she's fucking done nothing. As for the club, we've got no involvement. I'm only here because Zeke is my child."

"I can see that." The cop looks from me to Zeke and can't suppress a cruel smile. "Though apart from looks, I doubt he favours you."

Zeke's dressed in those harem pants again and has on a t-shirt sporting rainbows. The way the cop's smirking makes me want to hit him.

I refrain, of course. Having both Zeke's parents locked up won't help anyone, least of all my kid.

I notice the time, it's gone past midnight now. I might not have known I was a parent long, but I do know one thing, Zeke should have been in bed hours ago if they're going to make school in the morning.

"How long are you going to be here?" I ask impatiently.

Narrowing his eyes and looking around, the officer replies unhelpfully, "As long as it takes."

I wonder about leaving them to it and taking Zeke back to the compound but need to be here in case they try to plant evidence. From their behaviour, it appears they've not yet found anything. I watch as they pull out drawers and empty them on the ground, wondering what they're searching for.

When they pick up a laptop and put it into a plastic bag,

Zeke protests, "That's mine." When the cops show no sympathy, just take it out and store it in one of their cars, they turn to me in horror. "That's got my homework on it."

"Don't worry. Your mom can come up with something to say to your school." Even if she has to wait for a bail hearing, she should be back soon and can get everything sorted.

The cops are thorough, and the search of the small apartment takes a couple of hours. They take Cher's tablet and her e-reader, the latter I have no explanation for. Do they think they'll find she's been reading up on casino heists? They take some paperwork with them, but from what I can tell, all they have are bills.

When the door finally closes behind them, Zeke looks so tired they could drop on the spot. I send them to bed while settling myself down on the couch.

She'll be free soon, I tell myself. Either Jeeves will work his magic and show whatever evidence they've got doesn't stack up, or Keys will come up with some information that will clear her.

CHAPTER FIFTEEN

RED

Sometime during the night, I must have fallen asleep on the couch as the next thing I know, my phone is ringing. I fumble for a moment, as I extract it from my cut, then hit the accept key to hear Jeeves yawning.

"She out?" I ask, ready to go pick Cher up.

"No. She's going up in front of a judge later for a bail hearing."

Fuck! I run my free hand through my hair. "Okay. How much do you reckon they'll set it for?"

"They won't," he replies, chillingly. "With the figures involved, they're going to say she's a flight risk."

No, no, no, I scream in my head. "Her kid needs her," I shout down the phone. "She's done nothing wrong, Jeeves. This must all be a mistake."

He sighs. "If you ask me, what we're dealing with here is a customer counting cards, and she knew nothing of what he was doing. But they've got in it their heads that she was in cahoots with him. If it helps, I read her as innocent, but they seem to think they can prove their case or cast enough doubt on her assertion she had nothing to do with it."

Fuck, Cher. What have you gotten yourself into? "What have they got to go on?"

"This Parker Devonshire had been coming in for months, and always to her table." The most, in my view, they can criticise her for, is not noticing if he was card counting. But hell, that's hard to spot in a busy casino. "You got Keys looking into him?"

I'd told him that last night, so my *uh-huh* just serves to confirm it. "I'll get back to you when he comes up with something. Jeeves." I pinch the brow of my nose, trying to banish the lingering sleep fog from my head. "You get the feeling the casino has an underlying reason to go after her?"

"I've been wondering that myself. Unless they caught her red-handed, can prove a relationship between the two of them, or find funds in her bank account she shouldn't have, I don't see how they can make a case that will stick. I don't know what cards they'll be playing, Red, pardon the pun, so I can't tell you what, if any, evidence they're holding."

"She's innocent, Jeeves."

"As are all my clients." He chuckles, but then grows serious again. "In this case, I agree with you, and I'll do all I can to prove it. Now, I'm going to get my head down for a couple of hours as I'll be back at the courthouse later this morning."

"I'll be there." On hand and ready to pull together the bail money even if he thinks it's unlikely she'll need it.

"Don't get your hopes up." He throws that parting shot in warning.

A small voice speaks as soon as the call is finished. "Is Mom coming home?"

"Come here, Zeke." I stretch my arm out to my side, pleased when they sit next to me, and allow my hand to rest on their shoulders. I then tell them all that the lawyer had told me.

"Mom wouldn't steal anything," Zeke states adamantly when I've finished.

"I know," I tell them. "It just might take a while to prove it."

"I want her back."

Noticing Zeke's lower lip trembling, I decide there's nothing to be gained from sitting here listening to them ask questions I have no answers for. Instead, I take a stab at being a dad.

I stand. "I'll see what I can pull together for breakfast while you get ready for school."

"I can't go to school, not today."

I might not have been a father before, but I know how this goes. "What would your mom want you to do?"

"I can't go, Dad. Not when I'm worried about her."

"Come here." I pull Zeke in for a hug. "Your mom's done nothing wrong. This is going to turn out to be one great f… mistake. She'll be set free before you know it, and until she is, I'm going to be here for you both. She's not dead or dying, so life must go on. And she'd be the first to say your education comes first."

They look at me stubbornly. "I can't go without my homework."

"You can. I'll give an explanation the school will accept." I'll think of something, say it was stolen, perhaps.

"I don't want to go."

"I'm not leaving you here, Zeke. I've got things to do. Top of that list is me working to get your mom released. Come on, kid. You've got to play your part."

Zeke's eyes narrow. "You swear you'll get her out?"

"I promise." Even if I have to arrange a prison break, she's not going to be spending her life behind bars. Even if she was guilty, which she's fucking not.

Their lips purse, then a crafty look spreads over their face. "I've missed the bus."

"I'll take you on my bike."

Their eyes go comically wide, and they come up with another excuse. "I don't think Mom would like that."

Chuckling, I ruffle their hair. "And I'm your dad." I don't think she can say much about it. When she was only five years older than they are now, she rode on the back of my bike, and I was a total stranger at the time. If she complains, I'll simply remind her of that. As well as the fact I'm Zeke's dad and I'd die before I'd let something happen to them.

Deciding I've won this argument, I shoot a quick text, then go into the kitchen and raid the cupboards feeling relieved when Zeke says they're happy with just cereal. I fill two bowls, one for them and one for myself, and after making a quick cup of coffee, breakfast is over. I clean up and just when I've finished, there's a knock at the door. Waving Zeke back, I go open it.

I raise my chin at my VP. "You didn't have to come yourself."

He shrugs. "I brought Tom's along – thought that one of the twin's would probably fit Zeke the best."

He thought right. Tom's helmet fits Zeke like it was made for them, and I see by their grin that the anticipation of riding my bike has taken away some of the worry for their mom.

My bike's still the same one Cher had originally ridden on, still with the same sissy pad and pillion seat. I've enhanced the performance over the years and swapped out the belt drive for a more reliable chain, but in substance, it hasn't much changed. There seems to be a certain rightness about taking Zeke on the bike that was responsible for Cher and I getting together at the start. It had a big part to play in Zeke's creation.

While I close up the house, Crash has taken Zeke outside and is giving them instructions on how to ride pillion. As my VP seems to have it covered, I just stand back and, despite the circumstances, find myself looking forward to taking my kid for their first ride. I monitor the instructions Crash is giving but can't see he's left anything out. When he finishes, I approach the bike.

"Let's do this, kid."

I throw my leg astride and place my own lid on my head, wishing as always, I was back in Arizona and could feel the wind blowing through my hair. Though I am glad Zeke's head will be protected—not, of course, that I intend to drive anything other than cautious and slow.

Zeke places a hand on my shoulder as they steady themself

to get on. It shoots me back to the last time I took a pillion passenger, more than fifteen years ago. I've had no one riding behind me since Zeke's mom.

"Hold on to my waist, or the grips," I tell them as I turn around, ensuring their feet are secure on the pegs. "Ready?"

At their excited nod, I start my engine. Immediately, Zeke's hands come to my sides and grip tight.

Crash comes up alongside as we pull out onto the road and matches his speed to mine.

After half a mile, Zeke's death grip eases. When we pull up at lights, I turn my head to see my kid beaming wide. If nothing else, this has taken their mind off their troubles for now.

We arrive at the school at the same time as the buses. Deliberately, I pull up in a not very discreet spot, attracting the attention of a couple I know.

"Uncle Red!" Trist shouts delightedly and comes running across. "Hi, Zeke!" He holds out his fist and gets a fist bump from my kid who seems reluctant to get off.

"You're wearing my helmet," Tom states, but he's grinning. "Looks good on you, Zeke."

Crash sits with folded arms, grinning at the three kids. His eyes meet mine and he raises his chin. It takes a village to raise a kid, it's said, and I think all the members of the Vegas chapter can take a bit of pride in how Tom and Trist have turned out. I can't help but be pleased we've raised little protectors, who're now going to be looking out for my kid.

Tapping Zeke's leg, pleased to see they understand what I want and sling their leg over the seat, I then dismount, remove my helmet and place my gloves and shades in it and prop it on the seat. Crash says he'll stay and watch it for me. When he points at me and waves his hand up and down, I get what he's trying to say, and remove my cut.

"Hey, Zeke. Can you show me the principal's office?" As they come up beside me, I turn to speak to the twins. "Zeke's got some shit going on. Can you find them later so they can fill you in?"

"Sure we will, Red." Tom plumps up his chest.

"Catch you later, Zeke," Trist calls out as Zeke leads me away.

Even with Zeke swearing I'm their long-lost dad, I don't get far with the school. But I do speak to the principal's PA who notes Zeke had their laptop stolen, and that any homework they'd done can't, at this point, be turned in. They won't even add me as a fucking contact without Cher's say.

It makes me realise I've currently got no legal rights to them. I wouldn't even be listed on the birth certificate as she hadn't known my name.

I leave a mixture of frustrated and relieved, knowing the school takes security seriously, but with the desire to rectify and consolidate my rights to Zeke as soon as I can. I hate that his birth certificate probably has "father unknown" on it. That's something that will definitely have to change.

When I return to where Crash is waiting, I put my cut back on. I shrug when his eyebrow queries me, then jerking my chin, get on my bike and we head away.

Reaching the clubhouse, I make a beeline for Keys. As expected, he's in his office.

Pulling out the chair that's opposite his cluttered desk, I turn it backward then straddle it. "What've you got?"

Keys isn't taken aback by my non-greeting. He taps at a few keys to finish up what he's doing, then lowers the lid of his laptop, closing it partway.

"Not a lot. The casino doesn't seem to have much to go on, all circumstantial evidence. Parker Devonshire did only visit her table, and every time he did, he won quite a lot. Over the past few months, he's racked up five million dollars."

Not small change by any account. "You looking into him?"

"Yeah. I've also got Utah delving as deep as they can."

Utah, who far from being Neanderthals, are well up on this

shit, with technical abilities to seemingly hack into everything, including federal databases.

"This Devonshire ever play on other tables?" I ask.

"Not that I can find. I've looked through the security tapes, and it's always hers he aims for. Maybe his taste is the same as yours." Key's chuckle fades immediately when he sees the expression on my face.

"How the fuck do they think she was helping him cheat?"

Keys leans back, linking his hands behind his head. "I've no fuckin' idea. She opens a fresh sealed pack of cards just as she's supposed to. They can't be marked. But the fact is, he does win."

I rub at an itch on my nose. "Cops searched her apartment last night."

He presses his lips together and raises and dips his chin. "Presumably to find evidence of the money she's supposed to have obtained by aiding him. But they won't find shit. I've been through her bank accounts and there's nothing suspicious being paid in."

My jaw clenches. "What do they think, that she's got an offshore account?" My fingertips dig into my temples. As well as confused and riled by Cher's problems, I'm tired. "You should see her apartment. She's made a pleasant enough home for Zeke, but there are no luxuries there. If she had been bringing money in over the past few months, there'd be something to show for it."

Keys raises his chin to show he agrees. "The evidence they have is circumstantial at best. Unless there's something we don't know about."

I suspect that there is. I glance at my watch. "I need to get to the bail hearing in case she's released. I'll catch you later."

"I'll keep digging, Prez."

CHAPTER SIXTEEN

RED

Cher's brief court appearance was over fast. She'd look so wan and lost as she appeared that my heart broke for her. As I'd been warned, bail was denied, and she was to be held while the cops built their case.

I tried to telegraph that I'd look after Zeke when her pleading eyes had met mine. Then Jeeves caught up with me after the short hearing, and I heard those exact words relayed.

"She wants you to look after her boy," Jeeves tells me.

"Her child," I automatically correct. "And I will. There's no doubting that. They're mine, as well."

"She got more than one?"

"Zeke's nonbinary," I start, ceasing at the look of bewilderment in his eyes, and simply confirm, "Just the one."

He changes the subject fast. "I don't know what the cops think they have. I'll have to wait until they show their hand."

"They've got nothing," I retort. "Nothing at fuckin' all. I just don't understand."

He looks as perplexed as I feel. "They've got to have something. Keys found anything?"

Shrugging, I tell him, "Only that the fucker always chose her table. He can't find anything suspicious on her part, and she's no unaccounted-for money."

Jeeves seems to find the tip of his shoes interesting for a moment, then looks back up. "You need to find something, Red."

He doesn't have to tell me.

I return to the clubhouse in a foul mood. I'm tired from only having a couple of hours sleep and frustrated that there seems nothing I can do.

When Roller appears, I take my anger out on him. "Why the fuck weren't you at the barbeque?"

He rears back a step and holds up his hands. "Didn't think it was mandatory, Prez."

In a growling tone, I disillusion him. "I took it as disrespect. I expected it of Petty, but not of you. You got a problem with my kid?"

His eyes flick right and left as if looking for support but there are only the prospects around. "I couldn't come as I had something else to do."

Something with Petty, I suspect. Those two are tight as thieves. I'm itching to hit out at someone, and he would do. But before I can tell him what little I thought of his non-appearance, my phone rings. Having assigned a name to the unknown number that called yesterday, I answer Zeke immediately.

"Nah, no news." I walk away from Roller, as I answer their obvious first question.

"Um, I've got a dance lesson after school. Mom usually takes me."

I don't hesitate. "I'll take you. You need to take anything that won't fit on my bike?"

Zeke breathes a sigh of relief. "No, but I need my stuff from home. Mom usually brings it with her."

"I'll pick you up and we'll go collect it together."

When I end the call, I shake my head. If I'd ever envisaged myself with a kid, I would have seen myself taking them to football practice, not dance. But each to their own, and I wouldn't change Zeke for the world. The more I see of them, the more they have my respect. It's not easy being like them in a binary world.

Keys still hasn't gotten any further by the time I have to leave. This time, riding alone, I go to collect Zeke. I park in the same spot I had this morning and settle back to wait. Kids swarm past me, giving my bike admiring glances.

Most don't approach as I'm still wearing my cut, but for those that do, I raise my chin and grin at every, "Nice bike you got there, mister."

Eventually, three familiar teenagers approach. I watch them get closer, then leap off my bike. Closing the distance between them, I snarl, "What the fuck happened to you?"

One day in my care and my kid's already sporting a swollen eye. *Cher's going to kill me.*

Tom answers for Zeke. If I were to examine his expression, I'd say he looks proud. "Kid was bad-mouthing Zeke's mom. Zeke flew at him."

"We saw, Uncle Red. So, we stepped in." The twins knock their fists together. "He looks worse than Zeke now."

Placing my hand gently under Zeke's chin, I turn them so I can better see the affected eye. It looks painful, but not too bad. "You're going to have a shiner there. And what the fuck did that asshole have to say about your mom?"

Zeke's lip trembles. "He said Mom was going away for a very long time. That she's been robbing the casino for months."

What? Rapidly, I try to process their words. How would anyone have found out? Would the court docket have details of the crime? Surely it would only read, charged with robbery with no details or where or how. My instincts kick in, and then I tamp them down. I suppose there could be a simple explanation—she was walked out of the casino in cuffs. Still, I won't let anything pass me by.

"What's the asshole's name?"

"Brighton Ashton," Tom eagerly supplies.

"You should have stepped away and called me." My eyes fix firmly on Zeke. "You can't settle shit with fights."

"I couldn't let him get away with it, Dad. He said it in front of class. Now everyone knows." Zeke's trying to be brave but their bottom lip trembles.

"No one knows shit." I take a firm hold of their shoulder. "Your mom's innocent and we're going to prove that." I shift my eyes to the twins. "You gonna get into trouble?" It wouldn't be the first time they've been suspended.

Tom snorts. "We've got a dozen witnesses putting us somewhere else at that time."

While I'm pleased, I shake my head. This pair is going to be the death of me, and I'm not even their dad.

"Hey, the bus, Tom."

As the twins tear off, I turn back to my child. "You feeling okay? Still want to go dance?"

"Of course, Dad." They straighten their shoulders again, making me proud. "But my audition's on Friday. I just hope Mom's home in time to cover my black eye with makeup."

"She can do that?"

Zeke shrugs. "Sure. She's had to do it before."

"Just how many times have you had a black eye, Zeke?" I growl.

"Too many," Zeke grumbles. "Kids can be assholes." They brighten slightly. "At least this time it wasn't because of who I am, right?"

"What the fuck are you talking about?" I voice the question, suspecting I already know the answer, and by fuck, it will hurt if I'm not wrong. Cher had told me Zeke had been bullied, but I'd landed on the thought it was words not fists.

Zeke simply shrugs, their non-verbal response giving me the answer. My hands fist at my sides, wanting to put an end to that shit.

"I'm coming to speak to your principal."

My kid literally rolls their eyes, at me, their dad. I'd smile if it weren't for the seriousness of the conversation we're having.

"Dad, first, Mom's got to acknowledge your parental rights before you speak to anyone, and secondly, I'm not the only one targeted. Mia, now, she's overweight. Do they care she's been battling with her thyroid most of her life? No, they just tell her she's a fatty who can't control her appetite. Brent, well he wears these glasses with glass so thick they magnify his eyes. They love taking them off him and making him walk around almost blind. They'll pick on anyone who's different. If it wasn't because I was nonbinary, it would be because I'm slender and light…" Zeke pauses and creases their eyes. "School is something I've got to put up with. I don't hope it will be much better in the adult world, but hopefully, I'll be doing what I want and surrounded by people who see me for what I can contribute, and not criticise me for what I am."

Wow. There's an old head on young shoulders. Again, they make me feel proud. "And what do you want to do?"

The eye which isn't swollen lights up. "I want to dance. And that starts by getting this rehearsal under my belt and landing the part."

"You playing the lead or something?"

Zeke snorts. "I'll be no more than the chorus line, but that's where everyone has to start. Hopefully I'll show my potential."

I observe them for a moment, wishing there was some way I could accelerate them achieving their dreams. But as any parent, I suppose I need to step back and let them do it for themself.

"Getting back to school, Zeke. Where d'you have the most problems? Sports?"

Zeke grins. "Surprisingly, no. I'm crap at football, but I'm great on the athletics team. Coach doesn't want to lose his star runner, so he goes easy on me." He fidgets and looks around. "Dad, can we get going, else I'm going to be late?"

Immediately, I go to the bike and sit astride it, feeling their by now familiar weight settle onto the back. After a quick check around to make sure they've got their helmet fastened, I start the engine. I take them to the apartment, wait for them to collect their shit, then drop them off at the stage school. I've often heard about school runs and ferrying kids to one activity or another, but I'd never expected I'd be thrown straight into it, or at least, not without going through the baby stage first.

As Zeke walks away from me and goes inside the dance academy, I watch with not a small touch of pride. Despite the challenges their biological makeup brings them, Zeke's determined to make the most of their life.

I've a couple of hours to kill, so I ride back to the compound. I arrive to find Keys pacing. As soon as I'm through the door, he makes a beeline over to me.

"Cops have got a credible witness. That's why they're so sure of the case."

"A witness? To what?" I run my hands back through my hair. "They have to be lying." My confidence that Cher is innocent is unshakeable.

"It's a woman who goes by the name of Chantilly Lace," Keys tells me without hesitation. When my eyes rise, he says, "I know. She kept her maiden name when she got married so that handle must have come from the parents."

No wonder the woman's screwed up. "She a stripper?"

"No. She works at the casino but in the cashier's department. She's the one who cashes your chips. And..." he pauses for effect. It works. I raise on my toes and drop down again before he lets me out of my misery. "She's on the PTA at Zeke's school."

"And the connection is...? Other than they work at the same place and have kids at the same school?"

"No idea, Red. But if you're right and Cher's being set up, there's got to be a motive somewhere."

I take out my phone. ready to call Jeeves to dig and ask, without giving away that Keys has been delving where he shouldn't, of course. But wanting to get all updates out of the way, I add another query. "What about Devonshire?"

"I'm still looking into him. There's been no arrests, so it's not easy to dig up dirt on him. Utah's Stormy is giving me a lot of help."

"Thanks, Keys." I pat him on the shoulder, then turn away, but quickly turn back. "You say this Chantilly woman kept her maiden name. Her husband's not called Ashton by any chance is he?"

Keys goes to the table and leans over his laptop. His fingers dance over the keyboard, then turns and speaks over his shoulder, "Well, what do you know? He is indeed."

"I think you'll find they've got a kid in Zeke's class at school," I announce to him. "Brighton Ashton."

As Keys starts tapping away to confirm it, I turn and plant my fist into the wall. Fucking family. One responsible for getting Cher locked up, and her kid for blackening Zeke's eye.

"Prez?" Crash is staring at the dent in the plaster.

As I fill him in on the Ashtons, his face contorts. He takes a deep breath and holds it.

"Prez, you gotta stay cool. Let Jeeves have the info and leave him to deal with it."

I know I've got to fucking stay cool as my VP's put it. Doesn't mean I have to like it, at all.

CHAPTER SEVENTEEN

CHER

I've been warned if I'm kept here much longer, I'm likely to be transferred to a prison. I comfort myself with the thought at least there I'd have a room to myself. For now, I'm in a shared cell with other women, most of whom were thankfully released early this morning. Of the three remaining, one has been arrested for prostitution, one is waiting for her pimp to make bail, and the other's a drunk and disorderly which no one, least of all her, seems to care about.

If it wasn't that I'm in company and not quite trusting the women to have my back, I'd give way to tears.

I can't understand why I've been arrested. I've committed no crime, and even if guilty, I wouldn't skip bail. But here I am, incarcerated as if I'd murdered someone.

I didn't rob the casino, and I don't know why anyone would believe it would have even crossed my mind. I'm terrified that they've got the wrong person and I've been set up to do someone else's time. I suppose I've watched too many crime dramas, but you hear of people often being set up. There's no way they can have evidence that I've stolen money, but the way the police are acting, they seem certain they've got a case against me.

Thank Christ I had Red to call on and didn't have to rely on a public defender who may or may not have believed me. Christian Jeeves seems to be a solid, dependable type of man. His suit and bearing suggests paying his bill is going to hurt, but I'll do anything it if means I'll be released and get to go home to Zeke.

I'm beyond grateful Red has taken Zeke under his wing. While I worry about my child, I know Red won't let anything happen to them. Despite my concern about his role in the MC, I know he has Zeke's best interests at heart.

But what does Red think of me? Does he believe I'm a criminal? It's ironic that that's what I've thought him to be, when it looks like I'm the one heading to jail.

"Ms Samson, your lawyer's here." A bored-looking cop opens the door and ushers me along to a room I've been in before, leaving me freaking shackled to the ring on the floor, presumably so I don't throttle the man coming to visit me.

Setting my handcuffed hands on the table, I settle in to wait. It's not long before the door opens, and Christian arrives, carrying two cups of coffee. They're both clearly from a local shop and smell like nectar to me.

Offering a genuine smile, I take the cup he passes to me, cupping it awkwardly in my joined hands. Then, the brief moment of pleasure fades.

Christian sits opposite me, and studies me for a moment, then he glances to a point on the wall, then back at me. "We should be able to speak freely here. Client/lawyer confidentiality." But from his upward glance, I take it he's warning me.

I've nothing to say that would incriminate me, so don't really care.

"Ms Samson—" I open my mouth, and he grins. "Cher," he corrects. Well, after all the time we've spent together, a first-name basis is best. "As you know, we don't know what the police have that's got them so convinced of your guilt. I have to consider whether there's anyone who might want to do you harm, and who might have pointed the finger your way?"

My brow creases as I shake my head. "I've no enemies, or none that I know of."

"Take me through your life, Cher. Where do you go, who do you meet?"

An odd question but I humour him. "I'm a single mom with a kid. My life revolves around taking them to school, making sure they get where they need to be. Outside of that, I work. I might go to a neighbour's for coffee, but I've not been in Vegas long enough to make any friends."

"No other parents at school? Or during Zeke's activities?"

"Not really." The other parents I've spoken to have a problem with the pronouns I use for Zeke, but if they don't hide who they are, why should I? Most are nice enough but appear confused. Only a couple have been interested and want to know more. One asked why they weren't in counselling, and another, well, she was outwardly rude and said Zeke had no place in this school. The memory of how rude she'd been and how she'd stressed she was on the PTA and could get Zeke removed from the school makes my jaw clench.

"What's that thought?" the man who's clever and sharp immediately asks.

"There's one woman I really don't get on with. What's worse, she works at the same club. I can't seem to get away from her and her digs about Zeke." Huffing, I inform him, "She said Zeke should be in a school for freaks, or locked up in a mental institution. She didn't want them anywhere near her kid."

"Why's she so adamant?"

I sigh. "Zeke needed the bathroom one day. They were desperate with a stomach upset. The boys had prevented them using their bathroom, so they had to go into the girls. Zeke was really sick. I had to come and collect them, and the doctor said it was food poisoning. But despite them being as sick as a dog, one girl said they'd exposed themself to her."

"And he, sorry, they, said?"

"Their one compulsion was to get to a cubicle and lock the door."

"What happened?"

"The girl was out in the corridor shrieking about how a boy was using the wrong bathroom, and saying she'd seen a penis. I think she was probably exaggerating to her friends, but this woman overheard. She reported Zeke, and I was called in. The woman asked for them to be expelled immediately, saying she'd keep her son from school should they not. But the principal had a note from the school nurse confirming how sick Zeke had been. The principal sided with me." I give a small smile. "One reason I wanted to come to Nevada was the gender policies for bathrooms. He told her kids can go to the bathroom for the gender they identify with, and there was nothing wrong with Zeke using that bathroom. She flounced out, saying she was going to raise it with the PTA and that people like Zeke had no place in the school."

"And her name?"

Despite the circumstances, I grin. "Chantilly Lace."

He doesn't react to the name when so many do, making me wonder whether he'd heard it before, or whether he's just being professional.

"What does she do at the casino?" He makes a note on his tablet.

"She exchanges cash for chips and cashes them in."

"So, she would know about Parker Devonshire's winnings?"

I hadn't thought about that. "She might, I suppose. We don't get on as you can imagine. I ignore her when we cross paths at work. Oh, she wasn't successful with the PTA, inclusivity it seems is more important with the school."

"What would happen to Zeke if you went to jail, Cher?"

Again, my brow furrows. His words send terror through me, making me want to curl up into a ball and weep, but I force myself to stay calm and just answer his question. "Up until recently, my only option would have been Zeke's grandmother in Illinois." Not that she'd want them, or not as Zeke is. "Of course, now I've reconnected with Red, Zeke would have a father who I hope would take care of them." I pause, thinking for a moment. I'm far from stupid myself and can definitely make two and two add together. "Do you think Chantilly wants Zeke out of the school so much she'd get me arrested?"

He leans his elbows on the table and lowers his head into his hands. For a moment, he rubs at his temples. "Or it could be you got one over her. It sounds to me like it was her that was put in her place." He pulls his paperwork together. "Cher, I suspected the cops had a witness, and now I think you've given me a name. Hang on in there and I'll go see if I can knock some sense into them."

"Good luck with that," I murmur under my breath. But he hears anyway and as he leaves, turns back and gives me a grin.

I get taken back to the cell. For the moment I'm alone and all I can think of is how life is going on outside these four walls without me.

Did Red take Zeke to his practice yesterday? Or could he not be bothered? Is he staying with them, or just relying on Zeke to call him if they need help? Or is he stepping up and being a proper dad to his child?

Does Red think I'm guilty? Does Zeke?

Questions upon questions run through my head, not least, will I ever be free?

It must be a few hours later, in which time I've been joined by a shoplifter and another drunk and disorderly, the latter having collapsed on the floor and gone to sleep, when a cop comes once again and calls out my name.

This time I'm taken back to the security gates I was brought through two days ago, and with my mouth hanging open, once on the right side, have my personal possessions handed to me. It's what I've been hoping for, but hadn't expected.

"Don't go too far in case we have more questions to ask you," a detective warns me.

Then, as he indicates I'm free to leave, I have to restrain the urge to bolt.

Outside in the parking lot, Red's waiting for me. I run over to him, crash into his arms, put my face against his chest and sob.

"Cher, sweetheart. You're okay now. You're free," he murmurs against my hair while his hand rubs up and down my back. "You're okay. Zeke's doing fine."

For a moment, I can't control my sobs. Fresh air never tasted so good before. Then as my tears die, my need for answers emerges. "Why did they let me go?"

Red, still with his arm around me, turns me toward an SUV. "I'll tell you on the way, okay?"

And true to his word, he starts to speak as soon as we're headed away from the precinct. "Keys had found the connection with the Lace woman about the same time you came up with the name for Jeeves. Jeeves persuaded them their case would fall apart with an uncredible witness and no evidence."

"It was her? She made all that up?"

"Seems that way, together with other shit we turned up. Keys got some help from our Utah brothers. That dude who always played at your table? He's well known at, and banned from, quite a few casinos. He's a card shark who counts cards. A fuckin' expert. Once he hits on a casino, he tends to stick at the same table he first wins at. It has to do with the lighting on the cards supposedly, along with a heap of superstition."

"Did the cops arrest him as well?"

Red shakes his head. "No, he's already left town. There was a BOLO put out for him, but just in Vegas. They weren't sufficiently sure of their case to go to the feds. And anyway, as it turns out, like you, he wasn't stealing. Counting cards isn't a crime."

"What will happen to Chantilly now?"

Red flicks his indicator then turns to me briefly. "I doubt very much. She'll just say she was mistaken and had only been trying to look out for her employers."

"That's not fair."

"I know." His face tightens. "The law won't punish her, but let's just say she won't get away with what she's done."

"Red?" I turn my head and narrow my eyes at him. "What are you saying?"

When he responds, "Club business," I find I hate it as much as I was warned.

Annoyed, I tell him, "It's my business, Red. And don't you dare do anything that gets you into trouble."

He reaches out and puts his hand over mine. "Don't worry about me, Cher, but we won't let her go unpunished. But we'll take our time. Can't afford any mishap to befall her when fingers are likely to be pointed your way."

She tried to get me locked up and separated from Zeke, but I can't sanction someone being hurt on my behalf.

Red shoots a sideways glance at me. "Her son, Brighton, blackened Zeke's eye."

That does get to me. "That fucking family!" My fingers curl into a fist under Red's hand. Hurting me is one thing, but hurting my child?

"What's also not fair is that you've lost your job."

What? The blows just keep on coming. "Why should they sack me when I've done nothing wrong?" I narrow my eyes. "How do you know?"

"Keys found out you've been taken off the rotation. He delved deeper and saw you'd been given severance pay."

"So now I'm unemployed, and unemployable if word gets around." What casino would want someone who'd been arrested on suspicion of helping a customer cheat? "That's also down to fucking Chantilly Lace, isn't it?" I start to change my mind on retaliation. "Red?"

"Cher?" he answers cautiously.

"What kind of things might come under club business?"

He turns, looking amused. "Oh, I don't know. Ashton might have a problem with his job, Chantilly might be implicated and lose her PTA position, and Brighton might need to find a new school." He shrugs. "But I don't know. They might have misfortunes like that."

The first real smile since I left the police station crosses my face. For the first time, I start to wonder whether having an MC on my side isn't a bad thing at all.

"Where are you taking me?" Belatedly, I've noticed he's not travelling in the direction that will take me to the apartment.

"To the club," he replies. "To Zeke. I picked them up from school and brought them back. They were doing their homework with Tom and Trist when I left. Oh, and Cher, before you find out and throw a fit, I've let them ride on the back of my bike."

"You what?" I bristle. "Zeke's a kid, Red. They're too young. And that you've told me means you knew I wouldn't have allowed it if I'd been there to prevent it."

"Yeah, I knew." Red's mouth quirks. "And as I recall, you weren't much older than Zeke when you stepped onto a stranger's bike. And that, as their dad, I certainly would not allow."

My mouth opens and shuts. My face tightens, my eyes narrow, then I glance at my side to see Red trying hard not to laugh. Unable to do much else, I reach out my hand and poke him in his side.

"You're a dick." But he's got me there, and while I try to frown, it's another smile that ends up on my face.

He notices. "So, you won't be annoyed I bought them their own helmet?"

"How could I be?"

Red reaches out his right hand and takes mine and squeezes it. "I want to take on all Zeke's battles and fight them for them. I fuckin' love that kid and I've not even known them much more than a week." Releasing my hand, he now places his against the left side of his chest. "I feel them right here, you know?"

I do. That's how I'd felt immediately after Zeke had been born.

Overcome with emotion, I turn to look out the side window, biting my lips, trying not to let tears flow. Another man might have been angry to discover he'd had a kid and might have preferred never knowing. Zeke's dad might have turned out to be a transphobic prick and never given them a chance. That Red accepted them from the word go does things to me.

Why did I make such a mistake all those years ago?

"Where do you think we'd have ended up?" I start to ask. "If I hadn't gone home back then?"

He doesn't answer immediately, but he gives it some thought. "If you hadn't, do you see us with a house with a white picket fence and a brother or sister for Zeke? If you do, I think the answer is I don't think we'd have made a go of it. You were young, Cher, and so was I. Okay, I was older by a few years, but I hadn't yet lived. It might make me an asshole, but I needed to find the Devils to become what I am, and I wouldn't have done that with you around."

"You could have been someone different."

"Yeah? And who would have gotten you out of the hole you just escaped from? Not only would I go to the ends of the earth to keep you both safe, I now have the means of doing so."

I suppose there could be something to that. Not everyone has a computer hacker at their beck and call, or ready access to a competent and probably expensive lawyer. Which reminds me. "What do you think Christian will charge?"

"Christian? On first-name terms, are we?" He smirks. "Anyway, nothing for you to worry about. I've got it covered."

"No, Red, I always pay my way."

"Yes, Cher," he contradicts. "Put it like this, how much back payment do I owe you for bringing up my kid for fifteen years? In comparison, Jeeves' fee is probably small change."

I open my mouth to tell him he owes me nothing, then realise it's the measure of the man that he feels guilty about that.

Would money have been useful in the past? Could I have spent more time with Zeke if I'd had Red's support?

The answer is yes. But I can't hold it against him. It was circumstances that kept us apart. It was no one's fault.

I could so fall for this man again, probably have already. But the discussion about raining down punishment on the people responsible for causing me and Zeke problems has brought things into clarity.

Red's way of life is different to mine and the way I'd brought Zeke up to be. I taught Zeke to respect authority, while Red raises his middle finger at it.

While it would be all too easy to take what Red's offering, especially now that I'm feeling weak, I have to step back and think seriously about this.

Is Red good for me? And how close should I allow him and Zeke to be?

CHAPTER EIGHTEEN

RED

Cher's reunion with Zeke was so full of love that I longed to be a material part of their family and not sitting on the sidelines unsure of my place. Having spent more time with Zeke, I know I want to be an integral part of their life, not just on the outskirts of it. But their relationship has been tight for years, and while they're not actively excluding me, they're not inviting me in.

I sit, nursing a beer and smiling on.

I'd been so worried about losing Cher, about her being swept up in a fabricated case that we couldn't resolve and her being sent away for years that it's focused my mind. It's not a case of whether I'm going to make her my old lady, that's a positive. Surely showing how the resources of the club can be brought in on her side must have gone someway to convince her?

As it is though, I might have just saved her life, but I've no rebuttal or alternative argument when Cher instructs Zeke to tell me goodbye and says she's taking them home—if I can find someone to give them a lift that is. I haven't yet claimed her, and I haven't told her she's mine.

But I try. "You could stay. There's room for both you and Zeke here."

The shake of her head is adamant. "Too much, too soon, Red. I need my own stuff around me. I want to take a long shower and get clean. I feel filthy after being in that place. And I need to decompress and spend quality time with Zeke." Her mouth thins. "Never in my wildest imagination did I think I'd spend two days and a night in jail, locked up like a criminal. For a moment, I thought I'd never get out. It's a lot for me to process."

Which is why I don't want to leave her alone. "I'll drive you," I offer, with every intention of staying.

"No, Red. Let me have some space, please?" She shrugs. "I've no idea what I'm going to do now. I'm jobless and need to think what to do next." Her desire for independence reminds me she's always been on her own, has never had someone to lean on, while I desire that she leans on me and lets me share the burden.

"You're not leaving Vegas," I tell her, my brow creasing and my gut clenching at the thought.

She chuckles softly. "I certainly won't if Zeke has anything to say about it. I've never seen Zeke so relaxed about school, and that's thanks to the twins. It seems they've at last found a place here where they fit in. They might even be getting a part in a show, the start of achieving their dreams." She pauses, her eyes signalling while she's left the next to last, it doesn't come at the bottom of everything, "Then there's you. I wouldn't ever part them from you."

The relief settles through me like the sun's warmth on a rainy day. "I'm still giving you a lift," I tell her.

Frowning, she shakes her head, as if knowing it would be hard for her to object, and she comes up with an alternative proposal. "My car is still at the casino. Could you take us there so I can pick it up?"

Damn. There goes my plan of dropping her off at her apartment, using the excuse I need to check it out to get my foot in the door, and then coming up with some other reason why I should stay that I'm yet to think of.

I let none of my disappointment show. "Of course."

Zeke returns with their school bag hoisted over their shoulder. I raise my chin toward Crash and Twister, letting them know I'm heading back out. As I open the door of the SUV to let Cher inside, I notice how hard she's trying to keep herself together. An unguarded moment allows me to see how drained and tired she's looking. She looks completely wrung out, which isn't unexpected. I suspect she'll go home, take a shower, and sob her heart out where no one can hear. Gritting my teeth, I know I won't get my wish to be there to hold her.

"What was it like in prison, Mom?" Zeke asks with childish interest, as I slide into the driver's seat.

I try and catch Zeke's eyes in the mirror, but Cher rallies, and answers brightly enough, "Not as bad as some of the crime shows would have it."

"Cool," Zeke replies, while I know she's putting on a brave face. It was probably worse, especially as she was completely innocent, yet fearful that wouldn't be proven.

I've spent nights in jail on trumped-up charges, but it's part and parcel of the life that I'm living. It's degrading for a start, and the feelings of being trapped and out of control can be over-bearing. For her, it must have been unbearable. Once more I wish she'd let me stay with her and hold her when it all comes back to her in the middle of the night.

But I've no official claim on her, so for now all I can do is comply with her wishes.

It doesn't stop me saying in a quiet voice, "You call me, Cher. Anytime, day or night if you need someone to talk to."

I catch sight of her nodding, then I'm turning into the casino parking lot. She directs me to where she'd left her car.

"Fuck," I exclaim loudly as we approach it.

"Red!" Cher cries out, at the same time as Zeke swears, "What the fuck?"

It's a sign of how upset she is that she doesn't admonish them swearing as we approach the car that's sitting on rims. I pull up the SUV and get out. On closer examination, all the tyres have been slashed.

I take out my phone. "Crash? Could you arrange for someone to pick up Cher's car and put four new tyres on it? Hers have been slashed. It's outside Lucky—"

When he jumps to agree without me having to finish my statement, I next call Keys and ask him to check the security footage. I wouldn't be at all surprised if Chantilly Lace is found to be behind it. If she couldn't get Cher one way, she'd get her another. If I'm right, the thought makes me uneasy. What would she do next, and where would she stop?

Cher's sitting stoic when I return to the SUV.

"I'll sort it."

"You shouldn't have to, Red." Her voice is choked.

"It will be okay, Mom," Zeke, catching on to her distress, insists from the back seat.

But from the way Cher's jaw juts out, I know she's finding it hard to believe.

At her apartment, I now can use my excuse to check it out. As if Cher now accepts that the unlikely has become possible, she doesn't fight me when I insist on searching for a mythical intruder. But she still insists she prefers to be on her own. If I push her too hard, I know there's a good chance I'll lose her.

I linger long enough to say goodbye to Zeke, then, reluctantly, with instructions to lock and bolt the door behind me, respect Cher's wishes and leave them alone.

I drive away, feeling like I've left a big part of me behind.

I call her first thing the next morning. She's offhand, dismissive of my concern, swearing she's fine and over her ordeal, while I know she's lying. She says she'll be too busy to see me today. Finding a new job is the top of her priorities.

I spend a normal day on MC matters. Later that evening, I call her to check if she's okay. When I ask if she wants me to come over, she brushes me off.

The next day when I make contact again, I all but demand to

see her. Again, she palms me off with excuses she's got to write her résumé and keep looking for jobs. Biting back the comment that I'd support her, I know I'm in no position to push her. I leave her with a threat voiced as a promise that I want to see Zeke at the weekend, then, frustrated, end the call.

She hasn't even thanked me for getting her out of jail. It seems she wants to forget her association with the MC altogether, leaving me to wonder if I've found the family I've always wanted, only to land myself with a custody battle.

I might lose her, but I won't give up on Zeke. Never.

For the moment, I leave the ball in her court. If she needs me, she knows where to find me.

"Prez? Got a minute?"

Raising my chin, I approach Keys. "Whatcha need?"

When he jerks his chin toward his office, I follow him in. "Problems?"

Taking his seat, he grimaces. "I don't know. I've just got a bad feeling."

Quirking an eyebrow, I lean my hip on the desk. "In what way?"

Keys sits back and puts his hands behind his head. "This security contract with the Lucky Fortunes."

"It's going okay, isn't it?" For the past few days, I've been wrapped up in my own issues. Though what the casino did to Cher leaves a bad taste in my mouth, it's still good money for the MC.

"It's going good. We're getting paid. But there's just something I can't put my finger on."

Many a man's been saved by listening to his gut feel before. If Keys is uneasy, then I'm not going to ignore it. "In what way?"

He sits forward. "Considering our previous reputation with casinos, don't you think it's strange they came to us?"

Playing Devil's advocate, I dismiss his concerns. "Our security business has had many commendations. We do good work and are known for it. What happened with Tide and company was more than a decade back. People have short memories."

"Really?" he challenges with a raised brow. "Then why are Satan's Devils viewed as a violent and to be feared club? Most citizens don't think we've moved on from the old days. Yet the Lucky Fortunes have invited us in, much like a fox being asked to watch the henhouse."

My brow furrows, and I pinch the bridge of my nose. "You didn't raise your worries when we first discussed it."

Keys shakes his head. "I didn't have them at the time. Like the rest of you, I was blinded by the numbers and the confidence we could make this work."

"But?" And there is a but, I sense it.

His shoulders rise, hover level with his ears for a moment before they drop once more. "It's too easy."

I've known Keys a long time and know to trust his instincts. I also know what he's likely to want from me. "What do you need my permission to do?"

"I want to dig deeper into the owners."

I snort. "Okay, but haven't you already done that?"

"A cursory look for sure, but I'd like to hack into their phone records and emails. Get down to what they're talking about and what might be going on. I'll need Utah's help for that."

Pushing away from the desk, I drop into a chair. "Hit me with your thoughts, Brother."

He closes his eyes briefly. "I can't put my finger on it, and that's my problem. My nose is twitching, that's all, Red."

Utah has the amazing ability to hack into anything. But one of the reasons they kept their skills quiet was their fear that once known, they would be constantly called on, taking them away from their own work. It's one thing to ask them when we've got a real issue, like trying to find out what the fuck the police had on Cher, but to call them in on what could be a wild goose chase for nothing more than Keys' uneasy feeling, well, is it worth the flack I'd take from Snatcher if I loaded him up with more work?

Tapping the end of my nose with my finger, I question him. "The security plans we drew up for the casino, were they implemented?"

"Sure. With no objections or alterations. Crossman even thanked me for the good work."

Not quite good enough, however, the cameras didn't cover the whole of the parking lot, and Keys hadn't been able to confirm who'd damaged Cher's car. A problem Keys rectified immediately.

"Any problem with the club's security? Any push back against the changes you've made?"

Keys shakes his head and spreads out his hands. "None."

Cupping my face with my hands, I draw them down over my beard. It doesn't sound like he's got much to go on, but I'm loathe to dismiss his instinct and have it come back to bite us.

I make my decision. "I'll speak to Snatcher, warn him what you'll be suggesting, but I'll stress it's not a priority job."

He sighs and with the exhaled air, tension seems to fall away from him. "I don't see it's an emergency, Prez. That will work." He raises his eyes. "I just like to know what I'm dealing with. I think I'm bothered about how they treated Cher."

"Any link to us?" I ask quickly. I didn't think there was any, but I could be wrong.

Again, he shrugs. "I can't see it. But I didn't like the way they behaved."

Me neither. But how could I use that to justify taking a profitable contract away from the brothers? We're all benefitting from it.

"How's Cher doing?" he asks.

My answer is growled. "Damn woman's gotten so used to doing everything on her own, she won't let me in to help her."

His eyes widen. "So, you're staying away? Giving her space? Do you think that's the right thing?" He leans forward again. "Look, we're Devils. Getting arrested is par for the course. Getting arrested for doing nothing other than wearing our cut, yeah, again, nothing unexpected. Cher's a fucking civilian who never deserved to see the inside of a jail. It's got to be preying on her mind, Prez. And if she's got doubts about being associated with an MC, her experience is going to make it ten times worse. Left alone, lost in her head, she may turn her experience into a learning one, a warning she might take to heart."

He's fucking right.

"If she was my woman, I'd say she needs a good fuckin' to get her head straight."

Again, he's so right I stand so fast I almost tip over my chair. As I right it, he smirks. "Got a place you need to be, Prez?"

I bark a short laugh. "I'm going to see how Rosa's fixed on having Zeke over tonight." I raise my brow. "Think it's about time I focused on their mother."

"Go get your woman, Prez. Hey," he adds, getting my attention as I'm about to walk out of the door. "I like the kid, Zeke. Different, for sure, but I took to them."

I raise my chin in appreciation he's remembered the pronoun. Leaving his office, I'm a man on a mission.

First, I find Rosa. She has no objection to having Zeke hang with the twins this evening. Unlike Cher, she hasn't the same faith in her children. As, in her words, she's not leaving Tom and Trist without supervision, she'll be there to keep them all out of mischief.

Next, I shoot a text to Zeke, making sure they're okay with the arrangements. The one-word response I receive suggests that they are.

Zeke: Cool

Then I organise Owl to pick up the three of them from school.

After that, I'm free. I head out to Cher's, stopping off on the way to buy chocolates and wine. If I slip a box of condoms into the shopping cart, who's to ask why? A man can be hopeful, can't he? I'm only thinking of her. When someone's strung up tight, sex is a great way to relax.

Wondering whether the noise of my engine has pre-warned

her of my arrival, I pull up outside her apartment building. Putting my accessories into my helmet, I untie the bungee ties and remove the grocery bag, taking the condoms out and slipping them discreetly into my jeans pocket.

Then, hoping she lets me get my foot in the door, knowing I'm taking a risk in coming here, I walk up to her apartment.

CHAPTER NINETEEN

CHER

Knowing Zeke will soon be home from school, I splash cold water over my face, holding a cool wash rag to my eyes for a moment. They're red raw as I've been crying again.

Banging my hands against the sink, I could howl with frustration. I've spent a second day ringing around, trying to find a new job, but I've been blacklisted. Something I only found out when the recipient of my final phone call was polite enough to tell me. For a crime I hadn't even done, no casino will employ me.

It's so damn unfair.

In the past, I'd have packed Zeke and I up and headed out of town, but how can I separate them from their dad? And even if I did, my reputation might not precede me to a different state, but what would happen when they called up my references?

I'm half-inclined to walk back into Lucky Fortunes and give the owners a piece of my mind. It's only the thought that it would achieve nothing that stops me.

When my doorbell chimes, I wipe my face off with a towel, then plaster on a smile and go to accept the delivery or whatever it is. What I don't expect to find is the man I told to stay away.

I need some space. Being near Red fucks with my mind. He

makes me want to bundle my independence away and accept the safety and comfort of his arms.

Red's in an MC. He's the prez of it. He has a lawyer who drops everything on his command, and it doesn't take a genius to come up with the reason why. His relationship with the MC must be a profitable one. My sole brush with the cops is one I never want to repeat.

If I don't think of me, I've got to think of Zeke. If I take myself out of the equation, then Red can have a relationship with Zeke away from the MC, and far removed from the doings of it.

"Red," I say, tiredly, standing in the doorway. "Why are you here?"

"Bad day?" he queries, clearly noticing the cold water hadn't done a lot for my eyes.

"Zeke will be home soon." I avoid answering his question.

"Nah. I've sorted it. Rosa and the twins have got them."

"You what?" My eyes narrow. "Why should she have them?"

He shrugs nonchalantly. "I arranged for them to have a sleepover. Thought we could have some time together."

My temper flares. I've made call after call today and all proved fruitless. I'm already hanging by a thread and now Red's here, telling me he's rearranged my kid's night and clearly has plans to do the same for me.

I snap. "How dare you?" I inhale a lungful of air to hit him with the rest of what's on my mind, but he gets in before me.

"I think I've got fifteen years of dares in me," he retorts.

"I didn't keep them from you!" I explode.

Red stays eerily calm. "I know that, but the result's the same. Anyway, this isn't about Zeke, it's about you."

"What about me? Why can't you just leave me alone, Red?"

His eyes soften and he raises his hand, passing across a bag. Dubiously, I peer in. Wine, and chocolates.

Red gives a self-deprecating smile and shrugs. "I don't know much about women, but when you're down, I've heard these help."

I try to push the bag back. "I'm not PMSing. I've been locked up for something I didn't do and lost my fucking job. It's going to take more than chocolates and wine to help with that."

"I may have some ideas," he replies, stepping forward so I unconsciously move back. Then the bastard closes the door behind him.

"I don't want you here, Red." I can't think when he's this close. His muscles, his tattoos, the things that weren't there before make him so much more than the man I knew long ago.

"You might not want me, but you need me, Cher."

I fly at him. "Where were you when I needed a man to support me when I first found out I was pregnant? Where were you when I was in labour for hours, wanting nothing more than someone to be there to hold my hand? Where were you when Zeke fell and cut their head so bad, I thought they were dead? Where were you when Zeke came out and I had no idea how to take it? Where were you then, Red?" I pause for breath then beat my fist against his chest to make my point. "I got by without you then, I'll get by without you now."

He catches both my fists in just one of his, holding them tightly. He pulls me close, giving me no chance to get away from his grip. "I'd have been there, every fuckin' step of the way. Don't you think I regret not being able to share those burdens with you? Don't you believe I'd give anything to go back in time and stop you leaving that day? But I wasn't there, and you damn well know why not. It wasn't the way the cards fell, darlin'. That wasn't to be our way." His eyes gentle as he looks down on me, and his tone quiets. "I'm here now. Take me, use me. Lean on me. All I ask is that you never leave me again."

It's tempting, but I know it isn't right. "I can't live your life, Red. I obey the laws. I always have. I can't cross over that line."

"Whether you wanted to or not, and while it wasn't your fault, you already have, Cher. Now you can't get a job because of it." His free hand smooths over my hair. "I won't lie and say my life's always on the right side of the law, but we don't break it without good reason. I can't imagine how alone you must feel when I've got all my brothers behind me. Let me in, Cher. Give me a chance to do what I should have been doing all along. Let me support you."

It's tempting. It's so damn tempting. "I need to think of Zeke."

"Zeke needs their dad. And I'll be there for Zeke even if you won't let me be there for you."

I already know I can't keep them separate. Zeke's getting to the age when they won't be guided by me in all things, and if I tried to take Zeke away from Red, I think they'd hate me.

"I'm not sure about your club, Red."

He sighs, pulling me into him tighter. "I can't leave the club, Cher. I owe them too much. I've too many people depending on me. But they're good men. Give them a chance." I notice he doesn't remind me how much the club has already done on my behalf, or that I might still be languishing in jail if it wasn't for them. He doesn't tell me how much easier Zeke's school life is with the twins looking out for them.

He could, but he doesn't. Somehow, by him not bringing it up, I feel guilty that I've already taken advantage of what the club can offer. Instead of fighting to pull away, I lean into him.

His manly scent is invading my nostrils. His heart seems to be beating in time with my own. His warmth is enveloping me, and I feel myself weakening. Why insist on going it alone when I could have him beside me?

Without conscious thought, I raise my face. Reading my mind, he lowers his, placing his lips just above mine. Going on tiptoe, I close the distance necessary.

Sex, the union of our bodies, has always been good between us. If that was my only worry, I'd have no concerns. It's my worries about everyday life, like where we'd be living, how much he'd want me involved with his club that I should be considering, but for now, I leave that aside, and enjoy the comfort of being in his arms.

His mouth teases and slow glides across my lips with little pressure, forcing me to be the one to press against him for more. It's my tongue that insists on invasion. As his comes to meet mine, a growl comes from his throat, and he takes over.

Wrapping his hand in my hair, he angles my head for better access, and starts to kiss me like a starving man. His free hand presses me in tight against him and a warmth rises inside me, acknowledging I feel safe and protected when I'm in his arms.

Unbidden, a moan escapes and it spurs him on. His movements become more heated, his, and consequently my, heart rate speeds up. I breathe in only him, feel only him, and taste only the man who's kissing me.

If I opened my eyes, I'd see the man I'd walked away from, not the same person, but one with improvements.

Was he this dominating before? I can't remember. Did his kisses make my core throb? Did his touch make my pussy feel empty? Did I feel like I would die if I didn't have him inside me? Did I notice the hardness of his cock pushing against me, and did it elicit the same feelings of desperation before?

"Make love to me, Red."

He sweeps me up in his arms, unerringly heading for my bedroom. Once there, he lets me slide down his body, so my feet touch the floor.

For a moment his eyes examine me. "Say yes, Cher, and I'll make love to you like I never have before."

Before was so good, I'm not sure I can imagine what I'm in for.

"Make love to me Red," I manage to gasp out.

With his eyes staring into mine, his hands find the hem of my top and it's disposed with quickly. Likewise, my bra, which he unclasps and removes with sure expertise and no fumbling. Reverently, his hands come out to caress my breasts, his fingers and thumbs finding my nipples and pinching them.

A jolt goes through me. A connection I hadn't realised was

there causes tingles to run down my spine and congregate between my legs. I flush, I can feel it.

Then, this dominant man folds himself to the floor, and undoes the button of my jeans. As he pulls them down to pool at my feet, he takes my panties with them.

Last time was quick, fast, without us getting naked. I suck in air, pulling in my stomach, knowing the intervening years haven't been kind to my body. But he places a kiss against my stretch marks, tracing them with his tongue.

"Fuckin' beautiful," he tells me, softly, sounding in awe. "You grew my child in there."

I open my mouth to make excuses, but his knowing growl halts me. I'm soon distracted as he places his nose to my core and inhales deeply.

"Red?"

His hands put pressure on my thighs. Understanding his unspoken message, I part them. Then, his tongue is there, sweeping from my clit to my slit.

"Red." It's a cry, a plea. At least this time I know what to expect, but the sensations still overwhelm me.

I hang on to his shoulders, my fingernails digging in as all my thoughts flee, overwhelmed by the desire that's flooding through me.

His tongue circles that needy bunch of nerves, and when his fingers invade me, I shoot up onto my toes. My muscles tense as automatically I start to grind against him. There's no other thought in my head except worry how I'm going to survive this.

My stomach flutters. I can't breathe, can't take in air. I strain, as one hand leaves his shoulder and entangles in his hair, holding him tightly in case he has thoughts about pulling away.

His chuckle against my clit almost undoes me. I'm so close…

His finger rimming my forbidden hole and trying to force entry, the alien sensation is what completely unravels me.

"Come for me, Cher."

The vibration of his voice is all that I need to take off and soar so high I think I see stars. My legs tremble, but he's there on his feet, one arm supporting me, one hand still massaging my clit as he brings me down slowly.

"You're so fuckin' beautiful when you come." His voice is gruff, his own breathing heavy.

Gently pushing me backward, my legs hit the furniture behind me.

"Now," he says with a touch of humour in his voice, "let's do this properly and use a bed."

Enough of my senses have returned to enable me to say, "To do that, you have to be naked."

He chuckles and pushes me down so I'm seated. then proceeds to undress in front of me.

A twenty-five-year-old Red was good enough for me. This Red? I suck in air as he reveals the six-pack he's sporting on his stomach. His arms, muscular and tattooed, are finally fully revealed to me, and when he bends down to take off his boots, I see his back is covered by the same emblem they wear on their cuts.

He's a Devil. But a delighted shiver runs through me. For some reason, this sign of his commitment to his life doesn't scare me, instead, for unknown reasons, it excites me.

As he reveals the rest of himself, there appears to be no inch of fat anywhere, and I have to ask, what he sees in me?

His body isn't that of a young man, but one who's matured breathtakingly.

He's not shy. Once his boots are off, he pushes down his boxers and jeans at the same time, allowing his impressive cock to bob free.

He's had his mouth on me. Should I return the favour?

CHAPTER TWENTY

RED

I've given numerous women orgasms before, but never have I taken so much pride in their reactions as those that I've wrought from Cher.

When I first met her, she was only just out of her teens, and had a young girl's body to go with it. Now she's older, she's all woman and has more curves and a softness which really appeals to the older me. Those love handles will fit into my hands comfortably. Her tits, slightly bigger than before are more than adequate.

The stretch marks fill me with pride. *She'd carried my baby.* What greater sacrifice could a woman give her man?

Her whole body flushed when she'd come, a reaction broadcasting her pleasure, making me feel ten feet tall.

For a moment, I'm worried about what she'll think of me. I'm all hard to her soft. My hands are even more calloused than they were before from an extra decade of working on bikes and cars. But as I take in her expression as she looks at me, I see nothing but desire on her face.

She's viewed my body from head to toe, but now her eyes are focused on my dick. I inch closer, longing to feel her hands on me. But she does more. After licking her lips, she leans forward and places a kiss to the tip.

"Cher…" My word sounds like a plea.

With a cheeky grin up at me, she shuffles to put herself closer, then her hands are surrounding me, and she's pulling me toward her mouth.

"You don't have to."

"I want to." Already she's so close, the words vibrate through my dick. "Though I haven't done this before, I don't know if I'll be any good."

I don't need much more than her continuing to talk. With her hot breath fanning my cock, I'm on a hair trigger just thinking about her mouth enveloping me. If all she did was describe the act, I think I'd come like a shot.

The more appropriate question being, how long will I be able to last, once she gets those luscious lips around me?

It seems I'm about to find out, as her mouth closes over the head.

She's tentative, explorative, and her naïve touches do so much more than the experienced girls I've had working me. I've had more blow jobs than I can count in my life, but none have meant much to me except for how quickly they get me off. Cher? I'm already in the land of ecstasy, and she's barely touching me.

She takes me inside, using her tongue to lick me, then her cheeks hollow as she experiments with sucking motions. She's barely got more than the head in her mouth, but when she closes her hands around the rest of me, it fast becomes one of the best blow jobs I've ever had.

Her eyes are closed as if she's relishing the tastiest lollipop she's ever had in her mouth. I stare down, overwhelmed that I'm being pleasured by her. I've dreamed about this woman for so long, and now she's here, I know I'm never going to let her go. Every damn objection she puts in my way, I'm going to overcome.

Her technique isn't perfect, but she's making up for what she lacks with pure enthusiasm. It seems like she enjoys sucking my cock, which shouldn't surprise me, seeing as how much I like tasting her.

Christ, she's getting me close.

I stagger out a warning. "Cher, I'm going to come if you don't stop."

Instead of pulling away, she redoubles her efforts and I'm helpless to do anything but to let the sensations flood through me. My balls tighten, pulling up to my body, and I come with a fucking roar. My cum shoots out of my dick, flooding her mouth, spurring me on as she tries to swallow around me.

As if it comes naturally to her, she uses her tongue and licks me clean, and I swear she purrs like a cat as she does so. Her movements are so sensuous my cock stays semi-hard. When at last she releases me, she looks up with a satisfied smile.

"You can do that any fuckin' time you want," I tell her, my voice sounding husky.

I lean over her, taking her mouth with mine, not at all put off by the taste of my own cum. With her flavour still on my tongue, the combination of her and me does nothing to dampen my arousal, and even though I've just come, my cock's swelling again.

Putting my arms underneath her, I lift her enough to slide her up the bed. Then I come down on top of her, never once losing the contact between our lips.

Her legs fall open, creating a cradle for my pelvis. My hips buck as I rub my cock against her.

Grasping her right thigh, I pull up her leg, opening her to me, then start to push in.

"Condom!" she gasps out.

Fuck. At least one of us still retains their common sense. It's not that I don't want to father another child with her, but not right now. Not when there's so much left to be sorted out between us. Trapping her would never be my intention. As for her, it's Cher who'd have nine months of carrying a baby, and she's got the greatest say in the matter.

"Don't fuckin' move," I growl, pushing myself up on my hands, and moving so I can reach my jeans. I extract the condom from the packet I'd so fortuitously purchased earlier and slide it on in record time. I spare a moment to stare at her.

Obeying my instructions, she's not altered the stance I'd positioned her in. With one leg raised and off to the side, she's totally open to me.

Her pubes are trimmed close to her body, her labia a blood-engorged pink, her clit's still visible due to the orgasm I just gave her, and her thighs glisten with arousal. If I've ever seen a sexier sight, I can't remember it.

I'm back over her fast, and inside her with just one thrust. The urgency of my action has her sucking in a breath and letting out a shocked cry.

"Red!"

I pause, enveloped in her to the hilt, and allowing myself to enjoy the tightness of the warm channel that surrounds me.

"Red?"

Her change in tone suggests stillness isn't what she wants from me, confirmed when she squeezes her muscles. With a grin, I draw back and hammer home. Then I do it again. And again.

"Oh my God, Red," she stammers out, a flush spreading from her face down to her breasts. Her head rolls to one side then the other, and her jaw clenches.

Concentrating, I make sure my cock's hitting that part inside her which is going to send her wild. I move my fingers down, pinch her clit and that's all it takes to push her over.

I hold my breath, scrunching my face, concentrating hard so I don't follow her. Even though I've already had one release, I'm already so damn close. I gentle my strokes, drawing out her orgasm as long as I can. When the aftershocks which send such incredible signals to my dick start to subside, I pull out and turn her languid body over.

I position her on her hands and knees, noticing in her post-orgasmic fervour she's like putty in my hands. Without pause, I slam my cock back into her, and do what I'd dreamed about so often before, tangling one hand into her hair and using the other to grip her hip.

I let my inner beast go, fucking her like I've always wanted.

"Fuck, Red. Yeah…" she manages to get out. "Oh, Red… I can't."

But she can, which I'm on a mission to prove. She's still got another orgasm in her, and I'm a greedy man and want it.

I fuck her hard just like the biker I am. Swivelling my hips, I take no mercy on her. Her muscles start clamping down on my dick again. It feels like it's being strangled. My release is only seconds away, but still I hold back, wanting her to let go before I allow myself to take my pleasure.

So many times during the last fifteen years I've thought of Cher and promised myself if I had the chance again, it wouldn't be muted sounds of pleasure that I'd entice from her. Now the time has truly arrived when she comes shouting out my name with an ear-piercing scream.

My face contorts as I lose it. Even though I'd come only a short while before, it seems never ending. A loud growl escapes me as it seems to go on and on, my hips twitching as I empty my balls completely.

She's drained me.

Sated, now, my cock deflates. Holding the condom firmly, I let myself slip out of her. Raising to my knees, I pull off the latex and tie the end, dropping it by the bed to dispose of later.

Cher takes a moment before she changes the position I'd left her in, and then slowly rolls onto her back. Her face is red, her mouth swollen and her eyes leak. She looks thoroughly fucked. And that grin on her face? Well, that's worth the world.

Is it a grin, or a smirk? Looking closer, I narrow my eyes.

She chuckles. "I was just remembering a man who had to be reminded to finish me off with his fingers."

I feel my skin flush, but I wink at her. "Fuck, what a loser." I let myself drop down beside her, pulling her into my arms as lethargy floods over me.

"Do I even want to know where you got your new skills?" she murmurs.

I bark a laugh. Some things are better left unsaid.

She turns and nuzzles into my chest. "I would never have expected you to be celibate, Red. I didn't get much action as I didn't really have a choice. First Zeke was too young. Sure, I could leave them with babysitters, but I couldn't stay out all night. Then, when it was clear Zeke was different, I became even more selective. I dated, sure I did. But the couple of times I introduced someone to Zeke, it didn't go down well. Being told your child needs therapy or a beating to set them straight is not what a mother wants to hear."

I hate that I wasn't there for her, and while I wouldn't have liked it if she'd ended up with another man, I don't like that she had no one.

"It was a long time after you that I went with another woman," I tell her, softly, deciding to let her in on some of my past.

"Did I put you off?" The question isn't asked seriously. "I can't believe that. Not when you have sweet butts hanging around the club."

Quickly I glance at her, but she's said it as fact, not as an accusation. I chuckle. "I prospected in Tucson for a year. Prospects are tested in many ways, one of which is that they can't go with the club girls."

"Poor you. You must have had blue balls."

"Yeah." I pause, thinking back. "But we sure got sight of the action. Tucson was not a family club, and the men weren't shy if you get what I mean."

"They fucked in the open?"

"You got it. And it opened my eyes. A lot of that year all I could think of was what a disappointment I must have been to you."

"You weren't!" she says, indignantly.

"Babe," I begin to refute. "I didn't even know how to get you off on my cock. You even had to ask me to use my fingers as you just reminded me."

Her breath warms my chest, and a slight movement has me looking down. She's grinning again.

"So, you picked up tips from the live porn you witnessed?"

Snorting, I contradict, "The opposite. The club girls were used to men who knew what to do with their dicks. If you want the truth, I was fuckin' nervous. I was terrified of falling short."

She sits up and stares down at me. "You, nervous?"

"Better believe it, babe." I decide that as this disclosure is not causing distress, and instead seems to be amusing her, I gamble on telling her the rest. "At my patching in party, the club girls were queuing up, all wanting to put the new boy through his paces. The problem was, as you know, I didn't really have any."

"I never complained," she states firmly. "I've never looked back at our time together with those types of regrets. I hadn't been a virgin, and you were par for the course. No more or less than I expected."

"Babe, those club girls anticipated more."

"So, what did you do?"

I stroke her hair, pull her back down, and rest her face again against my chest. "You really want to know?"

"Yes."

The way I've positioned her puts my nipple close to her mouth. Her tongue reaches out and licks it, and my cock decides to come back to life.

"Keep doing that," I growl, "and I won't be able to finish my story."

She pulls back, and her body shakes with mirth. "Go on, tell me. Then you can demonstrate all over again."

And that's a promise I'll be keeping her to. Sighing, I admit,

"I'd had too much to drink, not enough to render me incapable, but to make my mouth slack. My best friend, Wraith, was trying to set me up, and I kind of admitted I didn't know what I was doing."

"Did he laugh?" She tenses as though she's about to become annoyed.

"Far from it," I reassure her fast, grinning widely as I remember. "He set me up with one of the girls and came into the room as well. He, well, he kind of gave me instructions. Pussy, that was her name, she did as well."

"What?" Again, she sits up, examining my face as if to check I'm being serious. "He gave you instructions on how to fuck?"

"Uh-huh." I chuckle at the memory. Fuck, but that night was enlightening. Perhaps I'm now too relaxed as I find myself over-sharing. "Then we both fucked Pussy at the same time."

Her widened eyes are to be expected, but her next question takes me by surprise. "Tell me about Wraith. What's he like?"

Perplexed, I tell her, "Loyal as fuck. He might be in a different club, but he'd always be there to have my back."

"No, I mean, what's he *like*?"

Unsure what she's asking, I try again, "Younger than me, fit, good looking, I suppose you'd say."

"Hmm," she murmurs thoughtfully. "Sounds like Pussy was one lucky girl. When am I going to meet Wraith?"

I sit up fast, my hands holding onto her biceps as I hold her a few inches away, trying to read her expression. The witch tilts her head and raises her eyebrows at me.

"Never!" I growl. "And he's already got an old lady." My betraying cheeks flush bright red as I remember how *well* I know Sophie.

Of course, she picks that up. "Red?"

Total disclosure? Or do I keep some things back? Gritting my teeth, unwilling to have something that might bite me in the ass later, I admit, "I might have had a kind of threesome with Wraith and his ol' lady." I add fast, "But I never gave her my dick, well not…" My voice trails off.

"Red!" She sits up. *Oh fuck, I've disclosed too much.* "How could you do that to me?"

"Cher, we weren't together. I didn't think I'd ever see you again—"

"You've just told me how hot Wraith is, and presumably, so's his old lady. What if I wanted a foursome?" Her eyebrows rise.

"What? You? Me?" I bluster. "Wraith?" I snarl as I add, "Not gonna happen."

She collapses against me laughing. "Your face, Red. You're so easy to tease."

I'm still far away from amusement. "I'm never going to share you, Cher."

Rubbing her face against me, she gives an exaggerated sigh. "Way to shatter a girl's dream, Red."

Again, I take hold of her hair and pull her up so I can see into her eyes directly. "I'll just have to prove I'm enough to satisfy you."

Pushing her over onto her back, I proceed to show her exactly that.

And, as it goes, it seems I leave her with no regrets. I successfully manage to fuck my woman into a stupor.

CHAPTER TWENTY-ONE

RED

While last night with Cher was amazing, I didn't want to push my luck. We'd eventually woken and devoured some of the chocolates and shared the wine which normally I wouldn't touch.

There was a growing intimacy between us which can only bode well. But thinking it's best I don't seem to be insinuating myself into her life, I didn't complain when after another demonstration of my abilities, she'd asked me to allow her to sleep alone.

It's Zeke's audition today, so I shoot off a text to them both, wishing them good luck and confirming I'll be thinking of them. Cher replies quickly, saying she'll let me know the results as soon as she has any news, but also warning me they may need to see everyone before making up their minds, and she doesn't know whether it's only today the cabaret are auditioning.

Seems fair to me, but I'm anxious to know. I'm aware how much Zeke has riding on this, and how many hours of practise they've put in.

"Hey, boys," I yell, as I walk into the clubroom, seeing Trist and Tom playing pool. Brought up in the club, they've held cue sticks from the time they were tall enough to reach the table.

Brothers have already learned not to bet against them, even if it's only candy that's up for grabs, considering their tender ages. They'll be ringers for certain once they're of age.

"Uncle Red?" Tom swings around immediately, while Trist finishes his shot.

"A word?"

Grabbing a beer from Owl, I take a seat at the table. It's not long before the twins come sauntering across. I hide my grin at the two young bikers in the making. Rosa might bitch about them eventually joining the club, but I doubt she'll have much option. They're Brick's kids through and through.

Trist pulls out a chair, turns it around and straddles it. The more serious of the two, his brow furrows. Tom, though, is all smiles as he plonks down beside him.

"I wanna thank you for helping with Zeke."

Tom beams, and Trist frowns slightly. "Ain't a problem, Red." I notice more and more often he's dropping the 'uncle' nowadays. In some ways it makes me sad, time is moving on.

"Zeke's great," Tom informs me enthusiastically. For some strange reason, he leans over and bumps fists with his twin.

Their gesture surprising me, I narrow my eyes.

One of the things I've learned as prez is that silence is a great enabler if you want someone to spill something. And after shifting awkwardly, the boys don't disappoint.

"I like Zeke." It's Tom who informs me. "They're a laugh."

The twins glance at each other and giggle.

Frowning, I grow suspicious. "Zeke doesn't play football, isn't into bikes. I admit I'm surprised you've taken such a liking to them."

The twins have been using non-verbal communication since they were in their cribs. Sometimes I swear they have some telepathic link between them. Although they seem to be simply staring at each other, I'd place good money that some kind of conversation is going on.

It's Trist who finally enlightens me. He shrugs. "Zeke's a girl magnet. They all love them."

"And now we've stepped up," Tom's got the confidence to continue, "the girls love us for protecting Zeke."

I snort. I can't help it. These kids are using Zeke to get pussy. Well, hopefully at their age, not pussy as such, but an in with the girls for a certainty.

Oh fuck. They're sixteen, I suddenly remember. I lean forward, clasping my hands, and growl sternly, "We've had the talk, haven't we?"

Trist rolls his eyes. "Sure, Red. We know how to glove up."

The age of consent in Nevada is sixteen. I decide I don't want to know anymore. At least the boys can't get into legal trouble, and as long as they use protection and discretion, hopefully nothing will come back to bite them on the ass. It's my kid I'm concerned about.

"So, you're using Zeke?" I ask casually, but inside I'm angry. I hoped they'd like Zeke for themself.

"No man, no way," both speak simultaneously.

Trist shrugs. "We've told you, we like them. But," he winks, "they do come with benefits."

Dismissing the boys, I sit drinking my beer, realising there's so little I know about the child who sprang from my loins. I want to learn more about them. They're surrounded by girls? The thought of Tom and Trist taking advantage does make me smile.

"Prez?"

"Yeah, Keys. What you got for me?"

Keys comes over. Sensible man, he'd stopped off by the bar and grabbed two beers. He hands one to me to replenish my empty one. He sits, sighs heavily, then lets me in on what's on his mind.

"Crossman contacted me. They have a bunch of their security out with the flu, and wanted to know if we could step in."

Raising the new bottle to my lips, I take a deep swig. When I've swallowed, I ask, "To do what? Guard duty in the casino?"

Keys shakes his head. "No, they've got their security truck coming in to take the casino's earnings. They had a good few days."

"Those companies know what they're doing." I rub my temples. "Got it down to a fine art, a smoothly oiled machine. Why would he need extras on his side?"

Keys shrugs. "It's his normal procedure. But his men who he normally has escorting the money through the casino are all off sick, and so are some of the others. He's spread pretty thin."

I eye Keys. Though I would have thought this was good news—that the casino trusts us enough to give us more duties—Keys doesn't seem particularly happy about it. "We're going to get paid for the extra work?"

Keys flutters his hand. "I did raise the issue, but Crossman baulked and said Greaves was the money man and wasn't convinced our contract wasn't too loaded in our favour already."

As a money man, he probably would think that way. I raise an eyebrow, interested in how Keys had handled it, and whether he needs any back up from his prez.

"I, er, hope it's okay, Red. I said we'd do it as a favour this time." He takes a sip of his beer, then glances up through his eyelashes at me.

I consider for a moment, then shrug. "It's still a relatively new contract so I'm happy to go with it. But next time we'll stand our ground. It could be he's trying to push us." After a pause, I get my thoughts together. "How many does he want, and who are you thinking of sending along?"

Now on firmer ground, Keys sounds steadier. "Five. I thought Cobra, Hammer, Indian, Twister and of course I'll go along."

"Nah, you stay. I'll go." I'm interested in seeing what goes on.

But it seems Keys is as well. "I'm happy for you to be there, Red, but if we're taking this contract seriously, I'd like to understand how they move the money, and what precautions they're taking."

That the computer guy and my de facto head of security doesn't seem particularly happy our role at the casino might be expanding doesn't escape me. "You got any problems with doing this, Keys?"

He considers my question carefully and takes a moment to answer. When he does, it's with a self-deprecating shrug. "As I've said before, securing this contract was like successfully landing a space craft on Mars as far as we're concerned."

"Our proposal was sound, well costed, and our references stacked up," I remind him.

His lips press together, then they relax and form a grin. "Of course, I might be overly suspicious of legit activities." I chuckle along with him. He catches my eye. "We just need to be careful, Prez. Run a mile if anything doesn't feel kosher."

His advice makes sense to me, but I put his concerns not out of my mind, but on the back burner. "So, we're doing this then. What time are we talking about?"

"Six p.m."

I suck in a breath. We'll have to move our regular church. Won't be the first time, but it's not often.

I give a nod as my confirmation that I'm going to be there. "Let the boys know church is cancelled. We'll reschedule it for tomorrow."

As Keys raises his chin and walks off, I glance at my phone. No message from Cher as yet. Still, it's only four thirty and though Zeke's audition was at four, it might still be going on. How the fuck do I know how long they'll be on the stage?

I'd wanted to go along, but Cher had persuaded me Zeke was going to be nervous enough without their dad being in the audience. Not wanting to be a distraction for them, I'd reluctantly concurred with their view. And there was always the danger that had the people conducting the audition not shown their appreciation of Zeke's performance, I might have been tempted to educate them with my fists.

I stop myself from begging for updates and ascend the stairs going to change my shirt which had gotten oil on it from helping out at the shop earlier.

Deciding to take a quick shower as well, I'm back in the clubroom just as Indian and Twister are coming in. Cobra and Hammer are at the bar waiting, and Keys is anxiously hovering, checking the time on his phone.

"I suggest we get going, Prez." He bounces up to me. "I want to make sure we know what we're doing and can get in position before the security truck arrives."

Sounds sensible, so I give him no argument. Within moments, we're all outside and getting on our bikes.

Vegas never sleeps, stops or slows down. The casino is as busy as normal when we arrive. The buffet is doing a roaring trade with families taking advantage of the low-cost food to feed their families, and my mouth waters as I glance in and see the piled-high plates and my stomach growls.

This shouldn't take long, I console myself. *Rosa will have saved some dinner for us.* Or, if she hasn't, we can get takeout. Thinking of Rosa makes me wonder whether I should have a chat with her about my suspicions about her boys. Would she want to know they could be sexually active, or would she prefer to stay in ignorance? Momentarily, I think of Brick and what he would have thought about how his twins had turned out. As fatherless kids, I reckon they've done alright.

They've been fishing with Hammer, ATV driving with Sarge, shooting with both Twister and I. They've not grown up wanting for male attention.

Should I do these things with Zeke? Hell, I'll be fucked if I know. My thoughts remind me I've still got a way to go before I can say that I know them. I'll need to find hobbies that father and kid can do together and have some bonding time. There's one thing for certain—with my two left feet, I won't be able to dance.

I'm grinning to myself, looking forward to the prospect of spending more time with Zeke, as we go upstairs to meet Crossman. One of the security guards, Bruce I think his name is, is there waiting.

He stands in his uniform, his thumbs digging into the sides of his utility belt. If ever there was a man playing cop, then this would be him. Like us, he's not wearing a gun.

Guns are not good things to have in casinos and it's been impressed on us that we can't carry them. Casinos' insurance premiums are already high, and if they have guns on the premises they go sky high.

Ignoring the guard who seems so full of himself, I approach Crossman.

He holds out his hand. "Thanks for helping us out, Red."

Brushing his gratitude aside, I ask for details. "What is it you need us to do?"

Staring at him, I notice there's a twitch in the side of his face. "All I need is for you to take the bags of money from the safe and take them out back to where the armoured truck will be waiting. You'll need to take them through the public area of the casino, so we'll need you to be on guard."

It sounds simple enough. Out of the corner of my eye, I catch the expression on Keys' face. His mouth is tight, and his cheeks are sucked in, bringing to mind the questions he'd raised just a couple of days before.

Should I have examined this contract more carefully? Looked the proverbial gift horse in the mouth? Perhaps I'd been blinded from the air of respectability it had brought to the club.

Providing a presence to back up their guards, installing and updating security and providing advice seems legit and above-board. But actually handling the money? Hadn't Keys mentioned something about foxes and henhouses?

"We'll stand guard while your staff transfers the money, but we won't touch it ourselves." My voice is adamant, leaving no room for argument. I catch Indian's eye and note the slight raise of his chin.

"But—" Crossman starts, and it's Twister who interrupts him.

"We," he nods toward Cobra and Hammer, "do as the prez instructs. Bruce, here, can handle the money."

"But," Crossman is undeterred, "that leaves us short on the floor."

"So, we patrol the casino," I tell him. "No biggie. Just swap the roles around."

His eyes flare. "I thought we had a good partnership."

So did I. But something's ringing warning bells so loud they're almost deafening me. "I need to make a call," I cut off whatever Crossman was about to say. Leaving abruptly, uncaring if it might appear rude, I descend the stairs, cross the casino and go out into the parking lot.

I make a phone call. "Crash. Need you to do something for me."

"Anything, Prez. What do you want?"

"There's an armoured truck which will be leaving the casino in about half an hour. I want you to follow it."

"We planning a raid, Brother?" There's a chuckle in his voice. "Didn't think our funds were as low as that." The thing about having brothers, even if I said such a raid is what's on my mind, he'd be right there behind me.

"I may be completely wrong, Crash, but this stinks of a setup to me. Crossman wanted our hands all over the money. What if he plans to rob his own truck and pin it on us?"

The VP intakes a breath loudly. "That's a bit of a stretch, Prez."

I know it is. "Call me paranoid if you want, but there's some-thing about this that doesn't smell right."

"We follow the truck, and…?"

"If it's attacked, be there to prevent it."

"Shadow and Titch have just come back from the shop. Fox is here with Sarge." Crash pauses as though he's looking around him. "Rope and Cuff might be around, but Petty and Roller are nowhere to be seen."

The latter pair have put in appearances in the shop but

haven't been to the clubhouse since the last church. Despite my differences with Petty, I'll have to have words if they stop pulling their weight.

"Call them in," I say sharply. "I want that truck followed."

"Bikes will be too obvious, Red. I'll grab the SUVs. Rosa's here. I'll commandeer her car as well. It will be less suspicious than us following on bikes."

"Crash…" I pause. "Stay fuckin' safe."

"Later, Prez. Gotta go get organised."

"Keep me posted." I end the call.

CHAPTER TWENTY-TWO

RED

"Something smells, Prez." Indian says quietly as Bruce leads us back down the stairs.

"Fuckin' reeks," Twister agrees, wrinkling his nose.

Keys is walking stiffly. "I'm getting the feeling we should never have gotten into this."

Him and me both. The problem is we make a hefty profit from this contract, and there's also the lure of giving at least the club's security business some respectability. But maybe I should have asked more questions in the first place.

My feelings aren't appeased as we stand by like spare parts when Bruce manages to summon a team. With a glare in my direction, he has them moving bags from the safe, then we escort them outside to where an armoured truck is waiting.

Narrowing my eyes as though to focus them, I look around carefully. Everything to my untrained eye looks just as it should be. The armoured truck has the name of a reputable company blazoned on the side, and the guys accompanying it have recognisable uniforms and look the part.

They go through the required motions, one knocking on the hatch which opens for the anonymous person inside to accept the money bags.

It all goes smoothly. The money from the casino is loaded without incident. The paperwork on the clipboard is signed, then the truck drives away.

Bruce huffs and hustles his men back inside. Twister stares in the direction the truck has disappeared in, worry lines creasing his brow.

But it's Keys who puts his finger on it.

"Fuckin' hell!" he exclaims, examining his phone. "That truck's not genuine. The license plate isn't registered to the company."

The truck looked kosher enough but could have been stolen.

I don't even waste a second. I'm on my phone before he can finish speaking. "Abort, Crash. Fuckin' abort."

The engine noise I can hear from Crash's end lessens and then stops completely. "Prez?"

"If this is a heist, it's already happened."

"You want us to come back? Not follow the truck?"

"Yeah. Meet us back at the compound and we'll have a sit-down and discuss." Fuck knows who's driving the casino's money away, but I want no part of this.

At least mine and my brothers prints won't be anywhere near those money bags.

"Crossman's fuckin' set us up," Twister growls, looking like he's going to march back upstairs and rearrange Crossman's face with his fists.

As far as I'm concerned, I'd like nothing better, but I want to be armed with information first and find out what the fuck's going on. I'm betting we wouldn't get near Crossman anyway. Bruce will have him well protected, and us causing a ruckus in the casino wouldn't go unnoticed.

"Get back to the clubhouse," I instruct, fixing Twister with my stare. "We've got things to thrash out."

Sharing a look that suggests they'd rather be getting imme-diate answers with their fists, Indian and Twister reluctantly head to the parking lot. Cobra, Hammer and Keys trail after them. I hang back for a moment, rubbing my temples and trying to work out what the fuck's going on.

My brain doesn't come up with more than one answer by the time we arrive. *They tried to set us up.* As I get off my bike, I see men milling around, as if trying to make sense of what's happened today.

Whistling loudly, I circle my hand in the air and lead the way into our meeting room. All eyes come immediately to me as I take my seat.

"What's going on, Prez?" my VP asks. "We could still have followed the truck."

I sigh, rubbing my fingers against my temples, then give him the answer that makes his and the eyebrows of others rise. "Finding who's responsible for robbing the casino is a job for the cops. I want no involvement with it. We can't afford to get caught anywhere near that fuckin' truck."

"The casino's been robbed?" Petty, putting in his first appearance since I handed him his ass, is the first to speak.

"I think it's safer to say the casino's fuckin' robbed itself." Indian speaks for me.

"You fuckin' what?" Rope looks mystified.

Titch though, well, he's been around a long time and it's easy to underestimate him. He's the first to give voice to what I really think is going on. His meaty fist slams down on the table. "They set us up."

Now roars go around. I bang the gavel hard a couple of times to get the protestations to calm down. "We figured it out, refused to have anything to do with it. But yeah, I think that was the whole point. It was supposed to be a setup."

Twister leans forward. "They wanted us to fuckin' handle the bags so they'd be covered by our DNA and fingerprints."

"How do you know, Prez?" Crash looks perturbed, as he well should.

This time it's Keys who speaks for me. "Because the

armoured truck wasn't legit. And neither, I suspect, were the guards."

Cobra folds his arms. "Why the fuck would the casino allow itself to be robbed?"

Fox snorts. "Casinos insure their money. They get hit, the insurance covers what they lose. I can only imagine if they rob themselves, they get the original money back as well."

"But why involve us?" I'm thinking aloud. "It wouldn't matter who did the crime."

"We're easy targets." Indian also seems to be verbalising his inner thoughts. "If their aim was to steal from themselves, get the payout *and* the original amount returned, they'd need something to muddy the waters of any investigation."

Hammer growls from deep in his throat. "What I want to know is, were they stringing us along all the time, or did they come up with this idea out of the blue?"

Flicking his eyes toward Hammer, Petty rolls his eyes. "Or this is a load of shit." He turns and points an accusatory finger my way. "Happenstance, Prez. They asked us to help with the money. Sure, Keys says the truck wasn't legit, but that's where the robbery started, not with our involvement. And," he glares at Keys, "who's to say their normal truck hadn't broken down and they borrowed one for the day. You fuckers refusing to do what they asked might have lost us the contract."

"Petty," I growl warningly. It's not that I don't welcome debate, I encourage different views to be put forward. But Petty's tone isn't just bordering on disrespect, he's trampling right over it.

He's unrepentant. "You're looking for things which aren't even there." His gaze encompasses the brothers one by one. "You know what Prez is setting us up for, don't you? He's going to pull out of the contract which will leave us all short in our pockets."

"Rather fuckin' short," Indian growls, "than locked up for something we didn't do."

"Face it." Petty's still got the floor and intends to keep it. "Prez isn't fuckin' thinking straight. Ever since he got with that bitch and her weird-as-fuck freaky-ass kid."

I'm on my feet fast but am beaten to it by Crash who, aided by Hammer who's also reacted like lightning, has got Petty off his chair and are holding him tight in their arms. I see Hammer pull back his fist and shout to interrupt him.

"Wait." Hammer pauses, raising an eyebrow my way. Moving like a panther, I stalk around the table until I'm in front of Petty. "I told you what would happen if you disrespected my kid."

"So, fight me," Petty yells. "You got lucky last time." He struggles against the men holding him tight. Then he appeals to anyone who'd support him. "Look, brothers. You gotta see this is wrong. Red's lost his fuckin' mind due to that bitch. Things ain't gonna get better if he brings her into the club. And who wants to be rubbing shoulders with a fuckin' freak?"

Cuff snorts. "Pot, kettle and black come to mind, *Brother*."

Ignoring him, I advance. "You challenging me, Petty?" Like laser beams, my eyes pierce him, then I turn and look over my shoulder. "Anyone else agree with Petty? Anyone else think I'm losing my touch? Anyone want to admit they've got a problem with Zeke?"

Roller's mouth I notice is opening and closing like a fish. It's clear he wants to support his friend. I wouldn't be surprised if there's steam coming from my nostrils as I focus on him. "Well, Roller? You keeping quiet as you don't have your brother's back, or is it that you're too chicken shit to tell me what you really feel?"

Looking down at his hands, Roller mumbles, "I always have my brother's back, Prez." At the intake of breath around the table, he quickly adds, "But in this, I don't agree with his views."

"Louder, Roller," I demand, turning my gaze back to Petty while he speaks.

"I don't support him. I've faith in you, Prez, and I've nothing against your kid." Without his support, some of the bluster visibly leaves Petty.

"Anyone else have a problem with me?" I ask, still focused on the restrained man.

"I got a problem with the fuckin' Lucky Fortunes who're fuckin' us around," Sarge states, loudly for him. "First, they set up your woman, now they look like they're trying to pin something on us."

My head tilts. For a second, I forget the man still vibrating with anger in front of me and focus on what Sarge has said. Could Cher's woes be tied up with the club? Is there a connection there? Surely not. How could the casino know that she meant anything to me?

"I think Cher's troubles are a coincidence," I say, half to myself.

"Worth checking out, Prez," Keys throws in. "Like who knew what and when. Chantilly fuckin' Lace might have known you and Cher were a thing. Things get around fast in school."

Petty snorts. "See, I knew Prez's bitch was at the bottom of this, she—"

This time I don't stop Hammer from punching Petty in his mouth. "Get him out of here," I snarl even as he shakes his head, flinging blood my way. "Take him down to the basement and I'll, er, speak to him later."

"You can't throw me out of church," Petty snarls. "I wear the fuckin' patch."

My brow furrows even as my lips turn up in an uneasy smile. "For now," I agree in a pleasant tone, then my voice hardens and I growl, "But maybe not for much longer."

"Come on." Crash and Hammer start dragging him out of the room, maybe to get him away before I lose any remaining control on my temper.

"Get a prospect to watch him," I shout after the three men. Hammer tosses a sharp nod back over his shoulder.

After they're gone, mayhem descends with everyone talking

at once. I bang the gavel a few times, and Indian lurches forward and shouts at them all to *shut the fuck up*. By the time Hammer and Crash return, there's some semblance of order.

"Right." I stare them all down. "Let's get things straight. I'm gonna lay all my cards on the table. I want Cher as my ol' lady, which means she and my kid will be involved in the club. This would have come to a vote sooner or later, so let's take this opportunity to clear the air now. Would you vote aye or nay?"

I'm not even sure if there's a written rule that old ladies have to be voted in, but it's something that's done in most of our chapters. It makes a lot of sense. A woman, particularly one who would become the first old lady, would have a big presence in the club. This isn't just a clubhouse, it's home to many of the brothers.

I could have Cher, live off compound, keep her and Zeke away from the club, but neither my brothers nor my family would have all of me, and I'm not even sure I could compartmentalise my life like that.

The Satan's Devils have been my family for so many years, I owe them everything that I am. But if they deny this part of me, would I ever be able to feel the same way about them again? How could I face my brothers, knowing they couldn't accept what I hope to be a massive part of my life?

I watch them. Titch looks thoughtful, Rope and Cuff seem mystified as to what the problem is about. Roller's still eyeing the door Petty was just taken out of. Cobra's looking down at his hands, and Hammer's staring into space. Sarge is tugging his ear, and Shadow's picking at his fingernails.

Crash clears his throat. "Speaking for myself, I trust Red implicitly. Whatever happens, I know he'll do the best for this club. Why the fuck shouldn't he take an ol' lady? Cher's alright from what I've seen of her."

"She kept your kid from you, Prez," Fox points out. I open my mouth to say not intentionally, but he doesn't give me the chance. "If you think you can make it work, then good luck to you. And I, for one, have no problem with Zeke." He pauses. "I wouldn't have had a problem with Joker had he decided to come out. I've great respect for the kid, at least he… they… don't try to hide what they are."

"Twisted," Rope says, making me start. Of anyone, I didn't think he or Cuff would have a problem. But he grins. "Zeke's twisted. As are we all." He circles his hand around the table. "Hell, we fuck anything that moves and has tits and an ass. As Fox just implied, we don't care if men rub dicks." Raising his fingers to form quotes, he adds, "'Normal folks' would see a problem with that. None of us are fuckin' normal."

"Not all of us use whips," Hammer drily puts in.

"What's normal?" Titch asks. Not getting an answer, he shrugs. "Some of us are born with dicks, some with pussies. Some even, as I've heard, can be born with both. Some guys like dick, some gals like pussy. Some," he stares at Rope and Cuff, like me well aware of the rumours, "can't make their minds up."

"It's called 'bi,'" Rope says drily, before quickly adding, "Not saying we are."

Titch glares at the interruption. "Joker and Lady were too fuckin' scared that we'd judge them for being true to their natures. Red's Zeke? Well, I admire the fuck out of them." He shakes his head. "I'm a biker. I get judged for wearing my cut and riding my bike. Zeke? Well, they could be like Joker, hiding in plain sight. That would make their life fuckin' easier. But do they hide? Do they give a shit?" He slams his fist on the table. "Like hell they do. And if you want to wonder why I try hard to get the pronouns right, it's because I give all fuckin' respect to that kid. Zeke doesn't hide, but also doesn't throw it in your face. What the fuck is it my business? That kid…" His voice continues to get louder. "That kid is going to have problems all their life. And you know what? None of those problems is of their fuckin' making. No, that's down to us." Now Titch stands, places his hands on the table and leans over. "What fuckin' right have we got to sit here and pass judgement about whether we bring Zeke in as part of the club? If Zeke was het, we wouldn't even be having this conversation. I say we've no fuckin' right. If anything, it should be down to Zeke to say whether they accept us as family or not." With one final glare, Titch sits back down, murmuring, "Fuckin' judgemental assholes," under his breath.

Hammer raises his hands, then exaggeratedly puts them together, parts them again, then starts a slow hand clap. Cobra, with a grin in his direction, copies him. Shadow joins in. Sarge just beats his fingers on the table.

Indian snorts and stomps his feet.

Twister barks a laugh and points down the table. "I'll give it to the old guy, he can tell us straight."

"I ain't got a problem with your kid, Prez," Roller says quietly, but loud enough to be heard. "I don't understand… them, but that's on me, not Zeke."

"I'm with Roller," Fox says.

Crash gives a sideways look at my mouth, still open. I'm staring at Titch in admiration for saying the things I couldn't voice. Then, my VP speaks. "I don't see any of us having problems with Cher, and clearly, there's none with Zeke."

I turn to him and wince slightly. "And me? Petty was raising a vote of no confidence."

"Petty should lose his patch for even thinking it," Twister snarls. "Craziest thing I've ever heard, Prez."

"Too fuckin' right," Titch pronounces from the end of the table.

As no comment suggests a hint of support for Petty's position, I begin to relax. Though I don't credit the asshole with much intelligence, a small part of me had questioned whether he was right, and I was letting my personal shit influence my duties. Had I a downer on the casino because it had fucked with Cher?

Now more confident, I'm pretty certain I'm right. I bang the gavel and get the meeting back on track.

For the next half hour, we kick around the events of the day.

In the end, we decide it's possible Petty could have been on the right track in one thing—just because the armoured truck had license plates not registered to a legit company, didn't mean it hadn't been hastily drafted in as a replacement. That I'd taken action to ensure there was nothing to link the brothers to any heist was given credit as there were too many unanswered questions.

We end the meeting unable to do more than tell Keys to keep digging and me with the resolve to ring Snatcher, with a request to move our non-urgent task up the agenda.

I want to know more about the assholes that run that casino, and if Keys has found nothing, then I'll ask Utah to dig deeper.

CHAPTER TWENTY-THREE

CHER

I'd watched Zeke's audition from one of the back-row seats in absolute awe at my child's talent. If the recruiters couldn't spot they were one of the best, then they had to be blind. They'd leaped and pirouetted faultlessly. Their jetés were perfect, their tour en l'air where they leaped and spun in the air the best rendition I've ever seen, and their arabesque could not be faulted.

Fairly unusual for someone born with a dick, Zeke danced en pointe. Then, ballet shoes removed, they'd effortlessly segued into a contemporary dance style, showing how diverse their skills were. The last music change and they'd paused, grinned, and then commenced a hip-hop routine, including breakdancing together with popping which put a smile on my face and raised a chuckle from the small audience.

Zeke ended looking spectacular in their final stance, one arm raised as if triumphantly. Still as a statue, their only movement was the vigorous heaving of their chest, the only sign of the effort that had gone into the show.

I could only just prevent giving a standing ovation and had to slap a hand over my mouth to stop myself yelling my appreciation. I was so damn proud.

That the organisers stood by silently as Zeke walked off the stage was a total anti-climax. When I'd joined my kid to overhear a disinterested voice telling them they'd be contacted as soon as a decision was made, I had to bite my tongue to say the outcome could be announced now. Surely no one could dance as well as Zeke? I'd sat through some of the performances of other hopefuls, and none had come close to my child's.

But then, I'm their mom, and have to admit, I'm probably biased.

Zeke's been anticipating this for weeks. To celebrate, I took them to their favourite restaurant without a thought to the fact that I'm now unemployed. As we ate, we dissected their performance. Perfect, in my view, with more than a few flaws in theirs.

I debate whether to call Red, unsure what to tell him. Any assessment I could make might lead him to think it went a different way. I decide to put the call off until we get home.

Zeke though was content they'd had some time on a stage, and although they could tell me where a foot had been placed wrong here, and a beat missed there, they were happy enough that stage fright hadn't frozen them.

As they told me, there'd be more auditions if this one didn't bear fruit.

When we finish our meal and drive home, I glance at the screen in my car, noticing my phone is connected and that it has a full battery. Not for the first time, I wonder why Red hasn't called or texted. I thought he'd be chomping at the bit to find out how Zeke had got on. When I dial his number, it goes through to voicemail. I decide to try later from home.

Zeke disappears the moment we get in through the door. I go to the kitchen and empty the dishwasher, then settle in front of the television. It must be an hour or so later when a screech from Zeke's room gets me to my feet, my heart beating fast.

We crash into each other in the hallway. "What's wrong?"

"I'm in, Mom. I got in!" Zeke's face is split into the widest grin that I have ever seen.

For a few moments, I can't stop telling them how proud I am.

They swing me around the room, Zeke expertly moving while I trip over my own damn feet. When the initial elation fades, I take out my phone.

"Mom, who are you calling?"

"Your dad," I respond, hoping I'll have better luck this time.

Zeke's hand settles on my arm. "Can't we go tell him in person?" When my brow furrows, showing a maturity well beyond their age, Zeke explains, "I know it was no one's fault, Mom, you always made that clear, but Dad's been excluded from everything in my life. I know he'd have wanted to be there for me." Their lips tremble. "When other kids had two parents show up to events at school, I used to tell myself if my dad knew, he'd have come too." They pull back their shoulders. "Maybe it was always a childhood dream, but I used to imagine him there watching with you." They give a shrug now. "He could have been an asshole, I accepted that too. But now I've met him, Mom, I know he'd have been the kind of dad who'd have always been there to support me. We owe him this. I don't want to tell him the biggest news of my life over the freaking phone."

But I do. I stare at my child for a moment, knowing there's a selfish part of me that wants to keep them all to myself. Of course, if Red and I build a future together, he'd be part of our family. But while I'm still not sure, I want to keep him at arm's length. Now my kid is showing me that's not fair.

Whatever the future holds for me and Red, Zeke will never just be mine again.

"It's late, Zeke."

In a gesture reminiscent of the man who sired him, they gesture dismissively. "You think I'll be able to sleep after hearing this news?"

Letting out a heavy sigh, I guess he's right. "Okay," I give in, but in an attempt to retain some parental control, I add, "But we go straight there, tell him, then come right back."

"Yay!" Zeke rushes to grab their jacket and has it on before I've picked up mine and found my keys.

On the drive, they go over the audition once again, marvelling that the recruiters overlooked the mistakes I certainly hadn't seen. Their enthusiasm is infectious, adding to the pride I already hold as their mom. Not for the first time, I wonder where their talent came from. Certainly not from me, and I doubt Red has ever performed a pirouette in his life.

It must be the way the stars aligned at their birth, I decide, shooting a fond look to my side. Whatever the problems I'd had bringing them up on my own, I wouldn't wish Zeke to have turned out anything other than the way they have.

I wave to Owl as he opens the gate, then park with the club's SUVs and away from the bikes. Noise and light are streaming out of the clubhouse as we approach, and I get a feeling of nervousness. When I've come here before, it's been at Red's invitation.

Beginning to have doubts about the wisdom of just barging into his world, my steps falter. Zeke, however, shows no such restraint or misgivings. Leaving me in their wake, they run forward, pushing open the clubhouse door. Flinging an impatient look over their shoulder, Zeke at least waits for me to catch up rather than letting the door slam in my face.

I step in, getting my first look at the Satan's Devils at play. Oblivious, Zeke has eyes for one man only, while mine roam, taking in Cobra with a girl on her knees in front of him. By the way his head's thrown back and the way her head bobs, it's pretty clear what he's doing.

But I've lost my chance to get Zeke out of here. They've spotted Red by the bar with a drink in one hand and another of the club girls I remember from the barbeque standing way too close to him. Of course, he'd explained who and what they were, but stupidly I hadn't let my mind go to how he himself might use them. A blaze of jealously rises inside me despite us never having had the exclusivity conversation. Following on Zeke's path, I storm across.

"Dad!"

Red swings around. The girl puts her hand proprietarily on his arm. To his credit, he ignores her.

"Zeke? What the fuck are you doing here?" The words might sound harsh, but the grin on his face though is welcoming.

"I got it!"

Red seems stunned for a moment. "Fuck, kid. With everything happening here, I forgot to ask. You really got it?"

Zeke nods vigorously, their face ablaze with pride at the achievement. Red pauses, then clasps his kid to him, slapping their back in that manly way I've seen him do to his brothers. The patting action continues for some time, and Red's eyes glisten as if overcome with emotion. I watch his Adam's apple bob a couple of times before he releases Zeke. "Of course, you did, kid," he tells them, his eyes finding mine, telegraphing his pride and pleasure in our child's achievement. "Of course, you fuckin' did. You're my kid, Zeke. You can do anything."

"What are we celebrating?" Rosa steps out of the kitchen, rubbing her hands on a towel.

"Are Trist and Tom here?" Zeke asks eagerly.

"No, sorry. They're spending the night with a friend." Rosa's slight roll of her eyes and the amused twist to her lips suggests she's got sympathy for whichever unfortunate parent has got them.

Then Red spies something behind me. "Zeke, I think there's leftover pizza in the kitchen. Why don't you go help yourself?"

Rosa looks confused for a moment, then clearly seeing what's caught Red's eye, snorts. "Yeah, Zeke. You come with me."

Zeke doesn't think anything's odd, never refusing the chance to fill their growing stomach, and happily steps off after Rosa. Once Zeke's out of earshot, Red steps toward me, blanching. "Sorry, Cher. We weren't expecting you. The twins aren't here..." He flutters his hands palms up.

"I can tell." I shoot a glare past him toward the club girl who's not moved very far away from him.

Red catches on. Moving closer, he lowers his mouth to my

ear. "Cher, you have no fuckin' reason to feel jealous. I would never step out on you, you hear? Hell, since I first saw you again, I've not been with anyone."

"But you've had her." I can tell, just from the way she's looking at him. Maybe not recently, but in the past he has.

"Cher." He gives a warning growl. "I've got history, you know that. Sure, I fucked the club girls when my hand wouldn't do." The said club girl doesn't seem at all put out by the way he's phrased it. "From here on in, why would I look elsewhere when I've got the best in you?"

Not certain whether to be righteously angry or complimented by his answer, it takes me a moment to know how to respond.

Red opens his mouth as if again to excuse his behaviour, but whatever he was going to say is left unsaid as suddenly there's a commotion. The main doors fly open with men in combat-looking gear pushing their way in, weapons in hand.

"Everyone down on the floor. Now."

Instinctively, I know this is a raid. Red pushes me behind him, hissing, "Get to the safe room with Rosa and Zeke. Now."

I don't argue. Whatever's happening isn't my business and is the main reason I was worried about getting involved with him. Sidling out, hoping I'm not noticed, I get to the kitchen. Rosa's brow is furrowed, and just one word has her ushering me and Zeke down the short hallway and into the safe room.

Once inside, Rosa shoots the electronic lock then immediately goes to slide out the panel which reveals the monitors.

"Mom, what's happening?" Zeke looks bewildered. Having been with Rosa, they don't have a clue what's going on.

"Shush," I hush them.

"Mom, is that a SWAT team?" they exclaim loudly, staring at the monitors.

"Quiet," I admonish them, not wanting anyone to find us here.

"It's soundproofed," Rosa throws over her shoulder. "I'm more worried about what's happening out there."

In two paces, I'm beside her, watching the same as she's seeing. The outside view of the clubhouse shows a number of squad cars, some of them armoured. The internal views show cops swarming in, and, Zeke was right, a goddamn SWAT team —all armed to the teeth and all currently handcuffing the men and none too gently.

"What the fuck is this all about?"

I'm more grateful than I can say that we can see and hear everything, as Red, refusing to comply with the instruction to lie down, challenges the visitors.

"I think you know exactly what this is about," one of the uniformed men answers sneeringly. "Now get on the ground."

"I know you can't come in here without a warrant," Red shoots back, undeterred.

"Oh, we've got warrants. We're here to round up the whole damn club. You think you can rob a casino and get away with it?"

"Rob a fuckin' casino?" Crash lurches to his feet. "What the fuck you talking about?" He gets pushed hard and off balance, making him fall back down to the ground. I wince as he's unable to use his hands to save himself.

"Arrest them all." Another man comes in.

"We haven't robbed anything." Red's reddened face shows the effort it's taking to fight to keep his voice level. "When was this supposed to have happened? And why pin it on us?"

The man who seems to be in charge snorts. "Play the innocent why don't you?" He points his finger. "We've got warrants for the arrest of all the members of the Satan's Devils MC."

"Let me see."

I see some paperwork passed briefly in front of Red's eyes. Even on camera, I see him straighten.

"This is the end of your fuckin' club," the man spits at him.

"Just tell me what we're supposed to have done." Red again questions him.

With a roll of his eyes, Red's at last told, "You've robbed an armoured truck transporting the proceeds of the Lucky Fortunes casino. Unfortunately for you, you left alive one of the guards. He clearly identified you from the cuts you were wearing."

I gasp, loudly. Rosa immediately turns to me with narrowed eyes. "They didn't," she tells me, firmly. "This is a setup."

But I'm not so sure.

"Mom?" Zeke's voice sounds quiet. "Dad didn't, did he? He wouldn't."

"He didn't," Rosa replies adamantly. "But they'll probably be searching this place to round everyone up. It won't do us any good being found here. We'll use the escape route and get out the back way."

I'm more than onboard with that plan. My eyes widen slowly as Rosa closes the door, covering the monitors, and quietly slips the lock on the door. Then she goes to the hidden door and opens it, ushering us through.

At my surprised expression, she gives a smirk. "Don't want them breaking the door down for no reason. Hopefully they'll see an empty television room and move on. That door cost a fortune and Red would have a fit if they broke it in."

She might have a good point, but I wonder whether Red will be in a position to care anymore. But the first priority is getting Zeke far away from here.

In a few moments, Rosa leading, me next then Zeke, we cautiously emerge into the garage. After a glance around and giving us the all clear, Rosa encourages us away from the vehicles. "Let's get to the back of the compound. Red keeps a Jeep out the back. If we use the main entrance, we'll have to pass the cops."

"Red keeps a Jeep in case of attack?" Again, I'm astonished.

Walking fast, Rosa satisfies my curiosity. "He didn't want me, Tiff or the boys caught up in anything. While there's been no problems for years, the Jeep is old, but well maintained. Though, it looks like a piece of crap."

Soon we come upon it. If she hadn't already indicated it was roadworthy, I'd have passed it without a second glance. I suppose that it's on four wheels is a giveaway, but its rusty windows are broken, and it resembles trash that no carjacker with any self-respect would give a second glance.

But when Zeke slips into the back and I position myself in the passenger seat, Rosa turns the key and it starts like a dream.

"Where are we heading?" I breathe a sigh of relief as we turn onto a main road.

"My place," Rosa says curtly. "Then we can start planning how to get the boys out."

Get them out? When they've just been taken away in handcuffs by a SWAT team? The people I'd like to get out of this mess are Zeke and myself. I don't want to go to Rosa's house and plan a prison break or get us mixed up in this any more than we already are. *Red's apparently robbed a fucking casino.* "Drop me and Zeke off at my apartment, please. Or here if it's easier. We'll get a taxi." Then I'll think how to retrieve my car later, hopefully before the cops start investigating whose it is.

She gives me a sharp look. "You running out on him at the first sign of trouble?" Shaking her head, she adds, "That's not who I took you for."

"I've got Zeke—"

"I'm well aware of having kids to think of," she snaps. "You really think Red was responsible for robbing a casino and shooting a guard?"

"Dad wouldn't," Zeke confidently contributes from the back seat.

"See? Kid knows his dad better than you do, Cher."

"You think they're innocent?" I gasp.

"Of course, they are. And there's a good reason why I know that." Rosa proceeds to drive in the opposite direction to my apartment, so I guess the decision's been made unless Zeke and I are to jump out of a moving car. While she seems convinced of their innocence, I'm still on the fence.

"You of all people should give him a chance." Rosa scoffs.

"Wasn't it you who was just behind bars for something you hadn't done?"

"She's got you there, Mom."

I stifle my comment that Zeke's interjection isn't useful. I bristle but can't deny that she's right. Instead, I allow my mind to wander in that direction.

"They don't send out SWAT teams for nothing. They must have something that led them to the club. The injured guard said it was the Devils," I remind her.

"People can say anything, as well you know." Again, she plants that little dig at me.

I suppose I deserve it. "So, what now?"

Rosa purses her lips. "Now they need their women to show what they're made of. We're going to get justice for them and get them out."

She makes it sound easy when I know it will be anything but. But wasn't that exactly what Red had done for me? When I'd been arrested, he hadn't run out. He'd gotten a lawyer, dug for evidence and freed me.

Don't I owe it to him to at least try?

I suppose since I reconnected with Red and found who he's become, I've just been waiting for a good excuse to run. Leave him just like I'd done before.

Perhaps this time, I should stand my ground.

CHAPTER TWENTY-FOUR

CHER

As soon as the Jeep comes to a halt, Rosa rushes us inside her home. While I'm not here to critique her homemaking skills, I do notice it's cosy and clean, even though filled with the paraphernalia that can't hide she's living with two teenage boys. Sports equipment is clearly on view through an open closet door, and the pictures on the wall are mainly of Trist and Tom, playing football.

One catches my eye. A man, in a cut, is standing with the twins. This must be Brick, Rosa's husband, with the boys before his untimely death.

Even with my level of anxiety as high as it is, I take a moment to admire her. Zeke had known no different from the moment of their birth, they had me, but no father. What had it been like to lose the man she so obviously loved, and have to cope not only with her own distress, but that of the two children he'd fathered?

Rosa had left us for a moment. She returns fast, tapping her phone in her hand. "That's sorted. Jemima, their friend's mother, is having the twins overnight." She blanches slightly. "I'm going to have to find some way of thanking her."

"What are we going to do about Dad?" It's Zeke who gets straight to the point. "He'll need a lawyer or something, won't he?" My kid turns to me. "What about the one you used? Red sorted him out."

Rosa grins widely. "Good thinking, Zeke. Cher, you got his number?"

I do have his card in my bag. I get it out, and Rosa takes it from me. Again, she moves away but I can hear her side of the call. I hear her repeat, yes, the whole club, and I wonder whether this is too much for him to deal with. But from Rosa's side of the conversation, it appears it's not.

"Coffee?" Rosa offers as she ends the call.

While I could do with something a hell of a lot stronger, I know I have to keep a clear head. Heaven knows at the moment, my brain is spinning. Questions assault me such as should I get myself involved in this, or just take Zeke and pretend apart from being the sperm donor, Red means nothing to us.

Unfortunately, that's not the truth. I have a depth of feeling for Red I so far haven't wanted to admit, and the thought of him languishing in jail or dying there fills me with dread. But the cops must have had evidence to arrest him and the club. I need to look out for Zeke and make sure none of that falls back on us.

"Zeke, could you go get the coffee started?" Rosa, her sharp eyes on me, asks.

Zeke looks like they'd prefer to stay with us, but good kid that they are, they disappear into the kitchen with only a pained look for protest.

Once we're alone, Rosa doesn't hold back. "You," she points a finger directly at my chest in case I thought someone was behind me. "You're in this up to your neck. You were recently arrested, wrongly, I admit, for stealing from the casino. You think the police won't connect the dots? Especially as you used the same lawyer."

Is she implying that I helped Red plan it? My eyes widen in horror. "Then Zeke and I need to leave—"

Her eyes harden. "You could go. You could run and always be looking over your shoulder. Or you could stay here and fuckin' help." Despite the company she keeps, the profanity from Rosa is unexpected and it pulls me up.

"But what can I do, Rosa?" I start to pace. "Red and I aren't even an item."

"Of course, you are," she throws back.

Checking Zeke's out of earshot, I hiss, "Sex between us is off-the-charts good, Rosa, I'll admit that. But is that a relationship? I didn't know him fifteen years back, and I still don't know him."

"Well, I do," she asserts, putting her hands on her hips. "I've known him for years. He's a good man, Cher. You say you don't know him, yet can you really think he'd be as stupid to pull a stunt like this? Honey, the club gets by, they don't need to commit robbery. And if they did, they wouldn't leave fucking clues."

I take a breath, trying to think clearly. "Okay, let's say Red has nothing to do with this, but it has to have been a member of his club."

Looking disappointed in me, she shakes her head. "First off, you're wrong. The club's history would attest to that. No member would go near money from a casino. Secondly, they were proud of the contract they'd signed with the Lucky Fortunes, and not one of the brothers would mess that up." I listen, acknowledging Rosa knows her boys in ways I've yet to.

She too seems to have a problem standing still. She walks to the couch and folds her arms as she leans on it. "Even if Red wasn't personally involved, in this situation, that won't matter." She dips her head but doesn't hide the wave of sadness which crosses it. "Have you heard of RICO?"

I'm not quite sure I have. I tilt my head to show I don't really understand.

"It's about racketeering and profiteering." Rosa shrugs. "Basically, it means if someone in the club committed the crime, Red and the officers can be held responsible if they can link it back to him."

"What if there's no link?"

Rosa snorts. "They'll say it's why they got the contract to provide security or something like that. They'll find some way to implicate them."

I start to get a bad feeling. "And if they do?"

"The club's assets will be seized and Red and the rest will be looking at a minimum of twenty years."

There's a crash as cups are dropped on the floor. Zeke's standing there, eyes open wide. "That can't happen, Mom. We've got to do something!"

If Red is indeed innocent as Rosa believes and I suspect, there's no way I want him going inside for a crime he didn't commit. As Rosa rushes over to mop up the spilled coffee, I come to a decision. While my desire to stay and fight had wavered when Rosa suggested the cops might think I was involved, what would Zeke think of me, or me of myself, if I didn't try to help?

Straightening my back, I ask for the wise woman's wisdom. "What can we do?"

"We speak to Drummer."

"Who's Drummer?" Zeke breaks off from apologising to Rosa as at the same time they prove to be as much of a hindrance as a help in clearing up the spilled coffee.

I'm not surprised when before she speaks, she waves Zeke off to complete the job by herself.

"Drummer's the president of the mother chapter of the Satan's Devils in Tucson," she informs us as she throws soaked paper towels in the trash, then rinses off her hands. "He's kind of the head of all the chapters."

I may be an independent woman, proud of looking out for herself, but under these circumstances, I'm more than happy to hand over the problem to someone who knows what they're doing. Some of my tension leaves me. "Okay, then. Let's call Drummer."

Rosa grimaces. "I don't have his number, and they've arrested everyone who would know." Her face screws up for a moment. "Tiff's working tonight, but there's no reason she would have his number." Again her mouth scrunches, then she suggests, "We can go back to the clubhouse and dig through Red's paperwork."

That doesn't appeal to me. The cops could still be there. "Don't you have any of the other club members' numbers?"

She shakes her head. "I've met some of their old ladies, but I didn't exchange details."

"Would Tiff know any of the other women?"

At that moment, Rosa's phone rings, and as if she was the Devil, it's Fox's old lady who's on the line. Rosa turns away as she explains the situation to her.

I expect to hear a wail of distress from the woman who's hearing her man's been arrested, but these women of the club have backbones stronger than that. It's clear she's telling Rosa while she can't help with any contacts either, she does arrange to meet us back at the club.

"Don't you dare," Zeke whispers into my ear, confirming they're a mind reader. "Don't you dare use me as an excuse to get out of this, Mom."

"But, Zeke, if we go back to the clubhouse, the police could still be there."

"So?" They shrug. "We're not members, they've got no problem with us."

"But they could drag us in as witnesses and question us."

Overhearing, Rosa snorts. "They know better than that. Deniable culpability is why Tiff and I are kept out of club business. Even if we were prepared to share information with the law, we don't have any."

Which makes me question why she's so certain Red's innocent.

She looks at me. "But there is a risk. With you working at the casino, they could pull you in anyway."

And there's the out I was looking for. Perversely, now she's given it to me, I don't want to take it. Or maybe I don't want to look weak in front of my kid.

Rosa picks up the keys to the Jeep again. "You coming or not?"

Zeke answers for me. "We're coming."

At Rosa's raised eyebrow, I nod once.

As if by agreement, we're quiet on the return journey. The thought is going around my head that I might never see Red again. I've heard too many stories of what can happen behind bars.

What's he feeling? If Rosa's right and he had nothing to do with what he's accused of, he'll be just like me, worried sick and angry that he's been caught up in something without a clue of how to get out of it.

I have to make a decision. Either I believe in Red and his innocence and put all my efforts into clearing him, or I sit on the fence, believing the worse of him, or at least, the members of his club.

By the time Rosa draws up at the clubhouse—now devoid of police cars—I know if there's any way forward for us, I have to trust him.

As the Jeep comes to a halt, I've decided. Heaven help me if it's the wrong choice, but I'm going to do all I can to get him walking free again. I vow if I can help it, Zeke's future views of their dad won't be behind bars.

Getting out of the car, I examine the building. All the lights are on inside, but for once, there's no music or voices coming from it. Feeling like an intruder, I follow Rosa.

The inside isn't completely empty. There by the bar, a full bottle between them, sits the three underdressed women.

"Scat," Rosa says sharply, approaching them.

"Can't tell us what to do," Jinx says dismissively.

"Can't I?" Rosa puts her hands on her hips.

One of the others pulls Jinx back. Brushing away tears, she asks, "When are our men coming home?"

Rosa looks at her kindly. "As soon as they can."

"Can we do anything to help?" the third one asks.

"Not unless you know the contact details for Drummer."

The three look at each other and shake their heads. Jinx tells us, "Had him a couple of times before he hooked up with his ol' lady. Pixie?"

Pixie shakes her head. "Same with me. He did us both together once, didn't he, Angel?" She pauses for the third girl to also gesture dismissively. "He was a tiger in the sack. Shame he got hitched."

"Not much help," Rosa retorts. "Unfortunately, it's not possible to trace a man based on his sexual prowess."

"We know where the clubhouse is," Jinx brightens up. "How about we drive down there and ask him?"

Rosa eyes the bottle and the empty one sitting beside it. "Maybe tomorrow if we can't come up with anything else."

Her original intention seemed to have been to banish them, but now she appears to be tolerating them. "Come on," she instructs me. "Let's start in your man's office."

"Her man?" Jinx snorts.

Rosa swings around, her face now darkening. "Her fucking man and don't you forget it."

Standing by Rosa's side, I stare at Jinx. I might not have claimed him as such, but I'll be damned if I let her think she can have him. Seeing the spark in my eyes, she backs down.

Following Rosa with Zeke trailing behind me, we go into Red's domain. It feels so wrong to be here, to see the Satan's Devils' flag over the desk where presumably Red sits and works.

"Any good at hacking?" Rosa asks, as she switches on the ancient-looking PC, taking a seat on Red's chair.

Zeke leans forward. "Try Cheryl." When Rosa shakes her head, he suggests, "Ezekiel? Zeke?" But that doesn't work either.

"Satan's Devils MC," I toss in.

Rosa snorts. "Keys would have flayed him if he'd used something as simple as that." She sits back and starts opening the drawers. She brings out piles of paperwork that we begin sorting through. Most seem to be receipts, a lot for motorcycle parts, but there's no phone numbers that we can see.

Unlucky, we move on to Keys' office, that is virtually bare and doesn't take more than a moment to discover our mission unfruitful. There's no paperwork at all, and from the charging leads lying around, any laptop has been taken.

By the time we get to the last office, Tiffany has arrived and is already in there. But she, too, comes up with nothing.

"Damn men are just too secretive," she announces as her eyes query us as we walk in and shake our heads.

"I'm beginning to think the sluts have the right idea. If we're to get a hold of Drummer, maybe we should drive down and speak to him."

"There must be something here." Zeke looks around, pulling papers toward them and shuffling through them again. "What about in the auto-shop? Would there be anything there?"

Tiff looks at Zeke with new respect in her eyes. "Can't hurt to look. Tucson might have ordered something from them." She picks up her purse. "I'll call you if I find anything."

As she disappears, we walk out into the clubroom to find Jinx behind the bar. She stands up guiltily. "There are invoices stacked here, but no notes or anything."

At least she's trying to help.

This is crazy. I know bikers are secretive, but someone must have left something. But then again, in the world of mobile phones, who has numbers written down anymore? And I doubt Satan's Devils carry business cards.

"There must be something here," I state. Now I've been frustrated in my search, it spurs me on to find something, anything that could help. It's not as if the Satan's Devils MC are going to have any business listing.

"Businesses!" I say at last, spinning around. "Does Tucson run any businesses that we could try to look up online?"

Rosa's eyes gleam. "I know they do. All clubs do. That's a good thing to try."

"I'll check online and see what I can find."

A gentle clearing of a throat interrupts us. "You want us to search the boys' rooms?"

Narrowing my eyes, I wait for Rosa to kick the sweet butt's offer back, but to my surprise, she shrugs. "It's not like you've never been in them. But no prying, huh? You're looking for something, anything that might help us get in touch with a different chapter."

Given something to do, Jinx, Pixie and Angel make their way to the stairs, a little unsteadily due to the amount of alcohol they've consumed. All I can hope is that their eyesight hasn't been impaired.

"I'll have another check around here," Rosa suggests. "Zeke, you with me?"

"Sure."

Feeling more purposeful and optimistic, surely something will turn up, I sit on a sofa and take out my phone and start googling. Not many results turn up for Satan's Devils MC in Tucson, or not any that would help. I try various combinations, then start searching for auto-shops.

Triumphantly, I at last find a number for an SD Construction and wonder whether that could be the one. But at this time of night, my call goes unanswered. Unsure whether there's any connection to the MC, I don't leave a message on the voicemail. SD Tattoos also comes up, but likewise, that one is also not accepting calls at this time of night.

"They've got a strip club and a restaurant." Rosa pauses her search. She's been checking down the backs of the sofas in case any notes or cards have found their way there.

Those businesses would be open, but I find none with the SD handle in front of the name. I'm just about resolving myself to ringing every such business when Zeke's loud voice exclaims, "Mom! Rosa!"

We both start and make our way over to them.

"What have you found?"

Zeke's standing by a door that leads down into the basement.

Rosa raises her eyebrows and shakes her head. "You don't want to go down there," she impresses on him, then exchanges a glance with me. "But we should take a look."

Is this where the bodies are buried? I cast a worried look toward my child, but they look back with a smirk.

"Too late, I've already been down. I've seen enough to know the Devils are a kinky bunch." He chuckles, but his eyes don't reflect his mirth. "There's something else down there as well. Something that's very rude."

Rosa glows red, and gives me an explanation, saying quietly, half under her breath, "Rope and Cuff installed some BDSM equipment in the—"

"Oh, I don't mean that." Zeke shrugs. "I've seen *Fifty Shades* so that doesn't bother me." *They have?* As I open my mouth to question what, when and where, they continue, "I'm talking about something living and breathing. One of the club."

CHAPTER TWENTY-FIVE

CHER

Rosa pushes past me and I'm right on her heels as she heads for the door that leads downstairs. When she comes to an abrupt halt at the bottom, I'm so close, I bump into her.

"What the hell?"

Her question is echoed in my mind. There's a man tied tight to a chair. He's obviously been there a while as his pants have a big wet patch on the groin area.

"Thank fuck. Get me out of here, Rosa," he demands.

Instead of complying, Rosa starts to advance. She's stands in front of him, then acknowledges she knows him. "Petty."

He rattles the chains that are holding him and snaps, "The keys are on the bench. Fuckin' untie me."

Rosa proves she's not retained the title of first old lady for nothing. "Brothers don't tie anyone in the basement without good reason." One of her fingers rests on her lips as though she's thinking. "Have you betrayed the club, Petty? Are you the reason they're all locked up?"

"Locked up?" Despite his state, Petty looks astonished. "What the fuck are you talking about?"

"Surely you heard the commotion?" I'd be astounded if he hadn't. "The cops came in and arrested them all."

"And I'm betting he knows just what for." Rosa's face is taut and she's vibrating with anger.

Petty seems to realise he's not getting far and tries a more conciliatory tone. "I know fuck all. It's soundproofed down here. Last thing I know, the fuckin' prospect went to ask permission to let me loose to take a piss, I've heard nothing since. That was fuckin' ages ago." Which kind of explains the state he's in. As I decide to be discreet and not mention it, he carries on, "And what the fuck are you talking about? Why would the cops round up the club?"

Rosa's still staring at him with no apparent sympathy. "Tell me why you're down here."

Zeke comes up alongside me. "He's a dick," they announce, as if that explains everything.

"Fuckin' freak," Petty sneers.

"Yeah, yeah," Zeke replies in a bored tone. "You said that before. Perhaps if you'd been more polite, I'd have freed you."

So that's what Zeke had meant by something rude. They hadn't been referring to the spanking bench or St. Andrews Cross which are on display in one half of the basement, along with an assortment of whips and chains.

"If Red put you here, he's got a reason." Rosa comes to a conclusion. "So, we're not going to release you. Quickest way for you to get free is to tell us what we want to know."

Zeke gives a chuckle and waves their hands toward the various implements hanging up. "Seems we've got access to a lot of persuasive equipment."

Petty seems to shrink back on his chair. "Don't let… *it*… near me," he snarls.

Mama bear comes to the fore. "Don't you speak like that about my child," I roar at him. I'm unwilling for Zeke to show any violent side, but by hell, I'll whip this man myself if he continues to insult them.

Ignoring him, Rosa walks closer. "I may not have been down here before, but I've been in the club for what feels like my whole life. I've seen men who they bring up. Men bloodied and beaten, or who aren't even breathing anymore." She glances around, her eyes settling on a workbench behind him. On first glance, it looks like the tools you'd find in any workshop. But I look closer and shudder when she adds, "I reckon Twister's got some toys I could use."

"You haven't got the balls," Petty growls. But there's a slight flicker in his eyes which could be fear.

"We haven't asked him any questions," Zeke intelligently puts in. "Maybe we should give him a chance to answer them."

"I've nothing to say to you, *freak*. Ouch! What the hell?"

The last is to the hard slap Rosa's just given him. The power behind the blow can be witnessed by the way she's now rubbing her hand, and how his head snapped back.

"You use that word one more time and I'll fucking end you."

Even Petty can see the promise in her blazing eyes. Deliberately, he turns his face away from Zeke and focuses on Rosa instead. "If I tell you what you want to know, will you release me?"

"Depends on the answer," she retorts. "For a start, what do you know about why the cops have come for Red and the others?"

"I know fuck all." To his credit, he looks distraught, as the predicament of the club starts to trump his own problems. "Look, I fucked up. Red was all about claiming Cher as his bitch, and I objected because of the baggage she brings with her. Who wants a… *person*… like that around the club?" He gives a stomach-curdling look toward Zeke.

"And Red objected and tied you up?" I'm impressed at the thought that he defended me, but I'm also worried in case Petty isn't the only one who harbours hatred for Zeke who can't help being what they are. Perhaps Petty was the only person who expressed himself vocally.

"Prez is being led by pussy. Someone needed to speak up."

"Seems not everyone was in agreement," Rosa remarks disinterested. "But now we need to get Red and his brothers out of jail and for that we need your help."

"Fuckin' untie me then."

"Uh-uh. You stay right there. What's Drummer's phone number?"

"What do you think I am? A fuckin' walking phone directory?" Petty rolls his eyes. "Let me go and I'll start the ball rolling. The brothers need a lawyer for a start."

"Already got one. Now we need Drummer here to take charge." As Petty looks like he's going to dispute that, Rosa stomps closer. "Looks to me like you're already in deep shit with your prez. How's he going to feel if you leave him one more moment in that jail than he needs to be there?"

"Presumably Dad restrained you for a reason," Zeke butts in. "I respect my dad, and if he doesn't want you free, I don't see why we should untie you."

I cock my brow at Petty. Zeke's made a good point.

"Look, kid." Petty at last looks Zeke in the face. "I don't get you or your type, it's not natural. Man's born with a dick that makes him a man not a fuckin' girl, and definitely not something in between. It's probably not even your fault. Your mom should have knocked some sense into you. If you'd been brought up with your dad—"

"I'd be exactly who I am now." Zeke doesn't sound annoyed or angry. "I am what I am, what I was born to be. Don't you think I'd rather fit into your binary world? Well, you're right, I would. But this is no fad nor fantasy, this is my reality."

"Zeke's been through shit that you wouldn't even dream of," I butt in. "They probably have more backbone than you. Would it be better if they tried to conform to your view of normal? Easier, for sure, but that's not who Zeke is. Zeke, at least, has the courage to stand up for what they are. Unlike you." I add the last scornfully. "You're a coward who can't admit you're scared of anyone who doesn't fit the boxes you're comfortable with."

"True," Rosa adds in support. "He freaked out when he found out one of our previous members was gay, as if it would infect him."

"You like dick?" Zeke asks, perceptively.

"What the fuck?" Petty sputters. "No, I do not."

Zeke shrugs. "Some guys like dicks, some like pussy. Some like both. Doesn't matter which camp you fall in."

"I am not gay," Petty screams out.

I wonder whether Zeke has a point. Oh, Petty might like the women, but he might feel tempted by, as Zeke had put it, dick. It's on him if he can't deal with that.

"Perhaps—" Rosa starts.

Petty seems to have had enough of this conversation, proving taunts can be more painful than threats of torture sometimes. To shut her up, he shouts out, "My phone's in my cut. The brothers took it off me—it's in here somewhere. Drummer's number's in my contacts."

I grin, while Rosa immediately starts looking around. It's not long before we find his cut, and indeed his phone just where he said it was. Zeke holds it up to Petty's face to open it.

Suddenly, Petty starts thrashing against his bindings. "Just call up the contacts then shut that shit down."

Ignoring him, Rosa hands the phone to me.

"What am I supposed to do with this?"

"Call Drummer."

"But I don't know the man." I try to give it back.

"I've no club standing, I'm tolerated as my husband was the old prez. But you're the first old lady."

"But—" I start to protest I'm any such thing.

"Club voted you in from what Petty just said."

"Mom, you know that's what Red wanted," Zeke prompts and nods to the phone. "If you don't make the call, I will. Perhaps I have standing as Red's child."

I hold the phone about the same way I'd hold a poisonous snake, as if it would suddenly strike and bite me. I'm apparently about to make a call to an MC prez, and not just any old one, but one who rules the mother chapter and all the Satan's Devils' MCs.

Gingerly, I scroll through the numbers. Drummer's is indeed listed under his name. I press the key and turn away embarrassed as I don't know what to say. While it's ringing, I clear my throat.

"You got Drummer, and you'd better have a fuckin' good reason for this call, Petty."

"Er, it's not Petty. I'm using his phone."

My female voice stumps him. Then he growls, "And who the fuck are you?"

Swallowing, I say the words I'm not sure I'm qualified to utter. Red might have claimed me, but I haven't claimed him. But if it's the only way to get Red help, I'll do anything at this point. "I'm Red's ol' lady." I may or may not cross my fingers with my free hand.

"What the fuck, woman? You one of the whores?"

I suppose it would come as a shock if he'd never heard of me before. "No, I'm Cher. I'm the mother of his kid. We've only recently reconnected." Realising I'm rambling, I stop. "The thing is, Drummer, Red needs your help. He and the rest of the club have been arrested."

"The fuck?" I'm beginning to think the mother chapter president has a limited vocabulary, before I hear muttering in the background. "Club business, babe. I gotta take this." There's a sound of rustling and then the stomping of feet. "Right… Cher. Have I got this right? Red and the whole of his club have been taken by the cops?"

"All except for one member."

"And who's that?"

"Petty. I'm using his phone."

"He there?"

I have to admit, "Yes."

"Give him the fuckin' phone."

"I, er, I can't do that."

"He injured?"

I glance at Petty. Inconvenienced maybe, and there's a slight swelling to one eye, but apart from the fact he'd been left so long he'd wet himself, he appears otherwise unhurt.

"No, but Red had him restrained in the basement, and we don't want to let him go."

"We?"

"Me, Rosa, and Zeke, my kid."

The other end of the line goes quiet for a moment, then Drummer makes a request. "Go to Petty and put the phone on speaker."

I do as instructed and walk closer to Petty. As soon as I near, Petty calls out, "Get the bitches to let me go, Drummer."

"Not so fast, Petty. Tell me why the fuck Red's got you tied up. And if I ever find it's not the truth coming out of your mouth, I'll let Blade at you. You'll be begging for death soon enough."

His threat is chilling, and the way Petty blanches, he believes every word. The name Blade seems to send shivers through him.

"Can you send the bitches away?"

"I'm giving you the fuckin' courtesy of listening to you. You don't get to make requests. Now tell me what's got Red twisted up about you, and whether it's anything to do with the arrest?"

Petty exhales loudly. After his next intake of breath, he snarls, "Red's kid is a fuckin' freak, Drummer. One of those kids who pretends he doesn't know what he is."

"I identify as nonbinary," Zeke puts in calmly.

"And, Petty, your problem is?" Drummer asks impassively, but something in his tone sends shivers down my spine.

"It's not fuckin' normal. Prez brings his kid into the club and we'll all—"

"What? Become infected?" Drummer pause then says, "How old are you, Zeke?"

"Fifteen, sir."

Drummer goes silent. "It's a different world we're living in, Petty. I've got two boys, Eli and Zane. Hell knows what's in their future and guess I won't find out for a long time. But whatever they want to be, I'll fuckin' support them. And probably like Red, I'd go to the fuckin' ends of the earth for them and kill any man who showed them disrespect. So no, unless there's a change in your attitude, I'm not going to tell the women to let you loose. Seems you could use some thinking time."

Petty's voice turns into a wail. "I've been here for hours, Drum. No one's coming back. I've…" He obviously thinks better of what he was going to say.

But Zeke steps up. "He's pissed himself."

Drummer snorts, then says, "Hold on, I've got something coming in on another line."

He goes quiet for a bit, then says, "Mouse has got info about a Vegas casino's cash deposits going amiss. Petty, you know anything about it?"

Petty stops glaring at Zeke, and stares at the phone I'm still holding. "We do security for the Lucky Fortunes. Tonight, we were asked to guard the money going into the truck. Red and Keys had some suspicions so refused to touch the money or the bags it was in. From what I gather, there's been a heist and fingers have pointed our way. It's a total setup, Drum."

"Cher, Rosa?"

"We're here," I tell him.

"I'm getting some boys together. We'll be in Vegas in the morning. In the meantime, I'll get a lawyer—"

"Already done that."

"That's good. I'll get in touch with Utah and see if they can do some digging."

"Keys has already contacted them," Petty puts in.

"Okay." Again, Drummer goes quiet. "Right. We've got an

unprotected clubhouse. I presume the prospects were taken as well?"

"Everyone." Rosa's voice breaks as if now someone else is taking charge, she's not so in control of herself.

"Petty, much as I hate to put a homophobic, transphobic and whatever else phobic dick like you in charge, you are the only member we've got there. Get yourself cleaned up and contact the lawyer to see what the police have got. But, Petty, I'll be asking Zeke and Cher whether you've been polite to them, and if they give me one sign you have not, you're a dead fuckin' man, you hear me? And don't expect a merciful shot to the head." He pauses, then chuckles, but it's cold and in no way merry. "Oh, and I'll be sending Lady and Joker across. And let me tell you, I don't take kindly to any of my boys being insulted." I notice Petty's face has gone white. But Drummer hasn't finished. "And if Red wants to complete what he started, I'll be there to back him up. You're on borrowed time, Brother. If you want to make amends, you'd best make the best use of it."

And that's it, he's gone.

Rosa stares at Petty for a moment, then calmly walks around to the bench and takes off a key. She unlocks the handcuffs holding his hands behind his back, then with a knife she'd also picked up, saws through the ropes.

I'd expected Petty to smirk and jump up immediately, but instead he groans, and seems unable to move his arms. Zeke goes behind him and starts massaging his shoulders, then running their hands up and down from wrist to elbow, then biceps. Petty freezes.

Zeke's unperturbed. "I know what it feels like. Some boys jumped me and tied me in a closet for hours. When the teachers released me, I couldn't move my arms."

"Zeke?" I ask in horror, not having heard this story before. The look they send me shows me they don't tell me everything.

Petty slowly turns his head to meet Zeke's eyes. "They did that?" Experimentally, he moves his arms and manages to bring them around in front of him. He then takes over his own massage, getting the blood flowing again.

"Yeah," Zeke answers him with a challenge in their eyes. "Because I'm different." Zeke holds Petty's gaze. "I don't know why you think I'm such a threat to you. I assure you, I don't want to fuck you."

I gasp at Zeke's crude words.

"You fuck with my head," Petty murmurs, looking away from Zeke's gaze. Then, as he groans and gets to his feet, Zeke nimbly steps away. Noticing they've put themself out of reach, Petty narrows his eyes. "I wouldn't hurt you, kid."

Zeke shrugs. "Words hurt bad enough. Trying to split me up from my dad? Yeah, that's pretty damn painful."

"Kid, I wish someone had taken me from a certain person in my life."

My head snaps around. Seeing Petty's mouth snap shut, I don't believe he meant those words to escape.

My feelings are confirmed when his face changes completely. He steps forward and takes his phone from my hands. "I'm just going to take a quick shower and get some fresh clothes, then I'll ring the lawyer. You going to be sticking around?"

CHAPTER TWENTY-SIX

CHER

While I'm not comfortable being dependent on any man, I do feel some measure of relief that someone who actually knows about the club and what they're doing is taking control. Even if it is Petty who's so obviously an asshole.

When he reappears, his hair is damp and he's in a fresh pair of jeans. I worried Petty might take his predicament out on Zeke. After all, if it wasn't for Zeke, Red wouldn't have needed to tie him to that chair. That Red is so protective about his child fills me with warmth, but that Petty might take retribution fills me with dread. I hoped he'd realise that if he hadn't been kept captive, he'd be locked up just like the others.

But whether he's taken Drummer's warning to heart or whether the club's problem takes precedence over any of his personal concerns, he doesn't say a word when he indicates Rosa, Tiff and I should sit at a table, and Zeke joins us.

Petty pulls out a chair for himself. "I've called the lawyer," he starts, his hands pushing back through his hair. "The cops haven't really got anything to hold them on. There's only the word of the guards who were jumped, both of whom are still alive, but pretty banged up. One swears he saw the men wearing Satan's Devils' cuts."

"What does this other guy say?" Rosa asks.

"Not much with his jaw wired shut." To his credit, Petty grimaces. "I can't see what else they've got. It's a fact that members of the club were at the casino when the money was loaded onto the truck, but Red made sure there was no fingerprint evidence or DNA as they didn't touch the bags. Oh, and where the truck was found, there was evidence of motorcycle tracks. But only four."

"So, it was stopped by men on motorbikes," I comment.

Petty widens his eyes. "Have you seen an armoured truck? That thing can withstand bullets and could easily mow a bike down. Hard to imagine how just four bikes could make it stop."

"Unless they were blocking the road, as if one had come off. They might have stopped if they thought there'd been an accident." Zeke's looking thoughtful.

Petty even gives Zeke a quick glance. "Good thinking, kid. But even then, they'd have instructions to report it in and drive around. If they were legit, it wouldn't be their first rodeo. Those guys are trained to look out for fake hazards."

"Unless it was." I'm thinking aloud. "What if they were inexperienced?"

"Or what?" Petty asks. "If the guards were in on it?"

I think it doubtful. "They got injured and badly by the sounds of it."

Rosa sits forward. "It was clearly a setup to trap the Satan's Devils. We know the club had nothing to do with it. Rather than focusing on logistics, shouldn't we be asking who and why?"

"The casino was behind it." Maybe it's my recent experience, but their employment practices aren't fair. I was proved innocent but lost my job all the same. I've no love for that company or those who run it.

"But why?" Rosa asks. "They gave the club the contract. Why do that if they didn't trust them?"

Petty shrugs. He's got no answer for that. But the way he raises his chin at me suggests he's on my wavelength.

Zeke gets up and starts pacing. "It's as if someone has a vendetta against them. First there was Mom, now the whole club. Who's got it in for the Satan's Devils?"

Petty tilts his head to the side and views Zeke intently. "Your mom had nothing to do with this. No one knew her connection to Red at that time. Well, I certainly didn't."

"They didn't," I confirm. "We know who set me up, and that was a woman whose kid is at Zeke's school." I think for a moment, then add, "But she does work at the casino and could have seen he was interested in me. It wasn't club related at all. She was like you, Petty, someone who didn't like who Zeke is. And she certainly didn't want them in the same school as her child."

"I'm not contagious." Zeke snorts.

"And she's crazy if she thinks Zeke can influence her son. Make him something he isn't," I add.

"Maybe she's worried about other kids as well," Petty states. "Bad things can happen if boys are allowed into the girls bathroom."

Zeke snorts. "You obviously don't know how this shit works, Petty. How many women have you molested?"

"I-what?" he blusters clearly shocked. "None!"

Zeke stares him in the eye. "But you've got a dick. If you strolled into a women's bathroom, they clearly wouldn't be safe."

Petty thumps his hand down on the table. His phone wobbles and threatens to fall off. He catches it, then retorts, "I wouldn't go near a fuckin' woman who didn't want it."

Zeke returns to the table, pulling out a chair, turns it around and straddles it. "So why assume someone transgender or nonbinary has less control of themself than you do?"

"Because they're lying to get what they want." Petty's fast with his response.

Zeke has inherited their dad's temper, though it's normally under control. Their face now flushes red, making their freckles almost glow. "So, I claim to be nonbinary. I spend every day of my life being judged and abused, just so I can jump on some unsuspecting pussy in a bathroom?" Petty blanches, taken by surprise at Zeke's sudden burst of rage. "Do you know how many examples there are of sexual abuse committed by transgender people in bathrooms?" When Petty doesn't reply, Zeke forcefully asks again, "Well, do you?"

Their loud voice makes Petty shake his head, admitting his ignorance.

"Zero. Okay? Fuckin' zero." Zeke slams their palm down on the table, then takes a deep breath and shudders as they calm themself down. "But abuse toward transgenders using the bathroom that reflects their sex at birth, well, that happens almost daily." Zeke's voice lowers, but their sadness shows. "I can't even use a public bathroom without the risk of being accosted, threatened, or subjected to verbal abuse."

I don't know the effect it has on Petty, but I hate hearing Zeke describe the circumstances which I already know. It hurts me down to the soul to know how difficult life is for them. Oh, I know changes are coming, but they seem to be too slow. And rather than accepting the small progress made to accommodate Zeke and the hundreds, thousands, maybe millions of people who are of the LGTBQ+ persuasion, the general public resents them. Non-gendered bathrooms, being able to choose a non-specific sexual description on government forms, is not accepted, and is frowned upon.

I don't know why. Sexual fluidity is not a new concept. People of different genders and persuasions have existed all through time. It's only during the last few centuries cisgender people, those whose gender identity conforms to the sexual organs they have at birth, seem to have become more worried about accepting that there are other types around.

But then folks are threatened by so many things—people whose skin is a different colour or who don't speak the same language, or even those who have a disability. Discrimination is everywhere, even within the same race.

I don't know what impact Zeke's speech has had on Petty, or whether it's done anything to change his mind, but I'm inclined to think not.

Rosa's been watching the back-and-forth between them like a spectator at a tennis match. She breaks the silence by changing the topic and getting us back on track. "How are we going to get Red and the boys out? That's what we're supposed to be talking about."

Petty visibly relaxes now he can move on to a safer subject. "Nothing except to dismiss that Cher's arrest and the club's is linked." He rubs his hands over his face, scrubbing at his eyes. "Look, it's late, or early, whichever way you look at it. Drummer won't be here for hours, and the lawyer's gone home for the night. There's no more to be done until the morning, so I suggest we all get our heads down."

But I'm too worried to sleep. "Rosa told me about RICO." I bite my lip. "Is this going to be enough to take the club down?"

Petty's eyes meet mine and now there's a hint of sympathy in them. "If they can find sufficient evidence to link them to the crime, it might." Then his large hand comes to rest on mine, and much as I dislike the man, I don't shake it off. "But the evidence isn't there, Cher. That's what we've got to hold on to. Soon as the cops figure that out, Prez and the boys will be home."

"Petty's right," Rosa states firmly. "We all need to get some rest. You and Zeke take Red's suite. I'll find another that looks clean enough. We'll sleep on it, get up our strength to face what the morning brings. There's nothing more we can do now."

It feels wrong for Zeke and me to share Red's bed with him being in jail. Zeke falls asleep fast, but I lie awake, trying not to toss and turn so as not to disturb my child. Having so recently myself been a guest of the law, I'm under no illusions as to what Red's going through. He's probably got the same emotions—

hope that he'll soon be out, and dread that whoever had set them up could have done their job too well.

I can only hope Drummer has some ideas when he arrives in the morning.

At last, I must fall asleep, and am woken by Zeke stirring. Feeling I've had no rest at all, I groan. "What's the time?"

"Six." Zeke pulls on the pants they'd slipped off the night before. "I think someone's arrived. I heard something downstairs,"

It's far too early for the Arizona club to have completed the journey. I'd estimated it would take them at least eight hours. But Zeke's right, I can definitely hear male voices downstairs.

This can't be good. We should have gone home last night, I think to myself, worried it might be the cops coming back with a search warrant. Or worse, could it be another motorcycle club or gang, seeing the clubhouse empty and stepping in to take over?

Trying not to let the worry show on my face, I throw back the covers and get out of bed, hastily visiting the adjoining bath-room to splash my face and apply toothpaste with my finger to my teeth.

"Stay here," I warn Zeke. "Let me go check it out."

"Mom—"

"No, Zeke. Obey me now." I accompany my words with my best mom glare.

Then, I go to the door and open it as quietly as I can. As I creep along the corridor, I hear multiple voices, but not those I'd associate with the law. The clinking of bottles and glasses also reaches my ears. Cautiously, I proceed down the stairs, pausing when I can see what's going on. A man's back is turned toward me.

I sigh with relief when I see the Satan's Devils' patch on the cut that he's wearing.

Hearing a noise behind me, I turn and see Zeke who's certainly not obeyed me. Sighing, I beckon them to join me, and slowly together, we complete our descent of the stairs. When we reach the bottom, I notice Petty. He's certainly not looking as though the other men shouldn't be there, but I do notice he's not entirely comfortable, as though he's out of his depth.

As if sensing our presence, several pairs of male eyes turn in our direction. A man, slightly older than the others, his greying hair betraying he's at least in his fifties, takes a few steps toward me.

"Cheryl Samson, I presume." He holds out his hand.

Automatically, I take the offered hand and shake it. He has the air of authority as though he's in charge.

"Drummer?" I query, even though I'd previously dismissed that as unlikely. But I've noticed this man has a patch on his cut denoting he is a president.

He gives a short laugh and shakes his head. "Name's Snatcher. I lead the Utah chapter, and these are some of my men. We flew in last night."

"Flew?" I must still be tired as I ask to clarify, "In a plane?"

He snorts. "Well, our bikes don't have wings, darlin'." His offhand comment leaves me reeling. The Satan's Devils have a private plane? Without offering more information, he draws me forward. "This is Preacher, our sergeant-at-arms-come-pilot. This is Stormy, and next to him is Bolt." The three men give me chin lifts. "Thor, my VP, is trying to scrounge up some food in the kitchen."

Which tells me Rosa's not up and about yet.

"And this must be Zeke." Snatcher again reaches out his hand.

"You seem to know a lot about us," I tell him, my eyes narrowing.

He grins widely. "Oh, I probably know more about you than you do yourself. There's not much my team and I can't find out. And, of course, we've been working with Keys to get to the bottom of what went on with that trouble you had with the casino."

I'm not sure I approve of him delving into my past, but if

he'd helped prove my innocence, then I haven't much ground to complain.

"Are you going to be able to get my dad free?" It's Zeke who asks the obvious question.

"I sure hope so, kid," Snatcher tells them.

"How come you're here?" I ask, still trying to gather my wits about me.

"You rightly called Drummer, he called me. Keys had already asked us to look into some shit. In fact, we were planning to enlighten Red this morning. Told Drum we'd be able to get here fast, so," he waves his hands with a flourish, "here we are."

"Why didn't anyone wake me?" Rosa appears, hurrying down the stairs. "Snatcher, welcome to you. You want breakfast?"

"That would be great, darlin'." Snatcher greets her warmly, planting a chaste kiss to her cheek. "Thor's got some coffee on, but one of your fry-ups would be most welcome."

"Zeke, you can come help me." Rosa beckons to them as she walks off.

I stay where I am, wanting to get more information. "What do you know about why Red's club has been arrested?"

Snatcher looks at me, and his eyes soften. "You're Red's ol' lady, huh?"

"Apparently." I shrug.

"Then you're well aware of the term club business?"

I start to seethe. Yes, I do, and I already hate it. I know it means he's not going to tell me a damn thing. "I don't see why you can't tell me. I've a right to know whether my man's going to get out."

"Oh, he'll get out, okay. We gave the lawyer some information last night, and the cops no longer have a valid reason to hold them." Snatcher's comment delivered in such an offhand way takes a moment to sink in.

When it does, my heart skips a beat. "Really?"

"Yup." He grins. "They should be getting out any time now."

CHAPTER TWENTY-SEVEN

RED

I don't think there's any biker club prez who wouldn't feel the bottom drop out of his soul when the word RICO is used in association with their club. That the MC is completely innocent of any wrongdoing doesn't count for shit when the feds have got you in their sights. We might be mainly legit, our businesses clean, but whether for envy of our lifestyle or that we live our lives without giving a damn, every MC is seen as a target to be taken down.

I try to be upbeat when I'm led into the police station along with the rest of the club, giving off a vibe of confidence to my brothers while there's dread in my heart. Whether evidence is fabricated or not, the prejudice against us might mean we'll still go down whether guilty or innocent.

If anything is made to stick, I, Crash, Indian, Twister and Fox at least are looking at twenty years behind bars. If they really go to town, the rest of the members might be faced with similar stretches as well.

Why hadn't I paid more attention to what Keys had said? Why was I so swept along by the promise of a lucrative contract with the casino?

Because I was lured by the idea of respectability for the club. Something I should have shied away from.

"You doing okay?"

There aren't enough cells to hold us separately in this jail, so once we were questioned, we've been put into groups. In answer to Crash's question, I just raise an eyebrow.

His face twists, suggesting he's doing about as well as himself. Twister's rhythmically banging his head against the wall, not hard enough to bruise, but enough to show his frustration. In a peculiar grouping, Owl is also in the same cell, and he's just sitting, looking bemused. Every now and again, he takes off his glasses and polishes them as if giving his hands something to do.

Cobra has his head in his hands with an air of defeat about him.

I've let these men down.

"It doesn't stack up, Prez. They can't hold us."

While I dip and rise my head acknowledging Crash's point, I also know that once bikers are arrested, it's hard to get out. Every part of our businesses is likely to be scrutinised, and I wouldn't put it past the feds to make up a case against us, even if the current one doesn't stack up.

Turning, I slam my fist against the wall. *Why the fuck has this happened now? Why, when I've just found my old lady? Why have the fates conspired to put a family in my sights, only to rip us apart?*

Me getting locked up is hardly likely to improve Cher's view of the club. Will she ever believe my innocence? Will I ever get a chance to know my child? Or am I destined only to ever see them, wearing orange and behind bars?

Fuck, Zeke has already had a hard life, and in today's world, it's not going to get any easier. I wanted to be there by their side, helping them, protecting them, doing what I can to smooth their path.

I'm already so fucking proud of them for taking a stand on who they are, and not conforming to society's expectations. I admire Cher so much for supporting Zeke, and not giving into temptation to insist on a gender identity for the sake of making her life easier.

I fucking wish I'd been there from the start. Now it looks like I'm not going to be there for anything.

The precinct outside of the cell area went silent some time ago. The drunk tank, though, is full. The sound of drunken complaints and the stench of vomiting reach me. In defiance of expectation, the other cells full of my brothers are relatively quiet. They know there's no point in protesting anything.

"Petty's not here," Crash again remarks. It's not the first time he's reminded me.

I only feel a twinge of guilt that I left him tied up. In view of the way he'd been treating my kid, he deserves everything. But I know that's not what's on Crash's mind. We'd been over this earlier, and the implications are so dire, I prefer not to think about it.

"If he betrayed us, he's a dead man." Crash's comment has caught Twister's attention. "They must have fuckin' searched the place, so there's only one reason why he's not here with us."

"They rounded us up," I tell him again. "They didn't check names. With us and the prospects, they must have thought they had everybody."

But Twister and Crash have ideas of their own. "Or Petty's fuckin' working with them, Prez. Working to bring us the fuck down." Twister states and Crash glares in agreement.

"He patched in," I tell them as I have a few times before. "What fuckin' reason would he have to betray us?"

Crash shrugs. "Satan's Devils are inclusive and he's a transphobic, homophobic, misogynistic, racist motherfucker. Maybe that was enough for him."

Yeah, since Petty joined, Joker and Lady have come out as gay, and Utah has a female enforcer. San Diego has a couple of black members. But surely, if a man didn't like the rules of the club, wouldn't he just leave it? Destroying it seems like too much of a retribution. A rather drastic way of avoiding a beatdown.

"I want more proof against Petty before I condemn him," I say sternly. "For all we know, he's still in the basement."

"I can't forget Skull." Crash clenches his jaw. "Petty could be a fed playing a long game."

While I think that's unlikely, I can't dismiss it.

Thankfully, Twister decides to lighten the conversation. "Cher did good getting Jeeves on board. That was quick thinking."

It's the one thought that's made me smile tonight. Cher must have been shocked out of her head to see a SWAT team arrive, but she'd gone straight to the lawyer who's since been working his ass off on our behalf, insisting on being present in all of our interviews.

By the time I'd managed to have a word with him and asked him to contact Drummer urgently, it had turned out Cher had taken care of that too. She's done everything I could ask of my old lady.

The night rolls on. Leaning back against the wall, I close my eyes, but get no other rest at all. I'm responsible for all the men who I've ridden beside, and whatever happens lands on my shoulders.

What should I have done? Where did I fuck up? What do I do? For now, we're relatively safe, but should we get sent to a penitentiary, all bets are off.

Will any of us be alive in twenty years' time?

Morning arrives. The drunk tank is emptied, and the smell of piss and vomit are replaced by the slightly pleasanter scent of disinfectant.

"Here we go again," Crash remarks, getting up and standing by my side at the bars as the sound of a door opening reaches us.

"Just keep practicing 'no comment'," Twister, joining us, states drily.

But the man leading the police officers down the hall is not who I expect. It's Jeeves. He stops in front of my cell and steps back so the cop can open the door.

When I catch his eye, he smirks. "You're free to go."

I raise an eyebrow but say nothing at all. Around me, brothers are starting to pipe up, but I signal them to stay cool. No fucking point annoying the cops when I can already taste freedom in the air.

In fact, I prefer to remain silent as my personal effects are taken out of the plastic bag and returned to me. I hold back, even when I could walk out the door, until I'm certain every one of my brothers is free.

When I at last get my first breath of fresh air, breathing it in and holding it deep into my lungs, I put my hands on my waist and bend at the knees, almost feeling weak with relief. When I raise my head, the first sight I see is Drummer and Snatcher approaching me.

As I start to grin, Drummer shakes his head. "Always knew there'd come a time when we'd have to bail Vegas out. Just didn't realise it would be literally."

I snort, and it's reference to the times we've ridden to help the other clubs out. I straighten, and go straight for the mother chapter prez, being enveloped in his arms immediately. We slap each other's backs, then smartly step apart. "I owe you one, Drum." My voice sounds husky.

"Nah, brother, you don't owe me. You've always had the other chapters' backs. And anyway, I did shit. Snatcher here proved your innocence."

"Snatch," I say, respectfully, then am subjected to the same rib-rushing hug that Drummer had just given me. "What can I say?" I add, when at last I can breathe again.

"Nothing here," Drum says fast, jerking his head to the transport waiting behind. I realise it's the club's two SUVs and the crash truck. Behind the wheels are Wraith, Bolt and Joker. And behind them, a car, the driver standing beside it, her hand lifting in a small, unsure, wave toward me. *It's Cher.*

I resist the urge to run straight over to her, and pause to say,

"We'll talk at the clubhouse." When I get the confirmatory chin lift from Drummer, I turn to Crash. "Get everyone home."

"Go get your woman, Prez." He grins at me.

I don't know what Cher was expecting when I approach her at a fast pace, but she doesn't seem surprised when I curl my hand around her nape and bring her face to me. Crashing my lips down on hers, I ravish her mouth as though my life depends on it.

I probably wouldn't have let her up for air any time soon had not a clearing of a throat made me aware that we weren't alone.

Reluctantly, I force myself away, and glance at Zeke. Releasing one arm, I reach out and pull them in. For a moment, the three of us stand there, while I relish in having my family together again. *There was a moment there when I thought I'd never see them outside of a prison again.*

The blast of a horn gets me turning, and I see Wraith gesturing. I give him the finger but acknowledge his non-verbal communication. *Time to get moving.*

Releasing Cher and Zeke, I go to the driver's door. Cher rolls her eyes.

"You're such a man."

"*Your* man," I tell her unapologetically. "Come on, let's get going."

While Zeke's getting settled in the back, and Cher's buckling her seat belt next to me, I push back the seat as far as it will go and alter the mirrors. When we're all set, I start the engine, eager to leave the precinct in my rearview.

Then I give a sideways glance at her. "Thanks for not running out on me." Her slight grimace suggests for a moment she'd been going to do just that. "And thanks for getting a lawyer and contacting Drummer."

"What else could I do, Red?" She bites her lip. "After what happened to me, I couldn't leave you if it was a wrongful arrest."

"I'm so happy you're free, Dad." Zeke can't be happier

than me.

"Thank fuck Rosa had Drummer's number."

"She didn't," Cher tells me. "And when we got it, she said it wasn't her place to speak to Drummer. She made me talk to him as I'm apparently your ol' lady."

I risk another glance at her. "And are you?"

Her lips press together. "I think we've got a lot to talk about."

"Petty had Drummer's number." It's Zeke who informs me.

"You found Petty?" *Oh fuck no.* If Cher knows I use the basement as a torture chamber, she'll never want to be with me. On the other hand, I'm filled with relief. If Petty remained where I left him, he obviously had nothing to do with this. Clearly, being tied to a chair in a soundproofed room had a lot to do with him not being arrested.

"Petty was, um, interesting." There's a lightness in Cher's tone which surprises me.

I ask sharply, "He tell you why he was there?"

"Sure." Zeke snorts from the back seat. "I set him right on a few things, Dad."

"You released him?" Petty has obviously not physically hurt my child, so I'm not certain they'd freed him. I'm not sure how far I'd trust him.

"We threatened to leave him there unless he watched his mouth. He'd wet himself, Dad." Zeke sounds amused. "We freed him as Drummer told him he'd let a man called Blade at him if he didn't behave himself."

A snort escapes me. Yeah, threatening to let Blade loose would have certainly made Petty compliant. Twister's good, but Blade's in a whole different league.

Cher doesn't seem quite so impressed. "Were you really going to torture him, Red?"

Of course, I fucking was. "He disrespected you, Cher. He had to learn a lesson."

As far as I'm concerned, he's still got one to learn. Unless he's changed his outlook on life, which I think is unlikely.

"You know anything about what happened to get us released?" I doubt she does, but it doesn't hurt asking. And hopefully, my question gets us off the subject of why I was going to torture a man in our basement.

"No. I don't know how you got out." Cher purses her lips. "Snatcher arrived and said it was club business. Then Drummer came and said the same thing."

"At this point, Cher, I know no more than you," I tell her, honestly. "All I know is that the club did nothing that it was accused of. I take it Snatcher could prove that."

"Snatcher's club sounds interesting," she comments.

She's not wrong. I may have my differences with Snatcher, seeing as he lied to us for years, but it seems I'll have to forgive him if he's cleared our name.

I pull into the clubhouse parking lot, which for a while I'd wondered whether I'd ever see again. When I turn off the engine, Zeke gets out of the back seat, slamming the door behind them, bouncing back with the resilience of youth, while I just sit there for a moment getting my bearings.

"Your basement is an interesting place," Cher comments softly. As I turn to her, I'm worried she's going to say she can't be with a man who leaves instruments of torture out on a bench and a restrained man waiting for them to be used on him. But instead, I see there's an odd look on her face, and a flush to her cheeks that I can't interpret. Though it falls into place when she adds, "I mean, some of it looks quite interesting."

Again, I curl my hand around the back of her neck, holding her by the nape. "You see anything that appeals to you, Cher?"

She sounds a little breathless. "Er, maybe?"

"Well, if you agree to being my ol' lady, Cher, I think it's only right that I give you a personal tour of everything the club has to offer. You know, all the facilities." I wink.

If there's anything that can top the euphoria I'd felt at being released, the thought of Cher in the club's basement at my mercy certainly comes close.

CHAPTER TWENTY-EIGHT

RED

While Cher blushes and seems intrigued by my offer, she doesn't commit to being my old lady, and after everything that's happened, I can't really blame her. Yet I walk into the clubhouse with my arm tight around her. Though our innocence would have eventually come out, her quick thinking in instructing Jeeves and contacting Drummer had facilitated our early release. I couldn't ask more of a first old lady than that.

I'm tired as fuck. I want nothing more than to drop into my bed, fuck my woman and then sleep for hours, but there's no immediate chance of that. I straighten my back and put my wants and desires on the back burner as I watch my brothers getting bottles of much-needed beer into their hands.

Welcome smells of cooking are already coming from the kitchen, and I know most of us must be starving. Jail catering leaves a lot to be desired.

Still unwilling to let Cher stray from my side, I greet Wraith, Joker, Lady and Peg one-handedly, then do the same to Bolt and Preacher, then with a little reluctance and a warning he's still not completely off my shit list yet, to Stormy.

"We need a sit-down," Drummer informs me.

"Everyone, or officers?"

"Everyone," he clarifies. "I think Snatcher's got information that will interest all of you."

I glance around, noticing Titch rubbing his back. A night in the cells must have played havoc with the old man's muscles. "Let them eat and drink for a bit first."

Drummer aligns his line of sight with mine, then meets my eyes and raises his chin. "Sure thing."

Rosa comes bustling out of the kitchen, heading straight for us. She gives me a smile that shows she's pleased to see me home, but that doesn't soften the frown on her face. "Cher, can you go help Tiff in the kitchen? Jemima just rang. I think she's had enough of Trist and Tom, so I'm going to have to go get them."

It's selfish, but I don't want Cher to leave my side, not until I have to. "Can't someone else go, Rosa?"

"All you guys and the prospects have only just gotten back. It's not fair to send them back out."

She's right. But looking around, I spy someone who has been here all night. The man who won't meet my eye.

"Petty!" I roar, getting his attention fast. "Got a job for you."

He comes across at a pace. "Go get Trist and Tom from the address Rosa will give you."

Petty stiffens and his eyes narrow. "I thought you wanted us around the table, Prez."

Hissing, I step closer to him. "You're fuckin' lucky I've not stripped the patch from your back," I remind him. "In fact, the fuckin' jury's still out on whether you're going to keep it or not."

As he opens his mouth, Drummer comes up to stand next to me. Petty snaps his lips back together.

"Anyway, you'll probably be back before church starts." I soften the blow because much as I dislike it, he currently wears the patch.

As he turns away grumbling, "I'm being treated like a fuckin' prospect now," I hear Drummer's low growl beside me.

"Dad?" Another voice gets me spinning around. Despite the

late night and the lack of sleep, Zeke has bounced back fast. *Oh to be young again.* When I tilt my head, they grin at me. "Can I go with Petty to get Trist and Tom?"

"They'll be here soon enough."

As his face falls, Drummer nudges me in the side. When I turn to him, he leans his head toward mine and speaks softly. "Kid's got currency and he wants to use it." At my perplexed look, he continues with a short, barked laugh. "One upmanship. The twins know fuck all about what went on last night and your kid wants to be the first to update them."

Canny fucker. Snorting loudly, I call Petty back. "Hey, take Zeke with you."

"What the fuck?"

As those words leave his mouth and I'm wondering whether it was such a good idea to ask him, Drummer emits a snarl.

"You want me to get Blade to Vegas?" Petty's face literally goes white. "You take your prez's kid and make sure they come back with not one hair on their head harmed. You feel me, man?"

I notice the omission of the honorific, *Brother*, and it occurs to me Drummer and Petty have already had words. Whatever had passed between them works, as Petty calls out to Rosa to give him the address, and then waves Zeke over to join him.

"You sure that's a good idea, Red?" Cher comes running over, looking up at me anxiously as the front door closes behind them. "He and Zeke don't exactly get along."

Drummer answers for me. "Petty's got too much to lose to risk hurting your son, darlin'. And that includes using words."

"Zeke didn't seem worried going off with him," I observe.

She grimaces. "Petty's got issues, and for some reason, Zeke brings them out. But Zeke's got a thick skin. They had to grow one."

That makes me fucking sad. I vow from now on, I'll be in their life. And no one, least of all Petty, will be allowed to insult them.

It was the right decision to keep Rosa here. The men from Utah and Tucson, and me and my brothers who'd been locked up all night, are ravenously hungry. Rosa's been feeding her boys for a very long time, and copes with a few more without blinking. Soon she has a kind of assembly line set up. Tiff and the sweet butts are keeping the coffee going, and Owl's behind the bar, topping up drinks for those who want something stronger.

When the last plate is scraped clean and the last coffee cup empty, I whistle loudly. "Brothers to the meeting room now."

"You going to let me in on what's going on?" Cher asks me, her lips pressing together.

I pinch the bridge of my nose. "I'll tell you what I can later, darlin'." It's all the promise I can give her, especially as, right now, I don't know everything myself.

To her credit, she accepts my limited offer with the narrowing of her eyes her only complaint and walks away to help Rosa and the women clean up.

For the first time since I accepted the title of prez, I don't take the seat at the head of the Vegas table, instead that's left for Drummer. I sit to his right, Snatcher to his left. My men shift themselves down, making space for the visiting officers and members, and for a moment, the prospects are kept busy bringing in extra chairs. I've never seen this table so crowded, with men bumping elbows each time they move.

Drummer picks up my gavel and bangs it. "Snatcher's got something you all ought to know," he announces without fanfare.

Snatcher clears his throat as all eyes look toward him. "Keys," he acknowledges my computer guy with a nod, "asked us to look into the background of the owners of the Lucky Fortunes."

Stormy interrupts his prez. "We didn't think it took priority, so I admit, we were slow to get on the case."

Raising his chin at the dark-haired man, Snatcher acknowledges his comment and adds his own apology. "We were some-what tied up in thwarting a kidnapping case. It was an all-hands-on deck situation."

"But you got there eventually," Drummer snaps. "Spit it out, man."

Snatcher sits forward. "The name Keaton Armstrong mean anything to you?"

A low grumble emits from the Vegas members sitting around the table.

"Fuckin' Tide." Titch spits the name as though he's using a swear word.

"Bastard's dead," Twister states.

"He hasn't sat around this table for fuckin' years. Why's his name surfacing now?" Crash asks the question that I want answered.

Snatcher raises his chin when the murmurings begin to pipe down. "His family wasn't happy that he died."

"Family?" Titch is shaking his head. "He never had any that I knew of. Keys?"

Keys shrugs. "None turned up when I looked. Of course, back in the day, my searches were limited."

"Men run from family to the MC," Fox states. "Tide never mentioned anyone close to him, or not that I recall."

Again, Snatcher's chin bobs up and down. "Tide was indeed running from family. He was the black sheep and they disowned him. Doesn't mean they stopped counting him as one of their own, or that they weren't pissed when he was killed."

"You better tell us more about his family," Drummer growls.

Snatcher leans forward and clasps his hands, resting them on the table. "Tide grew up as the adopted son of a moneyed family. They'd taken him in when he was eight years old. It's the old nature or nurture argument—was Tide born bad, or did his circumstances shape him?" The Utah prez shakes his head at his rhetorical question. "Whichever, he threw the chances life had given him away. Instead of appreciating all his new family could offer him, Tide fucked it up. He was in juvie, as you probably found out, Keys. Petty crime, but it brought disgrace on the family. When he was sixteen, he was either kicked out, or left on his own accord."

"You don't know which?" I ask.

"I'd say it was the latter as things have turned out." Snatcher's raised chin accompanies his response.

I'm puzzled. "He came from money, but turned his back on it to join the MC?"

Stormy gestures to Snatcher. When he gets his prez's nod, he takes over. "Tide was set up to go to a good college." At the disbelieving snorts, he sighs. "Yeah, you've probably guessed it. Money was involved. He'd never have qualified by himself."

"So, Daddy paid for him to attend?" Cobra sits back and folds his arms.

Stormy huffs. "Yeah, but it looks like Tide wasn't a fan of work."

"Got that fuckin' right. Lazy bastard." Titch's eyes crease as he remembers. "He was our road captain because the one talent he had was for routes and bikes."

Shadow coughs. "Is that a slur on road captains?"

Joker snorts. "Probably about fuckin' right." Then he and Shadow exchange glances, and Shadow reaches across the table and shares a fist bump with the man he'd taken over from a few years back.

"If Tide had money behind him, why the fuck did he end up robbing a casino?" Hammer asks.

"The thrill, the challenge?" Stormy proposes an explanation. "Or just a plain gambling addiction. He got out of his depth and could only see one way out."

"What you should know," Snatcher takes over again, "is he was no stranger to casinos. His adopted family fuckin' owned one. Maybe he thought by showing they were so easy to rob, he was thumbing his nose at his old man."

"His failed heist must have gone down like a lead fuckin' balloon," my old friend Wraith puts in.

Drummer looks straight at Snatcher and snarls, "Can you get to the fuckin' punchline?"

Completely unperturbed while lesser men would be shaking in their boots, Snatcher gives a twisted grin. "Tide was adopted into a family called Crossman. His younger brother, born after he was adopted, was called Jordan. Ring any bells?"

Bells? It rings a whole fucking belfry.

"Tide didn't use his adopted name," I state, trying to make myself heard over the comments coming from all directions around me.

Snatcher shakes his head. "No, when he left, he wanted to rid himself of that identity. Keaton Armstrong was his birth name."

I drop my head into my hands, then over my knuckles, raise my eyes to meet those of Keys. He was fucking right all along. There was something suspicious about us being given work at the casino. It was a setup from the start, and I didn't fuckin' see it. It's not hard to join the dots and wonder why. Crossman clearly thought we had something to do with Tide's death in prison.

Turning my face, I address the man by my side. "You want my patch, Drum?"

His fist slams down on the table so hard the rest of the table goes silent as he yells, "What are you fuckin' talking about?"

"I should have looked deeper. I should have known—"

"How the fuck could you?" Surprisingly, it's Stormy who jumps to my defence. "Keys was the only one who could have warned you, but he wasn't able to dig deep enough. Without knowing Tide's connection to the principal owner of the Lucky Fortunes, there was no way you could have known."

Out of everyone, I never expected it would be the self-confessed asshole who'd be defending me. But his opinion isn't worth anything. It's that of the brothers I ride with which counts.

Crash is looking at me with sympathy. "How the fuck could

you have linked Tide to Crossman, Prez? None of us expected it."

"Tide's been locked up for years, why has this happened now?" Titch stares down the table at Snatcher.

But I can answer that. "Tide died. Perhaps they thought we withdrew his protection."

"He died a fuckin' patch," Hammer contradicts.

Snatcher says calmly, "I suspect Crossman thinks otherwise."

"As for having your patch, Red, you can't blame yourself. You acted on your suspicions as soon as you smelled something off," Drummer states firmly. "With no fingerprints or DNA on the cash, all they had was the injured guard's say-so."

"And how did they get a fuckin' armoured truck to stop?" Sarge asks. "That stinks of a put-up job."

"According to the police reports, Lucky Fortunes employs a minor player in the cash collection security service. A small business with only two trucks, an office in a shared space, and only a handful of guards. It's a legitimate business, but a strange one for a casino to use. The ownership is hard to find under the many layers of corporate bullshit, but when we dug deep enough, at the bottom, we found Crossman."

Once again, I raise my chin to Snatcher for being able to figure that out.

"THAT'S CRAP," Keys states. "The logo on the side was the right one for the Security Corp I thought they were using."

"This logo?" Stormy slides a photo forward.

Keys grabs it first then slides it across the table to me. It's a photo of the truck, obviously taken at the scene where it was supposedly run off the road. In the same cursive script used by the international security firm, the writing on the side reads, *Securecorp.*

"It had decals too," Keys points out. "They're the ones we see all the time around Vegas."

As I take it in, Stormy explains, "I suspect the decals were stuck on to fool you so you wouldn't look closer. When the truck was found, the decals you saw were missing."

"Setting us up seems a hell of a lot of work," I comment, wondering how far back the planning went.

"Maybe it's the only thing that kept Crossman going after the death of his brother," Peg suggests in his gruff voice.

Drummer nods at his sergeant-at-arms. "One thing's for certain, they wanted to destroy the Satan's Devils."

"It was bound to fail." My brow creases.

"Was it?" Drummer asks, his voice deceptively calm. "The guard's identification might not have stood on its own, but if you had handled the money bags, then I don't think you would have gotten out of it. Feds would have leaped at the chance to bring a chapter of the Satan's Devils down. At the end of the day, the guard's loyalty wasn't enough for him to keep to his story. Just so happens, the other, who still has his jaw wired shut, is his brother."

And they probably hadn't signed up to the violence against them being so vicious.

"I want Crossman," Twister snarls. "Here, in my fuckin' hands."

I glance around the table and see no expression that suggests he'll have any opposition. "I think we all do, Brother."

"He's a dead fuckin' man," Drummer agrees amicably. "But any revenge has got to be planned carefully."

CHAPTER TWENTY-NINE

RED

Drummer's one hundred percent correct. After our night spent receiving hospitality from the local cops, I have no doubt there's been, or will be, fed involvement. Left alive, there's the chance Crossman will come after the Devils again, and while I want nothing more than to see him drawing his last breath, his disappearance has to be carefully managed.

I clear my throat. "No one's to go rushing off half-cocked. You hear me?" I give my best president's glare at each of my members.

"He failed once, Prez, he'll try again."

Rope's words are reinforced by utterings from the men around him.

"I'm not disagreeing," I respond. "He must be deranged to take on the Satan's Devils, and we had no fuckin' role in his brother's death though it seems he does believe it."

"We know anything about whether the other partners are involved?" Cuff directs his intelligent question at Snatcher who shakes his head.

"As far as we can tell, they're clean. Crossman put up most of the money for Lucky Fortunes. His parents died a while back and he inherited half of their estate. He sold his holdings in the family casino and moved to Vegas."

"How about we turn up for our shifts as though nothing's happened," Cobra suggests. "Call their bluff."

As I snort, Crash is raising and dipping his head. "Staying away kind of suggests we're guilty."

Drummer's giving a twisted smirk. "You could call Crossman, Red. Put him on the spot. Say the cops released you after making a wrongful arrest and see if he still wants your services."

"Or at least ask to meet him, man-to-man to discuss what happened," Snatcher suggests. "Or approach one of the other partners."

I suppose I can't argue with that logic but going back to the Lucky Fortunes feels a bit like sticking my head into the lion's den.

"I disagree," Indian says, his worried look toward me, showing my sergeant-at-arms has my back. "His plan failed, so we can assume he's now getting desperate. Prez going back there could be asking for a bullet in the head."

Which is clearly a scenario that holds no attraction.

Brushing my hair back from my face, I smother a yawn. Fuck, I'm tired as shit. I'm not even sure my brain is firing on all cylinders. "I want to talk to Crossman, but on my terms, and not at the casino."

"Pick him up from his home?"

"He married?" I query Keys. While it's a good option, I'd prefer no witnesses.

"Yeah. No kids." Stormy seems to have the information at his fingertips.

Suggestions start flowing about where and how to pick him up, but we come to no immediate conclusions. With the conversations circling around, I'm almost pleased when there's an unusual interruption—a knock on the door of our sacrosanct meeting.

Cuff, who's nearest, gets up to open it.

"I need to speak to Red," Owl stutters, shifting from one foot to the other.

With an apologetic look toward Drummer, I wave the prospect inside. "I'm here. What do you want?"

"Um—"

"Spit it the fuck out, Prospect."

"It's Cher and Rosa, they're worrying."

"Fuckin' women," Roller murmurs.

"This something to interrupt our meeting?" Drummer barks, and I swear Owl's on the verge of pissing himself.

"Worrying about what?" I take pity on him. It's not that I'm not concerned about Cher, but I can't think of anything that wouldn't keep until we've finished.

Owl looks like he'd rather be anywhere but here. He takes off his glasses, polishes them on the bottom of his t-shirt, then says hesitantly, "It's just that Petty's not back yet. Cher can't raise Zeke on the phone, and the twins aren't answering."

I swear my heart stops, but it's still pumping sufficient blood around to ask, "They were collected?" I feel heaviness settle in my stomach, a dread that I've never felt before.

Owl vigorously nods his head. "First thing Rosa checked. She rang Simone, the woman the twins stayed with. They left on time. They should have been back long before now."

"I fuckin' knew Petty couldn't be trusted!" Crash roars. "I said that, didn't I, Red? He must be in cahoots with Crossman."

"He wasn't arrested because he was tied up," I rasp back.

"Petty wouldn't betray us. He lives for this club," Roller shouts. "I know him better than anyone."

Drummer bangs the gavel, needing to do so more than once to calm down the uproar. My head's spinning with my fear of anything happening to Zeke, fuck, to any of the kids. The twins are part of the club. They're mine as well.

"This Petty," Drummer starts. "He out for revenge, Red?"

Numbly, I shake my head. *He couldn't be, could he?* Just because he hates what my kid is, he wouldn't harm them, would he? And not Rosa's twins. He's an uncle to them just like me. On top of all that, if he's taken off with them, it's not just his patch I'd be taking, it's his life.

"Can't see it, Drummer." But am I wrong? Could Petty's discriminatory traits be that ingrained? My stomach roils at the thought of a madman having my child in their hands.

My fists clench. I can barely think straight.

"Don't get hung up on Petty." Indian throws a glare toward Crash. "We could be missing the obvious. Crossman tried to get his revenge on the club. What better way than stealing our kids away?"

My eyes snap to him. That makes more sense. My brain's whirring, thoughts tumbling one after another. I've only been a father to Zeke for a short time, and if I've brought this trouble their way, then as a dad, I've failed. My sheer terror at the thought they could be harmed, or worse, makes it impossible for me to think. I can't settle on an action, and for once, I'm glad to have others around to do the thinking for me.

"Stormy?" Snatcher starts.

Stormy holds up his hand. He doesn't need to be told. He shouts at Shadow, "Make, model and license plate of the car Petty was driving." He taps the details onto his laptop as he's told them. Next, he snaps, "And the address where the kids were being collected from?"

Keys tells him and he too starts tapping on his tablet.

Bolt leaves his seat and comes up to lean over Stormy's shoulder. His eyes rise, and it's him who informs us, "Stormy's sending a message to Honor and Duty. They'll start monitoring the traffic cameras and see if they can find them. They'll also be checking the police reports to see if there's been a crash."

Owl's left the door open. Behind him, I can hear Cher shouting my name.

"Go see to your woman," Drummer instructs me.

I'm so fucking torn. I want to be here, talking about a plan of action to find out what's happened to my kid, but Cher needs me, and as a grieving parent, I need her. As much as there's no comfort I can give, I need to go to her. Leaving my seat, I tell them I'll be back immediately.

As soon as I'm outside, Cher's in my arms, shaking like a leaf. Behind her is Rosa who looks completely distraught, her normally tidy hair in disarray from the way she's been raking her fingers through it.

Rosa grabs my arm. "Where are they, Red? Has there been an accident?" she yells at me.

"It's okay." I try to reassure them, feeling none too confident myself. "Petty's with them. He'll keep them safe."

Cher's face turns up to me, tears flowing from her eyes. "What if they can't answer because they've been…" She can't even complete her sentence.

Rosa's frantic. "Could this have anything to do with last night, Red? Is whoever wants to take the club down trying again, this time with our kids?"

To my mind, that's far more likely than an accident which means none of the four could answer their phones.

My jaw clenches as I tell them both, "We're exploring every avenue. I promise you, we'll get the kids back." I've no other choice. Zeke might not have been in my life long, but they've got a place in my heart. I'm not sure I'd survive if I lost them. And if I feel this way, fuck knows what this is doing to Cher and Rosa.

Cher's eyes are blinking rapidly, her breaths coming fast. "You can't promise that, Red."

I grasp her by her nape, holding her tight, trying to inspire her with my confidence. "No one fucks with the Satan's Devils, Cher."

Her eyes blaze. "I want to call the cops."

It's Rosa who contradicts her. "We can't do that. Cops won't do shit." Then her weepy eyes meet mine. "They'll say they've not been missing long enough, that Petty might have stopped to buy them ice cream. Only we know different." She turns to me, and her voice catches. "Red will get them back. He has to. After Brick, they're all I have."

At least Rosa sounds like she's got confidence in me. I hope it's not misplaced. "Did Jemima tell you anything, Rosa? Were they followed when they left?"

She creases her brow. "No. She said everything was normal. Petty was waiting in the car. It was Zeke, or in her words, a boy she didn't recognise, who rang the doorbell. Tom and Trist greeted him then followed him out. The car drove off, and that's all she saw."

I feel a hand on my shoulder. Turning, I see it's Drummer. "Cher, I know you and Rosa want your kids back, and that's just how you should be feeling. But to do that, I need Red so we can try to get some answers. Try to be patient for now."

"Patient?" Cher all but screeches. "Have you got kids, Drummer?"

"Yes," he snaps at her. "Two boys. And if they were gone, I'd be a raging bull wanting to smash doors down to get answers. But even I know that's not the approach that will get the boys back unharmed."

Turning Cher back to face me, I stare into her eyes. "Zeke's *my* kid." I widen my gaze to encompass Rosa. "Trist and Tom are my boys too. I'll do *anything* to get them back safe. Just give me some time."

Cher's face reddens further. "Not good enough, Red. I'm not going to sit and wait while you men talk among yourselves. I'm either going to go to the cops myself or be involved with whatever it is you're going to be talking about. I'm their mom, Red." Her eyes blaze. "I can't sit here and wait without knowing who's got them, and why, and what we're going to do to get them back. I need to be doing something."

Drummer raises an eyebrow at me. "She sounds like my Sam. Doubt she'd be quiet under the circumstances either." He pinches the bridge of his nose, then sighs. "Okay, Cher, Rosa, join us in Red's office."

He walks off. I hold Cher back. "Are you my ol' lady?" I ask her quietly. "Because with some things we're probably going to talk about in there, I need to know I can trust you."

"If you're going to talk about killing the man who dared to take Zeke, then I'll be right beside you. That 'old lady' enough for you?"

I give her a sharp nod. "That'll do. And Cher, believe me when I say there's nothing I won't do to get Zeke back unharmed. I mean it. You hear me? Nothing."

When we reach my office, Drummer's clearly had a change of plan. He waves me on to the meeting room which is emptier than it was before. Snatcher and Thor are still there, as are Wraith, Peg, Joker and Lady. Of the Vegas team, only Indian, Crash, Twister and Fox are in attendance. I note the absence of Keys, Bolt and Stormy.

Drummer again takes my usual chair. I sit next to him, pulling Cher down beside me. Fox waves to Rosa and indicates she should sit next to him.

"Right," Drummer starts. "We're pretty fuckin' sure Petty and the boys have been abducted, and that it has something to do with the failure of what happened yesterday. Which gives us the culprit, a man called Crossman."

"Jordan Crossman?" Cher asks, her brow furrowed. "The casino owner?"

"Yes," I confirm, and then with a look toward Rosa add, "He's Tide's adopted brother."

Rosa starts, her eyes widening. "When is that asshole going to stop bringing the club down? I thought him being dead was the end of it."

Cher looks puzzled. "I don't understand the history, and that can't be important now. But you've got a place to start. I don't understand why you would, but if you think it's him, why don't we just go and find Crossman?"

Drummer gives her an indulgent smile, but his stare is steely when the full force of it lands on me. I lean into Cher.

"Trust us, Cher. We do know what we're doing."

She huffs a little at my veiled hint for her to stay quiet and purses her lips.

"He's got a wife," Keys reminds us. "How about we take her and offer an exchange?"

As again Cher stiffens, I plant my hand on her thigh and squeeze it hard. But it's not me who points out the difficulty.

"Unless it's carefully planned, then you risk being caught kidnapping," Wraith points out. "And with the feds already with eyes on you, you don't want to add that charge."

The door suddenly bursts open without even a courtesy of a knock. Why am I unsurprised when I see it's Stormy? His eyes are wild, though, and he's carrying his laptop in both hands, screen open.

Without so much as a hint of requesting permission, he spits it straight out. "Honor tracked the car Petty was driving through Vegas. It turned onto the main road, then, once out of the urban area, his camera access stopped. Looks like they got close to the clubhouse."

I stand. "Let's get—" Cher's already getting to her feet beside me.

Stormy interrupts, "Some of your boys have already headed out."

At that precise second, my phone vibrates in my pocket. Now with no apology offered from myself, I take it out and answer immediately and put it on speaker.

"What you got, Rope?"

"Prez. The car's here. Petty's been run off the road. He's bleeding pretty badly and unconscious."

I grow cold. "The boys?"

"Gone."

Cher goes white. Rosa gasps and drops her head into her hands, and a wail comes out of her mouth.

"Bring Petty here," I demand.

"He's in pretty bad shape, Prez."

"Right now! I don't care if the fucker dies, but I need to know who's taken the kids. If he goes to the hospital, they could drug him up so he's incapable of speaking, even if he did come around."

"You got a doc you can call?" Drummer asks.

"We've got Preacher." Snatcher shrugs. "He can do a pretty good patch-up job if he needs one."

"Bring him here," I instruct Rope again.

Preacher's already moving. "I'll go meet them to do a quick triage, let you know what you're dealing with, Red."

From how Stormy describes it, Petty was taken only about a mile away. As I put my phone back in my cut and start to think, Cher puts her hands on my arms.

"What are we going to do, Red? Someone's got Zeke, and the twins too." Tears stream from her eyes.

"What we're going to do is think this through." Drummer sounds like he's taking charge. It might be my clubhouse, but I'll be fucked if I give a single damn right now. I'll gratefully be told what to do. "Cher, Rosa, I know what you're going through, but hysterics ain't gonna find anyone."

"I'm not hysterical." Cher pulls away from me and turns on him. "But I want to find my kid."

Drummer's brow rises and seeing it's directed at me as well, I retake my seat, pulling Cher back into the one beside me.

Stormy clears his throat. "Honor and Duty are checking all the vehicles who headed into Vegas at that time. They're also checking the first traffic camera in the opposite direction on the highway. They'll run plates and check names."

"And if they don't find anything?" Rosa asks, patting a tissue to her wet eyes.

"If they haven't backtracked or moved on, then we'll look for places they could hole up in the locality."

"The first traffic camera is ten miles up," Twister informs him.

Stormy jerks his head up and down as if he already knows

this. He taps at his laptop, then his fingers move on the mouse pad. He turns the screen to face us. "If he turned off somewhere before then, it will be somewhere in this vicinity. Somewhere with vehicular access and out of the way."

Crash and Twister stand and go over to study the area he's pointing out. "There's not much out there. It's desert for miles. Unless he's got an ATV, he wouldn't get far."

"I want everything on Crossman." My brain has kicked into gear again. "Any properties he has access to in Vegas and the surroundings. I also want two brothers to go to his home. See if his wife knows anything." Glancing around, I see a nod of approval from Drummer. "Titch and Cuff can go." Both are members less likely to go off half-cocked. Titch has a lifetime of experience behind him, and Cuff, well, his kinky shit has honed an iron-clad dominant's control.

"What can we do?" Cher asks. Her eyes flicker around wildly. "There must be something. I don't understand why we don't call the cops. They could get out there searching."

"Cops can't do shit that we can't," Snatcher tells her firmly. "And that's when they do eventually get off their asses."

"Leave it to us, darlin'." Drummer's gaze softens as he looks at her. "This ain't our first rodeo."

Walking past Cher, Crash puts his hand on her shoulder, and squeezes it lightly. "They won't hurt them, Cher—"

"You don't know that," she interrupts.

"They want the club, darlin," he states, pressing his fingers into her skin lightly again. "They're more likely to use them as leverage."

But over her head his eyes meet mine, and I don't miss what he's signalling. *Taking our kids is a great way to get revenge on us.*

And Crossman is definitely a man looking for retribution.

CHAPTER THIRTY

ZEKE

I knew I was different from an early age. Mom had always had to work to support us, so at only a couple of months old, I was separated from her and enrolled in day care. I didn't mind, I knew nothing different. Maybe it was because I could choose who I wanted to associate with that from an early age all my friends had been girls. Later, at school, I preferred hanging around with them rather than kicking a ball around with the boys.

I was seven when the taunts first reached me. At the time, I wasn't sure what they meant, but other kids saw there was something different about me. It was mainly the boys who, both physically and mentally, bullied me, and deep down I knew I wasn't one of them.

I was eleven when I first tried on gay as a label, but even that didn't make sense. And when I wondered whether I'd have preferred to be born a girl, seeing as I have so much in common with them, I knew that I was happy in the skin that I was in, just mentally I didn't conform to expectations.

When I at last admitted my confusion to my mom, her answers had been to put me in therapy in the hope that I'd figure out where I belonged. Some helped, some definitely did not, but it all helped to focus me. I didn't feel like a boy, nor like a girl. I was me. That's all I wanted to be.

Words like son and boy started to annoy me, but the female alternatives were also not a good fit. When I started to look online and met like-minded folks, I hit on the term nonbinary. It was a revelation, *that was me*. Not gay, not transgender, but an undefined place in between.

When people respect my choice of pronouns, it does something to me. I feel seen, no longer invisible, no longer just an inconvenience to be ignored or made to feel I have no value.

I suppose I'm old for my age, and the internet can be a scary place, but I've read enough to know life won't be easy for me. I'll be victimised, joked about, and if I'm not careful, end up dead in a back alley. And all because I don't fit into someone else's neat little box.

But it's impossible to change what is essentially me.

Finding my dad brought a joy into my life which I didn't expect, and I love how easily he accepted me. Like Mom, I was worried about him being in an MC, but even there, Red had paved the way. Apart from the man currently driving the car, I've felt no real animosity from the other members. There's curiosity, but of course there would be. I'm even curious about myself. I certainly don't understand how I was born to be a misfit in this mainly binary world.

The MC has already given much to me, friends, more than that, champions. This week at school has been the best I've ever experienced, and that's down to the twins sticking up for me.

Would they have been my friends if it hadn't been for Red? I might be naïve, but a part of me thinks they might. I've witnessed them step up for the underdog a few times already, so I think it might be ingrained. They're good people.

I've had friends before, but they've mostly been girls. Tom and Trist are the first totally straight het boys who have befriended me. And I know a way to pay them back, give them a non-sanitised version of what went down in the clubhouse yesterday.

They'll want to hear it from me. Not a polite, *yeah, the club had some trouble, a misunderstanding, but it's fine today,* that I expect they'd get from Red and their mom.

As Petty drives, deliberately not talking to me, I bounce in my seat, full of anticipation, practising what I'm going to say. Last night was the most exciting thing that had happened to me in my life, well, perhaps except for finding my dad. Though it had been terrifying at the time, thinking I'd never see Red again, I had to admit in finding some satisfaction for being part of it, and a sense of the upper hand that Tom and Trist weren't. *They're going to be bummed they missed out.*

And I found Petty in the basement. I snort, remembering the state he was in. I'd have sympathy if it hadn't been he was tied up because he'd been an ass about me. I wished Dad had been there in my earlier days. I could think of a few other people I'd like to receive the same treatment.

Going on, I'll always have my dad there. The thought causes a warm glow inside me.

Glancing to my side, I notice Petty's tense. His knuckles are white as they grip the steering wheel. As the *don't-speak-to-me* vibe comes off him loud and clear, I get that he's resentful for being sent on taxi duty.

Not knowing this part of Vegas, I look in interest as Petty avoids the strip but takes us through some residential areas. When he pulls up outside a white painted single story, at last words come from his lips.

"Go get 'em. And tell them to be quick. I've gotta get back to church." He doesn't look at me, just stares straight ahead.

"Aye, aye, sir," I snap back, giving him a salute as I open my door. I hear his huff as I step out.

The front door opens, and Tom runs out. "Hey, Zeke." Spying the car behind me, he narrows his eyes. "What's Petty doing here? Why isn't it my mom or a prospect?" He looks behind him. "Trist! Something's up."

He got all that from Petty driving the car? Hell, that boy's smart.

"I'll tell you everything. Petty asked that you don't hang around."

"Trist?" Tom shouts to his rear more loudly.

"I… Oh." A frazzled-looking woman has come to the door. She glances at me, then the car waiting. "You know who that is?" she questions Tom. "I was expecting your mom."

"Yeah, that's one of my uncles." The twins speak as one.

As Trist sidles past her, I recognise the look of relief on her face. Guess the twins have been giving her a hard time. I grin at them. When we reach the car, Tom gets into the back seat and pulls me with him. He beckons Trist to slide in as well, and so I sit, sandwiched between them.

"We can talk better like this," Tom explains.

Petty tells us to *belt up*, starts the engine, guns it, then pulls away.

Tom doesn't wait. "Spill everything, Zeke."

So, I do. To their astonishment, which confirms the club doesn't usually have trouble, I tell them all about the raid and how we had to escape through the safe room, the ride in the Jeep and coming back to find Petty.

"Fuck, we miss all the fun," Trist complains.

"Hold it, brother, what happened then?"

"Mom got a lawyer and he got them all out. They'd been set up from what I could gather."

"Who by?" Tom asks, taking the lead again.

I shrug, my gesture acknowledging I have no idea.

"Hey, we got to teach you more of the art of eavesdropping. Behind the bar's a great place to hide." Trist reaches over and fist bumps Tom, while Petty snorts.

I remember something else I'd forgotten. "Oh, and Drummer and Snatcher arrived with their men."

Tom nods wisely. "I've known Drummer all my life, Snatcher too. Not had a lot to do with them, but Dad used to say they run a good crew. How did they know there was trouble?"

"Oh, my mom found Drummer's number and called him. Petty had it."

"How did you escape being rounded up, Petty?" Trist calls out.

I notice the populated streets of Vegas are being left behind us, and we're heading out into the desert now. When Petty grunts and doesn't offer a response, I answer for him, adding in the details I'd omitted in my brief summary.

"We found him tied up in the basement."

Tom snorts. "You what?" Then, showing what a Satan's Devils' kid he is, his eyes narrow. "You on the right side, Petty? Did you betray them?"

"No, I fuckin' did not," Petty snaps, flicking the indicator and passing a slow-moving truck.

"Well, why were you tied up?"

Again, he doesn't answer, but my eyes lighten. "He'd been saying crap about me."

"Petty, you're a fuckin' asshole," Tom informs him.

Petty snarls, "Watch your fuckin' mouth, kid."

Not being one of my favourite people, I decide to tell them everything. With a wicked grin on my face, I inform the twins, "He was in quite a state when we found him."

"Don't you fuckin' dare." Petty takes his eyes off the road and turns to face back as he snarls, "I'm fuckin' warning you, kid."

Undeterred, I state, "He'd wet himself."

Tom and Trist start to howl with laughter, then suddenly there's a loud crunch, and we jerk forward, then are jarred to a stop by the seatbelts. The sound is repeated and this time, we're pushed off the side of the asphalt and into a ditch. We're all screaming as the car rolls and lands on its roof.

For a moment, apart from the engine ticking, there's silence.

"Trist?" Tom's voice sounds shaky. "You okay? Zeke?"

Apart from the fact I'm hanging upside down, I think all my parts are in the right places.

"Fine," I gasp.

"Good," Trist says. "But Petty doesn't look so great."

There's a thump and an ouch as Tom gets his seat belt undone and drops to the roof of the car.

Trist does likewise, cursing as he lands. "Think I've done my arm in."

"I can't undo mine!" I say in horror, as my hands struggle with the lock.

"I got you." Tom takes charge, and soon I'm right way up alongside them.

"Shall we get Petty free?" I'm worried since blood is dripping from him and he's still hanging upside down.

"Let's get out first. It will be easier to hold him from the front," Trist says fast. "Tom, can you open your door? Mine's fucked."

Tom not only tries but gets his door open. I slide out after him, and Trist, supporting one arm, comes after. Now I realise what his urgent tone was for as the truck which ran us off the road has stopped behind us. The man approaching with a gun in his hand looks in no mood to help.

"Shall I put a bullet in the driver's head?" an overexcited female voice asks.

"Don't shoot Petty," I say quickly. "I think he's already dead."

"He's not moving," the female says. Out of the side of my eye, I see her checking the man hanging from the driver's seat.

Don't move, Petty, I silently plead. Hopefully, the fact blood's pouring from him means he's still alive—as long as he doesn't lose too much of it. Still, a bullet will leave him with no chance.

"Who are you?" I ask, wanting to get the focus on us. "Why did you run us off the road?"

The man cocks his head to one side. "What matters is that I

know who you are," he starts, his eyes roving up and down my companions. "You have to be Brick's infamous twins. But you?" His eyes stop on me. "Who are you?"

It seems this distracts the woman from trying to make sure Petty is dead. "Hell, that's the bitch's kid. He's Red's son."

The man's face lights up. "You mean we've got all the Satan's Devils' brats at once? Fuck, my day is made." He gives a delighted snort. "Now the three of you, go get in the back of the truck." He waves his pistol which I don't see how we can argue with. Both of them are armed.

Tom speaks out of the side of his mouth, "We could all make a run for it. Take different directions. They'd only be able to take two of us out."

As I'm thinking I don't much care for those odds, Trist objects. "Even Zeke wouldn't be able to outrun a bullet. And they've got semi's, Bro. How did you miss that?"

"In the truck now." The man glances up the road to where not too far up, the clubhouse lies. "We haven't got much time."

"The driver—?"

"Leave him, Tilly. If he's not dead now, he'll soon bleed out or roast to death under this sun."

I might dislike Petty, but I wouldn't wish that death on anyone. I've already guessed they won't bring him with us, so it's no good us begging for them to save his life, I might as well save my breath.

"Now take out your phones and give them to me."

Faced with the weapons, I do as we're asked. The man powers my phone down.

"I don't have one," Trist starts.

Suddenly, I'm being held with the gun against my temple. Tom and Trist do as they're asked.

I notice the twins seeming to have a silent conversation, but when the barrel of the gun is shoved in my back, I, at least, have no option but to step forward. I wonder if there's any way I could pretend to trip, spin around and get hold of her gun so as to give the twins a chance to get away, but that kind of thing only happens in movies. I'm out of my depth. I've never been kidnapped before. All I know is that I shouldn't get into that truck with strangers, but in the stranger-danger lecture Mom had given me, she'd omitted to give me advice as to what to do when held at gunpoint.

I hear the man shouting at the twins to get moving, then hear a shout of pain from one of them.

"Motherfucker!" Tom shouts the profanity in a way I doubt that his mother would approve of.

"Get in the back." The woman's pistol is used to indicate I should climb up into the back of the truck. It's got panelling and no windows, and a barrier between the rear and the driver.

Seeing no option if I don't want a bullet, I climb inside. Surely, it's better to stay in one piece and wait for the opportunity to escape later.

Apparently, the twins have decided much the same as they docilly climb in after me. The doors are slammed shut and bolted from the outside, then only seconds later, we're moving.

"Now my fuckin' head hurts as well as my arm," Trist complains.

I glance at him, then at Tom who's got blood running from a cut over his eye. "They hit you too?" I ask Trist.

He snorts. "Nah. But, twins." He snorts and glares at his brother.

"Hey, it's not my fault the asshole fuckin' pistol-whipped me. Fuckin' bastard. I'm going to have him."

I state the obvious, "I think it's them who've got us. Now what are we going to do about it?"

I should be scared. I should be petrified. I would be if I were alone. But the twins seem more angry than worried, and I'm picking up my cues from them.

"Red won't let them get away with this," Tom states firmly. "And they won't kill us. Or not immediately."

"Comforting, Bro," Trist states drily. "Very comforting."

CHAPTER THIRTY-ONE

RED

"A truck from the wheelbase," Bolt tells me. "Two sets of footprints. One so large, it's got to be male. One set smaller. Could be another man, or perhaps a woman. Nothing left at the scene, no bullet casings. Some blood on the back seat, but as the car rolled that's not unexpected."

Cher gasps. "They've been hurt?"

I'd be surprised if they'd survived the car rolling without any bumps or scratches, but I refrain from saying that to her. I also try not to show that I'm reeling at the thought of Zeke being in pain.

I force myself to concentrate. "Seatbelts cut or undone?"

Bolt raises his chin at my question. "Not cut."

I smooth my hand over my beard. At least it's likely they got out under their own steam. Or were helped out by persons unknown. *Fuck, Zeke.* I force my parental concern down, knowing I've got to try to be impassive to have any chance of helping them.

Cher's wandered away from me and is now staring down at the unconscious man on the couch. "Can't we wake him up?"

Petty is covered in blood. His nose is broken. Preacher reckons some of his ribs are probably cracked, and there's a large lump on his head which has probably caused a concussion. Hopefully his skull is in one piece.

Going to Cher, I put my arms back around her. She clings to me.

"Throw some cold water on him," Twister suggests.

"You can't do that!" Roller shouts, coming fast to his friend's defence.

Preacher approaches me. I disentangle myself from Cher and follow him into a corner. "If he's fractured his skull, the clubhouse is no place for him. I suggest we give it an hour or so, and if he doesn't come around, take him to a hospital."

There's no censure in his face, but we both know I'm playing with Petty's life here. If he's got internal bleeding or a swelling on his brain, he might need surgery. But it's my kid's life at stake, and my honorary nephews. We need to know what Petty has to say, and as soon as possible. We might not have time to wait until the doctors have treated him. Guiltily, I wonder whether I'd be doing the same if it was another brother instead.

Preacher has done his best for him, but first aid won't do shit if he's been injured too seriously.

"Petty should have picked up a fuckin' tail," I snap, partly to justify my delay in getting medical treatment for him.

Preacher raises his chin as if acknowledging Petty had been less than vigilant, and therefore bears some responsibility for the state he's in, let alone the kids being kidnapped.

My phone rings. "Speak to me."

"We've spoken to Crossman's wife. She knows fuck all, Prez." Titch sounds frustrated. "I mentioned we were friends of Keaton Armstrong, but she showed no recognition of his name. It's possible Crossman never spoke about him. Seems they've not been married that long. When I asked where he'd be now, all she mentioned was the casino."

"Fuck." A dead end. It was to be expected.

"Want us to go to the casino and check? He could be there, especially if he wants an alibi."

It makes sense he wouldn't do his own dirty work. "Yeah, Titch. You and Cuff go there. Just find out if he's put in an appearance. If he's in his office, we've got to find a way to tease him out. I'll want to talk to him, and on my own terms and ground."

"Gotcha, Prez. We'll find out how the land lays and report back."

Ending the call, I shake my head toward Drummer.

A groan suddenly gets my attention. Rushing across the room, I see Petty is stirring. "Back off now, give him some space," I bark, my gaze landing on Cher and Rosa who've stepped forward.

"My fuckin' head," Petty groans and puts his hand gingerly to his temple. "What the fuck happened?"

"That's what I want to know." My voice is forceful but low.

Petty looks at me, his eyes glazed and confused. "Last thing I remember, I was driving the kids." He groans again. "I think I'm going to be sick."

"Man needs a hospital," Roller calls out. "His brain's fucked."

His brain was always fucked in my opinion. Petty tries to pull himself to a seated position. Roller's there beside him to help. "Take it easy, Brother."

Petty's closed his eyes. He accepts the bowl that someone shoves in his hands, but just holds it. He purses his lips and swallows a few times but doesn't vomit. "I think I'm okay," he comments.

"Your nose is broken, probably some ribs," Preacher informs him.

"Nothing I've not had before," Petty comments, his voice sounding weak. His brow creases and he forces his eyes open. "What happened?"

I can hold Cher back no longer. "You were driving the kids back. You were run off the road."

"Kids?" Petty looks confused. "Kids?" he repeats, then wrinkles appear on his brow again. "Yeah, the kids. I picked them up. Zeke was telling them about last night, I looked round to shut him up about certain bits, then, fuck me. I don't know what happened until I woke up here."

Should I just kill him as he'd admitted he was distracted?

But then his eyes clear as he looks around him. "The kids. Where are the fuckin' kids? Are they alright?"

"They've been taken!" Cher cries out. "We trusted you with them, and someone took them."

Petty tries to get to his feet, but crashes back on the sofa. Preacher's hand is immediately on his shoulder, holding him there.

"Take it easy, Brother. You might have a fuckin' skull fracture."

Looking at me, Petty ignores him. "How long have I been out?"

I shrug and tell him, "About half an hour, give or take."

I hear the sound of an office door banging then footsteps approaching fast. "Red?" Stormy enters at a run, once again carrying his laptop. I raise my chin and hold the position. "Honor's been checking into all the trucks that returned to Vegas in the time frame. He's come up with this."

It's a traffic camera photo of a small white truck, one which you could hire to move a piece of furniture. It could easily hold three kids in the back.

"Where's it heading?"

"Honor's tracking it now."

"What makes you think it's worth watching?"

Stormy gives a wry grin. "We got video. Watch." He presses play and when the truck slows and stops at a red light, the back is clearly shaking.

"Could be the load's not loaded properly." I raise an eyebrow.

"Look again. It's bouncing on its axles more like something

jumping around. And no load I've ever carried has done that unless it's on springs."

"Let's get after them, Prez," Indian, having listened in and clearly hearing enough, states.

I'm unsure about putting all my eggs in one basket, but I have to admit it's a lead. The erratic movements of the truck could indeed suggest it's transporting Zeke and the twins.

"Indian, take Twister, Cobra, Hammer," I pause and look around, "Rope and Shadow. And Meat with the crash truck. Head to where the truck was last seen. Stormy will update you with further directions."

Stormy jerks his chin to show he agrees.

"Want me to go?" Wraith asks, knowing I need to be here to direct operations until we have something more definite to go on.

"We're in." Joker indicates himself and Lady.

I count up how many that will leave us. "Thanks, Brothers."

As the rest of the men grab their bike keys and head outside, swiftly followed by Meat, Wraith pauses and leans in.

"I'd be out of my fuckin' mind with worry if that was my kids, Red. I know how you're feeling. We'll do everything to get them back."

I wouldn't wish how I'm feeling right now on anyone. I'm numb and suffering immense pain all at the same time.

"Do you really think it's them?" Cher comes over, her face managing to appear both hopeful and doubtful.

"No fuckin' idea." I put my arm around her, needing her close to me. "But, babe, it's a lead."

"You're staying here," Preacher suddenly snarls.

"No. I'm going." Petty's protest has me glancing around.

"Bro, you'd be better off in bed. I'll stay with you, make sure you don't have a concussion," Roller tells him.

"I'm not fuckin' going to bed," Petty growls. "Not until the kids are back."

I could admire the man's determination, but Petty's no use to anyone. He's managed to get to his feet, but only with the help of balancing his hand on the back of the sofa.

"Get your ass to bed, Petty. You're no fuckin' use as you are. But, Roller, I might need you. Send one of the club girls up to sit with him and make sure he doesn't die."

"Sweet of you to care, Prez," Petty chides me.

I snarl back, "I've still not determined your punishment for your disrespect and now losing the kids. I'd be careful if I were you, Petty."

Cher watches Roller and Preacher help Petty to the stairs. When they disappear up them, she turns to me. "Don't you think he's already suffered enough, Red?"

I give her a twisted grin. "Maybe. But the fucker fucked up, Cher. Let him suffer a bit longer before I let him off the hook. I still want to know why he was so fuckin' distracted he didn't notice the truck trying to run him off the road. That car's souped up. He could have shaken a tail if he'd noticed it."

"Ever driven with kids, Red?" Rosa appears. "They're distracting by their very definition."

I point my finger at her. "A member entrusted with the Satan's Devils' kids should never take their eye off their surroundings."

I suppose it's easy enough to say, and in truth, I think Petty's current suffering is probably enough for him. Unless harm has befallen Zeke. Then I'll want vengeance on anyone and everyone who had a hand in it.

My phone vibrates. Taking my arm away from Cher's waist, I pull the device out of my pocket.

"You got Red." I hadn't even bothered to check the number.

"Well, that's good. That's who I wanted."

"Crossman?" I quickly wave my hands to get the brothers remaining to keep quiet and mime putting it on speaker. They'd all turned around when I'd gotten a call, expecting it to be an update.

"Keaton Armstrong's brother. Remember him?"

"I do." I'm thinking fast on my feet. "We were sorry to hear what happened to Tide. He was halfway done with his sentence."

"Save your fake sympathy. You withdrew his protection."

"You're wrong," I tell him, trying to sound as convincing as I've ever been. "Tide died a Satan's Devil. I don't know what the fuck happened to him inside, but it had nothing to do with the club."

"I don't believe you," Crossman replies, and I know it's not worth my breath to tell him the same thing again. "You took my brother from me. Only fair I destroy you like you destroyed me. Keaton and I were fuckin' close."

"If you fuckin' hurt our kids—"

"Yeah, your kids. The twins seem normal enough, but that other one? What the fuck is he? Seems like I'd be doing you a favour if I ended him."

"You touch one hair on their head," I roar, "and you'll beg for death long before I've finished with you."

Stormy's miming something at me. *Keep him talking.*

So, I embellish my threats. "You've got a wife, Crossman. You hurt mine and I'll go after yours. I'll slice her into pieces and send them to you."

Cher gasps at my side, so I step away from her. "You give me our kids back, Crossman."

"Oh, I'll give them back, but I want something in exchange."

"What?" I have a feeling I know what he's going to ask me.

"Three lives for three lives. Seems you, Crash and Indian would have been the ones who took away the protection from Keaton. Yeah, he often spoke to me. Said you were the ones on his shit list when he got free. You didn't want him to get out, did you? Of course, I'd prefer Brick, but he's gone already."

"I'd fuckin' die for my kid," I tell him. "So, tell me where and when to meet." I notice Drummer's got hold of Cher and has his hand over her mouth. "But I can't sacrifice men to whom the kids mean nothing. And as you said, the twins' dad is dead, so there's no one here who'd sacrifice for them."

Hammer, I notice, is fighting to keep Rosa quiet just like Drummer is Cher.

Crossman is quiet for a moment. "You then. Come alone."

"Where to?"

I hear a snort. "You ride, drive or fucking crawl, but make your way to the casino. And you come on your own. Once I know no one is with you, I'll ring again and give you directions as to where to come to see your kid. I might even be kind and let you speak to him for one last time."

"You got to swear to me you'll set them free."

"Put it this way, Red. You don't appear in half an hour, then I'll start shooting. Might even start first with the freak."

My jaw clenches. "I'll be there."

It will be pushing it, but there's no way I'm risking my kid.

"You're going to sacrifice yourself for Zeke?" Cher's eyes are wild.

"Cher—"

"No, Red," she cries. "There must be some other way. I don't want to lose either of you."

"You're losing no one," Drummer barks so forcefully it stops her tirade. "Trust your ol' man, woman." His tone and piercing eyes make her go quiet, then he moves his gaze down the table. "Stormy?"

"Yeah. Got them. Fucker must think the Satan's Devils don't know how to track phones. And," he points to his laptop, "Honor's tracked that van to the same location. We know where they're being held."

I raise my chin.

Breathing deeply, I try to think myself back into the role of a hard-ass MC prez, and not an out-of-their-wits-scared parent. Satan's Devils have got this.

I push back my chair. "I better get going."

"Hold on, Red," Snatcher barks. "You head off to the casino, but you don't go elsewhere. You leave this to us. We're experts in kidnap extractions."

There's no way in hell. "With all due respect, Snatcher, I won't turn down your help, but I'm not leaving the fate of the club's kids to your abilities for negotiation."

I'm not suicidal, I know what I'm doing. Or hope I do. But if sacrificing myself means my kid will have a future, then I'll gladly face Satan and account for my misdoings.

I'd left Cher after subjecting her to a blistering kiss on the mouth, then walked away without listening to her remonstrations.

Bikes are already starting up around me. I'm not the first to exit the gate. They'll be heading straight for the location where we're certain Crossman has the kids, while I'll be making my way to the casino to await further instruction.

CHAPTER THIRTY-TWO

ZEKE

"**Y**ou okay?"

"My fuckin' arm's busted," Trist complains, trying to brace himself as the truck swings around a corner. "What do you fuckin' think?"

Tom and I try to balance him to prevent him knocking into the side.

When the truck gets going straight, I tear off the long-sleeved t-shirt I'm wearing, and quickly construct a makeshift sling. "Here, that should help support it." Gently, I help him ease into it.

Then I turn to Tom. "You need to hold something to your head." It's bleeding profusely, and he keeps having to wipe blood out of his eyes.

With a grin, Tom strips off his own t-shirt, bundles it up and holds it to the cut on his head.

"You dying, Bro?" Trist asks, drily.

I snort. "Head wounds always look worse than they are."

"And you'd know, how?"

I grimace at the memory. "Because I fell down some concrete steps and split my head open. Still got the scar, see?" Pushing back my hair from my forehead, I show them the small lightning-shaped scar. "Mom thought I was dying. Got me to the ER. When they cleaned up the blood, it didn't even need stitches. They just used glue."

"Cool," Tom comments. "You look like Harry Potter with a wizard mark. How's your head feeling, Trist?"

"Throbbing. Why the hell did you let him hit you? You could have let him hit Zeke then I wouldn't be hurting." He glares at me as if I should somehow have thrown myself in front of the pistol, but then he winks to soften it.

"Hey, I never thought I'd be kidnapped. You think they're going to ask a ransom for us?" Tom actually sounds excited.

Trist's eyes glisten. "How much do you think they'll want for us?"

"Millions," Tom states, confidently.

I'd been so scared when we were thrown into the truck, but if I had to be kidnapped, I reckon these two are the best company I could have. But it doesn't mean I'm comfortable with the situation. Not at all.

"What do you think will happen to us?" Now I've tended to their injuries, grateful I'm at least unscathed, I start worrying again.

"We'll be alright, Bro. We've got the Satan's Devils coming for us. Whoever's driving this truck will be faced with their worst nightmare."

"They'll wish they'd never been born." Trist holds out the fist on his sound arm and Tom bumps it with his. They turn, both holding their bunched hands toward me, and I touch mine to each of theirs in turn.

I just wish I could feel so confident. But their lack of concern does bolster me.

"How will they know where we are?" I ask, wishing I could see out of the truck and know where we were heading. *Back into Vegas, or out into the desert to God knows where?*

But here too, the twins are confident. Trist enlightens me.

"Keys. Or maybe he'll call in Utah to help. They'll go back over camera footage and track the truck."

"Utah has already arrived," I remind them. "They flew in last night."

"Then we'll be fine," Trist says, confidently. "Utah can find anything."

Tom's lips press together. "Hate to rain on your parade, Bro, but where we were run off the road, there were no cameras."

I drop my head into my hands, my brief period of hope evaporating. But Trist's undeterred.

"Utah will track all vehicles for anything that looks suspicious."

At that moment, the truck makes a sudden turn. We slide across the slick flooring, crashing into the opposite side, landing sprawled in a heap with Trist crying out as even the sling didn't prevent his arm being jostled. My back crashes into the side, and I know I'm going to have bruises.

"Fuckin' be careful," Tom yells out. "You've got live cargo."

But the driver doesn't hear, or ignores us. Whichever way, he doesn't adjust his driving.

Righting myself, I sit forward, excitement growing inside me. "You say Utah will be looking for anything that raises their suspicions?"

Tom looks at me warily. "Yeeeesss."

"Well, why don't we make the truck look suspicious?"

"How?" Trist asks, eyes gleaming as I've caught his interest. "Spit it out."

"We jump, make the truck bounce, run side to side and unbalance it."

The twins have some kind of silent conversation, after which, they speak in unison, "That's a great fucking idea."

Trist continues, "But best we wait until the truck comes to a stop, else they'll just think it hit a pothole or something."

"Yeah, we wait until we hit a red light."

But the truck heads on. Either the driver must be having the luck of the Devil and hitting all green lights, or we're heading out of Vegas. But the turns make me think we're heading into the city, as does the speed which is slowing.

"Yes!" Tom fist pumps the air as the truck finally comes to a halt with the engine still running.

Ignoring the jarring to his arm, Trist jumps up and down on the spot, while Tom and I throw ourselves at the sides of the truck. I don't know what it looks like from the outside, but it's certainly rocking and bouncing. A loud banging comes on the partition from the front, but it doesn't make us stop.

"Let's scream as well," Tom suggests.

We start shouting various versions of *"help, we're being kidnapped"* but after a pause, the truck resumes its journey.

We've attracted no outside help, but hopefully, if someone's hypervigilant, they might have picked up the unusual movements of a truck's cargo.

"Let's do it the next time the truck stops," Tom suggests, eagerly. But shortly after, the truck comes to a halt and the back doors are flung open. In climbs the man carrying the gun. He braces himself, lodged in the corner with his feet apart. His weapon's aimed on us.

"One more shout, one more move, and I'll shoot one of you." He sneers. "Fuckin' kids aren't getting the better of me. And for fuck's sake, put your clothes back on."

"I can't," I protest, not upset that my bare chest is somehow offending him. "Trist needs it."

"And I need mine." Tom holds his to his head once again. The activity has restarted the bleeding. "You some fuckin' paedophile or something?"

The man's face blazes red. "I'm not into fucking kids," he rasps out, and points at me. "But I don't want to see that naked."

I might not look entirely masculine, but I have to point out, "I've no tits, man. I'm not a girl."

"You're a twisted freak, that's what you are."

Tom snorts. "I think he fancies you, Zeke."

Trist reaches out his good arm and pulls me down beside him. He shoots a message with his eyes to his twin. I can't interpret it, but I've got a good idea what he's signalling. *You don't taunt the man with a gun.*

Tom sighs and sits down beside us. After a moment, he turns to me. "How did your audition go, Zeke? I forgot to ask you."

In the ensuing excitement, I'd almost forgotten myself. "Oh," I say breezily. "I got in."

"Fucking ace!" Again, Trist fist bumps me, and Tom follows with the same action.

"That's fuckin' brilliant. When's the show start?"

"Not for a few months, but I'll be going to all the rehearsals."

"You won't be going anywhere if you're dead," the man with the gun states, as if he feels he's losing control. Instead of three scared-out-of-their-minds kids, we're speaking normally.

"Ignore him," Trist states. "Tell me more, Zeke. What part are you playing?"

"Oh, I'm just part of the chorus line. But it's a start, you know?"

"Fuckin' kids," the man roars. "Shut the fuck up. Don't you understand the danger you're in?"

Tom turns his head slowly and so far around, for the moment it reminds me of the kid in the *Exorcist*. Especially so when he focuses our captor with scary eyes.

"And I don't think you understand the Satan's Devils will be coming for us. I can't wait to see what they do to you when they catch you."

"Kid…" The man takes a step forward at the same moment the truck brakes. When he stumbles, I start to brace in case I can make a leap for the gun. But unfortunately, he rights himself and goes back into his corner again. After a quick shake of his head, he continues, "Hate to break it to you kids, but the Satan's Devils will have fuck all idea of where to find you. And you won't be leaving alive unless they fulfil my terms."

"Your terms being?"

"Red, Crash and Indian will give themselves up for the part they played in the death of my brother."

At that moment, the truck makes another turn, then comes to a stop. The engine dies, and moments later, the back doors open.

For a second, the man stays motionless. "And even when I've killed Red and his officers, that might not be enough. I'll destroy all the fuckin' Devils, and that includes their brats."

It's the cold way he says it that sends shivers down my spine. I get the feeling he really means it.

He waits a beat and fixes us with his eyes, then slowly feeling his way, moves to the opening. The woman has her gun directed at us when he jumps out of the truck.

Once he's steadied himself, he instructs, "Out."

I jump out, Tom follows me, and we both turn to help Trist get down without jarring his arm. Once all our feet are on the ground, I look around. We seem to be around the back of a deserted diner. The woman gestures us to go inside the door that's hanging open.

"Cool," Trist states. "I'm hungry."

Tom snorts. "If there's anything to eat in there, the place will be crawling with rats."

"Probably is anyway," Trist retorts. He glances at the woman who has blanched, and grins. "Huge big ones with teeth. Probably starved and just waiting for a nice bite of human flesh."

"Inside!" the man yells. "And shut your mouths." In an aside to his companion, he hisses, "Tilly, I assure you, there are no fucking rats."

Tom raises his eyebrow at me. Guess we've discovered one of Tilly's weaknesses.

"Hey," I whisper to Trist as we walk inside. "I'm sure I've heard that you're supposed to try to get on good terms with your kidnappers. Make them see you as human." When he looks at me as though I'm stupid, I add, "I'll pretend I don't much like rats either. Maybe we can bond over our common phobia."

When I wink, he snorts.

The kitchen's been stripped bare of anything usable, so I doubt it's likely they'll have left any useful utensils in the cabinets. But as we're led through, I jump to one side and point down.

"Rat droppings. See?"

Tilly screeches, and once again the man snarls, "Keep it together, Tilly. They're trying to scare you."

"Scare her?" I purposefully make my voice sound like a squeal. "I'm terrified of rats too. Can't you take us somewhere else?"

"There is nowhere else," the man barks, clearly riled. "Now just keep on walking. And Tilly, no rats are going to get you."

"What about snakes?" Tom asks. "Abandoned places like this make good homes for them."

"Well, you're about to find out." Moving past us, he opens a door. It looks like it used to be a big freezer. "Get inside."

"I'm not going in there," Trist states, backing away. "I get claustrophobic."

Now completely incensed, the man fires his gun up into the air, bringing plaster down all over us. "I'm not kidding. I'll shoot the freak first. Now fucking get in there."

Tom pretends to cry but it doesn't help, and we're pushed inside. When the door slams shut behind us, it's totally dark.

"Hey," I start nervously. "I wasn't entirely messing around about rats. I'm okay when I can see them, but not when I can't."

"Me neither," Tom moans. "About the snakes."

Trist sighs loudly. "Babies, both of you. Let's check it out." Suddenly there's a small beam of light.

Breathing out with relief and looking down, I see Trist holding a keyring with a miniature flashlight on it. He takes a moment, scanning the place. "Look, nothing can get in."

"Or out," Tom says, glumly. "No windows and that's a fucking sealed door.

"It's a giant fridge," I tell them, also glancing around. "If they don't let us out, we'll suffocate."

"Nice, Bro. Nice." Tom shakes his head.

Trist walks to the door and examines it. "There must be some way to unlock it from the inside. It's a safety hazard if not."

"You reckon that bar opens it, Bro?"

"Could be." Trist reaches his hand out to press down on it, but I stop him.

"They think we're locked up in the dark. They think we're just kids." When I pause, the twins glance at me, curious where I'm going with this. "You say you think the Satan's Devils are on their way, but I don't think we can depend on that. I think they're trying to lure Red here, maybe Crash and Indian too. Let's not show our hand. Let's wait for a bit and come up with a plan."

Tom raises his chin to me.

But Trist objects, "We don't even know whether we can get out."

I shrug. "Whether it's then or now, the door will either open or not. Leaving it to find out will give us our best chance of taking them off guard."

"What's the plan then?" Trist settles himself down.

We toss ideas around for a bit until deciding we'll wait half an hour to let them relax. Of course, the next step depends on the door actually opening, but we don't think about the implications if it doesn't.

The plan involves me distracting the kidnappers while the twins try to get a hold of a gun. They apparently know how to shoot one.

"Can I borrow your flashlight?" When Trist hands it across, I shine it into a corner where I just spied something we'd missed earlier, lying low on the ground. "Oh, look there. Now that I think we can use, what say you two?"

The twins give equally wicked grins. "That'll do," they say together.

CHAPTER THIRTY-THREE

RED

Applying my brakes and shifting into neutral, I pull to a stop in the closest space to the casino door. I roll my shoulders which have been tense during the ride, take a couple of deep breaths, then dismount and walk toward the entrance.

I'm not surprised to see Bruce waiting for me, holding a sealed envelope in his hand. Eyeing him with suspicion, I take it. "You know what's going on?"

Sneeringly, he replies, "I hope it's your marching orders. We don't need the types of you around here."

Although I'm on a schedule, I pause enough to say, "I'm guessing you're up to your neck in that theft yesterday, Bruce. If I were you, I'd watch my back."

He snorts. "From where I'm standing, I've got nothing to worry about. If I were you, I'd be more concerned about myself."

Having confirmed he's deep in this shit, using two fingers, I point to his eyes. "I'll be seeing you," I state, ripping open the envelope.

"Somehow I think that's unlikely," he tosses over his shoulder as he walks away, seemingly having lost interest.

I put him to the back of my mind for now as I see there's a single phone number written on the paper. Keying it in fast, I walk back to my bike. It's answered by the time I'm astride the seat.

"Glad to see you're a timely man, Red."

"I want to speak to the kids. Hear for myself that they're alright."

"Nah, you'll just have to take my word. They're safe, for now. That's all you need to know. Get yourself fast to this address and come alone. If I see or hear another bike, then I'll start killing them one by one."

"I want proof of life first."

"What we want isn't always what we get. Your kids are still breathing, but I'm not giving you more than that."

The kids are missing, that's a fact, and I know the man I'm speaking to was responsible. I'm taking a risk with my own life that he's still got them in his hands, and that he hasn't harmed them. What choice have I got? If he hurts Zeke or the twins, then I might as well be dead already.

"If you kill me, you won't get away with this," I snarl. "The Devils will never stop hunting you down."

"I'm not afraid of your MC. It's you who should be scared for yourself. And if you don't get here in half an hour, you won't see any of the kids again."

He ends the call without me being able to express the rage that bubbles up inside. I swallow hard and breathe deep a few times, trying to tamp my anger down. There's a time when I'll let my rage have free rein, but right now I need to keep my head straight.

While I had him on speaker, I'd texted Crash the location as soon as he'd told me. Now I read the text I got back.

Crash: We're already here. Dilapidated diner. Dumpster round side. Bolt reckons roof for a sniper.

Relieved we were right on the location and that Crossman is unawares he's got company, my blood pressure drops to a manageable level. I translate Crash's text to mean Bolt will be taking up position on the roof, and brothers can get close as there's adequate cover.

Red: Can you get the kids?

Crash: No, no sign of them. When you appear and distract Crossman, we'll try the back entrance. That's where his truck's parked.

Red: Anyone with him?

Crash: Can't tell.

Damn Petty for being unconscious when they were taken. Crossman could be working alone or have a team with him. If he's unaccompanied when he appears, I still need to be careful. There might be one or more inside with instructions to hurt the kids if I take down Crossman.

Red: Focus on getting the kids.

What's my life worth if those of Zeke and the twins are forfeit?

Crash: We've got this.

Red: Kids before your prez, VP. That's an order.

Putting my phone back in my cut before he can answer, I mount my bike, turn the key and press start. Pulling my cut down more firmly over the Kevlar vest Indian made me wear before I stepped out of the clubhouse, I calculate the quickest route, and then set out on it.

I try to blank my mind from any fear that Crossman might have lied and focus on taking him and any of his co-conspirators out. *Zeke and the boys will be fine.* If I don't believe that, I'd be unable to ride. Or breathe. Or do anything to keep my heart pumping blood around my body.

I make the journey in twenty minutes, cautiously slowing my speed as I close in on the shuttered diner. It's not hard to see why the business shut up shop. I've passed three of the major named-brand diners close by it, and this one is set back from the road. Even if the paintwork wasn't peeling and faded, it would look out of place in today's world.

Have I ever been here before? I cast my mind back to all the years I've spent in Vegas just in case something will trigger a memory of the layout inside, but nothing comes to mind. Unless I once staggered here for a hungover breakfast and then I'd be unlikely to remember anything.

Accepting I'm a sitting duck, I park outside and wait still seated on my motorcycle. I'm banking on Crossman coming out to see me face-to-face, and not just shoot at me through the window.

Subtly raising my eyes, I see Bolt seated on the roof with his sniper rifle pointed down to the doorway. *How the fuck could he get up there with just one hand?* Then I remember, it's impressive and bionic and possibly more functional than the one he lost.

There's movement in the doorway. I focus my attention ahead, and carefully dismount my bike. Taking my helmet off, I lay it on the seat, then stand, my hands at my sides.

"Show me the kids," I call out.

Crossman just walks a few paces forward but says nothing.

Taking it for given Crossman expects me to walk closer, and calculating Bolt's already got him in his line of sight, I take a step forward. My brow creases. I don't see a gun. *Is this going to be like an old Wild West battle where fastest on the draw wins?* I, of course, have a weapon in my belt, and at the first sign of him going for his, I'll draw it.

"Bring the kids out," I demand again.

There's something wrong. My senses, already on high alert, kick into overdrive. All the bravado he showed on the phone is gone. I start to wonder whether Crash indeed got in the back way and is in charge of everything.

Suddenly, Crossman falls on his knees and places his hands on his head. *He's surrendering to me?* Utterly perplexed, I take another step forward and give an upward glance to Bolt to ensure he's still got this covered. Bolt doesn't acknowledge me or even see my look. His eyes are focused with a single intent on making sure Crossman doesn't so much as twitch his hand in the direction of a gun.

Suddenly, a figure appears behind Crossman. He stands in the doorway, feet apart, hands holding a weapon steady in a shooting stance.

As I tense, the figure in the shadows calls out, "It's okay, Uncle Red. I've got him covered."

The relief that floods through me almost has me dropping to a similar stance as Crossman. Well, I'll be fucked. "Tom?" From this distance, it could just as likely be Trist.

"Trist's inside," he says, which at least shows I've guessed right. "He's with Zeke. They've got the bitch under control."

"They sure have." Crash appears behind Tom and is laughing as he rests his hand on Tom's shoulder. Carefully, the VP takes the gun from the boy's hand. "We've got it from here, son." Crash beckons me forward. Still stunned, it takes a moment for my legs to start moving.

When I'm close enough, he throws me a pair of cuffs, and I make quick work of putting them on Crossman whose eyes are glaring daggers at me.

"Underestimated the Devils' spawn, did you?" After that taunt, I ignore him with a simple instruction to my VP, "Keep an eye on him, will you?"

I want to see Zeke to make sure they're okay. When Crash steps out, I take his place in the doorway, and then step inside.

"Over here, Dad."

My eyes close briefly at the proof Zeke's alive, and from their tone, unharmed. "You okay, kid?" I call out, unable to see them immediately.

"Zeke's good," Tom says from beside me. "It's me who got fucking hurt." He gestures to a wound on his head which looks sticky with blood. "That fucker out there pistol-whipped me."

"And I've got a fuckin' broken arm," Trist's voice complains from behind the ancient counter. "It will probably need surgery to have it set and pinned, and then I'll have metal in me which will set off every metal detector in sight. I won't be able to go anywhere without being searched."

"You are not fucking going to have an operation," Tom screams out, horrified. "You'll be under anaesthetic, but I'll feel everything."

"Yeah? Well, it might get you back for this pounding in my head," Trist retorts.

I palm my hand over my face. That the twins are back in form means they can't be too traumatised from their ordeal. I move past the bickering pair to where I can see an amused Twister standing, training a gun on a woman who looks almost catatonic. Zeke's behind the enforcer, and he's grinning.

I suspect every parent knows how the relief at seeing their kid unharmed can morph into many emotions—love that knows no bounds, along with the rage that what they did scared you, as well as the desire never to let them out of your sight again. And there are the words on the tip of my tongue, *don't you ever do something like this again.*

Anger isn't right. It's not Zeke's fault they scared me. Zeke didn't ask to be kidnapped or stolen away, but in that brief fleeting moment, that's the initial reaction that goes through me.

"How's Petty?" When I don't speak, it's Zeke who takes the lead, showing concern for the man who's never had any compassion for them.

"He'll be fine," I tell Zeke dismissively, then, narrowing my eyes, rasp, "Why the hell are you half-naked?" *Did Crossman try and molest them?*

"That would be me." Trist raises his arm encased in Zeke's shirt as a sling.

"And I had to use mine to mop up the blood. It was everywhere, Red," Tom says rather too gleefully to be someone dying from a head wound. Belatedly, I realise he, too, is shirtless.

"What the fuck happened?" I ask, proud as fuck, but confused as hell, wondering how three kids turned the tables on two adults with guns.

Trist snorts. "They locked us in the freezer. Stupid twats didn't realise it had a safety bar on the inside. We waited until they didn't expect anything, then Zeke comes out and goes into this dancing routine."

"Yeah, Zeke looked like a stripper ready to do a lap dance," Tom adds, admiringly. "I think Crossman thought they were coming on to him, and started to back away—"

"But I'd gotten behind him and tripped him, then took the gun when it fell out of his hand." Trist and Tom give each other high fives.

"Then Zeke produced that and threw it at her." Tom snorts and points to what's in the motionless woman's lap. "She's been like that since. She dropped the gun as she fell."

The woman, proving she's not completely out of it, raises her wide-opened eyes, and whispering, as if speaking louder could wake the dead, demands, "Someone get it the fuck off me."

"No please?" I murmur, as I stare down, unable to keep the grin off my face. This is a story that will go down in the annuls of the Satan's Devils MC and will probably get mileage for years —how the Satan's Devils' kids fought off their kidnappers armed with nothing but a dancer shaking their wares and a dead mummified rat.

Moving to Zeke, I ruffle their hair. "I'm proud of you, kid." In fact, I'm so choked up, it's hard to speak.

"Eh, what about us?" Turning, I open my arms, and the twins come forward to let me hug them.

"Fuckin' proud of you too." And ain't that the truth.

"So," Tom asks slyly. "This seems a good time to ask if we can patch in."

I huff a laugh at the same time as Twister snorts. "When you're eighteen." I give the standard answer, the same as I provide every time they ask.

"Will you get this fuckin thing off me?" the woman now screams, so high pitched it hurts my ears.

"What thing?" Drummer's deep voice sounds beside me.

"You here?" I turn, surprised.

"Couldn't leave you to have all the fun. Now what's she making all that fuss about?"

I point, he guffaws, quickly summing up it's not the threat of the gun keeping her immobile. "Whose idea was that?"

Proud as fuck, I announce, "Zeke's it seems."

He gives into his laughter for a second, then, slapping my back, gets to business. "Got the crash truck on its way. Guessed you're going to want to have words with these two back at your compound."

That most certainly is my plan.

Moments later when the truck arrives, brothers swarm in. Crossman's been loaded already, and now they drag the woman, who's apparently Chantilly-fucking-Lace, out to join him. As an afterthought, I carefully pick the dead rat up and throw it in the back of the truck with them. Chantilly gives an immensely satisfying scream.

"Hey, kids." When they turn around, I toss them my phone. "Give your moms a call on the way back, will you?"

When they squeeze into the truck, I instruct Owl in a growl, "Drive fuckin' carefully."

"Gotcha, Prez." He nods, starts the engine and the crash truck pulls smoothly away.

I stand for a moment, watching the Vegas members, as well as those from Utah and Tucson who'd come to assist me, get to their bikes. *I could have died today.* But I didn't. I had the Devils behind me.

"You okay?" Wraith, hanging back, comes up alongside me.

The adrenaline drop makes me yawn. "I could sleep for a fuckin' week."

Wraith chuckles and kicks at a stone. "You know, if you don't patch the twins in, Drummer would have them."

"Now?" I ask hopefully.

He chuckles loudly. "When they're old enough, you fucker."

Breathing deeply, I wonder if I'll survive until then.

"Oh and," he adds, barking a laugh, "I overheard Cobra and Hammer. They think you should have that rat mounted."

Now that is an idea. "I'll think on it. But for now, I may have a better use for it."

He slaps the back of my cut. "I hear you, Brother." Then his eyes become dark and determined. "Now I think I'd like to see how well equipped your basement is."

CHAPTER THIRTY-FOUR

CHER

I never want to go through the last few hours, scrap that, few days, again in my life. I certainly don't want to repeat being arrested and held on false pretences, and neither do I want to worry about my man being put into prison for possibly the rest of his life.

But above and beyond that, I never want to let Zeke out of my sight. Unrealistic for certain, but to know they'd been taken and not knowing whether they were alive, hurt or dead was something I don't think I'd survive a second time.

Had it not been for Rosa, I'm not sure I'd have gotten through. Her twins are her last remaining link to her husband, and just like Zeke is to me, they're her whole world.

Her confidence that Red and the club would sort it and get them back had been unwavering, and, despite my doubts, she'd been right.

When we've received our respective calls from the twins and Zeke, we'd both clung together, fresh tears flowing, though these were of relief rather than the fear that had haunted us during the past few hours.

After a moment, we'd pulled apart, both wiping our faces and looking sheepish.

"Food," Rosa announced, dabbing her eyes on a tissue for the last time and then throwing it away. "The kids will be hungry." Turning around, she spies the sweet butts who'd been hanging around but keeping out of the way. "Hey, girls. Kitchen now."

Jinx, whose eyes which had lit up after gathering all had ended alright, now grumbles but slides off her stool, Angel and Pixie following her lead.

Pixie glares at Rosa. "The boys will need us when they get home."

"They'll need feeding first," she snaps back. "Go on, shoo." She bats with her hands. "I'll be there in a moment. Jinx, get some meat defrosting. Pixie, Angel, you can start preparing the vegetables. I'll do a Spaghetti Bolognese." When they move off, obviously knowing what Rosa wants them to do, she now turns to me. "We need to talk."

I'm still full of elation that my kid's on their way home, barely suppressing my desire to do a happy dance around the room. Unsure what she wants to discuss, I tilt my head to one side.

She takes a deep breath, then lets it out. "You're good for Red, Cher. It's easy to see he's besotted with you." Again, she takes in air. "But these past few days have shown you the worst of life with the Satan's Devils MC."

They certainly have. "Are you expecting me to leave him?"

She places her hands on her hips. "Well, are you?"

To be honest, that thought hadn't entered my head while I'd been so wrapped up in getting Zeke home, and the idea that might only be at the expense of Red's life had confirmed just how much he means to me. The idea I'd never see him again had made me die a little inside.

But what Rosa's clearly put her finger on is that while the Vegas Satan's Devils have assured me they haven't had trouble like this for a very long time, it was something they were inherently prone to. Delaying my answer, I turn away.

Zeke hadn't been directly put in danger because of their

connection to the club, or not this time. For Crossman, the twins would probably have been enough. That he'd swept up Zeke along with them was just icing on the cake. But a surefire way to get to Red would always be through his kid.

Would I be able to keep Zeke safe if I took them away and moved out of state? Or would their relationship with Red always haunt them? Now it's known Zeke's the child of the Satan's Devils' prez, could there be a chance they'd always be at risk of being used as an instrument against him?

Would it be possible in any event to separate Zeke from their newly found dad?

Even if Zeke would go along with it, I owe Red. I had the first fifteen years of Zeke's life. It would be cruel to take them from him now. Red loves Zeke in the best of ways a man can love his child. Their relationship should be given a chance to develop and strengthen for both their sakes, and I want to be there to see it.

Then there are my own thoughts about Red. It's impossible to deny I still love him. Or maybe the word still is wrong. Back when I'd first met him, there was an attraction that neither of us could deny and that certainly hasn't died. But now I've grown to respect the man he's become—the way he leads his club and cares for every one of his members, well, maybe with one exception.

He's a fair man, strong, dominant and caring, and handsome as all get out. What more could a woman ask? If I've never found an equal to the younger version, what chance have I now? Would I even want to go looking? I'd never have another Red in my life.

Does staying with him commit me and Zeke to a life of constant danger? Quite possibly the answer is yes. On the other hand, I'd have to be blind and deaf to deny how this club jumped into action when their own had been threatened. Rosa had been right all along. Even if the kids hadn't had a connection with the MC, the police would have been slow off the mark.

We'd raised the alarm less than an hour after they'd gone missing. The police would have wanted to wait, especially knowing there had been an adult with them.

If I'd gone to the cops, without the MC and the resources at their disposal, I might not now be waiting for Zeke to come back, happy and cheerful from what I'd picked up from their brief call.

Zeke by their very nature is not going to have an easy life. Too often I read in the news about someone in the LBGTQ+ community being murdered just for being who they are. If I allow myself to follow my inclinations to be with Red, then Zeke will have not only their dad, but a club full of feared uncles at their back. That surely can't be a bad thing.

What it comes down to is, following my own wants and desires could just coincide with what's best for Zeke.

Though it sounds like a point in their favour, the one downside of the Satan's Devils MC is how protective they are. They like to keep their women cocooned and safe, and in the dark as to what's truly going on. But then, when it mattered, they had involved me when I'd put my foot down.

I've seen how they are with Rosa—respectful and caring—and I suspect being Red's old lady, they'd offer me nothing less. Would I feel that my own dominant streak was being smothered? Or would I be able to make my own place and hold a position where I could feel valued in my role as the woman standing beside their prez?

Rosa's still standing, her hands on her hips, giving me time to process and think things through. She'd warned me at our initial meeting that to be the club's first old lady, a woman needed to be strong. Did I have the necessary strength had been the question she'd been asking?

Now I think the answer is yes. If I can go to battle for Zeke, then how different is that from battling for members of the MC?

I raise my face and stare Rosa straight into her eyes. "None of what's happened is of the club's making. Red and the boys were trying to go straight. You know what really pisses me off?"

Rosa's brow furrows at my unexpected words, and at the sudden fury I put behind them. "Red was so obviously pleased they'd gotten the security contract at the casino, but that was all fake. It was Crossman's chance to control them, a plan put in action to see them locked up." My face glows as I grow ever angrier. "That's going to knock them all back. They can sit around in church, hashing out the details, but they're going to need reassurance and some TLC. They've stepped into the citizen world, and it shoved them back into their box. This wasn't Red's fault. It was all down to Crossman."

Rosa raises her chin, her own face red. "It all goes back to Tide and his gambling addiction. If he wasn't dead, I'd kill him myself."

"And you know what, Rosa?" My lips curve, but it's a kind of cross between a grin and a snarl. "I'd be right there beside you. They didn't deserve what happened to them."

Rosa's mouth also moves, but she forms a smile. "Does this mean to say you're going to stand beside him?"

"Whatever he does?"

Rosa's head bobs up and down. "Whatever he does."

I raise and lower my shoulders. "Most of the time, I expect he'll be right, but he might need a woman's hand to guide him."

Rosa snorts and reaches out her hands to take one of mine, clasping it firmly. "I knew a day would come when I had to hand over the mantle as the club's first old lady, the mother hen if you like. Or rather, I'd hoped, as Red didn't seem on a path to find his woman, even though it was obvious he wanted one." She squeezes my hand. "I had doubts about one who returned to his life having once left him. But now I see you, Cher, I know you'll be good for him. And what's more, you'll be good for the club."

My mouth quirks. "Is this your seal of approval?"

She chuckles. "It certainly is." She cocks her head to one side and cups her hand to her ear. "They're back," she tells me excitedly. Without letting go of my hand, she starts to drag me to the front door.

Seeing I'm as eager as her, we reach the entrance together, comically both trying to get through the door at the same time.

Outside, under the hot Vegas sun, the club's crash truck pulls up, followed by the earth-shaking roar of numerous motorbikes.

But my eyes are on the truck and the kids spilling out as soon as it comes to a halt.

Zeke heads for me at a run, the twins, more nonchalantly stroll toward Rosa. But the effect is the same. Zeke's quickly enveloped in my arms, and Tom and Trist in Rosa's.

Lost in our own world for a moment, I just hang on to my child, holding them tight. When they protest with an ouch, I hold them at arm's length and examine them carefully, then turn them around. A clear nasty-looking bruise is forming on their naked back.

Naked?

"What did they try to do to you?" I ask through gritted teeth. "Where's your shirt?"

Zeke snorts and jerks their head over their shoulder. "It's now a sling for Trist's broken arm." They see my expression and roll their eyes. "Mom, he didn't try to molest me."

Now that I can more easily breathe, I ask, "What happened? How did Red get you free? Is your dad okay?" I'm anxiously looking behind at the row of bikes but can't find him. I'm assuming Red's fine as I hadn't heard differently, but I won't be satisfied until I see him with my own eyes.

"Dad's good. But we didn't need him. We freed ourselves, Mom. It was awesome."

"Hey, you were awesome." Tom comes over and slaps Zeke's back. With a wink to me he adds, "You should have seen them. Scared the hell out of those perverts."

I narrow my eyes. *The kids freed themselves?* Not liking that Zeke sounds like they'd put themself in danger, I ask, "And what did you do, Zeke?"

"They fucking danced!" Trist, shaking off Rosa's concern, joins us.

Danced? Hell, they're not that bad.

"Trist, get back here. I'm going to take you to the hospital. You need that arm set."

"Mom," he moans and shakes his head. "Not yet."

"Yes, yet. You too, Tom. I want your head looked at."

Trist grins at his twin and elbows him with his good arm. "It's too late for that, Mom. His head's too fucked to be fixed now. Should have done that when he was a kid."

"Language!" Rosa yells, but I see her eyes twinkling. If the kids are laughing and joking, despite the injuries they've picked up, they're going to be alright.

Zeke exchanges fist bumps with the twins as it becomes clear Rosa is going to get her way. When she ushers the boys toward her car, Hammer and Cobra intercept her.

"A prospect will go with you."

Rosa looks set to argue, but then she shrugs, turns back to me and winks. After a quick word with Hammer, Owl stoically walks to his bike. When Rosa's car leaves the compound, it's with the prospect in hot pursuit.

Finally, the last two bikes draw up, and at last, here's Red.

My eyes are fixed to him as he has a few words with the mother chapter prez, and then, his gaze meeting mine, he strides over.

This is the man who's the love of my life. The man I'd had to question whether I'd lost forever only a short while earlier. This is the man I vow never to run from again.

I close the distance between us, throwing myself into his arms. Surprised, he picks me up and swings me around. Of their own volition, my lips find his and it's me who's kissing him with everything I've got. After he gets over the initial shock, being him, he takes over.

Whistles and shouts sound around us, but it's a few more seconds before we part. When we do, he rests his forehead against mine.

"Now that's how a prez likes to be greeted by his ol' lady."

His eyes sparkle as he looks down. Then he reaches out his hand, beckoning Zeke over.

When he clasps Zeke to him, I swear Red has tears in his eyes. He looks at me over the top of their head and we share a parental moment of sheer joy that our kid is safely home. For a moment, the three of us stand, lost in our own little world until life starts to intrude as a banging and shouting from the back of the truck sounds.

I raise an eyebrow. "You got the kidnappers in there?"

He doesn't try to deny it. "Sure have. Crossman, and would you believe it? Dear Chantilly Lace."

"And the rat," Zeke puts in, their eyes screaming mischief.

"That fuckin' rat." Red ruffles their hair, then looks at me. "That accounts for the screaming, by the way."

"Sounds like you've got some work to do." I know Red's going to get his revenge on Crossman and the bitch who set me up. Surprisingly, I'm not at all bothered about it. I'd like to dish out some vengeance myself.

"Dad, can—"

"Don't even ask, kid. The answer is no."

Red's tone of voice is such that Zeke knows not to argue with it. Hiding my grin, I reckon Red's going to make a great dad.

"Come on, Zeke, let's make sure the girls in the kitchen know what they're doing." In Rosa's absence, I suppose I better step up. I'm not the world's best cook, but I can direct operations. Rosa was right, it won't just be the kids, her, *my*, boys will soon be wanting to be fed.

It turns out that Zeke's in his element. They pass no judgement on the scantily clad girls and quickly the sweet butts accept them. While not much help, Zeke sits on a countertop, swinging their legs regaling us with stories of how they escaped. When they mention how they danced, Zeke's asked to demonstrate, and gets admiration when they oblige. When Jinx tries to imitate them, and Pixie and Angel want to be taught some moves, well, let's just say, dinner gets a tad later.

A still unsteady Petty emerges in the midst of all the fuss, and eyes Zeke warily.

It's Zeke who makes the first move. "You okay, man? I thought you were dead."

Petty's voice sounds choked. "I fucked up. I should have seen that truck."

Zeke shrugs. "We're all okay, just minor injuries, so it turned out alright. And at least Dad got the man who's been fucking with the club."

"Zeke…" I growl.

"Messing with the club," they correct hastily. But if we stay here, I suspect I'm fighting a losing battle, just as Rosa clearly has with Trist and Tom. All I can hope is Zeke learns when it's appropriate for them to let loose, and when to mind their language. Having confidence in my kid, I suspect they already do.

"What the fuck happened?" Petty gets himself to a chair and groans as he sits. He massages his temples, then looks up, and for the first time I can remember, gives his full attention to my kid.

Gleefully, Zeke relates the story, adding a few embellishments, I suspect. Zeke's got the gift of storytelling and when they get to the rat part of the story, Petty ends up in hysterical fits. As it's just as funny the second time around, the girls and I join in.

Petty goes so far as to reach out his fist, and Zeke touches their own to it.

There's clearly not room for all the men to assemble in the basement, so gradually those left out wander in, and Zeke has to go through the tale, and demonstration, all over again.

Dinner does get made, eventually. But I, for one, don't give a damn about the delay. I'm so proud seeing Zeke cement their role in the MC. Zeke will never be one of the men, but to be accepted and not judged by them is all I can ask. Even Petty is showing a new respect for them.

It's an ill wind that blows no one any good, they say, and in this case, being kidnapped has done wonders for Zeke.

Not that I'd have wanted it to happen that way, but I can't be sorry for the outcome at least.

Eventually Tiffany arrives, and I'm pleased as without her appearance, I doubt anyone would have gotten any dinner at all. She grins an easy smile at me, hugs Zeke warmly, then gets to checking what's in the pot Jinx is half-heartedly stirring.

When Red finally joins me, despite that his knuckles are bloodied and sore, I feel that my life is complete.

CHAPTER THIRTY-FIVE

RED

Everyone lives in fear of the legendary Blade, so I sense Twister thinks he's got something to prove to Drummer. Being enforcer doesn't just mean doling out pain before death but knowing how to use it to get the information needed. Just the name Blade puts fear into those who know it, and it seems Twister's hoping that his will become much the same.

He's standing, flexing his muscles, eyeing Crossman as though assessing his weak points while Drummer, Wraith, Snatcher, Crash and I stand in the corner. We're putting our heads together and coming up with a plan.

"How much do you want to hold on to your security business involvement with casinos, Red?"

Right at this moment, I want nothing to do with it, but that's not thinking with my prez's hat. Shaking off the remnants of my emotional reunion with Cher and Zeke, I try to focus on the club's priorities.

"Can't deny this has left a bad fuckin' taste in the mouth," I tell him, having got my thoughts together. "But it's been a lucrative business for the club, and we'd hoped to spread out further. Not to the big players of course, but to the small joints. We're always happy to add to our portfolio." I pause and pinch the bridge of my nose, then look up to meet Drummer's eyes. "Even without bragging, we did a good job. Their security was shit until we stepped in. Keys has a good handle on this business."

Wraith, who seems to be on Drummer's wavelength as Crash so often is on mine, jerks his head toward our prisoners. "We need to know whether the other partners had any involvement, or whether Crossman was acting alone."

"They stood to gain from the fake robbery," I explain. "They stand to get back the original funds as well as the insurance payout."

"Or hope to," Snatcher says drily. "The cops have had to let you go and haven't caught anyone else. Insurance companies love to try to prove it was an inside job. They don't pay out unnecessarily."

"What are you thinking, Prez? You've got that gleam in your eye." The VP raises his brow.

"I'm thinking," I start, deciding how best to give voice to my ideas, "that we help the cops along in this instance. Get the info out of Crossman about how exactly he arranged this. And," I pause again to grin, "if his partners weren't involved, give them the evidence to deal with it."

"And him?" Drummer's eyes sneer in our male captive's direction.

We all ignore Chantilly. Someone hung that rat right in front of her nose so if she even breathes too hard, it sends it swinging. She's totally transfixed by it. I wouldn't be surprised if the experience hasn't traumatised her for life. Or, at least what's left of it.

"I want to bury him. He went for my woman and kid, and Brick's. Brick would be turning in his grave if I left him breathing." I shrug. "But it depends on what evidence we have if we lose the main culprit. If it stands on his own, he's signed his death warrant. If not, he'll end his days in prison."

Drummer places his hand on the back of my cut. "If it has to be the latter he won't last long in there. I've friends in low places who can guarantee it." Then proving why the shrewd man is in the position he is, he jerks his head toward Twister. "I think we ought to move it along. Your man there wants to show me what he's made of."

I grin. "He does. Is it so obvious?"

"Fuck, Red," Wraith snorts. "So far only Swift can come up with more interrogation methods than Blade."

Snatcher chuckles quietly. "They still talking about that MC enforcer conference? Because Swift's still willing to hold one."

"Heaven help us," Drummer breathes out with a smirk. "But as long as it's only Satan's Devils involved, I have no objection with it. Don't want to put any tools in the hands of our enemies."

"I'll get Swift to set something up." Snatcher raises his chin. "But for now, let's see what Red's boy has got in him."

I beckon Twister to come across. Once he's here, I put my arm around his shoulders. "We need information, Twist. To start with, encourage him to talk. Depending on his answers, we'll decide how far to take it."

Twister nods. "Make him hurt but leave minimal marks?"

"You got it." My mind drifts back fifteen years to that innocent man setting out on the road to find his dreams. Never would I have dreamed all these years later, I'd be discussing methods of torture with my kid waiting upstairs. The thought amuses me, remembering how naïve of the world I'd been back then. At the time, I wasn't equipped to look out for a family, and now I feel I am. Anyone can say they'd die, or kill, to protect their child, but not many have the guts to mean it. But with the Devils on my side, I can do anything. If Satan had decided to call my number today, I'd have known Cher and Zeke wouldn't be left unprotected, nor without family.

"And if he gives the right answers?"

An evil grin spreads over my face. "Then we make him hurt and mean it. He'll be heading for a nice spot six feet under in the desert."

"And her?" Twister jerks his head backward.

"She was out to get my wife and didn't care if Zeke got hurt. She held a gun on him." I take a breath before pronouncing sentence. "She's already dead, Brother."

"Do we bury the rat in the grave with her?" Twister asks, so seriously that I bark such a loud laugh everyone looks at me.

"Or we could bury her alive with a few lives ones in with her."

I blink fast, then bellow with laughter again. "You're an evil man, Snatcher."

Drummer rubs his hands together. "Well, seems we've got a plan. It's over to you, Twister."

Twister seems to grow a few inches as he strides forward toward Crossman. He leans on the arms of the chair Crossman's fastened to and gets right into his face. Now I love my fucking brother, but I know he occasionally has problems with halitosis, so when Crossman rears back, I'm unsurprised.

Twister starts talking quietly to the man who soon begins to squirm. Even from where I'm standing, I see the growing terror in his eyes. As Twister eases his body to the side, there's an obvious wet mark on Crossman's pants. He's already wet himself and my enforcer's yet to put a hand on him.

Drummer looks at me with a raised eyebrow. "Impressive," he remarks.

And me, being all team Vegas, feel a glow of pride.

I start asking questions, and Crossman, encouraged by Twister, begins to provide answers, hesitantly at first, then they come faster. The enforcer's using a sharp thin ice pick type instrument that doesn't leave much mark on the skin but that apparently hurts when it's pushed right in. Becoming bored, he then proves himself a master at twisting a limb to the exact point of breaking.

I'm almost disappointed when it's over and we've got everything. Twister's performed his task to even Drummer's satisfaction, making Crossman spill the beans and only leaving the barest of marks on him.

Snatcher's a great help. While he's been listening, he's been texting his brothers in Utah, getting them to verify everything. At the end of it, we've got names, addresses and all the details to prove Crossman's guilty without having to present him to be questioned. No one would raise an eye at him going missing. Any criminal as inept as him would run when his setup misfired.

By him being totally honest, I'm going to get my revenge. By the end of this session, he won't ever be able to kidnap a child again.

It's then, when I know I'm going to give Twister free rein, that I let my stoic mask fall. Waving the enforcer to stand aside, I take his place. As I allow myself to remember the fear when Zeke disappeared, my fury rises. My first punch breaks his nose, my next, hopefully his jaw.

"You threatened my kid's life," I spit in his face. "You threatened to take Zeke's future away. You tried to destroy this club full of innocent men." Now I go for his ribs, hearing a satisfying crack.

It's not often that I let my redheaded temper have full rein. Over the years, I've learned to control myself. But red is the only colour I now see before my eyes, both in his blood flying and metaphorically.

He resembles a limp bloodied rag by the time Crash pulls me back.

"Thought you were going to let us all have some fun." But when I turn, there's a huge grin on his face. He examines my eyes, then nods. "You needed that."

I certainly did. But now I can afford to be magnanimous. "Finish him off," I tell them, waving imperiously with my hand.

As they proceed to do so, I go to stand in front of Chantilly Lace.

Slipping my knife through the string holding it up, I bounce the mummified rat in my hands. She seems to come back to herself with the rat now out of her face.

"You've got to let me go," she says fast. "I won't say anything about what happened here." Her nervous sideways glance toward Crossman's almost dead body shows what she's talking about.

Putting a foot on the edge of the seat she's sitting on, I lean forward, resting my elbows on my knee. "You kidnapped my kid."

"We didn't mean to. We were going to take the twins, but he was there so he came along."

"They," I correct, deceptively calmly. "My kid prefers to be referred to as they."

"Can't you see how wrong that is?" she hisses, leaning forward. "You're a real man—" *Fuck me, is that batting of her eyelashes meant to be her flirting?* "You surely can't go along with how his mother's brought him up. Poor kid should be in a mental home or having therapy at least."

"Yeah?" I retain my position, as if the conversation is just between the two of us, but I'm fully aware that my brothers are listening. "And you've done so well with your kid, bringing him up to be a bully."

"He's not a bully. He was just pointing out the facts of life. Your son is a freak and shouldn't be mixing with normal kids."

"Hmm." I nod my head. "You're sure doing a good job of bringing him up right. Encouraging him to pick on those different from him. And what a good example you set. Getting Zeke's mother fired from her job and locked up for something she never did. Oh, and how could I forget? Aiding and abetting a kidnapping because Trist and Tom punched your kid to stop him from hurting Zeke."

I feel a nudge to my shoulder and straighten up. Snatcher's behind me, showing me the screen of his tablet. He also whispers an explanation into my ear. "Her husband, Ashton, is filing for divorce and custody of the kid."

"Ashton clean?"

Snatcher nods. "As far as we can tell. He's citing unreasonable behaviour as part of the reason for the divorce."

I raise my chin, reading the undercurrent. I'd already thought young Brighton might be better off without a mom like Chantilly. Presumably, his father thinks so as well. Of course, at his age, he might be too old to change, but without her, Brighton might have a chance.

"Let me go and I won't say a thing about your club," Chantilly tries again. "I'll even tell the casino I was mistaken about Cher."

"And you've proved yourself to be honest and trustworthy, haven't you?" Getting annoyed, I raise my hand and rattle the rat in her face. She rears back. "The thing is, I love my kid, love my woman, and respect family enough that I'm going to give yours a chance, without you to contaminate them."

"Wh-wh-what do you mean?"

"I mean," I tell her, sliding my gun out of my cut, "that for all our sakes, a woman like you is better off dead."

I don't give her long to think about it. I'm not into mental torture like that. But I do throw that long dead rat right there into her lap to take her mind off what comes next. While she shrieks and rears away from it, I put a bullet into her head.

"At least she wasn't worried about dying," Twister remarks drily as he comes up to my side.

"Looked to me like she died of fright before Red's bullet hit her." Wraith barks a laugh and slaps my back. "Like your style, Brother."

"Well, I think that's our cue to get out of here," Drummer states, giving a cursory glance at the bodies.

It's been a long time since Vegas had to deal with cleanup, but I still remember how it goes. We're one prospect down as Owl's escorting Rosa to the hospital with the twins. I glance at Crash and inform my VP, "Seems Meat's going to learn how to get his hands dirty."

It's surprising it's Roller who offers first, "I'll stay and help."

"You trying to get back in my good books?" My eyebrow rises.

Roller smirks. "Is it working?"

Feeling lighter now there's two less assholes in the world, I laugh. "Yes."

"Me, me! I want in with Daddy's favour." Rope's leaping up and down and raising his hand.

"If he's in, I'll do it too. Anything for Daddy," Cuff says, making me roll my eyes.

"I'll give you worse jobs if you ever again call me Daddy," I growl, while around me my brothers laugh.

I'm tired as fuck. I've had no sleep for two days, and my brothers are no better than me. While I've ribbed them, I'm eternally grateful for their offer to sort this mess out. The sooner we clean up, the sooner we can put this behind us and get on with our lives.

"I owe you," I tell them, meaning it, as I turn and follow Drummer and Snatcher up the stairs.

"Good set of brothers you got here," Drummer states as he reaches the top.

I raise my chin. "We're Devils, whatcha expect?"

Drummer grins and gives me a nod.

"Hey, Red? Preacher says the plane's fuelled and ready, so we're going to be heading back to base." Snatcher comes up behind me.

Turning, I reach for the hand of the Utah prez and pump it up and down a few times, then pull him in and slap his back. Releasing him, I tell him honestly, "I had misgivings about your chapter, but that's in the rearview now. I can't thank you enough, Brother."

Snatcher looks at me earnestly and says quietly for only me to hear, "Remember, Red, when anything's stored electronically, it can be altered."

As I look confused at his enigmatic words, he chuckles and

turns to the men he'd brought with him. "Apparently Utah's okay in Vegas's books, Brothers."

"Does that mean you no longer think I'm an asshole?"

I growl as I turn to the speaker. "Don't push it, Stormy."

"Everyone thinks you're an ass, Storm." Bolt clips him around the ear good-naturedly. "Including your Cat."

Instead of objecting, Stormy agrees. "Especially my Cat. Talking of whom, I can't wait to get back to her."

As the Utah brothers move through the clubroom, it takes them some time to reach the door. Everyone has a word or another to say to them, especially Keys, who corners Stormy for a while before letting him move on.

Before they've completely left the premises, Drummer sniffs the air. "If I'm not mistaken, there's food on the go, or at least being prepared."

The aroma's reaching me too. "You going to partake of our hospitality, Drum?"

"With an eight-hour journey ahead of us, and barely no fucking sleep last night, of course we fuckin' are."

"I'll get someone to sort you out." I pause then reach my hand out to him. "Can't thank you enough, Brother, for having my back."

Drummer, as he's prone to do, shakes my gratitude off. "I still think we're in the red as far as help from Vegas is concerned."

And long may it stay that way. I've had enough excitement over the past few days to last me for life.

The smell of garlic gets stronger, and I hear Zeke's voice from the kitchen. Unwilling to stay away from my family one minute longer than I need to, I make my excuse. "I'll go check when we can eat."

Pausing in the doorway, I take in the sights. Tiff's checking that Jinx and Pixie are following the instructions presumably Rosa had left, while Cher's looking on. Surprisingly, Petty's sitting at the table, looking a bit pale, but looks like he'll be staying the land of the living for a while.

Sarge is chatting to Titch, repeating the rat story again as if no one has already heard it. And Zeke's in deep conversation with Angel. They appear to be discussing makeup of all things. As I look on, Zeke carefully paints lipstick on her lips, and then demonstrates the action on their own. And you know what? I see fuck all wrong with it.

When Cher catches sight of me, I realise I look a mess, and that I should have cleaned up before coming to her, I'm still covered with Crossman's blood. Hell, Zeke shouldn't be seeing me like this, but luckily, they're otherwise engaged.

Cher, though, without missing a beat, comes straight over to me, and takes my bloodied hands in her own, turning them over and checking them.

"We better get these looked at," she tells me, without questioning how I'd gotten my injuries.

"Have I ever told you, you'd make a great ol' lady?" I ask, right into her ear.

She looks at me seriously. "What if I want more, Red?"

More? There's nothing more to a biker than claiming a woman as his, and her being the only female to ever ride on the back of his bike. What more of a commitment to her could I make?

I could make her mine in the citizen world.

As the penny drops, hoping I'm right and not making a fool of myself, there in the kitchen, in front of the sweet butts, my kid and a selection of my brothers, I drop down to my knees. That I'm covered with the blood of mine and her enemy isn't lost on me.

"Cher, will you do me the honour of becoming my fuckin' wife?" I grin up at her.

She squeals and drops down beside me, encasing me in her arms. Her lips come to mine, but I don't allow her long before it's my arms around her, and my mouth taking control.

"Guys, we're going to be plating food in a bit," Zeke's sarcastic voice sounds. "I'm all for PDAs among my parents, but there is a time and a place." Glancing up, I see them grinning so widely it looks like their expression is going to split their face.

"A wedding?" Tiff spins around from the stove. "A fuckin' wedding?"

Vegas has seen its fair share of funerals over the years and has even hosted celebrations from members from other chapters tying the knot. But it's been almost beyond living memory that we've celebrated such a union of our own. Not since before my time when Brick married Rosa, and Tiff and Fox had had theirs.

Word gets around. Soon the congratulations extend beyond the kitchen as news spreads, and behind me the clubroom is full of hollers of excitement. I get to my feet and reach down my hand to pull Cher to hers.

"I hope you weren't expecting something quiet," I say drily.

"I don't give a damn how we celebrate, Red. I feel like I've waited a lifetime to become your wife."

CHAPTER THIRTY-SIX

CHER

I was happy enough with the old lady title and know for some that would be enough. But if I was going to commit to Red totally and to form a proper family with Zeke, then I wanted the whole shebang and a ring on my finger, and hopefully one on his.

I didn't expect him to propose right there and then, but Red obviously didn't need time to think. And immediately dropping to his knees was somehow more romantic than something arranged.

Wraith rushes in as soon as he hears the news and I blush as I remember how it's thanks to him my man has such good moves in bed. That their friendship is long and enduring is easily seen, though Red does get gently teased by the man who beat him to the altar by a couple of years. They start making plans about getting together as a foursome, when it can be arranged, and yes, my mind goes there. I do have doubts about meeting Sophie, or what exactly a foursome might entail.

Red knows exactly what I'm thinking and shakes his head. "Not sharing you," he growls possessively into my ear.

I still have to come to terms that Wraith's woman has some

idea what Red's like in bed. I decide to reserve judgement until I've met her.

Everyone wants to congratulate me. Somehow, the sweet butts and Tiff get dinner plated and served, and people are soon sitting on every available surface with filled plates. If the food suffered from Rosa's absence, no one complains. Halfway through eating, she returns, Tom sporting a Band-Aid on his head and Trist a brand-new cast which the brothers all start signing. Or, when I sneak a look, writing profanities and drawing dicks.

Rosa notices and starts berating them, reminding them he'll need to wear it to school, but it doesn't seem to bother Trist one bit.

When she hears the members from Tucson will be staying the night, she immediately starts allocating accommodations, shoving some brothers out of their beds. Rope and Cuff, who are missing, will be told they're going to share, likewise Roller and Petty. With her no-nonsense approach, no one complains. I stand on, watching and learning, realising soon I'll be expected to be like her.

When I'm introduced properly to two brothers from Tucson, Joker and Lady, it's immediately apparent they're gay, and don't try to hide their relationship. No one baulks or says anything at their outward displays of affection, nor the comments that Lady's not going to allow anyone else near Joker's bed.

I do notice Petty seems uncomfortable but is polite enough. Not for the first time, I wonder whether there's a story as to why he's so adamant that people shouldn't deviate from being straight. Is he still in the closet? Or is it something else? As a permanent fixture here, I'll have time to get to know him and maybe get to the bottom of what his problem is.

Although the boys are in the mood for a celebration, they're all tired as fuck. Red can barely stop himself yawning.

When the food's eaten, and a few drinks have been downed, he crosses over to me.

"I don't know about you, Cher, but I'm dead. I need my bed."

I glance around to look for Zeke, but with the resilience of youth, they're yet again demonstrating the moves they used to distract Crossman. They don't look tired at all.

"Cher, Red." Rosa chooses that moment to approach. She winks at me. "I guess you're looking to celebrate, and I can tell you from experience, Red's suite has paper-thin walls. How about I take Zeke home with me and the twins tonight? Then you don't have to restrain yourselves."

I blush. It's Red who thanks her and, after a glance my way, accepts her offer eagerly.

It seems we're not the only ones heading upstairs, and some haven't even waited to get into bed. Sarge is already snoring, his head laid back on the couch, which I suppose leaves another room free.

I enter Red's suite, *ours* now, I suppose, in front of him. He closes the door behind him but doesn't step far inside.

Tired as he is, he starts a conversation. "Rosa's right and living here all the time will not be good for Zeke. They need a place they can invite friends to. What say you, we start to look for our own place?"

"A home?" Joy leaps inside me at the thought of Red and I searching for our dream house.

"A house. A home. A place to raise our family." He pauses and brushes his hands over his face. "I've lived at the club the entire time I've been a Devil, Cher. I've good money put away. You can have whatever you want within reason."

"I'm starting to feel overwhelmed, Red. You and Zeke, home safe, a proposal, a new house, all in one day." I approach him and lean my head against his chest. "Seems all my dreams are coming true at once."

"You're my dream come true, babe." He rests his chin on my head. "This is all I've ever wanted. It feels so right, like this is our chance and we just have to reach out and grab it."

Gently, his arms start to move, and he takes hold of my shirt and eases it over my head. His tired eyes brighten when he undoes my bra and reveals my breasts.

"I thought you just wanted to sleep."

"Sleep's for the dead," he says, quickly, with one of his trademark grins. "I'm a biker, babe. I need me some loving first."

That I'm definitely willing to give him, to reconnect after those awful couple of hours when I thought I might never see or feel him again.

He nuzzles my neck, obviously in no hurry, but that's fine with me. With no Zeke, no time pressures, we can enjoy just being together.

His voice vibrates against me. "How do you feel about having another kid?" When I don't immediately reply, he retracts. "I missed so much with Zeke. I'd love to experience that with you. But if you don't feel the same, then that's okay too. It's you who has to suffer for nine months."

I'm still silent, thinking it through. I always hoped I'd find someone, have a brother or sister for Zeke, but things hadn't turned out as I'd planned, and I gave up on that dream. But I'm not too old, I'm thirty-five, not ancient.

When I think of a response, I chuckle. "Did Wraith bring up some water and slip it into your drink?" I'd heard from Rosa about the rumours around the Tucson club. Once Wraith had found his woman, many others had fallen too. The club is now overrun with babies and toddlers.

Maybe that could happen here too? I kind of like the thought of the clubhouse being filled with childish laughter.

Red snorts at my comment. "I doubt it. Though it would be nice to breed a new generation in Vegas. Perhaps I should ask him to ship us a few gallons. Who d'you think would be next? Crash?" He chuckles. "Twister? Fuck, I can't see it, can you?"

Not immediately, I can't, as there are elements missing. "They'd have to find the right woman."

"As I found you." His brothers' future romance forgotten, he returns to what he was doing. My shorts are unbuttoned and pushed down my legs, my panties too.

"It's been too long since I've tasted you," he says, walking me back to the bed.

Whether it's been minutes, days or hours, I don't think I'd complain.

He pushes me down and my legs apart in one fluid motion, and huffs a breath over my already eager clit.

I can't prevent the next question escaping my mouth. "Should I thank Wraith while he's here, for teaching you?"

He snorts so hard he has to wipe his nose. "Woman, if you keep making me laugh, I won't be able to do my job." His mirth fades as he attempts a stern look.

Then, when he gets down to demonstrating his talents, joking is the last thing on my mind.

Under his talented mouth and tongue, my orgasm comes fast. While I'm still recovering, he removes his pants and underwear. Then I feel the heat of his body as he comes over me.

"I love you, Cher."

My response is fast and feels so natural. "I love you too, Red."

"Condom, or…?"

It takes only a moment's thought. I'm not getting any younger, and I doubt I'll fall as fast as I did before. And if I do? Well, who the hell cares?

"Bare."

He breathes a heavy sigh. "I was hoping you'd say that. Fuck, Cher, I've never forgotten what it felt like the first time I was inside you."

"I try to," I say drily.

"You what?" He rears up fast. "Hell, Cher, I wasn't *that* bad."

When I can't stifle my laugh, he slaps my thigh. "I'm going to have my hands full with you."

He slides inside, stretching me, making me feel whole. This

feels just so damn right. No man could ever compare because they're not him, and our coupling wouldn't be fuelled by love.

Red glides in and out, taking his time, ramping up my desire all over again. I clutch at him, as he holds on to me. I forget everything but his name as he takes me higher and higher, then after I reach my peak, he lets himself go, flooding my body with his sperm, just as he'd done when we created Zeke.

And if we bear fruit this time, I won't have to do it alone. I'll have Red, and his whole club of brothers beside me.

Red's utterly exhausted as he rolls over onto his side. He makes a move to get up, but I wave him to stay where he is, while I go to the bathroom and clean up the mess which comes with having thrown caution to the wind.

When I return to the bed, he's already asleep, but when I curl into his side, he rolls over to spoon me.

Soon, I'm following him into sleep, not waking until well into the morning. And then, he makes love to me all over again.

Once we're sated, I lie back, remembering the highs and the lows of the day before. Diplomatically, I ask, "Will I ever be seeing Crossman or Chantilly Lace again?"

He stills, then replies without embellishment, "You will not."

I know what that answer means. Do I care? No. It means justice has been done, and neither Zeke nor I will have to look over our shoulders for the rest of our lives. Have I changed? Or is this the woman I've always been? Somehow, I don't think it will be too hard to sink into the role of the prez's old lady.

Turning onto my side, I play with his hair. "Can we discuss what I saw in the basement?"

He stiffens, thinks, then a grin comes over his face. "Somehow I don't think you're talking about the tools of Twister's trade. You mean the BDSM shit?"

My confidence slips a little. "Yeah."

His eyes sharpen. "You interested, Cher? You want us to spend some alone time down there?"

"I've never..." I start to admit, but my voice trails off.

"Babe, I'm here to give you any experience you want to try. You want to be tied up? For me to have my wicked way with you?" The thought makes my stomach clench.

He rolls me onto my back. "For me to spank that luscious ass?" My legs press together.

"For me to torture you with feathers and see how you respond to touch?" I feel my skin flush.

He gives a wicked chuckle. "Oh my, Cher, I think underneath everything, you're a kinky bitch. And as long as you're my kinky bitch, I think we're going to have a lot of fun down there in the basement."

I writhe against him. "My down there could do with some fun right now."

It seems Red's happy to oblige.

By the time we come up for air and make it downstairs, it's to ribald comments and cries of *about time*.

Wraith comes up and bumps his fist against Red's. "I was just about to come up and rescue you, Brother. Thought you might need resuscitation."

"Fucker." Red grabs his arm and wrestles with him. Wraith fights back and they both end up sprawled on the ground while I'm covering my mouth, laughing.

A deep voice beside me growls, "Some things never change."

I glance at Drummer and say shyly, "Thanks for your help."

"Anytime, Cher. You've got my number. You need me, Red needs me, hell if your kid Zeke needs me, just call and I'll be there." He kicks at the bodies on the ground, and snarls, "Break it up, or I'll bust you both back down to prospects." Then he gentles his voice as he turns to me again. "You and Red need to bring Zeke to Tucson sometime."

I go to thank him, but he's already gone. Red stands and brushes himself off, then does that manly hug with Wraith again. The Tucson VP, following his prez, walks for the door with a wave of his hand in my direction.

Red's eyes narrow when he spies Lady talking to Petty, but it seems amicable enough. Then the gruff man called Peg, and Joker, walk past, respectfully saying their goodbyes to the prez of the Vegas club.

I go with my man to wave the Tucson men off.

As the bikes disappear into the distance, Red kisses the top of my head.

"You complete me," he says softly. Then adds as a car comes into view, "You and Zeke."

As Rosa pulls up, the twins and Zeke almost fall over themselves getting out. Zeke comes running across and starts boasting about scores they got on one of their computer games. If the events of yesterday had left any mark on them, I've yet to see any.

When Crash comes up and murmurs into Red's ear, he nods his head.

"Gotta get to a meeting," he explains.

"Go do your prez thing." I laugh, waving him off.

Rosa examines my face, and what she sees satisfies her. She links her arm through mine and together we re-enter the clubhouse.

Already it feels like home.

"Bodies disposed of," Rope starts. "We buried Chantilly deep and threw the damn rat in with her." A round of laughter greets him.

"May they both rot in hell. They deserve each other." It's the normally quiet Sarge who makes that observation.

"Crossman?" I query, while wondering whether it was fair to the rat.

"Hammer came up with the idea." Rope raises his chin and gives credit to his brother sitting opposite him. "We got Crossman's car, drove it up to the mountains, set fire to it and pushed it off into a ravine. Hopefully they'll think he was running, afraid of being accused of his crimes, driving too fast and sliding off the road."

"Accident spot, so no one will care." Hammer shrugs as though it hadn't been his very good idea. "Car bounced and rolled a few times on the way down."

Not for the first time, I think what a good bunch of brothers I have around me.

"Basement's sparkling clean courtesy of the prospects," Cuff announces. He winks at me. "So, it's open for business."

I can't hide my grin. After Cher raised the topic this morning, I can't wait to get my ol' lady down there.

"What are we going to do about the casino?" Fox gathers some papers together and taps them into a submissive neat pile. "We're going to feel the loss of that contract in our pockets."

"And none of it our fuckin' fault," Titch growls.

Keys settles back and links his hands behind his head. "Who says we've lost it? We haven't been told anything yet."

"Not officially, you're right, Keys." Pulling at my beard, I wonder what to do next. From Snatcher's research, Crossman was doing all the shit on his own, and his partners were probably in the dark as much as we were. But probably is the operative word. We can't be certain.

"I need to talk to them," I decide. "Head it face on. Am I correct that if we can continue the contract, we all want to?" Dealing with Lucky Fortunes certainly hasn't been propitious for us, and I wouldn't be surprised if some of the brothers said to hell with it.

Cobra raises his hand. "It's a sweet deal, but was it too sweet because of Crossman? He obviously had plans for us from the start."

Hammer pokes him in the side. "They should give us a fuckin' raise because of the shit we've had to deal with."

Crash taps the table with his hand. "We've got to be fuckin' careful to show we know nothing about Crossman's setup to rob the casino." His eyes narrow as he looks around.

In sergeant-at-arms style, Indian leans forward as if checking for himself, no brothers would let slip anything that would see us end up on a murder charge. Then he sits back again and raises his chin to me. "You go to the casino, Prez, I'm gonna be right there beside you. Snatcher might have said they're clean, but I want to see for myself."

Gazing around the table, I see no one in disagreement that, if possible, we continue our contract with the Lucky Fortunes. "I'll go over there today," I tell them. "Indian, yeah, you're coming with me, and so too are you, Keys."

"Want me, Prez?"

I consider for a moment then reply to my VP, "I don't want to go in heavy, so you stay here."

"Zeke over their ordeal?" Titch asks from the end of the table.

"What ordeal?" Shadow laughs. "Those boys are treating their kidnapping as if it's the most exciting thing that's ever happened to them."

Twister shakes his head. "That's down to the fuckin' twins. They saw it as an adventure."

"Trist is wearing that cast like a badge of honour." Roller grins.

Petty's mouth opens, then shuts again. Hardening my eyes, I ask, "You got anything to say?"

Directly challenged, he shrugs. "Was just going to point out that Zeke's a sensitive soul. On his own, things might have gone differently."

"Fuckin' sensitive?" Sarge challenges. "That kid's got balls of steel. You did hear the part they played in their rescue?" He rolls his eyes, and sneers.

Like me, he seems to think Petty's up to his old game again.

Petty's not going to be quiet. He leans forward. "Yeah, sensitive. What other fuckin' kid would care for the comfort of a man who insulted him?" He lets that sink in for a breath, then admits, "It was the first thing he asked me when he saw me. And that night, when I'd been tied to the chair, he saw I was in pain after I was freed and massaged my fuckin' arms to get the blood running again." His fist hits the table. "I say sensitive but it's not a bad thing. He's plucky, though he's not got the hardness of the twins."

I'm confused. "Where are you going with this?"

Petty sits back. His shoulders rise parallel with his ears then dip back to their starting point. "I'm saying he needs this fuckin' MC behind him." His eyes find mine.

"You had a come-to-Jesus moment, Petty?" Indian challenges. He nods toward me. "And prez here has already said, Zeke prefers different pronouns. You gonna show them respect?"

Petty grimaces. "It won't come easy for me, but I'll try, okay?"

Crash snorts. "This is Petty trying to avoid another beatdown from the prez."

But I'm not so certain. I think the account that Zeke has given of themself has made Petty see them in a different way.

Titch raps his fist against the table. "Zeke's here to stay. As is the prez's old lady."

Rope grins widely. "And we're going to have a Vegas wedding."

There are a few fists banged on the table and a stomping of feet.

"Are we thinking Elvis?" Cuff asks.

"Alice Cooper," Shadow announces decisively.

Keys gets in on the act. "How about a *Star Wars* theme?"

Even Sarge joins in. "A James Bond one." While eyes go to him, wondering what on earth he's on about, he adds his justification, "I heard they have a Bond girl dancing at the end."

Hammer reaches over the table and gives him a high five.

Fuck. I grin at them. Vegas offers more kinds of themed weddings than you could dream of—Rock 'n' Roll, Western, Pirate, Gangster or Camelot. Whatever your jam, Vegas can cater to it.

"It will be up to Cher to decide." This will hopefully be the most important day of her, *our*, life. Apart from the day Zeke was born of course.

"Why not do what Slick did? Get married on your goddamn Harley?" This idea comes from Titch.

My grin widens. I like that idea. I like it a lot. My mind goes back to the first time I met Cher. If it hadn't been for my big two-wheeler waiting outside the diner, I might never have caught her interest. There's a certain poetry in us using my old girl at our wedding.

"Set a date, Prez, and I'll get invites sent to the other chapters," Keys offers.

Hmm. Any thoughts Cher might have of keeping this small might only be in her imagination. When a Satan's Devils' prez ties the knot, it's a big cause for celebration. It occurs to me that maybe that's why Drummer and Sam have never done that shit legally. Or maybe, for them, it's just sufficient that she's his old lady. I want something more. A ring might be no guarantee, but I'll tie her to me in every way so she never runs as she did once before.

"I'll let you know, Keys." I raise my chin, showing I'm grateful for his offer. I get back to the topic at hand. "Let me get to the casino and see whether I'll be offering Cher richer or poorer."

That raises a chuckle.

I bang the gavel and we close the meeting.

In the clubroom, Tiff, Rosa and Cher are drinking coffee. I go over to my woman, reach down and claim her mouth. When I let her up for air, I question them, "What are you three reprobates planning now? World domination?"

"Your wedding," Rosa retorts sharply.

"And do I get any say in it?"

"No, you do not." Now Rosa's grinning.

Cher turns, and her eyes run all over me. It's a bit convenient as that heated look in them makes me harden, but my cock comes back under control when she announces, "You would look good in a tux."

"A fuckin' tux?" I bark. "Woman, I'm telling you, I don't care where or when or whether we get married by a fuckin' penguin, but I'll be wearing my cut."

Rosa's eyes sharpen. "We'll see about that."

Tiff bends at her hips and her body shakes with her laughter.

I decide it's time to change the subject. "Kids get off to school okay?"

We'd debated letting them have a day off, but Cher thought they needed to get back to normal, and agreeing, earlier Rosa had dropped them off.

"Yes." Rosa complies with the change of subject. "After I had a good talk to them about not discussing their recent adventure." She purses her lips. "A car accident will suffice to explain their injuries, and it's not far from the truth."

I have no doubt the twins will keep their mouths shut, that's if they're serious about becoming prospects.

And Zeke? Well, I'm finding they'll do about anything for their old man. Long may it continue, but I'm under no illusions. When the first elation at having a dad starts to wear off, I'm betting I'll be in for some teenage angst and rebellion. *Bring it on.* It's all part of being a parent.

Behind me, I hear Indian jangling his keys. Turning, I give him a nod.

"I've got some business to deal with," I tell Cher, pleased when I get an upward lift of her chin, but no interrogation.

Rosa makes a shooing motion with her hands. "You go do your manly stuff. We'll get on with planning your nuptials."

As I start to walk off, I overhear Tiff saying loudly, "I know this place that does tuxes…"

"You're in fuckin' trouble now." Indian snorts and slaps my back as I walk with him toward the door where Keys is already waiting.

Don't I know it. But what I also know is, I wouldn't change any of it for the world. Not Cher and I reconnecting, not Zeke, and certainly not if I end up wearing a fucking tux if that's what it takes to put a smile on the face of my old lady.

"I managed to get in touch with Rodgers and told him you wanted a meeting," Keys informs me, snapping my mind back into business mode as we walk to our bikes. "He fuckin' leaped at the idea."

That's interesting. As I ride in front of my brothers, I try to think of how this meeting's going to go down. Is Rodgers eager as he wants to show us the door, or is he willing to consider having us back on the job?

My thoughts aren't any clearer when we turn into the parking lot, nor when we walk into the casino which seems to have carried on, just like it had before. My eyes harden as I pass the blackjack table, and there's someone else in Cher's spot. Shaking my head, I lead the way to the stairs, and raise my chin to the guard who, I notice, isn't Bruce.

He greets me with a smile. "They're waiting for you in the boardroom." Unsnapping the rope, he holds it to one side, and lets us walk past.

I exchange a glance with Indian. If we're to get our marching orders, the security staff haven't been forewarned.

Cautiously, I knock, then push open the boardroom door.

"Red." Rodgers actually gets off his ass and comes over to greet me, shaking my hand warmly. "Indian, Keys." To them, he nods.

"Come and join us," Carson offers cordially.

"Can I order refreshments?" This comes from Greaves.

Keys raises an eyebrow toward me. His unspoken comment is right. This is no execution squad.

When we turn down the offer of drinks, it's Greaves who sits forward. "I don't know what the hell the cops were thinking when they arrested you." He draws in a breath and his lips press together. "We told them you've been doing a stellar job."

I shrug. "Par for the course, I'm afraid. Our previous reputation is hard to shake off." Looking around, I ask, innocently, "Crossman not here?"

Carson's face hardens. "No, he's not."

Rodgers sits back and folds his arms. "Go on, tell them," he directs.

Greaves' face reddens. "Crossman's taken off. Seems he got himself deep into gambling debt and tried to steal from the casino himself."

"And we were the fucking idiots that went along with it." Carson shakes his head. "He convinced us having our own security guards to transport the money was a good business venture. Thought we could build something up, offer our services to other casinos."

"Instead, it was a setup, right from the start. He was planning a heist on his own casino."

"And put the blame on us."

I'm surprised they figured it out so quickly.

"How do you know?" Keys asks, obviously on my wavelength.

Greaves snorts. "Pretty damn obvious when he didn't turn up. And one of his cohorts, a woman who worked in the cash office, is also gone." He shakes his head. "One of the security guards was in on it. When rumour got round that Crossman had taken off, he tried to make a run for it."

Rodgers takes over, "One of the guards you trained saw Bruce acting suspiciously on camera. Brought him in and he spilled everything on condition we kept it quiet. Took us to the money and admitted everything."

"Reckon Crossman and Lace are on the other side of the country by now," Carson adds. "We also paid a visit to the hospital and spoke to the fake guards from the armoured truck. They filled in the gaps we were missing." He shrugs. "Seems their loyalty to their boss didn't trump staying out of jail."

Rodgers's eyes flicker as though he wasn't quite in agreement. "We told the cops we didn't want to press charges. We got the money back, so let the matter drop."

Indian's brow creases. "You said Crossman was in debt from gambling? How does a fuckin' casino owner not know the house's odds were stacked against him?"

Greaves gives a mirthless laugh. "Oh, he knew that alright. It was the gee-gees that brought him down. He bet almost everything on a sure thing—"

Carson interrupts, "We suspect the race was rigged—"

And Rodgers finishes it off, "But a horse that falls and breaks its leg hasn't ever been known to win anything."

Well, that's just convenient for us. Crossman managed to give himself a reason for disappearing.

"What happens now?" I ask, wanting to get down to the main issue. "Do you still want our services or not?"

Greaves' eyes widen. "You think we'd get rid of you because of a misunderstanding? Fuck no. You," he points to Keys, "have come up with some great plans. We jumped when you wanted to meet us. We were worried you might have been put off, so this meeting is to reinforce we still want you working security."

"I, er, we," Carson looks around at the other partners, "owe you an apology. We didn't exactly rush in to defend you when you were arrested."

My shoulders rise and fall. "Understandable."

"Have to admit, I had doubts before we employed you. But your references were sound, and you've proved your worth. Now I've seen what you can do, I have no hesitation in continuing our contract."

"And as an incentive to give us one more chance, we'd like to offer you a onetime ten percent bonus," Greaves finishes off.

All three men look at us with expressions ranging from caution to eagerness, while I have to stop myself imitating Zeke and doing a literal happy dance.

Keeping my face impassive, I glance first at Keys, who, equally, stoic, gives me a nod. Then I raise my eyebrow toward the sergeant-at-arms. His face contorts slightly, making me think he's trying not to smile.

Of course, I know what they're both thinking. There's no way in hell we're going to turn an already very rewarding contract and a damn bonus down.

Finally, I raise my chin then lower it. "We'll give it one more try."

CHAPTER THIRTY-EIGHT

CHER

"So, Prez says, oh so fuckin' coolly, 'we'll give it one more try.'"

I smile on as Indian regales the story of their meeting at the casino for what must be the tenth time. It's easy to see how important this contract was for them. It doesn't seem to matter how often he relates it, the boys still listen on, encouraging him by slapping their thighs or stomping their feet and yelling their pleasure at the way things have turned out. Many bottles and glasses have been raised toward my man this evening.

I admit I'd had my doubts about Red's assertions they ran legal businesses at the start, wondering why the hell they called themselves an outlaw club if they stayed the right side of the law. But clarity had come to me when I saw the lengths they'd go to, to protect their way of life, and whatever belonged to them, people or bikes.

I'm under no illusions what happened to Crossman and Chantilly, and I have no problem with it. My kid had been threatened and kidnapped, and I'd have happily pulled the trigger myself.

"What was the verdict?" Red, still grinning at Indian doing an impression of him and the way he said those final words, flops down beside me. When my brow creases, he clarifies, "What have I let myself in for, wedding wise?"

I wonder whether I should lead him on, confirm we'd agreed on putting all the brothers in monkey suits, along with button-holes and the whole regalia. Possibly I could tell him I'd decided on a church, though whether we could find one which wouldn't be struck by lightning and thunder when the Devils entered, I wasn't sure. I could torture this man beside me, or I could put him out of his misery.

Turning myself to face him, I take his hand in mine, toying with his fingers, and finally glance up through my eyelashes.

"Uh-uh." He puts his free hand over his face, covering his eyes and peering out through the gaps in his fingers. "I'm in trouble, aren't I?"

I swallow a couple of times, not knowing how he'll take it.

Red removes his hand from his eyes and places it on top of mine. Now my hand is enclosed by both of his. "Cher, babe, love of my life," he starts, earnestly. "All I want is to see you in my cut, and my ring on your finger. I don't give a fuck how they get there. You want to go all out and want me to dress like something from *Star Trek*—"

"*Star Trek*?" My eyes widen.

He waves that off. "What I'm saying is, give me a time and a date, and I'll be there." He pauses for a moment and then smirks. "Might be interesting to see the brothers dressed like they're going to Comic Con."

I giggle at the thought, then grow serious once more. "Much as that idea appeals to me, it's not what I want. I, er..." He squeezes my fingers in encouragement. "Rosa said there's a chapel that's Harley themed. Where you can ride your bike down the aisle. I sort of thought you've still got the same bike, the one that brought us together..."

I have to stop because of the expression on his face. He's gone totally blank. Then, when he speaks, it's in staccato. "You. Want. To. Ride. On. The. Back. Of. My. Bike. Down. The. Aisle?"

I'd thought it was a great idea when Rosa suggested it. Apparently, a couple from Tucson had done that before. But Red clearly can't see the appeal.

Suddenly his hand raises from my lap and snakes out around my neck. Dominantly, he takes hold of my hair and forces my face up so my eyes match his. His pupils have dilated.

"Have I told you how much I fuckin' love you, Cher? Have I told you, you're perfect for me?" He pauses. "This is why I'd never found anyone your equal. You're my other half."

"Er, does that mean you're okay with it?" I tentatively ask.

He snorts. "Okay with it? I can't think of anything better."

"I told you he'd love it."

I startle and turning, see Rosa leaning over the back of the couch.

"Mom?"

As another voice interrupts, I turn to see Zeke running into the room. There are advantages of being an old lady. When I'd mentioned I'd have to leave to collect Zeke from their practice, Rosa had told me to send a prospect, that that's what they were there for.

I won't always take advantage, but I'd been pleased to be able to continue discussing the wedding with Tiff and Rosa.

I smile at my kid. "You get on okay?"

"Yeah. Oh, hi, Dad," they greet Red offhandedly. "Any food going, I'm starved."

Red winks at me. I suspect he was going to ask me to celebrate our forthcoming nuptials in a way we'd both end up dirty, but he's being thrown into parenthood in a big way.

Instead, he stands. "I'm hungry too. Let's go raid the kitchen, kid."

My heart feels like it's going to burst as I watch my man and Zeke walk off together.

Rosa takes his place beside me. "Now, let's get started. Now Red's agreed, we can hone our ideas."

Planning this wedding wasn't going to be an evening's work

as I soon find out and it's not long before I start to wonder what I'm letting myself in for. Apparently, the legal joining of a Satan's Devils' MC prez and his old lady is a big deal.

All the chapters need to be invited, and of course, places arranged where they can stay, with all due deference given to the presidents and officers. I'm beyond grateful when Rosa takes charge.

All the significant others of the members who have them will also be invited, and Rosa gives me a rundown of each and every one. There's of course, Sam, from Tucson, who I've already heard about, and Sophie, who's Wraith's, who I'm a little dubious about meeting. Also from Arizona are Carmen, Sandy, Ella, Darcy, Marcia, Becca, Tash, Mariana and her brother Drew, and Allie, who apparently used to be a sweet butt.

From San Diego, there's Lost's old lady, Patsy, Saffie, and Alex who's the club lawyer, also Mary, and her daughter, Alicia.

Swift, from Utah, we don't know how to classify as old lady or member, and Stormy's Cat, who I'd heard mentioned when he was here.

There's also several more from Colorado, Violet, Stevie, Melissa, Jayden, Beth, Vanna, and Moira, who's the wife of the ex-prez, and Jeannie, two older women who even Rosa finds a bit on the intimidating side. *Heaven help me.*

I do draw the line at inviting sweet butts from the other clubs, but agree Jinx, Angel and Pixie can't be left out. It's amusing how they throw themselves into choosing their outfits, a task in which Zeke helps them out. They've really taken to Zeke, and Zeke's often found helping them with their makeup or giving the girls dancing tips.

The latter being an offer Zeke also extends to me. Red and I will have to have a first dance after all. But while I'm willing to try out a tango or something that will impress, Red puts his foot firmly down at learning to dance. Apparently, shuffling around together to a slow song will be his limit.

Which brings us to music, and I'm stuck for a choice.

It's one night when I'm lying in bed after being thoroughly loved by my man, that the ideal song hits me. Red was on a journey, just heading where the winds blew, when he stopped off at a diner and picked up a girl. She rode with him for a while, then left him because the weather had turned and she'd got cold.

"Roll me away" by Bob Seger.

Okay, so Bob wrote the start, but we've written the ending. The song seems to fit so well.

When I tell Red, he barks a laugh, but backs up my choice. It will be our secret, the story of how we met played on our special day.

Zeke has some great ideas when I ask their opinion on what I should wear. A long fairy tale dress is out, as I'll be riding on Red's bike. Zeke has the idea of cream satin trousers, a short diamanté encrusted tunic, and a detachable train that will make me feel like a bride.

Tiffany apparently has a friend who's a seamstress, so she gets to work. When my ensemble is finished and I get to try it on, I feel like a million dollars. *The corset top with the deep cleavage will drive Red wild.* Though I'll need to use tape. Lots of tape. I don't want to flash my tits on the ride down the strip that we've also got planned.

Over the top of my outfit, I'll be wearing my cut, something that Red presented me with a week after all the tumult over the kidnapping had died down. It's butter soft leather and fits like a glove.

I now know it's that garment that means so much more to the Devils than a ring on my finger, so I'd traced the words *Property of Red* with pride. It might be a sign that I belong to him, but it also shows to the world that he's mine.

The venue for the reception is booked, various cakes tasted to Zeke's delight, and several brothers warned not to let Peg from Tucson near the DJ that night. In fact, Indian volunteers for that duty, a job you'd think was the most serious of the day.

As there are no little girls in the Vegas club and Zeke will be standing alongside his dad as his best person and I don't want to exclude the other kids in the club, bucking tradition, Tom and Trist will follow me down the aisle as ring bearers.

Zeke got some mileage trying to persuade them they'd be wearing lacy outfits to make up for me not having bridesmaids. Of course, all the brothers got on board, even Red warning if they didn't do what I wanted, they'd never be wearing a prospect's patch.

When they'd taken the threat seriously, the ruse continued, much to their growing disgust.

One night, Red suggested he was warming to the idea of making them wear bridesmaids' dresses. It would, as he said, give them a taste of the hazing to come, and what they'd experience as prospects.

The topic was apparently even discussed at church.

A week before the wedding, it's Zeke's first night on stage, and Keys managed to block book seats in advance. The whole damn club turned out to watch them dance. And if the chorus line got a standing ovation at that particular moment, only Zeke knew it was directed at them.

Zeke, in my eyes, was the star. In their element they'd shone.

For the past six weeks, I don't think I've ever been this happy.

And tomorrow I'll be happier still, when I stand up beside my man and finally say, I do.

CHAPTER THIRTY-NINE

RED

"You're a complete asshole, Uncle Red."

I narrow my eyes at Trist, pleased to see he's had his cast removed, though his left arm now looks a shade paler than his right.

Tom backs up his brother but uses a stronger term. "Motherfucker."

"Hey," I snarl. "Watch your mouth."

Unrepentant, Tom shrugs. "Well, you do fuck Zeke's mother."

Raising myself to my full height, I do my best to loom over them. The trouble is, they're growing so fast they're now almost as tall as me. "You mind your fuckin' language." Inwardly, I smile. Sure, I do fuck a mother, and I'm very happy doing it. I'm especially looking forward to doing so tonight, taking her for the first time as my legal wife.

The twins stand their ground, and I'm not surprised. It was only today they'd found out I wasn't really going to insist they put on cream satin pants and flowing shirts to accompany my soon-to-be wife up the aisle.

The pretence we were going to put them in dresses had been a step too far but tricking them out in a girly style had had them fooled. Every time they objected, which was roughly every hour, one of the brothers reminded them what it was going to be like when they were finally allowed to prospect.

It's been great playing them along, but now I've had to come clean and admit it. Rosa will be dressing them in their normal style. In fact, all my brothers and I will be doing is making sure our jeans and t-shirts are clean and free of grease and oil, and that none of our cuts or boots have dust or mud on them. Thanks to my soon-to-be wife, she's quite happy for me to come as I am. Just as long as I'm there to put a ring on her finger.

At the last moment, I decide to swap my t-shirt for a crisp white button-up shirt, just to show I've made an effort for her.

"Get lost, boys. I've got to get ready now."

"Red, you've got hours." Trist rolls his eyes.

And I've got to get mentally prepared for it. This morning's been the first time I can steal a few moments for myself. Over the past couple of days, brothers and their old ladies have been rolling in from far and wide, some coming early to make an occasion of staying in Vegas, which means my back's been slapped so often it already feels raw, and I'm sure I've got a lot more of that coming later.

Drummer's here, Wraith, Snatcher, Lost and Demon, and they've brought almost all of their chapters along with them along with the old ladies. It's going to be one hell of a procession when later I'll be heading the column that intends to drive along the strip in Vegas on the way to the wedding chapel.

As Tom and Trist leave, I sit on my bed with my head in my hands. Cher and Zeke are off in another room getting themselves ready with Rosa and Tiff, along with a sampling of women from the other chapters. I've seen Sam and Sophie, and sweet Ella, whose own wedding happened in Vegas. Mel's there as well, and last night I'd had a chance to catch up with Pyro. With a grin on my face, I've seen a few bottles of champagne heading into the room which I'm forbidden to enter.

In the background, I hear the incessant roar of engines as bike after bike arrives on the compound.

Yeah, it's good to take a moment for myself. I roll my head back and shake out my shoulders, feeling any tension dissipate as I close my eyes and think about how happy I am.

But as if fate has destined not to allow me the moment's peace I think I deserve, my phone rings. I curse as I take it out of my pocket.

"You got Red."

"Red? It's Greaves here."

Why the fuck is he calling? "What's up?"

"I'd like you to come down to the casino." His voice sounds odd, but I can't put my finger on it.

Not immediately worried, we've developed a good relationship over the past few weeks, I remind him what day it is. "It's my wedding day, Greaves. Can't this wait?"

"I don't think it can, Red. What time's the ceremony?"

"Two o'clock."

"Then you've got time to get here and then back again."

"What's this about, Greaves?"

"I'd rather discuss it in person. Can I tell the others you're on your way?"

Now I am starting to get worried. While it's not how I wanted to spend my last few hours as a single man, I agree and tell him I'll be there as soon as I can make it.

"Brother! A drink?" Drummer calls out as I make an appearance. Then, having assessed my expression, his eyes narrow. "She run out on you?"

"The casino wants to fuckin' see me. Now. Apparently, it's important."

"Fuck, Brother. Can't Keys go for you?"

I shake my head. "They asked for me personally."

Drummer sighs but gives me a look of understanding. "You'd better make it back in time, that's all I'm saying."

"I'll be here," I snarl. Nothing is going to keep me from attending my wedding.

Glancing around, I see Crash deep in conversation with Beef, the VP from Colorado, who, of course, I remember from Tucson. Walking across to them, I interrupt their discussion.

"Greaves wants me at Lucky Fortunes. You coming with?"

"Today?" At my sharp nod, Crash rolls his eyes, then agrees immediately. We might work for them, but none of us like having meetings with the partners without a witness being present, especially when we have no idea what the summons is about.

It takes more than a minute for me to cross the room, having to reassure too many people I've not gotten cold feet. Then, once the VP and I are on our bikes, we have to wait our turn in the stream of bikes entering the gate before making our way out.

I carefully keep to the speed limits even though I want this meeting over and done with, knowing Cher would not be impressed if I got arrested. When we park our bikes side by side in the parking lot of the casino, I turn to Crash.

"Let's get in and out fast. I want this over and done with." If I sound irritated, I make no apology for it.

"Any clue what this is about?"

"No fuckin' idea," I growl. "Just that it's important enough to disturb my wedding day."

"It better fuckin' be." Crash seems equally upset. He was enjoying himself, catching up with brothers from the other chapters.

It's just another day in the casino. Machines clatter out winnings, and chime. Drowning out the familiar cacophony, I head to the stairs. The security guard nods and lets us up, then I head straight for the boardroom.

Greaves, Rodgers and Carson are already seated, and the former waves us to the spare chairs opposite them.

"I've not got much time. Can we get down to it?" I can't help but snap as I sit myself down.

Greaves sits forward, resting his clasped hands on the table. "Crossman's been found dead."

"Yeah?" My gut goes cold as I wonder if they've suspicions we had anything to do with his demise.

"Yes. He didn't run far. They found his car burned out at the bottom of a ravine. He didn't even make it out of Nevada."

I splay my hands. "What can I say? I'm sorry doesn't sound right under the circumstances."

"That's about how we feel about it," Carson agrees.

"Couldn't you have told me that on the phone?" I narrow my eyes at Greaves.

"I could." Greaves returns my stare coolly. "But there's more to it." I feel Crash tense by my side. "His death will have an impact on the casino."

"I thought it had been running well in his absence," I remark. It didn't feel like anyone had missed him.

It's Rodger who grimaces. "His will makes certain there will be changes."

Now chills run up my spine. Crossman fucking hated us. Could he have implicated the Satan's Devils in anything from beyond the grave? I cast a sly glance toward the door in case cops are waiting outside. Only slightly eased when I see no one, I bring my attention back to the men in front of me.

"Are we allowed to ask how?"

"Did you know Crossman had a brother?" Instead of answering mine, Greaves asks me a question, pulling some paperwork toward him. He checks something then raises his head. "A Keaton Armstrong."

Purposefully, I crease my brow and rub at my temples, then I look up and snap my fingers. "The only person I know of that name is an old member of the club who we knew by the road name, Tide."

Crash nods as though the penny's just dropped. "Not thought of him in years. Before your time in Vegas, Red."

"That's the man," Greaves confirms, while I wonder what on

earth that paperwork is, what exactly it says, and whether I should have had Jeeves on standby.

"Apart from his wife, Crossman had no family. They predeceased him," Carson announces. "Crossman's will," he dips his head toward the papers in front of his partner that I'd been concerned about, "clearly hadn't been updated for a while. Other than the woman he was married to, his other main beneficiary was his brother, Keaton Armstrong."

"Who sadly died a couple of years ago." I hope I've got a sufficiently sombre expression on my face.

"Indeed," Carson continues. "As we've recently discovered. But there was also a caveat put in place." He breaks off, and surprisingly, he smiles. "Armstrong, or Tide as you knew him, obviously thought highly of the Satan's Devils. In fact, your club is described as the people who brought meaning to Tide's life."

How I do it, I don't know, but I refrain from turning to look at Crash's face. I fight to retain control, and definitely not to snort.

"To cut a long story short," Rodgers clearly thinks matters are going too slow, "in the event of Armstrong's death preceding his own, Crossman left his share of the casino to the Las Vegas Satan's Devils MC."

I suck in air.

"Which means," Graves sits back and folds his arms, and adds deferentially, "Your club's now the majority partner in the Lucky Fortunes."

What the actual fuck?

"This is a joke," Crash gets in before me.

"No joke," Greaves confirms.

For a moment, I can't think let alone speak. "Can I have a copy of the will? I'd like my lawyer to look over it." Luckily, I've already seen Dart with Alex in tow.

Carson pushes an envelope across. "That's the paperwork that you need. It names your club as part owners."

But how? Crossman hated us. He blamed us for his brother's

death. He'd have never left anything to the club. How the fuck has this happened?

Suddenly, something snaps into my head. "Where was Crossman's will?"

"An electronic copy was filed online at the courthouse. It was dated a few years ago. It was signed. It's all legal, I assure you."

Snatcher's voice suddenly echoes in my head. *Remember, Red, when anything's stored electronically, it can be altered.* Again, I try to keep my face expressionless. *The fucker. He had known.* More than that, he was responsible for this turn of events.

Will this stack up? It seems unbelievable, but if I know anything about Utah, they know what they're doing.

Suddenly, I notice Greaves grinning and holding out his hand. When I stand, reach over and take it, he shows he's got a firm hold. "Welcome aboard, Red. We've said before we've been impressed with the improvements you've made to the security here. Well, now you're even more invested in making this work."

And my club has a buy-in to a legit business. If I dare to believe it, that means there's nothing out of our reach.

Other chapters have strip clubs, tattoo parlours, restaurants... well ownership, even in part, of a casino, surely trumps the lot. Well, maybe not Snatcher's trade in Utah, but even so.

"Thought you'd like more good news on your wedding day, Red."

"Yeah, congratulations in advance, *partner.*"

"Speaking of which, Prez." Crash nods toward the clock. "We should really go."

We should, but I hesitate one moment longer. Using their first names for the first time as their partner, I extend an invite. "Clancy, Austin, Trent. If you feel yourselves inclined to accept an invite to a biker wedding, consider yourselves duly issued with such."

"When and where?" Carson, or Austin now, pulls a notepad toward him and picks up a pen.

I tell him the details, then apologise, and say I really must go.

CHAPTER FORTY

RED

I don't remember the ride back to the clubhouse. All the way, I felt I was on cloud nine. In a few short hours, Cher will be mine, and the club will be sorted for life.

Curious eyes greet me as I walk in the door, with Twister being the first to ask, "How did it go? What did those fuckers want?"

Instead of answering, I look around. "Have you seen Dart?"

He narrows his eyes and jerks his head. "By the bar."

I tap his shoulder then set off. As expected, Alex is close to her man. Being a bit rude, I ignore the VP from San Diego, and just push the documents into her hand. "Just run your eyes over this, will you? Tell me if it's legit?"

With only a curious glance toward me, the beautiful curvy woman takes Dart's hand to help her off the stool, then slides the paperwork out of the envelope I'd carefully nursed safely in my cut all the way back, and places it on the bar. Her eyes widen as she scans through.

"What's up, Red?" Drummer's fast at my side. "It must be trouble if you need the club's lawyer's help."

"Red, you fucker!" a loud voice barks, then Snatcher's hand

lands on my shoulder. Turning, I see him sporting a wide smirk. "I see you got my wedding gift."

"Snatch—"

The Utah prez brushes me off. "No, Red. No thanks required. You'll find it's legit. It will all stand up."

Drummer's been reading over Alex's shoulder. His body stills. "A fuckin' casino?"

"The majority share," Alex murmurs. "Satan's Devils have fifty-one percent, the other forty-nine divided equally between the three other partners."

Now our lawyer's confirmed it, it's time to let my brothers share the unbelievable news. I jump onto the bar and whistle loudly enough that the packed room starts to quiet. When I think I can make myself heard, I shout out the information.

There's a stunned silence.

"You lucky fuckin' bugger."

I spy the owner of the voice and raise my middle finger toward Wraith.

His statement raises a flood of comments and questions heading my way. Crash and I answer them as best we can, and slowly the implications start to sink in. If we don't fuck this up, the Vegas chapter will be made for life.

"You know grand gestures are expected on your wedding day," Drummer remarks drily as the hubbub begins to calm down. "But getting your old lady a casino kind of looks bad on the rest of us."

My face is aching with all the smiling I've done. My pleasure amplified by those on the faces of my brothers. This day starts a whole new chapter in the life of the Vegas club, hell, a new book.

Fox already has a calculator in his hands as Alex passes the financial information across.

Then, in the midst of it all, again, silence falls. It's first broken by a sharp whistle, which is quickly followed by murmurs of appreciation.

Turning my head in the direction everyone's looking, I see

the best sight I've ever seen in my life. A vision of beauty descending the stairs, ready to become my wife.

I'd had no clue what she was going to be wearing today, nor how she'd be doing her hair. It's been swept back, but not up, leaving her able to accommodate the helmet, but still revealing a cascade of blond curls.

The helmet she's carrying has a fucking veil attached.

She's a combination of the epitome of a biker's old lady, and a bride any man would be proud of.

My legs feel weak. My hands go clammy. The crowds part as I walk unsteadily forward. When I hesitate, feeling I've been brought to my knees, Zeke steps forward, takes my hand and hers, and joins them together.

I clutch at her fingers as if I'm never going to let her go, and she does the same to mine. Her eyes smile, and her mouth moves, saying silently, *it's time*.

Accompanied by cheers and whistles, we lead the procession out of the clubhouse and to the bikes.

I'd love to say I remember every moment of my wedding day, but it passes in a blur. I don't notice the tourists with their cameras out as we head down the strip and ride the Harley to the altar as that's where I'm directed to go. I'm only vaguely aware of Zeke, both giving her away then standing by my side as my best person.

I've only eyes for her. My ears only hear her agreement to be my wife, and I could have eaten cardboard at the lavish reception for all that I know.

I will always recall taking her in my arms and sharing a secret smile when Bob Seger's words ring out, about a big two-wheeler, a biker, and a girl who met him briefly before leaving, followed by the optimism, the hope, that the next time he'd do it right.

If my eyes water, who can blame me?

It took fifteen years, but now she's home.

RED

"This is crazy." Cher looks around at the boxes that are piled sky high, and the large number of envelopes scattered around.

"If you've got a pair of decent pipes in there, let me know," Rope calls out.

"Or a clutch lever, mine broke," Sarge puts in.

"They're all for us?" Cher asks me, sitting on the floor and ignoring the brothers crowding around.

Our celebration had lasted a couple of days, but now we've seen the last of the stragglers off, and Cher and I have a chance to look at the mountain of wedding presents that have been given to us.

"Hey, don't just look, get opening," Titch grumbles, settling himself on a stool.

Cher glances at the old man and grins, then pulls a box toward her. She reads the label, then starts trying to decide how to unwrap the paper.

"Give it here," Twister demands, impatiently pulling it to him. With his knife, he slits it open, then passes it back.

"Who's it from?" I lean over her shoulder.

"Blade and Tash," she answers, distracted as she pulls out a box. "Oh, it's a set of kitchen knives. And there's a note." As she reads it her brow creases. "Chosen to be dual purpose?" Her head shakes.

Fucking Blade. That cracks me up.

"Next!" Cobra impatiently shouts.

Shadow eagerly picks up a box, tears off the label, hands it to Cher who passes the parcel to Twister who makes quick work of the wrapping.

"This is from Swift and Road," Cher announces, before she opens the box. Then her eyes widen. "What the hell?"

Taking out the contents, I laugh loudly. It's a his-and-her pair of the very latest in Kevlar vests. I only hope we never have need of them.

As we move through the pile and Cher opens the third Instant Pot, she shakes her head and states glumly, "I should have had a wedding list."

But Tiff takes one of the spares and Sarge the other, both saying they'll come in handy.

There are tool kits to spare. I pass them around, keeping the best for myself.

An odd-shaped package holds a pair of fleece lined handcuffs and a crop from Rope and Cuff which make Cher blush but which I know will come in handy. She does enjoy her time in the basement, and I love how her ass reddens nicely.

When a large, elongated parcel is opened, I do find an exhaust, but not one I'm giving to anybody. It's a hard-to-find original replacement part for my forty-year-old Harley. The sender is Drummer. He'll be getting my personal thanks.

Wraith's present makes everyone howl with laughter. There's a How-to Manual on sexual positions together with a pregnancy test and a note, warning, *Watch out. I brought some of the Tucson water to Vegas.*

Cher leans into me and speaks to me quietly. "I don't think he's kidding. I need to use that test later on."

"Yeah?" I beam.

When she nods shyly, I kiss her soundly, ignoring the comments to move it on already.

A slim square box is opened next, its contents stunning Cher and starting her crying. My eyes narrowed, I take it from her, then my gaze finds Zeke and I raise my chin to them. It's a framed professional shot taken at one of their first performances. Zeke's been caught in mid-air and looks amazing, and I know we'll both treasure it forever.

There are chocolates, spirits, wines and beer from most of my brothers, and I give them all chin lifts to thank them.

As the pile, *at last*, begins to diminish, the door opens, and Trist and Tom walk in carrying a large rectangular box. When they place it down in front of Cher, there's a suspicious rustling.

"What the fuck?" I glare at them, not putting it past them to get me back for the way I'd teased them.

"Open it," Tom instructs, eagerly. "Hey, Zeke. This is for you as well."

Rather gingerly, as cautious as myself, Cher pulls the paper apart. For a second, she stares down silently, then her hand covers her mouth as she starts first to giggle, then snorts as the chuckles come fast. She laughs so hard she falls back into me, and my arms come round her automatically, holding her tightly.

It's a fucking rat in a cage. I have to admit, it's a cute little thing, standing on its hind legs and looking around curiously.

"Wow. Thanks, Bros." Zeke seems delighted.

Seeing Cher's seen the funny side and is not upset, I lift my chin to thank them. Then warn them before they can ask, "No prospecting until you're eighteen."

It takes a good couple of hours to open everything, and when the contents of all the envelopes are counted up, we must have well over four thousand dollars in gift cards, all from various establishments.

"I can't believe all this." Cher rests back in my arms, staring at the pile surrounding us. She leans her head back and looks up at me. "All this, *and* a casino."

"For better or worse, babe," I remind her of the vows we'd spoken earlier. Seems right now some god of fortune is shining down on this. And even I can't believe my brothers' generosity. But I joke quietly, "I warned you I come with a big family."

When Zeke comes over and artistically arranges themself beside us, I realise however many people I have riding alongside me, it's these two here that complete me.

As the prospects start gathering the discarded paper, brothers drift away to get themselves drinks, and Cher talks to Zeke about helping her with the mammoth task of writing the numerous thank you cards, I let my mind drift.

Fifteen years back, I'd left Vermont with nothing but my dreams, a rough southerly direction to head in, and a vague desire that at some point I'd have my own family.

Now I've got more than I ever thought I'd have.

Prez of the Satan's Devils Las Vegas, married to a woman I love more than life, Zeke, my kid who I couldn't be prouder of, and, if that test proves positive later, maybe another child to add to the mix.

They say good things come to those who wait for them.

They are one hundred percent right.

Satan's Devils MC Second Generation #4

Marvel

I became a member of the Satan's Devils MC to escape from my past.

I love this mismatched family that I've joined, would give my life for the club, but something always keeps me slightly apart.

I've watched as my brothers have found partners and settled down, seen them have kids and have played a sideline role in their upbringing, but never had any yearning to find someone for myself.

More than thirty years back, I learned women can't be trusted. It's a lesson I took to heart.

If I never fall in love again, I can't be hurt and my world won't be torn apart.

Virginia

I was betrayed in the worst of ways by the man I loved. Even now, it's hard to put what he did into words.

But I don't need to speak for myself, everyone knows. And everyone blames me. Me, who'd had no idea what was going on.

Traumatised, I try to hide from the world.

But even a reclusive woman has to emerge sometimes. I didn't expect to get caught up in a major incident, nor to be forced into close proximity with a biker named Marvel.

I didn't expect we'd have so much in common.

Can two broken souls come together to make a whole?

Pre-order: https://books2read.com/u/b6vpZ0

Warts an' All

Toad

I've seen her around with her airs and graces, making out she was better than the rest of us. Head held haughtily high, nose in the air as if everyone else was beneath her. She had it all – a rich daddy, a fine mansion, fast cars. Yeah, that princess wanted for nothing.

I've seen her, but she's never seen me. Until she needs my help, that is. Then she comes crawling, words sticking in her throat as I make her beg.

Grovelling to a biker obviously hurt, and every word out of her mouth was a lie. She said she'd thank me with no thought to paying her debt.

But I know not everything in her perfect life is what it seems. I've got the power to bring this snooty princess down to my level. I've got her daddy in the palm of my hand.

She owes me, but his debt is bigger. He won't think twice, giving her to me as payment.

Love? Nah, that doesn't come into it. I'll show her who gets looked up to around here, and it's not her.

ACKNOWLEDGMENTS AND AUTHOR'S NOTE

I am fully aware that I may have divided the audience with Red's Peril Part 2. I could have taken the easy way out and made Zeke a character more in fitting with societal norms. I'm also aware some readers may have found Zeke's chosen pronouns too difficult to read.

I didn't so much write Zeke into this story to make a stand for the LBGTQ+ community, but more to show that they have as much right to be a character in a story as anybody, and as much chance as anyone else to live a normal life unimpeded by prejudice.

We live in a rich society, full of people of all colours, of all races, of all religions, of different sexual orientations and genders, and I like to write about this varied tapestry.

In saying that, I'm no expert in nonbinary. My son identifies as queer and has a rich variety of friends, one of whom is transgender and who prefers the they, them, their pronouns. Listening to my son and discussing various elements of this story was an interesting experience as I found there are more questions than answers and a whole spectrum of how people define themselves. If I've oversimplified things with Zeke, then I apologise.

I was nervous when the beta readers first got their hands on this book, but not only did they make the usual suggestions for changes (or correct inconsistencies), they also gave me the encouragement to send Red's Peril Part 2 out into the world. So thank you once again to Sheri, Danena, Jo, Tami, Tera, Alex and Zoe.

Once again, a huge thank you to Maggie Kern my long-suffering editor.

Darlene, thank you again for proofreading this book. I know I was again late getting it to you and rushed you to complete it, but you came through for me again. I really am very grateful.

A huge thank you to Andrew Flanagan for once again becoming Red, and of course to Golden Czermak of Furious Fotog for the photo and to Dar Dixon of Wicked Smart Designs for the cover.

Finally, last as always, but definitely not least, thanks to all of you, my wonderful readers who've taken a chance on this book. If it wasn't for your encouragement, I wouldn't keep writing. I have recently received messages and emails telling me how much you like my books, and I love reading every one. A positive message inspires me to write more.

This book, like all of my works, has been to beta readers, through editing twice, to a proofreader and then to ARC readers, but there could still be the odd typo that's crept through. Please message me if you've found anything, so I have a chance to correct the book. I love to hear from readers, even if you're pointing out something I've got wrong.

If you've enjoyed this book, please consider writing a review. Reviews are essential to us authors, and I appreciate and read them all.

I'm also writing a much shorter book as part of the Bleeding Souls Saved by Love anthology, a collaboration of some great authors. Each book is a standalone and based on a fairy tale. My contribution, Wart's an' All is based on the Princess and the Frog. My chapter of the Wicked Warriors MC has its home in

Arizona. It will be published on Jan 3, 2022, and is available to be pre-ordered now.

The next Devil will be Saving Marvel. Although a story about one of the original Tucson chapter members, it's set in the Second Generation time line.

OTHER WORKS BY MANDA MELLETT

Blood Brothers – A series about sexy dominant sheikhs and their bodyguards

Stolen Lives (#1) Nijad and Cara

Close Protection (#2) Jon and Mia

Second Chances (#3) Kadar and Zoe

Identity Crisis (#4) Sean and Vanessa

Dark Horses (#5) Jasim and Janna

Hard Choices (#6) Aiza

Satan's Devils MC - Arizona Chapter

Turning Wheels (Blood Brothers #3.5, Satan's Devils #1) Wraith and Sophie

Drummer's Beat (#2) Drummer and Sam

Slick Running (#3) Slick and Ella

Targeting Dart (#4) Dart and Alex

Heart Broken (#5) Heart and Marc

Peg's Stand (#6) Peg and Darcy

Rock Bottom (#7) Rock and Becca

Joker's Fool (#8) Joker and Lady

Mouse Trapped (#9) Mouse and Mariana

Blade's Edge (#10) Blade and Tash

Heart Mended: A Satan's Devils MC Novella

Truck Stopped (#11) Truck & Allie

Satan's Devils MC Boxset 1 Books 1-5

Satan's Devils MC Boxset 2 Books 6-8

Satan's Devils MC Boxset 3 Books 9-11

Satan's Devils MC - Colorado Chapter

Paladin's Hell (#1) Paladin and Jayden

Demon's Angel (#2) Demon and Violet

Devil's Due (#3) Beef and Steph

Devil's Dilemma (#4) Pyro and Mel

Ink's Devil (#5) Ink and Beth

Devil's Spawn (#6)

Satan's Devils MC - Next Generation

Amy's Santa (#1) Wizard and Amy

Hawk's Cry (#2) Hawk and Olivia

Twisted Throttle (#3) Throttle and Gwen

Satan's Devils MC - San Diego Chapter

Being Lost (#1)

Grumbler's Ride (#2)

Avenging Devil Part 1 (#3)

Avenging Devil Part 2 (#4)

Satan's Devils MC - Utah Chapter

Road Tripped (#1)

Stormy's Thunder (#2)

Satan's Devils MC - Las Vegas Chapter

Red's Peril - Part 1

STAY IN TOUCH

Email: manda@mandamellett.com

Website: www.mandamellett.com

Sign up for my newsletter to hear about new releases in the Satan's Devils and Blood Brothers series.

Facebook reader group: https://www.facebook.com/groups/mandasbadboys/

facebook.com/mandamellett

twitter.com/manda_mellett

ABOUT THE AUTHOR

Manda's life's always seemed a bit weird, starting with a childhood that even today she's still trying to make sense of, then losing her parents in the late teens. Going from the tragic to the bizarre, who else could be unlucky enough to have had two car accidents, neither her fault, one involving a nun, and another involving a police woman?

There isn't enough space to list everything that's happened to Manda, or what she's learned from it. But by using the rich fabric of her personal life, psychology degree, varied work experiences, and amazing characters she's met, Manda is able to populate her books with believable in-depth characters and enjoys pitting them against situations which challenge them. Her books are full of suspense, twists and turns and the unexpected.

Manda lives in the beautiful countryside of Essex in the UK, the area's claim to fame being the Wilkin's Jam Factory at nearby Tiptree. She can usually find jars of jam which remind her of home wherever she goes. As well as writing books and reading, Manda loves walking her dogs and keeping fit. She lives with her husband of over 30 years, who, along with her son, is her greatest fan and supporter.

Manda is thankful that one of the more unusual, and at the time unpleasant, turns her life took, now enables her to spend her time writing. Confirming, in her view, every cloud has a silver lining.

Photo by Carmel Jane Photography